Torn Asunder

A Novel of the End Times

PRAISE FOR MARK ALAN LESLIE'S NOVELS
THE LAST ALIYAH

"This could turn out to be a definitive book, from the shame of replacement theology to the Christian involvement in the rescue of the Jews."
—**Frank Eiklor**, president of Shalom International

"*The Last Aliyah* is one of the most intriguing stories written about the plight of the Jewish people in the End Times. What makes it memorable is the author's resurrection of the use of the Underground Railroad that originally brought the slaves freedom to Canada, and now used to bring Jewish people home to Israel. A must read for Christians who stand with Israel."
—**Mitch Forman**, vice president of Chosen People Ministries

"[*The Last Aliyah*] is a compelling, fast-moving and timely story, and unfortunately begins with a very scary, but very plausible scenario. I enjoyed the book and kept wondering how [Leslie] was going to get out of the corner he had painted Omri into. Very clever using the sci-fi version of 2 Kings 6:18."
—**Neil Lash**, co-founder of Jewish Jewels

CHASING THE MUSIC

"A gripping story told with the maturity of a seasoned wordsmith. I'll put this one in the class with John Grisham or other secular novelists touted for producing today's best fiction ... Readers can't go wrong with the intricately woven plot, intriguing characters, and crisp writing style."
—**Randall Murphree**, editor, *AFA Journal*

"One word to describe *Chasing the Music*? ADVENTURE! ... This was *Indiana Jones* wrapped up in *Romancing the Stone* overlaid with *National Treasure*—all my favorite action movies between the covers of one book ... It definitely reads like the best action adventure movie I've ever seen ... I definitely recommend that adrenaline junkies read this book."
—**Pam Graber**, *BookFun* reviewer

"I was blown away at the many scientific connections and historical ones in *Chasing the Music*. The extensive depth of information was exceptional. Well done!"
—**Lynda MacDonald**, Heart to Heart Ministry, Nova Scotia, Canada

"Fast action and high suspense... The read was exciting, following clues and moving from place to place. I loved it."
—**Randy Tramp**, freelance writer and author of *Night to Knight*

THE CROSSING

"Mark Alan Leslie includes a meticulous attention to historically accurate details with respect to the KKK's presence in Maine and their attempt to target Catholic immigrants, Jews, blacks, and illegal alcohol. With a genuine flair for compelling, entertaining, and deftly crafted storytelling,

The Crossing is very highly recommended, especially for community library Historical Fiction collections."
　—Midwest Book Review

THE THREE SIXES

"Leslie's insights into world politics and contemporary culture are staggering and frighteningly realistic. He and his co-writer, son Darek Leslie, will make readers think they're living too close to catastrophe."
　—Randall Murphree, editor, *AFA Journal*

TRUE NORTH: TICE'S STORY

"Leslie vividly describes the plight of runaway slaves ... Tice exhibits a deep religious confidence that will endear him to readers of inspirational literature. While the main plot is a work of fiction, the well-researched historical elements make it believable and even, at times, educational."
　—Publishers Weekly, naming *True North* a Featured Book

MIDNIGHT RIDER FOR THE MORNING STAR: FROM THE LIFE AND TIMES OF FRANCIS ASBURY

"In a world of namby-pamby Christianity, along comes a story of a man who played no games with God. The life and exploits of Francis Asbury read like the biblical Book of Acts. Mark Alan Leslie did not write 'just another book.' I couldn't put *Midnight Rider for the Morning Star* down. Neither will you. This one is a 'must read.'"
　—Frank Eiklor, president, Shalom International Outreach

"An exciting, exhilarating story that challenges the reader in an intense way."

—**the late Dr. Dennis E. Kinlaw**, past president, Asbury College, founder, The Francis Asbury Society

"Again and again it spoke to my heart."

—**the late Merlin R. Carothers**, founder, Foundation of Praise, author of *From Prison to Praise*

"A stimulating and imagination-provoking book."

—**Patch Blakey**, executive director, Association of Classical and Christian Schools

Torn Asunder

A Novel of the End Times

MARK ALAN LESLIE

PUBLISHING THE POSITIVE
ELK LAKE PUBLISHING INC
Plymouth, Massachusetts

Cover and Interior Design: Derinda Babcock

Editor: Deb Haggerty

PUBLISHED BY: Elk Lake Publishing, Inc., 35 Dogwood Drive, Plymouth, MA 02360, 2020

Library Cataloging Data

Names: Leslie, Mark Alan (Mark Alan Leslie)

Torn Asunder: A Novel of the End Times / Mark Alan Leslie

456 p. 23cm × 15cm (9in × 6 in.)

Description: A cataclysmic earthquake and tsunami—could the world be ending? Reporters Darek and Jillian with friends Ty and Bethany are there ... and report the truth to the end of times?

Identifiers: ISBN-13: 978-1-951970-20-8 (paperback) | 978-1-951970-21-5 (trade paperback) | 978-1-951970-22-2 (e-book)

Key Words: Christian, Apocalyptic, End Times, Action/Adventure, Charismatic Leader, One World Religion, One World Government

LCCN: 2020934888 Fiction

DEDICATION

To all those in my former profession, journalism, who double check their facts and report the truth of a world gone horribly askew even as they face animosity from peers who deny and defy God and strive to destroy Christianity.

ACKNOWLEDGMENTS

To my publisher and editor, Deb Haggerty, and her continued support of my work whether it be historical novels or this end-of-history book.

To my beta readers Dave and Suzy Shaub and Kerrie Faye Herron, thank you for your help and suggestions.

To Bill Fielding, a hero of the Vietnam Conflict, without whose help I could not have written one key scene in this manuscript.

To Loy, forever at my grateful side.

And a special thank you to my cover designer, Derinda Babcock.

How beautiful upon the mountains
Are the feet of him who brings good news,
Who proclaims peace,
Who brings glad tidings of good things,
Who proclaims salvation,
Who says of Zion,
'Your God reigns!'
—Isaiah 52:7, NKJ

PROLOGUE

The first indication the world we know was about to end eluded the world's most alert seismologists. In the earth's upper and lower crusts, where massive tectonic plates slide across one another, their jagged edges sometimes catching and grinding, a mild movement caused the earth above to quake.

As people slept in Japan, the massive Ring of Fire plate shifted ever so slightly over its entire breadth from the Pacific Rim to Chile to New Zealand. That shift caused just a burp in the seismograph charts.

The second clue might have forewarned a veteran of seismic monitoring.

As Starbucks-infused Seattleites hurried to work early to beat the morning rush, the small Juan de Fuca tectonic plate off the coast of Washington and Oregon suddenly plunged obliquely beneath the North America plate. A cough erupted on seismometers.

The third signal? As soccer players in Liverpool, England, practiced in the late-afternoon sun, the Eurasian plate nosedived below the eastern edge of the North American plate. At that point even sleepy-eyed scientists jerked awake with a jolt.

In places little known for earthquakes, something ominous, something dreadful was about to tear apart the earth. By now, time had run out for seismologists to warn the masses. Some called home to warn their families. But escape the carnage? That was another matter.

CHAPTER ONE

At Maine's famous Knife Edge ridge marking the northern end of the Appalachian Trail on the summit of Katahdin Mountain, Darek Field's internal thesaurus for "danger" kicked into gear when the earth moved under his feet like a slow waltz—then a salsa.

Darek shot a worried look over his shoulder—a reassurance his wife, Jillian, and friends Tyson and Bethany Cole were standing upright as the mountaintop shimmied.

They were, but he didn't know just how startled he would have been to find them missing. Nothing would surprise him—not at this point, not after the last few months.

Jillian's eyes were wide in fear, and she struggled to keep her feet under her. Darek grabbed her hand and pulled her to him.

Drawing a deep breath, he scanned the panorama around them. Rocks of all sizes, remnants from the glacier's retreat thousands of years before, lay strewn along both sides of a two-to-three-foot-wide ridge at its widest. The view was a full three hundred and sixty degrees.

A hundred or so miles to the southeast was the Atlantic Ocean. On exceptionally clear days, a person could see Cadillac Mountain down on Mount Desert Island.

Even the agonizing circumstances which led to this week in the wilderness couldn't dull the splendor—the crystal-bright colors of the Maine forest in the full panoply of fall. The woods glowed in kaleidoscopic beauty in the mid-morning sun.

The pale rainbow to the east a couple of hours before—a strange sight on a clear day—had disappeared.

Even Sam, the Canadian blue jay who'd been following them, had vanished. Darek looked to his northwest where the Knife Edge opened onto a wider tabletop area. The usual horde of hikers on the mountaintop this time of year was diminished, certainly due in part to the depleted human population.

Darek slapped at his neck. "Boy, a mosquito even in October and at fifty-six hundred feet. We are indeed part of the food chain."

Despite being winded, Jillian found enough oxygen to laugh.

Again the mountain trembled, and Darek tugged Jillian down to the ground with him. Fall off Knife Edge and you plunge to your death. He glanced at Ty and Jess, now clutching each other, their feet set wide apart.

Darek caught Jillian's eyes in his own. A look of terror filled her pretty face. Then the noise commanded their attention. Rising from the southwest, the sound began as a dim grumble. Drawing nearer, the commotion grew louder, and as the ground began a severe shaking, the rumble overwhelmed everything.

Looking over his wife's shoulder, Darek gasped. About ten miles to the southwest of the mountain, an earthquake ground its way toward them, tearing the earth apart, splitting open a gaping, ugly crevice a hundred yards wide.

The quake was like a giant tumbler churning rocks against an immoveable object, Maine's granite ledge.

"Whoa!" Jillian exclaimed as the quake exploded through the deep, thick ledge. Piles of rock exploded out of the ground. The noise amplified, grating and screeching. The motion was like the bowels of the mountain were churning.

Then, the quake curved southeastward just below the mountain. The Knife Edge heaved and flipped Bethany out of Ty's arms and into the air as if off a bucking bronco.

"Help!" she screamed as she slid down the steep face. She tried to grab a rock big enough to hold her weight. Her feet kicked stones over the precipice.

Ty scrambled toward her, dove belly down and reached for her arm. He found and clutched her wrist.

Darek had risen to a crouch and put a strong hand upon Jillian's shoulder, the pressure demanding her to stay put. Standing up was akin to riding a two-by-six plank in a rough sea.

Darek lunged toward Ty's feet, and on his knees, grabbed Ty's ankle as his friend struggled to pull Bethany up the incline.

"One! Two!" Darek yelled. And when Ty pulled Bethany, Darek in turn pulled him backwards.

"One! Two!" Again Ty pulled Bethany in sync with Darek's yank.

"One! Two!" This heave got Ty to solid ground and Bethany close enough for the two men to grasp her forearms and haul her to them. She spun on her knees and clutched Ty around the waist, weeping in relief.

Then they all fell to the rocky ground as a thunderous sound cracked the air.

"Look!" Ty pointed at Millinocket Lake below them.

Darek gasped, stunned, then leaped back to Jillian's arms. They watched entranced. The water level rose sharply to the top of the lake's banks. Then a loud sucking noise bellowed from the basin—a goliath's burp—and in a sudden, swift whoosh, the water drained completely out of it, swallowed into the earth's core.

Just as Darek exhaled, another loud trembling rumbled from the southwest followed the precise path of the first.

Eyes wide, he and the others leaned forward to look over the edge of the precipice.

While its predecessor pummeled northeastward, this second earthquake shrieked ear-splitting, terrorizing decibels.

The ground rolled like waves pounding to shore, then weaved, then bucked like a frenzied rodeo bull, tossing the four people about on the mountaintop that seemed to grow narrower by the second. The foursome hugged the ground as rocks slipped away from under their feet and disappeared over the cliff.

Below them, boulders once piled atop one another by the first temblor flew into the air like so many tennis balls, and the earthquake elbowed its crevice even wider.

The first eruption had created a fissure wide enough to swallow a train. This one?

It must now be half, three-quarters of a mile wide. Darek raised his head to see.

Just then, a monster boulder that moments before had lain waiting for them to skirt around, dislodged and, with an ominous sigh, began to roll directly at the hikers. Darek spotted the rock through the corner of his eye and screamed, "Look out!"

He jumped to his feet, and realizing he didn't have enough time to escape death, pleaded to God for safety.

Time stopped for Darek Fields.

As though he were suspended in air ten feet above his body, he watched the scene below—the others glanced up at the boulder, which was already upon them. He grabbed

Jillian around the waist, pulled her to him and dove to the side of the path. Ty and Bethany landed beside them.

Inches away, the boulder rolled past, gained momentum with the downward slope, and tumbled down the side of the mountain, jumping from ledge to ledge until crashing into the thick mat of forest below, bowling over dozens of trees before coming to a stop. Chunks of ledge and an avalanche of rocks, loosened from the mountainside, spewed down in its wake and plowed into the forest, snapping saplings off at their trunks.

As his friends let go a collective sigh of relief, Darek was startled to find himself back within his body. *What just happened?*

But he had no time to decipher. Before his eyes, the land on the far side of the earthquake's fissure began to shift away. Some kind of invisible force was at work.

No, this can't be.

A hundred miles of land—from Mt. Katahdin to the sea—was moving. Slowly, yes, but surely. Edging away.

A shiver ran down Darek's spine. He glanced at the sky. The expanse was blue and beautiful. Glorious. But below, the town of Millinocket about twenty miles distant slipped away as if in quicksand. The village seemed to be dipping below the level of the land on the near side of the crevice.

"Millinocket," Ty exclaimed. "It's sinking!"

They were all slack-jawed.

"Cities and towns, *people*," Darek managed.

"The land mass could stretch all the way up into New Brunswick," Jillian gasped. "And who knows how far south— Boston, New Yo—?"

She cut off the last word as the immense tract of land— from the jagged coastline out of sight to the forest land just ten miles away—sank in slow motion, down and away. A heavy groan, an empty complaint, then a deafening belch echoed into the growing abyss.

The distant fields and rivers, then Millinocket closer by, then the tops of the trees nearer to them dropped out of view like a hanged man through a gallows trapdoor.

The four friends gasped, gulped, exhaled—their eyes wide in amazement.

Jillian screamed in hoarse terror. She grabbed Darek around the neck. Ty and Bethany clutched each other. None could force their eyes from the horror before them.

Suddenly, an other-worldly wall of water began to rise on the horizon. A thousand feet, two thousand feet into the air. The wall seemed to swell out of the ground, then hesitated— ominous, posing like a bodybuilder, proud and motionless.

Several seconds of silence followed, then the colossal wave rushed landward, taking aim at what was now not an inland mountain but the shoreline. Nothing could stop this monster from surging forward. A mass of sea plants siphoned up from the ocean's floor topped the wave which smashed through the woods and bore down on Katahdin.

A memory flashed in Darek's mind of Pamola, the Abenaki Indian god of thunder and protector of Katahdin, who was said to live beneath the mountain. Pamola was about to get pummeled, so where was he now?

Pushing the thought aside and putting his trust in the one true God, Darek embraced Jillian, his cheek aside hers.

Our last moments together on this side of heaven.

They were five thousand and two hundred feet above sea level, but nowhere seemed safe in the path of this killer force. They could do nothing, except pray. So they did. Shotgun prayers. "Dear-God" pleas. "Save-your-people" appeals.

Then the wave plowed into the mountainside, striking halfway to the peak. The ground shifted like someone shaking a mattress. His left arm wrapped around Jillian and right arm around Ty, Darek squeezed tighter.

The end would not be unwelcome.

But in a few moments, the innards of the mountain stopped swaying—and the wave ebbed backwards from the bulk of the mountain range, draping trees with masses of sea urchins, kelp, and other salt-water vegetation.

Fierce splitting sounds rose from the forest where branches and trees broke from the force of the water. Cracking noises ascended along the mountainside as rocks bounded downhill. Otherwise, silence reigned.

Darek and the others stood and looked eastward. Nothing—nothing but water as far as they could see. The ocean had laid claim to a mass of land spreading from here in central Maine to—to who knew how far in either direction?

"Incredible." Darek's exclamation was barely audible.

"All those people," Jillian whispered. "All gone. Oh, my—all gone."

Her shoulders sank, she sobbed convulsively, and Darek clutched her slumping body.

Bethany shuddered, her lips trembling, and spoke softly. "Everything's so quiet. All those thousands, those hundreds of thousands of people perishing. There should have been more—more sound. A human sound. A scream. A whimper. This doesn't seem—real."

Ty gripped her securely, speechless.

"What are we going to do now?" Bethany asked.

Their senses assaulted, no one had an answer. No wisdom from on high.

So this is what happens to your brain after an IED attack—in this case an attack on steroids.

Finally, Darek scrambled for the satellite phone in his backpack. "We've got to call Jake."

CHAPTER TWO

Jacob MacMillan sat with his back to the long, wide mahogany desk, facing the view through the glass wall on the third floor of his Truth Publishing and Broadcasting Network headquarters. Fog from Boston Harbor was moving into the city now—a thick, white mass streaming across the wharfs, down Atlantic Avenue, creeping around the corners, advancing, obscuring. Like the sandstorm that engulfed his division in an Iraqi village during the Gulf War, he mused.

Jake pulled on his meerschaum and sweet-smelling smoke wafted about him. A contraption in the ceiling quietly siphoned the smoke out of the room.

Lost deep in thought, he was impervious to the activity behind him. No penthouse suite for Jake. From his early days as a newspaper reporter, he had always preferred to be in the midst of the action, the epicenter being the newsroom.

And his Truth Publishing and Broadcasting Network newsroom was buzzing, the keys to three dozen computers clicking and reporters speaking into video-phones—the rapid heartbeat of his news organization whose broadcast television and radio signals circled the world and whose printed news filled a web site and his national-distribution newspaper.

Facebook had long ago placed Truth in permanent "jail" for political incorrectness.

Jake was supposedly a racist, bigot, misogynist homophobe—any one of which was enough to "imprison" him. Never mind more than half his employees were women, and about forty percent were people of color of various shades. He pleaded guilty to having a problem with the idea some people were in search of a sex that suited them.

Jake was unaware of the record-shattering earthquake splitting the earth apart in its path. The quake's arc swept from its epicenter in southwest Maine both northeastwardly into New Brunswick and westward into New Hampshire, through Conway, south of Concord, then curving east-southeastward through Manchester and into Massachusetts, tearing its way through Lawrence and Danvers toward the north shore of the great city of Boston, cutting into the Atlantic Ocean at Salem, demolishing the courthouse of the Salem Witch Trials fame.

Portsmouth, New Hampshire, along with Portland and Bangor, Maine, would soon be gone. Mansions in Bar Harbor, Boothbay Harbor, Camden, and the shanties of Washington County, the country's easternmost point, would soon gurgle under water. And millions of people with them.

Without warning, the floor of the giant Truth building began to vibrate and pulsate—then rock. In the newsroom, ceiling tiles fell, sending reporters diving for cover or the stairwell. Computer monitors went wild with flashing bars and crosses.

Hanging lights swung crazily like berserk high-wire trapezes. Window panes shattered, sheaths of glass shooting inward as if smashed by a giant hammer.

Odd, but Jake felt strangely detached. The place looked like the Jerusalem restaurant destroyed by a homicide bomber. He'd survived the attack. Would he survive this?

He knew he should get under his desk. But he turned to look outside, and what he saw mesmerized him. An earthquake had struck, for sure, far greater than the one he had experienced in Japan.

Instinct told him the quake was ferocious and grinding closer. Up and down Atlantic Avenue, huge buildings jounced in convulsions as their walls shattered. Bricks and mortar crumbled and supposedly quake-proof structures crashed to the ground. Clouds of dust billowed up from the earth, blending into the fog.

Shivers ran down Jake's back. *People. People perishing in those buildings.* Corpses in gnarled heaps of steel and wood and bricks. A few frightened victims ran out onto the streets.

New York's Twin Towers flashed into his mind, but this far surpassed even the 9/11 devastation.

Then the sister quake struck—gleefully, it seemed—doubling, tripling the carnage. The few remaining structures crumbled into rubble. The sight was staggering.

Jake gripped the edge of his desk to stay upright and looked quizzically about him. Truth HQ still stood.

A minute later, the quake finally subsided, and Executive News Director Carlos Martinez burst through his door. Then stopped, stunned. He eyed Jake and then, in obvious wonder, scanned the room. Jake followed Carlos's eyes and slowly realized—not only did the building survive, his office was unblemished. The ceiling, mammoth window, the books on the shelves lining the northern wall were intact and in place.

"Unbelievable. Surreal," Carlos murmured. "You're, you're all right."

Jake nodded, acknowledging the hand of Providence on him, and waved an arm toward the window. "But look, Carlos."

The wharfs across the street were all destroyed. The Boston Aquarium just a hundred yards away was ruin. The several beautiful hotels lining the waterfront were piles of brick and twisted steel. Smoke and flames rose from their guts.

"The people!" Jake gasped.

Carlos walked closer to the window and surveyed the wreckage. With an empty exhale, he sat on the edge of Jake's desk.

Jake nodded toward the newsroom. "It's the hand of God we're still standing. How is everyone?"

"Scrapes and bumps. People hit by chunks of falling ceiling, minor cuts from flying glass. But nothing serious. Annie, Sam, and a couple others are downstairs checking out the communications room. Others have gone upstairs to broadcasting."

Todd Livingstone, the US news editor, charged through the doorway, mouth agape.

"Any idea of the magnitude of the thing?" Jake asked.

"Jeff Warren's contacting Boston College's Weston Observatory seismograph station and the National Earthquake Information Center in Denver." Todd caught his breath. "Andrea's on top of the police and fire departments and the hospitals. Jonathan's getting in touch with Civil Emergency Preparedness and the Red Cross Disaster Team. And the statehouse and Washington bureau folks are covering their end.

"I mean, the Washington people are. We can't seem to reach the statehouse office. Probably Beacon Hill got wiped out, so I hope Ted and Alison are all right. Land lines are dead. Thank heaven for cells, though I'm sure the towers still standing are overloaded with calls."

Jake blew out a breath. "Todd, I want every available news staffer who isn't in the building to get in here, if they can get here at all. Call the DC office and have them check with Homeland Security to see if terrorists set off a bomb of some sort on a fault line to start this thing. Also have them get in touch with the White House, FEMA.

"Our staff up here? Have them contact the Army, Navy, and Coast Guard rescue units, the Civil Air Patrol and Power Squadron, and the departments of Defense, Public Works, and Health."

Jake turned to Carlos. "And have someone check Logan Airport, the FAA, the docks, the subway, the rails—anything moving people. Meanwhile, let's get LaShawn and his crew up in the copter for aerials. And, get someone over to the statehouse to see if our folks there are all right."

"We'll GPS their cells if all else fails," Carlos said.

"Right." Jake paused and bit on the stem of his pipe. "Listen, we'd better check with the Nuclear Accident Center and Nuclear Regulatory Commission, and then get hold of our stringers to look into the nuclear power stations wherever this thing flattened. We could be in even worse trouble."

The muscles in Carlos's and Todd's faces seemed to let go and their mouths fell open, a stunned look in their eyes.

"You're right. Oh, my goodness," Carlos said.

Todd simply stared, apparently caught short by the vision of the possibilities.

"Tell me as soon as you get the Richter reading, will you?" Jake said. "That quake, or quakes if there were two of them, must have registered off the charts.

"And Todd, if this *is* related to terrorists I want to know immediately."

Both men nodded assent.

The private satellite phone on Jake's desk rang a sharp jingle like an old-fashioned dial-tone landline.

He leaned over and picked up the instrument.

"Jake," he answered.

"Jake!" Darek Fields sounded frantic. "Jake, a mammoth tsunami is heading your way!"

Crackling static followed.

Jake was flabbergasted. He'd heard wrong. "A what?"

"A gargantuan wave," Darek said. "It's wiped out ... Maine ... to Mount Katahdin ... where we are!"

Jake held onto the phone and ran to his office door.

"Get everyone back to the secure room," he hollered. "Now!"

As the two men hustled away, Jake turned and looked out the window beyond the nearby rubble to the horizon. *How can this be? The entire East Coast shoreline is supposed to be too shallow for tidal waves.*

He hadn't stood there a minute when Ann Stapleton stuck her head in the doorway. "Jake, come on! Everybody's downstairs. You can't stay here."

Jake drew a wooden match from the pocket of his vest and turned to her. "I'll be all right, Annie. You just get back down there and watch out for yourself and the others."

"But, Jake!, you'll be smashed to smithereens!"

"No buts, Annie. Don't worry about me. Get safe."

"B-but—"

"Annie!" Stern finality filled his voice.

Annie shrugged as if slapped, then ran.

Jake turned back toward the window, snapped the match into life with a fingernail and took two steps forward so he stood only a foot from the glass. A wall of water appeared over the horizon beyond the crumbled buildings lining Boston Harbor. The mass rose higher, and higher still, pointing its crest toward the few faint, wispy clouds in the sky. A thick, yellowish-white foam hung on the curl of its lip—like a monster frothing at the mouth, preparing to devour prey. But, was this a monster, really, or a message from God?

Jake looked at the beast, and the words came softly. "My dear Lord, what is your plan? Is this your wrath?"

God's plan—as seen by those who believed in him— seemed obtuse at the beginning of this latest series of afflictions. At first, Jake considered the sufferings a low-grade blight, but the bad news had escalated quickly.

In a millisecond, the recent past flashed before him, and Jake confirmed while the One World movement had accelerated, this was not a good thing.

CHAPTER THREE

3-1/2 YEARS EARLIER

About four hundred recognized terrorist groups operated around the world. Ninety percent of them were Muslim, and they wrought death and destruction in the name of their angry god, killing Christians, Jews, Buddhists, Hindus, and any other "infidels" wherever and whenever they had the chance.

Even while a new peace reigned in the Middle East— an accord authored by the Premier of the One World Government—terrorists continued killing sprees. As jihadists were jailed, more recruits sprang up—by all appearances.

Since the early 1990s, Sudanese and Nigerian Islamists had been enslaving and murdering Christians by the score. Since the late 1990s, Islamists were doing the same in Indonesia and the Philippines. Since the early 2000s, terror had spread to other African countries—not to mention the United States and Europe.

In January 2019, in Jolo in the Philippines, twenty worshippers at a Catholic church were killed by Muslim bombers, and a dozen believers were murdered during Fulani violence.

And in recent months, terror had rained down like a hailstorm on Christians worldwide. The Chinese government had replicated the Romans' gruesome crucifixions, torturing Christians in public squares in a show of force aimed at squelching the revival-in-hiding that had festered there for decades.

When asked to intervene, the One World Government stood mum, and the fledgling Church Universal shrank into a corner like a child in a dunce cap.

In the United States, materialism ran rampant with a scary lust. Hate filled the streets, and socialist activists called out the wealthy to pay "their fair share." An odd dichotomy, that. "We want more wealth, but if we can't earn a fortune, we'll take yours." This was the mantra of socialists who demanded a eighty-percent income tax rate.

As Alex de Tocqueville had predicted in the mid-1800s, America would remain a great nation until the general populace discovered they could vote largesse for themselves from public coffers. Jump-started by Franklin Delano Roosevelt's New Deal in 1937, the federal government had unraveled with money grabs from myriad entitlements.

And with a population diluted by sixty million aborted babies who would have contributed to the dwindling government-assistance and Social Security assets, the government resources were on the brink of bankruptcy.

At the other end of the spectrum, people who had lost loved ones in terror attacks had become upset when they didn't get their "fair share" in government moneys paying them for their loss. No one seemed to ask why they would expect such a windfall from fellow taxpayers, or why their life-insurance payoffs weren't enough.

American companies spent fortunes to remove the last one percentage point of air pollution. Only when those US businesses went bankrupt, while Chinese and Indian manufacturers flourished, did environmentalists realize they had killed the goose that laid the golden egg.

Thinking themselves enlightened, the "people" had so decimated corporate America—the corporate world, except for Russia, China, and India—with stifling bureaucracy and taxes they had lost their own jobs *in* those companies as bankruptcy followed bankruptcy.

Crime rates had risen through the stratosphere, driven largely by illegal immigrants from Third World countries. Bands of bandits—gangs of all races and nationalities—roamed city streets, pillaging entire stores, robbing individuals. Supermarkets were prime targets. Jewelry stores had been at one point, until most of them shuttered.

Believing the myth America had more mass killings than any other country, the masses called for an end to the Second Amendment and for the government to take people's private arms.

In the countryside, the moon shadows of the trees that in earlier years had inspired poets, now sheltered highwaymen—lurking marauders of the underworld.

And what *could* have brought improvement often made life worse. The prime example of this was the Alliance, an amalgam of political-action and social-justice organizations. The Alliance was positioned to help fix problems, but emotions had driven its leaders to horrible ends.

Enraged by the Alliance one day, Jake had editorialized before his hundreds of millions of world viewers:

> Forgetting what we as a society have, we demand more. Upon receiving more, we ask for still another measure. The circle of people drawn into this new spiral toward socialism grows—encompassing, consuming. In America, for instance, most everyone, somewhere along the way, has forgotten they or their ancestors came here from scores of

other countries but pulled together to make this one nation, indivisible.

Our ancestors answered to God. To whom do we answer? How many have left religion? How many defy it? And even attack God and anyone who dares stand up for the integrity of his word?

The count is mind-boggling, but one group in particular stands out. Like leeches, the members of this organization prey on society in a crazy, carnivorous crusade to break the laws of good men and, more importantly, to violate the commandments of God. Among this group are such unlikely colleagues as heroin- and cocaine-legalizing advocates, *Mother First!*-ers, Black Power League renegades, abortion crusaders, some of whom even champion killing newborn babies, LGBTQ, et al, socialist activists who have amnesia about the corpses of Soviet Republics, Venezuela, etc., and sundry underground organizations.

We find this bully sniffing around the entrails of once-treasured values, demanding handouts, and declaring all who side with them are reprobates, deplorables, homophobes, Xenophobes, you-name-it-ophobes, and are not worthy to live.

Contraceptives being covered by government-mandated insurance isn't enough; religious groups must conform. Gay marriage being legal isn't enough; law demands a baker must bake the wedding cake. Not just demanding everyone listen to scientific arguments on the environment, the left insists Americans commit economic suicide with "green new deals" or be judged as child-haters. No moderation is acceptable, no

22

incremental change tolerable. Any movement must be comprehensive and definitive, with knee bent in supplication.

This legion of **true** haters calls itself the Alliance. At first a non-violent, political-action force in which each of its member groups would support the other in return for the backing of the whole, The Alliance has devolved into a potentially violent, selfish, megalomaniacal bully. They are, and all apparently, on board with the destructive tactics of *Mother First!*

Dialogue with this creature is a monolog, for its leaders won't accept two-sided debate. Interrupt their soliloquies and they bludgeon you— figuratively, that is ... So far.

Theirs is a diverse mob, yet our political leaders beg away from confrontation with them, even sidle up to them as buddies. Why?

By giving *special* rights to every minority conjured by man, shall we take away the rights of others? By allowing every other narcotic known to man, do we preempt the right to security of drivers on the highways who are *not* high? By kowtowing to violent socialist activities, are we not depriving others of the right to safety?

Do you recall when former-US Attorney General Eric Holder refused to prosecute Black Panthers for threatening voters? One man decided to stick his thumb in the eye of the law.

And today? When we stand idly by as adult mobs calling themselves Black Hebrew Israelites (really?)

bully teenagers at a Pro-Life Rally, what is our defense?

By legalizing even after-birth abortion—which is truly infanticide—and calling the act a 'Right To Choose,' have we not only destroyed our own future generations but declared life is as worthless as anyone might choose to think?

"In 2004, some states began the practice of giving drivers' licenses to illegal aliens—*illegal* aliens—who, in turn, used them as identification to collect welfare and vote. This was a slap in the face of the millions who have immigrated here legally and a worse slap to all working Americans who have paid for the illegals' welfare ever since.

Some states started giving illegal aliens free tuition at state colleges—a gift citizens don't receive.

Some cities and states have long broken the law by refusing to inform Immigration and Customs Enforcement (ICE) when an illegal alien is in custody until after the alien is released and free.

We're far past time for this country, this world, and its leaders to draw open the blinds and wake up to the consequences of their decisions. We are going down one highway, in the direction of the Alliance and the One World Government, and this path is 180 degrees away from the road of righteousness.

We are traveling down toward despair. We must change the course of our individual consciousness, and our collective will, before the clock ticks twelve. Time *is* running out!"

World Premier Clifford Sardis read this editorial and stood silent in his Brussels headquarters, mentally placing one more check mark next to this troublemaker Jake MacMillan's name.

He crossed his arms, ground his teeth ... and plotted.

CHAPTER FOUR

THE NEXT DAY

The next day Jake faced a series of crises.

His wife, Dawn, woke him up with a kiss and the words, "Boy, are you popular this morning."

She turned her iPad toward him and scrolled down a list of combative tweets, Instagram posts, memes, and one podcast calling Jake the evil pawn of Satan—and spawn—just add the "s" for a double whammy.

"Several have gone viral," Dawn said. "Globally."

Jake sat up and shook his head. His checked his watch. Six o'clock.

"Among them, darling," Dawn said and pointed to a virulent slapping-down given him by the bishop of the Roman Catholic Archdiocese of Boston.

"Some people you've gotta love getting angry," Jake said with a smile.

"Well, if you enjoy his worship," Dawn continued, "I don't believe I can repeat the words of the bishop of the Episcopal Diocese of California."

"Well," Jake deadpanned, "might as well get fans coast to coast, eh?"

"Do you think you're getting more opinionated as you get older?" she asked, eyebrows raised.

"More reasons to be," he said.

Dawn shrugged. "Can't argue with you."

A shave, a shower, a bowl of cereal later, and Jake's cell rang. The sound of bagpipes told him the caller was Ted MacDonald.

"The enemy's at the gate," Ted said. Rough, gruff, and no-nonsense.

"I'll head right in," Jake said.

He leaned over the breakfast table, grasped Dawn's hands in his and prayed for wisdom.

Her response was a prayer against anger.

"Anger?" he asked.

"People are people—most of them lost, many with little purpose but to stir up little storms. Don't expect them to act like the folks the next pew over."

"Um-hm."

He planted a kiss on Dawn's lips.

The drive to Truth proved people had lost any semblance of patience. McClellan Highway was like a sea of maniacal balls in a pinball game gone haywire. Pray your way down the freeway and hope you don't break down in one of the tunnels. Had the infamous Big Dig fixed Boston's transportation problem? More torture than cure.

Nevertheless, eventually he chugged along Atlantic Avenue, wishing now as he approached the Truth building that he could stop for a while at Boston Aquarium to his right. What he did know was although people had alternatives with hydrogen-powered and super-battery-operated vehicles, oil remained king, especially since the discovery of fracking as well as huge deposits beneath American land.

The Truth building rose before him to his left, set hard across the street from Boston Harbor. A famous minister had recently said the building contained a creature of immense might standing for righteousness. He'd noted while print media had been floundering for years, even calling for a Marshall Plan to subsidize newspapers' existence, Truth's news empire had flourished.

The minister had died a day later, the victim of a hit-and-run driver who to this day hadn't been found.

As Jake drew near the front entrance, a crowd spilled out into the street. Frenzied whoops and hollers and rowdy tirades filled the air.

He turned down an alleyway and circled around and into the private parking lot behind the Truth building. He slid his entry card through the security reader and entered through the rear door, then hustled through corridors to the front of the building.

Ted MacDonald stood erect in the broad front foyer, pointing here and there as he spoke to four security guards. He spotted Jake.

"It's the Alliance," Ted said, "and they want blood."

"Whose?" Jake asked.

"Yours."

Jake looked out giant windows. Bulletproof panes. Jake had learned the lesson well.

No surprise. Stephen Russell, chairman of the Alliance's board of directors, stood on a large wooden crate on the sidewalk only feet from the front door.

His rainbow-topped hair was spiked on the crown of his head. His face was crimson. One fist was clenched. The other held a wireless microphone. And his mouth was flapping nonstop. Typical.

Jake stepped to the double-door, which was bracketed by security guards, and opened it a sliver to listen.

"Stronger unity is what we need!" Russell said.

A set of high-powered speakers boomed his message into the crowd.

Cheers greeted his call. "Unity! Unity!"

"Backbone!" he hollered. "Especially in my own organization, Gay Rights Resolve. Gays need resolve to get all our rights, everywhere. Not just Massachusetts. Not just Maine and Colorado and here and there but everywhere!

"Resolve! Backbone! Unity with our trans-brothers and sisters, our cis- and pans- and allo- and andros- and poly-friends. Opposing oppression of all sorts. Oppression as espoused by those in this very building!"

Russell turned on his crate and shouted invectives in general and at Jake in particular.

"MacMillan," he yelled, "you belong in the sewer, not running a publishing empire. The ministers who speak out on your behalf are delirious. 'Man of vision,' they say. More like a purveyor of doom. We can see your ruin, MacMillan, and the calamity of those who speak up for you. You are anti-American and sacrilegious—the worst kind of Christian, a far cry from my minister and his wife."

He slandered Jake's name, then demanded, "Pack your bags and close down your stinking lie machine. May the monster rot in hell!"

Picketers waved damning placards high above their heads and roared, "Rot in hell! Rot in hell!"

Obscenities laced the air.

"MacMillan, come out and face us. Coward!" a man in the mob roared.

Cheers greeted his challenge.

"He wouldn't dare. He hides behind his security guards and his paper's skirts!" cried another.

Cheers redoubled. "Coward! Coward!"

The heavy glass front door swung open with a powerful burst, and the jeers died and shouts caught in picketers' throats.

Hands on hips, Jake stood straight and strong before the crowd.

One of the security guards tried to step in front of him to protect him, but Jake gently moved him aside. "It's okay, Tom. Just stand by," he said.

Jake looked squarely at Russell about ten feet away. Surprise, Jake thought, and a touch of fright, filled the man's eyes.

"You're a vile-mouthed little man, Stephen," Jake said softly.

Russell didn't respond—couldn't, perhaps—his mouth twitching, his left hand balling into a fist, his right hand strangling the mic. He appeared barely under control.

Jake turned his attention to the mob. *A flock of mind-numbed sheep.*

"I'll face you, Stephen," he declared loudly. "I'll speak the issues with you. I'll debate you. Any peaceful confrontation you contrive."

"Word games!" cried an old man from the center of the mob. "Lies and word games!"

"You'd prefer *gun* games?" Jake responded. "Would you rather prove your point with wisdom or with blood—

like ISIS, Hezbollah, Al Qa'aida, Hamas and the Muslim Brotherhood?"

He redirected his eyes to Russell. "We can have a debate, impartially moderated. I'll broadcast our get-together worldwide. Podcast, YouTubed, whatever you want. Your choice."

"Empty rhetoric, MacMillan," drawled a girl in a halter top—and with piercings in all sorts of unnatural places.

"Here's what we think of your deceit, you pompous Cretan," came a man's voice at the rear of the mob. A large red tomato arced over the heads of the crowd toward Jake. Jake watched its flight and a smile played on his face.

"Oh, no!" Russell stammered and began to duck. But too late and with too much force. As he toppled off the box the tomato struck him squarely on the top of his head and he fell to the ground with an "Oomph!"

Fighting back a chuckle, Jake stepped toward Russell and offered him a hand.

"Get away from me!" Russell screamed. He awkwardly pushed himself backwards on the sidewalk, then stood up. As he did, a barrage of tomatoes flew from the crowd. Only this time they found their mark. Jake put his arms up in front of his face, but a full dozen of the missiles hit him squarely, forcing him backwards.

Six guards stepped forward toward the crowd. Jake stopped them with an outstretched hand.

"No, no," he said. "Leave them be. Just come inside."

The soft, runny pulp of squashed tomatoes ran down his shirt and dripped from his arms.

The confrontation appeared the next morning on Truth Publishing and Broadcasting's *Sonshine News Hour*.

Truth's e-mail and phone lines were packed with cries of support as well as anti-MacMillan outrage. "We must be doing something right," Jake told Carlos Martinez, "with all those people mad at us."

"But, look," Carlos replied, "look at all the supporters. Many, many people out there still recognize and endorse righteous behavior."

Jake simply nodded in agreement.

If he owed her nothing else, he owed his wife that much—to trust God to deliver His believers into a bright eternity beyond the dark, ominous present. Dawn had bubbled enthusiasm and optimism. They had escaped through her every pore, and she had made a project out of converting Jake to see things her way. She saw a glimmer of good in the dusky tunnel of wickedness called time, just as you could see a ray of sunlight sparkle along a thread of cobweb in a musty cellar.

Jake's memory of Dawn was vivid, even and especially as the tsunami hung high before him.

CHAPTER FIVE

Two days after the May incident with Stephen Russell and the Alliance, Dawn rushed onto their terrace, her brilliant, blue eyes sparkling.

"Jacob." Dawn's joy was contagious. "Guess what, darling. We're grandparents. Me, Grandmama. You, Grandpapa. Lisa just had a big baby boy. One minute she had a contraction, the next a baby!"

She ran—no, glided—to him and he wrapped his arms around her, feeling strangely youthful despite the news. He held her close. Warmth spread over him, taking calm control, its serenity fueled by the love he had for this woman, some twenty-five years his wife and roommate, his confidante, his lover.

He leaned away, held her at arm's length, and studied her face with mock seriousness. He took in her prettiness.

"Ah, but my love, you don't look like a grandmama. Not a wrinkle here." He gently touched her cheek. "Not a wrinkle there." He playfully patted her taut tummy. "I *am* a lucky man."

"More specifically, my dear Jacob," she feigned an aristocratic, queenly air, "you are a lucky grandpapa."

Their laughter was simultaneous, and hearty.

"All right, sweetie," Jake said, "I'll call our pilot. How long do you need to get ready to catch a flight for San Francisco?"

"Get ready? For more than two decades we've shared bed and board and you need to ask such a question?" Her eyes were mischievous, deceiving a sharp tongue. "Mr. MacMillan, not only am I already ready, but you are, too! Our bags have been packed for a week. You're a newsman, a news executive, you even own your own broadcasting empire, and look how easily I keep the truth from you. I needn't even try!"

"Why, you—you'll have your way with me, will you? I think instead I'll have my way with *you*, Grandmama!"

Jake bent, scooped her legs out from under her and carried her back into the house. He moved swiftly toward the stairway leading upstairs, and she hit him rapidly but softly on the chest with balled fists and called out, "Help! Help!" to an empty house.

He had her in his arms, yet he was her captive.

Later, they lay quietly, a mellow feeling of content enveloping them. Dawn turned to look at Jake and said, "Tell me how much you love me, Gramps."

"Oh, darling," he said poetically, "but the words would be like pouring the ocean into a seashell, or counting the stars."

She nudged him with her elbow and said accusingly, "That's someone's words."

"You expect originality from someone you call 'Gramps'?"

She laughed, then her brow knit. "Either I get originality, or I shop for a new Gramps."

He looked pained, then put an arm around her and drew her to him. He smelled the sweet fragrance of Shalimar perfume touched lightly on her neck and he could feel, actually feel a life force between them, as if their love united into a being which played upon the very fibers of their senses.

The axiom "Love makes two one, and one two" came to mind.

"My sweet," he said, "to describe my love, a man would have to climb the highest mountain in the land, and, reaching its pinnacle, behold the most magnificent sunset ever seen by humankind, and then imagine a sight thrice as breathtaking. And, if he could transfer what he saw into words, he might approach doing justice to describing my love for you."

Dawn examined his thick silver-laced hair, his bright brown eyes which spoke to her when no words left his mouth.

Tears welled in her eyes. "Oh, my handsome husband," she sighed, "how beautiful."

He gently kissed the tip of her nose and whispered, "I climb that mountain whenever I'm alone with you, sweetheart. A wonderful climb."

"For me, too," she said softly.

An hour later, Jake held their large suitcase in his right hand and a smaller one in his left, with a makeup case tucked under his left arm. They had showered, he had called his pilot to prepare Truth Publishing's jet for the trip, and he was about to set the large suitcase down to open the door when his cell phone rang.

Dawn was halfway down the walkway of the spacious front lawn when he answered.

The caller was Carlos Martinez.

"Dawn, hold on," he called.

Dawn waited and watched. He knew she knew something was wrong. Seriously wrong.

Jake walked toward her with the large suitcase in one hand and phone in the other, listening to Carlos.

"A bomb just detonated beneath the newsroom, Jake!" Carlos said.

A bomb? A bomb would be a step up for Stephen Russell and his gang. But, then again, the mob the other day had transgressed the tipping point.

Jake felt a shock down to his toes.

"Thankfully," Carlos said, "no one's hurt. The wire desk crew was in the coffee-break room, or they all would have been blown to pieces."

"Security!" Jake nearly screamed. "Where was security?"

"Jake, that's exactly who we think bombed us. We don't have any proof but I think the Alliance—"

"What?" escaped Jake's lips.

"Fred," Carlos said, referring to a guard, "was assaulted on his way out of his apartment building this morning and was found in a heap in an alleyway. He's in Mass General now. But the man who worked the shift told the guard in charge Fred was sick with the flu. They just never checked out the story."

A heavy pressure filled Jake's temples and a stitch-like pain hit him in the upper rib cage like someone had delivered a blow. The thought anyone would want to harm his people was no longer overwhelming but expected. But a bomb?

Jake recalled the anthrax sent in the mail to television and media outlets back in 2001, but that seemed so distant. He wanted to strangle whoever planted the explosive.

Noticing his teeth were clenched, his chin drawn tight, he stopped and drew a deep breath, then another. Everything will turn out all right, he thought. Other acts of terrorism, plunder, even murder, would happen. Events far beyond the control of any person, or earthly power. But through all the turmoil he needed to remain adamant in his belief good would prevail and "this too shall pass." At least such was what he told himself at this moment.

Jake peered ahead, concentrating on what to do, yet noticing the sweet aroma of Dawn's presence. He looked her way, then approached her.

"All right, Carlos. Get all the technical folks in to look over the situation and have recommendations when I get there. I'll be down as soon as I drop Dawn off at the airport."

He slipped the cell into his pocket. "Someone blew up part of the newsroom. Probably the Alliance. Maybe some ISIS-like gang."

Dawn gasped, and he quickly added, "but, miraculously, no one was hurt. I've got to get down there. You go out to Lisa's and Andy's and I'll fly out as soon as possible."

Dawn looked worried. "Okay, but you've got to promise me one thing."

"Yes?"

"You get a security system installed in this house right now—today. Those people are beyond talking to now, and I don't want you and me blown up here." She paused a moment and flashed a quick smile. "It would be no fun being a grandparent alone, you know."

"Today. Security system." Jake held up three fingers. "Scout's honor."

They loaded the luggage into the car and he drove Dawn to Truth's private hangar at Logan International Airport.

As men loaded their luggage onto the Truth jet, Jake held Dawn in a long embrace.

"I can't stay to see you onto the plane, darling. But I'm with you in spirit." He gave her a long, warm kiss. "Don't worry. Everything's going to be all right. Give my love to Lisa, Andy, and the new little munchkin."

Driving away from the Logan, Jake commanded his phone to dial their daughter.

"Hello." Her husband Andy's face appeared on the monitor. "Dad!"

"Hey, son. Congratulations."

"Thanks. I'd give you over to Lisa, but she's sound asleep. The delivery was quick, but she's wiped out. Can't wait to see you."

"Exactly why I'm calling. Dawn's flying off right now. I have a problem I have to tend to, so I'll be out later."

"Sounds great."

"Give Lisa and the baby a kiss for me, will you?"

"Sure will."

They said their goodbyes, and Jake drove to Truth Publishing and Broadcasting, feeling especially lonely and alone. Dawn was flying out to San Francisco. He was driving through a city he loved but whose warmth and hominess had cooled considerably, through seams tattered by sins of all sorts. A sanctuary city turned inside out by rampant crime, Third World diseases, and bedeviling drugs imported by deadly cartels.

A loud boom snapped Jake back to reality. Wondering what the racket was, he scanned the highway, checked the rearview and sideview mirrors. Nothing.

How he'd love to toss his hands up in the air and fly off with Dawn. But he had thousands of employees depending on him at this moment and a crucial situation to oversee. Put duty aside and his little empire might crumble, and all the king's horses and all the king's men ...

The bombers' message was abundantly clear: Beware if you support this Jacob MacMillan and Truth, and be wary if you cling tight to your Christian beliefs.

The vilification approached the vitriol during a presidency when conservatives were attacked for merely wearing Make America Great Again (MAGA) hats.

Little made sense any more.

A couple of years earlier, Jake had sought and not found any racial statement by the ex-president, yet opponents called any who supported him racists. He had searched for but not found any Trump statement against the LGBTQ crowd, and yet, opponents called him and his supporters "homophobes."

Special counsel Robert Mueller's scores of lawyers had investigated for two years to find evidence of Trump Soviet collusion and come up empty, yet opponents continued to declare a complicity existed.

The point where debate would solve differences had passed. Jake had used verbal warfare. He was exceptionally good at the game. He had won battle after battle, visiting campuses like Boston University and Harvard here at home and at UC-Davis and University of Notre Dame thousands of miles away. So now the opposition was resorting to force.

"Might don't make right," Reverend Jesse Jackson had said some years before. But then again, even the aged Jackson's power among the people was a shadow of its past ever since scandals broke out around him.

At the same time, as the number of issues grew, the odds rose against Jake's campaign—with each passing day. And so he had to select his battles. He felt overwhelmed sometimes. Society had been breaking so many rules since the Supreme Court approved abortion rights more than fifty years before. The State of New York in 2019 had led the way for other states in passing law legalizing abortions up to the last minute of pregnancy.

Virginia legislators had upped the ante to include killing newborns; but the legislation was voted down.

Simple carnal knowledge marked the days of Jake's youth. A half-century later, carnality was a full-grown, many-headed viper.

First the pregnancy rate among teenagers had risen astronomically; then intercourse had become common among younger and younger youths—16-year-olds, 15-year-olds, 14-year-olds, and finally 13- and 12-year-olds.

Venereal disease clinics abounded but were overloaded. HIV and AIDS had crushed the gay population and drug addicts. But with curative medicinal mixes, the Hammer of Damocles over their heads no longer hindered their practices.

And now, another sexually spread disease was infecting the gay population—super-gonorrhea. This new strain of the old venereal disease was even featured in editorial cartoons, commonly characterized in a long, black monk-like cape exposing just its hands, bony and wart-covered with long, jagged fingernails, and its face, dark and eerie with a mangled, crooked nose and twisted, sneering lips.

Such characterizations were severe, but not enough to dissuade those who contracted the disease. Indeed, as with AIDS, gays seemed to wear this new epidemic as a crown— laying claim to the killer as their very own.

The epidemic had surpassed the syphilis plague of 1495.

Not constrained to the urethra and vagina, the affliction attacked the heart, kidneys, eyes, bones and joints—disabling, blinding, killing tens of thousands of victims.

Unlike common gonorrhea, this strain could only be contracted through sexual contact. How many people had discovered their spouses' transgressions because of this? Just one minor side effect of the disease.

How ironic, Jake thought, this disease struck only those who indulged when they shouldn't. But such irony faded when considering super-gonorrhea's deadliness.

Jake had toured a special ward at Massachusetts General Hospital set aside for victims of the disease. The place was a horror-picture show, the frames of which kept him awake nights for weeks afterward. People writhing in pain only slightly dulled by even the most potent pain-killing drugs; patients groping for objects with hands unused to the chore of seeing for themselves; women weeping in agony, with no help in sight.

The One World Government had declared an all-out effort to curb the disease, demanding cooperation of all seven of the New World's Regional Governments, including the Americas.

The Center for Contagious Diseases in Atlanta was working twenty-four hours a day, but nothing seemed to work. Penicillin and antibiotics were ineffective, as were sulfonamide and other drugs. The "soups" created to wage war against HIV/AIDS were useless.

Flushing distasteful recollections like these from his mind was difficult, but Jake was doing better.

And, at this moment, his immediate concern was Truth's employees.

He steered his vehicle into his reserved space in a parking lot beside Truth Publishing and Broadcasting. Stepping out, he looked over the face of the structure.

Deceiving. Looks no different.

There were no tell-tale signs of the Alliance's mob picket two days earlier. His maintenance staff had removed the garbage left behind and sand-blasted the graffiti spray-painted on the brick building. The heavy, acrid smell of pot was just a memory.

As Jake stepped to the sidewalk and entered the building, a familiar feeling washed over him. He felt comfortable, at home, almost cozy. This was *his* building, *his* newspaper, *his* broadcasting network. And he loved them all.

He had always thought if he didn't have Dawn, Truth would be his entire life. He'd work, dine and sleep within its confines, venturing out just for church, close friends and civic events. He'd be in touch with the world and yet protected from the craziness.

But any feeling of safety was shattered. He balled his fists.

Jake hadn't felt the fear Dawn showed when she asked him to install an alarm system installed at the house. But now, as he noticed the uneasy look in the receptionist's eyes, the first tickle of anxiety moved along the back of his neck.

Beyond the receptionist, in the Marketing and Advertising Department's large, open room, a dozen men and women lifted their eyes in his direction. They looked puzzled.

Even Ted Anderson, the security guard who was planted by the receptionist's side, seemed ill at ease.

"Sir," the receptionist said, "Mr. Martinez and Mr. MacDonald are waiting for you at the wire desk.

"Thanks, Marcey. Are the police here investigating the bomb?"

"They've come and gone, sir."

Jake was mystified they'd finished so soon.

Reaching the third floor, he walked briskly into the newsroom. The four rows of reporters' desks were half-filled, normal for this time of day.

The wire desk was a large, kidney-shaped table seating five people.

But the entire wire area was in disarray. A hole was blown in the wall and the surrounding floor.

"Jake. Hey, Jake, over here!" Tom Burns perched his tall, stocky frame on the edge of his desk and held a telephone pressed against his chest. "I've got Owens of Universal Satellite Systems on the line. You'd better talk to him."

Jake walked to the desk and took the phone. He could see Owens in the video-phone monitor on the desk. The man's heavy jowls quivered and he looked like he was perspiring profusely.

"Charlie, what's up?" Jake asked.

Owens sounded distant and strained. "Jake, I can't get your replacement satellite up in space—the one to broadcast into Europe."

"What do you mean? The launching schedule's locked in."

"Jake, we're getting a lot of heat for supplying your satellite service around the world. This would set off a backlash we're not prepared to withstand."

Jake stepped closer to the monitor and looked, incredulous, at Owens. He knew the man could readily read his expression. "Charlie, count up the business I've given Universal over the years. Millions—tens of millions—and you're worried about a bunch of hatemongers? What's the real story?"

There was silence as Owens fumbled for words. At last he said, "Jake, our board of directors are very important people. They own real-estate businesses, department and clothing stores; one's a restaurateur, another's president of an advertising firm. The response to this could severely harm their businesses. Then there's one on the board of Planned Parenthood. I've got to face realities. Most of the public don't care much for your television and radio stations, not to mention the newspaper and Internet. I'm really sorry, Jake."

"So am I, Charlie, but more for you than me."

Owens hung his head and his image faded from the monitor as Jake cradled the phone. He turned to Tom. "Find a new satellite service ASAP. We need to reach Europe *now*, to tell those people what's up the sleeves of the Alliance and One World Government."

Jake turned to the others gathered around. "Let's all agree in a brief prayer. We need the Lord's help now more than ever."

With one voice in agreement, everyone reached for their neighbors' hands and bowed their heads.

"Dear Lord," Jake began, "the forces of evil continue against us. We know you are greater than they and your hand is not too short to accomplish your purpose. Father, go before us as a breaker, to discover a satellite provider who will stand with us and provide the services necessary, and to open the doors for a launch so we can inform the people in that area of the world what the enemy plans to do—what the enemy is, in fact, doing as we stand here. Thank you, Lord, for inclining your ear to our prayers and for accomplishing your will in this matter. Amen."

Jake could sense a new feeling of hope pervade the office.

A phone ringing broke the elation. Sue Haynes took the call, then, ashen, wailed.

She looked at Jake. Their gazes locked.

Jake flashed a "what's up" look.

"Jake, who was on your plane?"

The question itself was like a shiv in the gut. Why would she ask?

Jake stammered, "Wh-why?"

"Your jet just blew up during takeoff from Logan."

CHAPTER SIX

At the moment Jake was hearing of Dawn's death, Darek Fields was driving to New York City from Buffalo. Leaving a mild form of desolation, he thought, and hopefully not heading into tragedy.

Darek's immediate hope—permanently connect with the love of his life.

The world's hope?

*We'll just have to wait and find out, try to tread water until that's unveile*d.

To be determined was how many would drown along the way and how many would escape with water-wrinkled fingers.

Darek knew the journey ahead would be rough. Trying to envision the days ahead was like driving into a dense fog on an unfamiliar road at forty miles an hour, knowing sooner or later you'd likely run smack into something, or someone.

The future was written, the obstacles carefully mapped. But no human had access. The script was Captain's log for the future and only he knew the specifics.

What Darek did know was he was about to change his career, his life. He'd had his fill of this constant travel. The brief interludes of live broadcasts on the weekly *American Magazine* news show were just too fleeting. At first, he'd been fascinated with his job, had greeted every trip with yearning expectation, to see more country, the great sights of the world, meet fascinating people and all kinds of exotic nature. He wanted to greet the sun rising from behind the Atlantic, bid farewell when it set behind the swells of the Pacific.

The possibilities mesmerized him. The Rockies, Yellowstone, Death Valley, the Mississippi, Palm Springs, Miami, the Bahamas, Greenwich Village and Haight-Ashbury. There were just so many places Darek wanted to see, and this job was his ticket.

And besides, reporting was more an innate part of him than a vocation. He couldn't *not* write. His college friends could never understand the feelings he got from "his scribblings."

They'd congregate in a room and pass around a joint for their high. He passed a poignant, telling phrase through his keyboard and his high was higher still. And while they were smoking their brains to Timbuktu, he at least thought he was enhancing his little gray cells as Agatha Christie's Hercule Poirot would say.

He recalled an old man who had visited the University of Maine at Orono campus back when he was a senior. The fellow was a self-proclaimed guru, but he'd shot up and smoked up and snorted up so much he was more like a dried-up old sponge—too parched to absorb anything new, and with nothing left to give. But the school's potheads and drug-heads gathered around him like sheep.

A latter-day disciple of the long-dead Edward R. Murrow, Darek nevertheless began his career in the print media to build a solid foundation. Since then, he'd quickly reached his goals. Immediately upon graduating from college, he got a job working on a medium-sized daily newspaper. A general assignment post on a large Boston daily came less than two years later. A year passed, and he was covering the statehouse.

His superiors recognized his talent so much so they struggled to retard his progress.

But the big break, his final-goal-reaching break, came at the one time he wasn't producing copy through his keyboard, not digging for information. He was on a television talk show, invited there to discuss a bloody order of the Muslim Brotherhood called the Takfir wal Hijra, about whom he had written a series later awarded the Pulitzer Prize.

John Cannon, the executive vice president of news for a national cable network, was relaxing on an overstuffed couch in his Upper Manhattan apartment, drinking a nightcap, when the talk-show host on the television before him introduced Darek. The moment the camera zoomed in on the young man, Cannon sat up. When Darek and the host exchanged pleasantries and the usual informal repartee, Cannon leaned closer to the set. When Darek began to answer a serious question about a Muslim cleric in Chicago, Joanne Cannon entered the room.

"Do you want your drink refilled, dear?"

Cannon shushed her with his hand as he concentrated on the zoom-in of the young man.

"Takfir wal Hijra means 'excommunication and exile,'" Darek said. "Outwardly, the Takfir appear to have spurned Islam. They're drinking, going to strip clubs, wearing Western clothes, clean-shaven and with short-cut hair. These actions would have them excommunicated from Islam. But, inwardly, they are devout Muslims."

Cannon loved the resonance of Darek's voice.

"This imam in Chicago agrees with many others around the world, that this behavior is justified as a tactic of *jihad*, holy war. In other words, crime can be committed for the good of the cause. The idea is parallel, in a way, to Mohammed agreeing to a treaty knowing he would break the agreement.

In his view, breaking his word was all right if the result was brought victory."

The host leaned forward. "So, in this view, religion approves crime?"

"The perfect belief system for a criminal, or someone bent on destruction," Darek answered. "A Takfir imam offers his followers redemption that allows them to remain criminals. In fact, their crimes can even be their means of redemption. Very good news for those whose lives are overloaded with bad deeds, to find out they don't have to change their ways. Their ticket to paradise is punched when they die killing an infidel. And you and I," Darek pointed to the host and back at himself, "are considered infidels. Are you watching your back?"

The host coughed uncomfortably.

When a commercial cut into the interview, Joanne Cannon said to her husband, "Captivating young man. Has a presence about him."

His reply: "I've got to have him, Joanne. He's perfect."

Cannon had investigators dig into Darek's personal and professional lives.

Weeks later, his lead investigator walked into his office, a thick file folder in hand.

"What ya' got?" Cannon asked.

"Whistle-clean kid," he said. "Colleagues, classmates, professors, editors, nobody'd say anything negative. Even played a mean shortstop up through college. If not for a shoulder injury he'd be in the pros. That's the only blemish we could find." He shrugged and shot Cannon a half-smile. "Kid fell short athletically."

That's all Cannon needed to hear. He himself had checked out Darek's writing career and graded:

Adaptable. From the non-personal to the highly personal, he writes both well.

Contacts and sources. He accumulates them with ease and quickly,

Communicates. Child or senior citizen, hillbilly or sophisticate, he communicates equally well with them all.

Darek's past editors reported astonishment at his capabilities.

Before the Muslim story, his biggest assignment was traveling to England and France, scrutinizing multi-national corporations and proving they price-fixed and performed dark market manipulations. He dealt with death threats throughout that investigation.

Thus, at the age of twenty-eight, Darek joined the reporting staff of *American Magazine*, the most widely acclaimed and respected newscast in the world. His television "presence" captured viewers immediately.

The obstacles to success on such a highly rated news documentary seemed to flatten out before him, much like the New York freeway as he passed Syracuse. And he wondered if, indeed, his rise had been too fast. If he could go back and start over again, perhaps he would. But then again, if so, he wouldn't meet Jill, the prize of his life. She'd be impossible to replace in any other maybe-life ... and, thankfully, she was getting closer every minute as he drove down this highway.

Darek had met Jillian before *American Magazine*, while working on a series about religious cults. He'd been in Washington, DC, and had gone to the offices of Truth Publishing and Broadcasting's capital bureau to check its files. As soon as he stepped foot inside the carpeted office, he sensed an atmosphere atypical from the other newspapers.

It was calm, serene even. A hubbub, yes, but constrained. Everyone went about their job, but with a quiet confidence, not the frazzled tenseness normal among his colleagues.

As he stood staring dumbly at the scene, he felt a tap on his shoulder. When he turned, he looked squarely into the most startling emerald eyes he had ever seen. Noticing nothing else, he fell immediately in love. Well, no, he admitted later, rather infatuation. But love wasn't far behind.

The owner of the eyes asked sweetly, "May I help you? Are you looking for someone?"

He stammered, unable to form a word, let alone a sentence. He'd felt like a fifth-grader. Grown-ups didn't bumble like this. He bumbled some more.

The young woman smiled and waited, letting him find his tongue. Then he noticed her smile. Her face was as stunning as her eyes. Sun-striped blond hair flowed down to the nape of her neck, then curled softly up, held by a barrette. Full lips parted in amusement as he assessed her.

Finally, thankfully, he found the words to break the silence. "I'm from *American Magazine*, and I'm in town working on a story."

"Oh?"

"Could I possibly access your historical archives and check some back issues?"

She led him through the office toward a side door, looked over her shoulder, and said, "My name's Jillian Down."

"Mine's Darek Fields," he managed.

"I know," she repeated. "I used to read you when you were at the *Boston Herald*."

Certain he was blushing, he wondered how well she could read him now. Like a book, probably. A first-grade primer.

He extended his hand, she laid hers in his with a firm squeeze, and he again felt like a schoolboy—a schoolboy with puppy-love jitters.

Over dinner, they learned more about one another.

Over a glass of wine, Darek told her how the atmosphere at Truth impressed him. "Why the aura?" he asked.

"I believe I know the answer," Jillian replied. "Most journalists are skeptical. If they believe anything at all, it's in evil. They look for evil everywhere because, hey, what's more exciting to write about? Therefore, they tend to turn away from positive things that might suggest unity, accord, a purpose of good."

Darek looked hard at her, intent on what she was saying, recognizing he was observing more than her beauty.

"Most news people don't believe in God," Jillian continued. "But at Truth we do. We see his hand on things everywhere, in circumstances all around us. Psalm 91 talks about God giving his angels charge over us, to watch us in all of our ways, to lift us up in their hands so we don't strike our feet against a stone. And then, even when the end comes, we know where we're going. I think that's why everyone seems more at peace there."

"At peace," Darek said softly. "Maybe you're right. But, you know, I always thought of ministers and priests and nuns as being 'at peace' with God, being happy, always in good health, things like that. Then one day I was in a drug store and saw a nun buying half a dozen huge bottles of Maalox antacid."

They laughed.

Thinking back, Darek felt the pleasure from the warmth he felt when he was with Jill. And he reflected on what she'd told him over their first dinner—about "money people" and "thing people."

She wasn't talking about him, though she might just as well have been. In his advances in his career, he'd told himself money and possessions weren't motivating factors, rather his stories were the only overriding issues. But as Jillian spoke, he was forced to reassess. Exactly how dazzled was he by his possessions, by being a respected, highly paid journalist and celebrity? God knew there weren't many of those in the world.

Over Lobster Newburg, Jillian had made a point setting him to thinking.

"I'll tell you one thing," she said, "you speak of nuns and their Maalox, but I'll make a comparison between Truth employees and those from nine out of every ten other publications or networks—we have fewer ulcers, fewer drinkers and fewer smokers. And we have fewer people out to get all they can get—monetarily, I mean."

She swept her arm in an arc encompassing the plush DC restaurant. "Look at these people. Upper-class or upper-middle-class. How many of them, do you think, chose what would make them happy over what would make them wealthy when they were confronted with choices?"

Darek's mouth went dry. He had to tear his eyes from Jillian's. He fixed them on his wine glass and took a sip. He faced such a decision before. In fact, he'd once decided he wanted to move to beautiful San Diego. But the *Herald* had made an offer he'd convinced himself he couldn't resist. Ever since then, he'd had a rough time facing up to that decision where he placed finances above all else. He'd be reading a book, or watching television, or driving down the highway, and his mind would divert to that milestone. The paths would cross but just miss, like bumper cars on a carnival. The inner debate had become more and more fleet—did money rule his life—propelled by his conscience unwilling to grapple with the idea.

He never did get to San Diego, but *American Magazine* had come along. And since then, the job's challenges had filled his life, as much as they could—for since the night with Jillian, there was a void in his days, a tangible hollowness when they were apart.

Every instance where he could get to see her, he would. If he were in New York City on a story and had just one free night he'd catch a flight to DC. Dinner, a show, one of the Smithsonian museums, a picnic in the park, a bike ride around the capitol, a car ride out into the country.

On occasion, they'd meet elsewhere. They'd both fly into New York for a weekend on the town. Once they met at Niagara Falls, walked down into the tunnels beneath the great, cascading falls, boated out into the river below, then watched the shimmering light show on the falling waters at nightfall.

Cape Cod showed them its attractions once, but fell a poor second to Boothbay Harbor in Maine, where craftsmen proved people could still create with their hands and where the sharp, salty air snapped them to attention when they approached the docks for a ride out to an island for a lobster and clam bake. And they found snug, beautiful hideaways in the Cascade Mountains.

They always took separate rooms. For Jillian, there was no other way. But they were so often together, they'd become an "item."

The tabloids, the *Washington Star* in particular, and the gossipy magazines stayed hot on the tracks of this new, young TV news star.

"Darek Fields Falls for Ravenesque Vixen," barked the *Tattler*.

"Who Is the Beauty on Darek Fields's Arm?" asked *Star*.

Answering this, *People Magazine* gossipers did a piece on Jillian, delving into her career accomplishments, speaking with her coworkers, editorial bosses, and parents. They found God did not bless her only with beauty—her journalistic credentials were impressive as well.

After graduating from the Missouri School of Journalism with minors in political science and history, she'd gone to work for a small, award-winning investigative newspaper in Upstate New York. Her forté was covering the inner workings of the statehouse, a perfect stage for her investigative talents. She became an antagonist to everyone persuaded by money or anything else but facts, to legislators whose votes on key issues seemed oftentimes to take quirky turns at crucial moments.

Her exposés reached a boiling point when she discovered a powerful state legislator's stock in a particular power company spiked in value shortly after an important committee vote.

In the wake of economic fiascoes where one party's national chairman earned hundreds of thousands of dollars in stock profits, Jillian considered this as one more nail in the coffin of political largesse.

But although the public hollered and griped, the party leader vilified Jillian at a press conference, claiming she was a witch-hunter, and the rest of the press, who had picked up her story, were her puppets. The party leader had equated Jillian's story to tossing a hunk of red meat into a school of piranha.

The next day, when Jillian walked into the state Senate chambers during a recess, the senators' glances cast her way were killer looks. The feeling was like stepping into the caverns of hell with venom dripping from its roof like stalactites.

Darek read the story and said to her, "I have to read these things about you in the magazines. Why didn't *you* ever tell me this?"

"No reason to," she'd said. "That was then—this is now." And she had leaned over and kissed him warmly on the lips.

"Great kiss, but you're straying. Those must have been very difficult times for you, personally."

"Yeah. But I learned a good lesson from that one news story in particular, or from the people involved." Jillian pushed her chin to her chest and squinted like she was in pain, then added, "I knew I was violating protocol, but I was dating that legislator. I thought he was terrific. Charming, handsome, great conversation even." She chuckled ruefully. "Then I found out about the payoff, and I was knocked off my feet, stunned. I couldn't believe a man I liked, a man I trusted, was caught up in such corruption.

"He wasn't representing his constituents—he was selling them out. Legislators considered me a spy and backstabber. They thought I'd dated this guy in order to 'get him.' I became taboo. The story killed all my legislative contacts."

She flashed a hurt smile, then continued, "But I learned a lesson for a lifetime."

"Yeah?"

"The old axioms 'beauty is only skin deep' and 'appearances deceive' are valid."

Darek put a hand on hers.

"Funny," Jillian said, "but when I thought about what transpired, I realized I very often judged people by their looks. An ugly-looking person equaled a nasty individual, a beautiful person? Nice. People are led astray simply by good looks—good-looking businessmen, beautiful actresses, handsome clergymen, good-looking politicians."

She sighed and went on: "But now, I'm wary of first impressions. Making an initial, impulsive, and incorrect evaluation of a person can be detrimental for years later. I made too many errors, too many impulsive categorizations. I had to learn or stagnate."

"And," Darek interjected, "you've *got* to be able to admit you've erred, to realign your feelings. Then cope with your disgust. I used to just go out and holler and scream at the person I'd misjudged. They'd think I was crazy."

Oh, my darling, brilliant, Jillian. Darek drove eastward along the outskirts of Utica. *So beautiful—inside and out, every which way I might look at you.*

In her case, her beauty far transcended the skin-deep kind, reaching deep into her soul. Her smile never ceased to brighten his days, and her love sparkled the nights alive. The electricity between them played lively music on his skin, and when they were with each other they belonged totally to one another.

Those moments even out-dazzled the adrenaline-rushed broadcast nights of his career. Those were the times he felt whole. He could barely wait to marry her, so "the two could become one flesh." For Jillian had promised herself to remain pure until she was married.

"Wrapped in the sunlight of your arms, babe," he sang out loud. "Just gettin' a taste of all your charms. Hangin' out together as the dusk turns to night. Lovin' 'til the dark turns to light."

A movement to his left caught his eye. A teenage girl in the passenger seat of a passing car was watching him sing and was smirking. He turned his eyes forward, a little embarrassed. But, yes, he was feeling those words.

Hulking out of the farmland along both sides of the road was Binghamton. He drove on, soon thereafter turning south and toward New York City.

The wind whispered over the ocean, carrying the salty fragrance on twisting paths through the air. Jillian stood at the railing of the tour boat taking her and a couple of dozen others on a cruise around the Statue of Liberty and Ellis Island. The haze of New York Harbor dimmed the bright sunlight that had shone through her hotel window and awakened her this morning.

She never tired of this boat trip, and when she had deep thinking to do, the ride especially quickened her senses. Today was a deep-thinking day. But her decision was eighty-percent certain, dependent only on Darek's opinion. The question would shock him, for the whole situation had arisen too quickly for her to share with him yet.

As a matter of fact, the phone call she had so casually answered the day before had stunned her. She had settled down to a late-morning brunch on her terrace in Washington. No reason to believe the call was out of the ordinary. The one thing she did not like about telephones was they never gave you a hint of what was to come so you could prepare yourself. And she certainly wasn't prepared for *this* call.

When the caller's famous face appeared on the monitor she was startled.

Jake MacMillan. Oh my.

"You're a marvelous, gifted writer," Jake said, "and I'd love for you to work directly with me up here at headquarters."

The voice was warm, the words sincere. She was flattered—and flabbergasted. A promotion coming out of the blue.

"Thank you," she said quietly, then stopped as myriad thoughts and questions flooded over her, visions of a new life breaking the even flow of her existence.

He caught her hesitation. "Take your time, Miss Down. Your work for the *Truth* is valuable wherever you do so, whether you stay in DC, or move up here. But I'd rather have you here. There are some crucial projects we'll be undertaking, and I need our very best people at my side. Please think over the offer. If you'd like to speak with me, I'll fly you up here in our corporate plane. Or we could get together when I come to DC in a couple of weeks."

He mentioned a salary, but Jillian didn't hear the particulars; she didn't need to—they didn't matter. She was lightheaded, trying to catch up to this new development. And when he said his goodbyes and flashed his strong-jawed smile (the one the world either loved or hated), she barely heard him.

Then, as they were about to hang up, she said hurriedly, "It was wonderful talking with you, Mr. MacMillan." As she placed the receiver on the hook, she realized she'd hardly said a word.

But now, she had recovered from the shock and overcome her anxieties. She'd been beset by a befuddling combination of exhilaration and nervous anticipation. But, beneath all her emotions, she believed the offer was an excellent, perhaps even Utopian opportunity.

The Truth had become the epitome of a no-nonsense conservative news empire in a deadly time for such an attitude, defying warning overtures from a government grown self-indulgent, even bordering on lawless. Lawmakers, and especially the US Supreme Court, had weighed heavily to the left and decided they could improve on the Constitution ever since 1963 when the Justices took prayer out of schools.

The Constitution had always stood as a mountain of rock in America, its face spelling "Freedom."

But Congress and the Supreme Court had decided they'd like to sculpt the mountain face. Chisels in hand, they'd begun slowly at first—a chip here, a chip there. But they had gained momentum when they discovered the citizenry didn't stand up en masse to demand a stop, or call for their resignations. Oh, the Liberty Institute and Americans for Jurisprudence would scream, but their protests always faded with time.

It hadn't taken long for these people to get to the news outlets. They'd started by letting confusion reign in the late 1970s and early 1980s about the laws encompassing freedom of access, right of privacy, right to bear arms, right of newsmen to protect their sources. The latest incursion saw Congress pass a law mandating any radio or television station broadcasting a conservative talk show to broadcast a liberal talk show of equal length of time. Since the courts began tightening their grip on these rights, the First Amendment had slowly been choking to death.

Of all the multi-platformed news organizations, Jake MacMillan's the *Truth* had been the most vocal and emphatic at trying to stir the public to back the founding fathers' demand for unabridged freedom of the press, freedom of speech, and call for the sanctity of life, no matter at what stage.

MacMillan himself was up in arms when the 9th Circuit Court upheld a lower-court ruling allowing doctors to inject patients with deadly pharmaceuticals to end their lives, and the Supreme Court refused to hear the appeal. His editorial screeched at the top of its lungs: "Death Court: Jurists' Rule

Threatens Elderly, Others." He compared the High Court's action to those of Hitler, whose minions murdered mentally and physically handicapped persons.

And when the Supreme Court, in the continual fallout of the 9/11 massacre, made a monumental decision the First Amendment did not imply the press's right of access to government information or sources of information within the government's control, MacMillan was livid.

The ruling was a major tear in the fabric of the free press, and MacMillan had verbally climbed all over the leading liberal Associate Justice Tia Hernandez and her colleagues. "Right of access is as essential as the right to publish, for without one you cannot have the other," he'd argued.

"How can citizens examine the government's actions if its records are denied to the press?" he asked. "How can we investigate the handing out of multimillion-dollar bids to industry, disbursement of public funds for the military, maintenance of county jails, without being allowed access to public documents and those jails? Without these rights, we have a totalitarian press, not a free one, and without a free press how far are we from having a totalitarian society? Like the 9th Circuit, the Supreme Court doesn't want to preserve a republic, but rather to impose martial law."

In a rare public statement, Associate Justice Hernandez had demanded a retraction from MacMillan and the *Truth*. MacMillan had declined but said he would be glad to debate his claim with her or the entire court, if she wished.

Jillian smiled as she recalled the debacle—the first, and now probably the last, time a Supreme Court Justice had debated in a broadcast of any type. Surely Associate Justice Hernandez would have preferred to keep quiet if she'd known in advance the outcome of the telecast by Truth Broadcasting.

Near the end of the hour-long show, having grown tired of the Hernandez's defending the belief federal, state, and municipal documents are government documents and the public, therefore, has no right to view them, MacMillan had stared sternly at his opponent, his brown eyes piercing.

"Justice Hernandez," he said, "our founding fathers were brilliant men. There are few—I dare say none—like them today. In their wisdom, they declared: 'Congress shall make no law ... abridging the freedom ... of the press.'"

Slowly, he repeated the words, then held up a thick, hand-bound booklet. "This is filled with news stories of local, state, circuit, and Supreme Court decisions involving the media you and your colleagues are dismembering. Our sacred cows, our Constitutional safeguards for a free press, your honor, they're being *slaughtered*. You just can't see the blood dripping from the pages—just like you can't see the blood of unborn, aborted children flowing in the streets of America."

The Associate Justice twisted uncomfortably in her chair. Her face turned shades of crimson.

In one hand, Jake lifted a loose-leaf document of several pages. "This, Justice Hernandez, is a copy of the United States Constitution. If this could speak, I'm sure it would ask for prosecution of the High Court for violating its intentions, for dragging its values, character, integrity through the torture chamber—stretched on the wheel, lashed with a cat-o-nine-tails of poisonous legal tongues—en route to its death!"

Hernandez, her white mane flying, shot out of her chair, stuttering something incoherent—more like blubbering, Jillian thought now—and shaking her fist at MacMillan. So out-of-character for the aristocratic-looking lady in her black, pin-striped suit.

The moderator of the debate, sitting between the two, had hurriedly thanked them for appearing on the show, and the station had cut quickly into an advertisement.

The running battle between the two had not stopped, and indeed was continuing to this very day.

Indeed, so famous had the debate become that when Jake invited the Speaker of the House and President of the Senate to debate him, they refused. The subject was to concern America's sovereign rights being handed over to the new One World Government.

Jillian stood on the boat deck looking at the New York City skyline soaring high on the shore, a dim background to the torch of freedom held high by the famed lady of the harbor.

The chance to work directly with Jake MacMillan—wow! Darek might not be upset. He might very well be ecstatic. Yes. Yes, he would. He'd be thrilled for her.

As Darek pulled into the below-ground parking lot of the Manhattan hotel where he and Jillian were staying, he started to push the Off button for the radio when news-alert music blared. He hesitated and waited.

"We have just learned a private airplane has exploded upon takeoff from Logan International Airport. Aboard the Gulfstream G650 jet were Dawn MacMillan, wife of Truth Broadcasting magnate Jake MacMillan, and a crew of three—"

Darek slammed on the brakes, stunned, oblivious to the other names.

"FBI and Homeland Security are on the scene along with Boston Police, and a National Transportation Safety Board investigative team is en route."

"Bomb," Darek blurted out.

"Eyewitnesses say the cause appeared to be a bomb rather than a mechanical problem."

"Muslims." Darek gritted his teeth and squeezed the steering wheel.

"Jake MacMillan has famously made enemies of groups ranging from Muslim terrorists to homegrown socialists and received numerous death threats."

"No kidding," Darek deadpanned.

"No one has yet taken credit for the explosion. Stay tuned for further updates. This is Tony Gillette for WTTH radio."

Darek hung his head and wondered how Jake must feel. How would Darek feel if he lost Jill? And the MacMillans had been married for, what, ages.

A car horn blared, jerking Darek out of his thoughts. He hurried to park the car and get into the hotel. Jillian must be there already.

When Jillian opened her door to his knock, she was red-faced and tear-stained, distraught. Truth Broadcasting Television was blaring a news report in the background.

Darek wrapped his arms around his fiancée and held her close as she convulsed and buried her head in his chest.

"Oh, Darek. Oh, Darek. I can't believe this," she wailed. "Poor Jake. I met Dawn MacMillan once. What a gracious, fun lady. How could this happen? Who in the world did this?"

"Someone who wanted Jake MacMillan dead," Darek replied despondently. "There's a legion of them."

Once she'd finished a long cry, Jillian sealed the subject, saying: "She was a devout Christian, outspoken about righteousness and virtues. The only way I can cope with her death is to think, well, she beat us to heaven."

"Yeah," Darek said, "but poor Mr. MacMillan. How does *he* cope?"

Later, as they sat down over a room service dinner, Jillian broke the news about the job offer. She'd been right on target about Darek's reaction, but she wasn't ready for what followed his initial jubilation.

They were standing on the terrace off her hotel room, looking toward the very harbor Jillian had cruised earlier. The autumn night air was nippy and Jillian crossed her arms for warmth.

"Can I get you a sweater?" Darek asked.

"No." She cozied up next to him. "You'll do quite nicely."

"My pleasure." Darek folded both arms around her shoulders. "You know, I've been wondering ... how do you think Jake MacMillan would like to add two to his staff instead of one? Say, a husband-and-wife team. Like Jill and Darek Fields?"

Jillian took a moment to decipher the sentence. Then she turned as if pinched. "Darek, did you just ask me to marry you?"

He smiled and raised an eyebrow.

Jillian wrapped her arms around his neck and raised up on her toes to plant kisses over his face.

He leaned back. "Is that an acceptance?"

She laughed in spite of her mourning. "You got it, kid."

Four days later, at Dawn's funeral in a downtown Boston cathedral—the MacMillans' own Protestant church was too small to accommodate the thousands of people who attended—Jake stood erect at the outer door of the church, shaking hands with every person who'd come.

Rich and powerful, poor and of lowly stature—people had poured into the cathedral until even the building overflowed. Few could tell, as he smiled and spoke pleasantries, what he had gone through in the days since the murders.

Jake had struggled with God, and the Lord had won. He'd yelled at God in the privacy of his home, and found little solace in Psalm 116:15: "The Lord holds dear the death of His saints."

Scripture, he'd told God, didn't send sweet whispers into his ear. He couldn't share his hopes, dreams or love with Scripture. Scripture didn't talk to him over the breakfast table, or respond to his jokes. Indeed, there were no jokes on his lips these days and perhaps never would be. No, Scripture played a poor second to the one woman he'd ever loved—loved as he was supposed to love—as Christ loved the church and gave His life for her. He felt an overwhelming emptiness. There was no hole in his heart because his heart was missing. On hiatus. Gone.

"I *would have* died for her. I would have *died* for her. I would have died *for her*," Jake had said aloud to God, his voice shaking, his shoulders shuddering as he sat on his bedroom floor, his back against the footboard, one of Dawn's scarves wrapped in his right hand.

A still small voice had answered, "I died for you. Now mourn, but then get back to the work I have set before you. I've got Dawn here with me."

Jake's back had stiffened and he'd turned behind him, thinking the voice was that of someone in the room.

Quiet. Dead still. Then he felt a strength he didn't know he possessed. Unnatural. Supernatural, even. He blew his nose on an over-used handkerchief and pushed himself to his feet.

"Okay, Lord," he'd said softly, then in measured cadence added, "but I am not happy."

And now, here he was, after hearing the eulogy about his wife, the readings of her favorite verses from the Bible, the hymns she loved best, capped by *Amazing Grace*. Their daughter, Lisa, was unable to fly cross-country with her newborn, so Andy stood at Jake's side. That was the extent of his family.

Friends, acquaintances, friends, acquaintances, friends, acquaintances slow-stepped by, many of them weeping and saying they were available for whatever support he needed.

He knew they wondered about the strength he displayed, but he realized it was not his. From this time forward, only God would be his strength. Only God *could* be his strength.

Friends, acquaintances, friends, acquaintances. His feet ached and he wished he could just disappear, vaporize into some realm where the pain wasn't so sharp or deep.

Beam me up, Scottie.

Friends, acquaintances, friends, acquaintances. Then, through the threshold of the innermost doorway came two faces that surprised him—Jillian Down and Darek Field. They were sober-faced, and yet Jake could tell they were made for each other. Just like Dawn and him.

Jillian, eyes red and face flushed, put her hand in Jake's and said softly, "I am so, so sorry about Dawn's death, Mr. MacMillan ..."

"Jake," he corrected her.

She laughed lightly at how he had put her at ease. "Jake."

She hesitated, then added, "I met Dawn two years ago, at a Holocaust Museum fundraiser in Washington. She was so sweet. She didn't know me from Eve. Didn't know I worked for you. She simply approached me and began asking about me and saying how she admired me, a gentile, for being at such a function."

"Really?" Jake said.

"Yes, and it was *I* who admired *her*." Jillian smiled sadly. "The whole world will miss her, though not half as much as you, I'm sure."

"No, not half as much." A tear left his eye, and he dried the moisture with a forefinger. "Thank you for your kind words. I remember the occasion you referred to. Dawn told me she'd met you. You impressed her."

Jillian blushed, then moved aside for Darek.

"Kind of you to come, young man," Jake greeted him.

"Sir, I'm here with Jillian to pay our respects. And I hope for an audience with you whenever you return to work."

"Tomorrow then, son, and you can meet me at nine a.m."

Obviously startled by Jake's quick return to the trench warfare, Darek stammered, "Nine tomorrow, then, sir."

The next morning Jake sat at his desk at the Truth when him Darek and Jillian arrived.

Jake had wondered why Darek wanted to see him, but this morning he'd been busy forcing himself back to work, compelling his thoughts to divert from Dawn, making himself press onward as the Lord had spoken to him.

So here he was, writing an editorial about one of his major issues—political correctness. He'd harped again and again on this topic, yet even with myriad thoughts tugging at his mind about the funeral, loneliness, and how best to console his daughter, this commentary was going particularly well, and he was savoring the feeling of a compelling, well-turned phrase.

More than this, he savored the thought of the distraught and angry responses he would get from some of the Speech Police. Of course, Dawn would defend them: "Now, Jake, you can't expect unsaved people to act with God's common sense rather than nonsense."

That argument always made him bristle—because he knew she was right—but he nevertheless was compelled to at least speak and write the truth.

His mouth curled at the thought of Dawn, and the smile still rested there when Jillian and Darek crossed the rebuilt newsroom and entered his office.

Jake waived them to a leather couch and sat across from them in a matching, leather chair.

"Darek, what a surprise to see you at the funeral. Of course, with Jillian there, I wouldn't think you'd be far away—if possible."

"Well, I try to be as close as I can be, as often as I can be. Actually, maybe more so pretty soon."

"Oh?"

"You're the first person to hear this, so I have to swear you to silence."

"Sure, son. What's the secret?

"We're getting married."

Jake shot out of his chair, extending his hand to Darek, his face beaming as he recalled his thoughts in the reception line the day before.

"My. Wonderful news. Congratulations."

He shook Jillian's hand as well.

"Thank you, sir. But there's another thing," Darek continued. "I'm leaving *American Journal* in two months and would like to interview for a job with you—either print or broadcasting, if something is open."

"Interview? You? Darek, I'd love to have you here with us. Sit right there for a minute."

Jake sat back down and put his unlit meerschaum to his lips, thumbing the bowl, thinking. He swiveled his chair to look out his window.

Darek exchanged a look with Jillian. Jillian smiled and shrugged her shoulders, then put a finger to her lips.

The man's thinking. Give him space.

A minute passed, and Jake turned to grab his cell phone. He typed and sent a text, then turned his back to them. A minute later his cell jingled and he checked the message.

Darek smiled at Jillian and shrugged.

At least the man didn't outright say, "No."

Jake turned back around, a sparkle in his eyes. "You said print or broadcast, right?"

Darek nodded.

"Then I have an idea I think might rank as inspiration."

Jake leaned forward, his handsome face intense, the hand holding the pipe waving in the air.

"Husband-and-wife team. A dynamic duo. I want you to work together, both writing as a team and—well, I've been toying with the idea of creating a new, hour-long news-magazine program called *Truth Be Told*, but the right personnel mix has eluded me. Until now."

Jake eyed each of them. "I think you two would be perfect. Jill, have you ever been on-air?"

Jillian frowned. "No, sir."

Jake waved his hand. "No worry. With your personality and charisma ..."

He peered at Darek. "You with me so far?"

Excitement added an edge to Darek's voice. "Yes, sir."

"The broadcasts will only be every two or three weeks, or once a month—we'll call them 'news specials.' Meantime, you'll be lead investigative reporters. We'll send you out to cover the biggest in-depth stories. First, they'll appear in the morning publications—both in *Truth* and on the web site. Then that night, an episode of *Truth Be Told* will broadcast, exploring and expanding the story.

"What if we have a breaking story?" Jillian asked.

"You can report on the daily *World Watch* news. You know the broadcast business, Darek. You two'd be covering the world beat. You're the world's 'Most Beautiful Couple,' according to *People Magazine*." Jake held his hands apart as if holding a banner. "You'd be snappy and crackly. Perfect."

Darek laughed. "Snappy and crackly? Between you and Jill, I'm having some interesting conversation lately."

He winked at Jillian as she drew up close to him.

"Be straight," Jake said, eyeing each in turn. "What do you think of my brainchild?"

Darek turned to Jillian. She returned a dynamic smile and nodded yes.

"Our inclination is yes. But we should pray on the idea tonight and let you know in the morning. Is that okay?"

"I wouldn't have a decision any other way," Jake said. "If the Lord says, 'Yes,' that's confirmation."

Darek nodded.

"Here's the deal-maker." Jake extended his hand to Jillian, then Darek. "But, Darek, if you're going to work for me, the 'sir' has to go. It's 'Jake.'"

As they left, Jake smiled to himself. A man and a woman falling in love. Just as life should be—not this man-and-man and woman-and-woman "matrimony" that first Massachusetts, then the country, and now most of the world, and even most churches, sanctioned. He looked down at his editorial, headlined "The SS (Secular Socialists) of Political Correctness."

It read: "Yes, 'diversity' certainly has morphed over the last ten to fifteen years. Pretty much the same as 'tolerance.' Once proud words that could carry their own weight, now they drip venom. 'Diversity' means 'enlightened liberal uniformity.' And those who preach 'tolerance' are *in*tolerant of anyone favoring traditional, moral values. Meanwhile, 'inclusion' means all should be included—unless, of course, they believe in biblical morals.

"God was correct when he predicted at some point right would be considered wrong and wrong, right—dark would be considered light and light, dark. Such a time was to be the End Times. Logically, then, we're in those End of Days."

Jake's smile morphed into a frown. As a lover of history, he found the notion obvious—the founding fathers, whom he admired, those men who gave birth to tolerance, would not be tolerated in this day and age. They'd be pronounced bigots and worse—just as, in many circles, he was.

The next day, a chill Boston morning, Darek and Jillian stepped hand-in-hand into Jake's office.

Jake looked up and chuckled at the glad sight of them. "Well, what did the Lord tell you folks?"

"We're thrilled at the opportunity," Jillian said.

"Can't wait for our first assignment," Darek added.

"And to hear more about this *Truth Be Told* show," Jillian continued.

For two hours they talked through the parameters of their new jobs, discussed who else would be important additions to the *Truth Be Told* broadcast, and even ideas for the first segments.

CHAPTER SEVEN

Ian Ryan was counting his Irish good luck for getting this job delivering newspapers for *The Truth*. Good pay and benefits. Cordial boss. Early-early morning hours. Nobody around. The streets were quiet at three in the morning.

Ian loved how the streetlights shone off the pavement from an earlier rain shower.

On Charles Street in Malden, he pulled the truck to the sidewalk and stopped to drop a bundle of papers into a vending machine next to Pisa Pizza. The bulk of Macdonald Stadium loomed behind the store. Boy, this place brought back memories every time he stopped here.

He'd played football for Malden High School at Macdonald Stadium, and after the games the gang would celebrate at Pisa's. Now every once in a while he'd bring his wife, Ellen, to the stadium to walk the track surrounding the football field and relive his last game against Medford High. His best game, ever—one against their rivals. What a way to go out.

He could hear the announcer now: "Touchdown, Ian Ryan! And as time runs out!"

Half the crowd went wild, his parents among them—half stood in dull, stunned resignation to defeat.

"Thank you, fans," the announcer said, "for attending the annual Thanksgiving Day showdown between our Golden

Tornados and the Medford High Mustangs. Final score today, Golden Tornados, twenty-three, Mustangs, twenty-one."

Ian pulled open the back door to the truck. As he reached for a bundle, a noise like shoes scuffling on the asphalt echoed behind him. He turned, but all he could see was a glimpse of three or four figures, silhouettes really, then wham! Something hit him in the face like a Mike Tyson punch.

The blow laid him down like a piece of meat. Flat on his back and dazed, he didn't move. Couldn't budge. Rough hands hauled him up off the ground and pinned his arms behind him. This was not good.

Police! Someone!

He wanted to call out, but his mouth didn't work.

Suddenly, these figures started taking turns wailing away at Ian like a punching bag. Splitting pain from a broken rib. Gasping for air from a blow to the chest.

Ian blanked in and out of consciousness. Then he was back on the ground and one of the men was kicking and kicking.

The poor guy'll wear himself out.

Pain seared his ribs when he laughed at his own morbid thought.

Then one of the men growled, "This will teach ya', buddy. Keep workin' for Jake MacMillan and we'll double the pleasure next time."

A couple of others ranted curse words about "MacMillan the Nazi" as Ian blanked in and out of consciousness.

Where are the police anyhow?

As Ian lay there, the rough asphalt digging into his cheek, the distinct smell of gasoline filled his nostrils.

Oh, no.

A loud *whock* and the heat from flames. Struggling to maintain consciousness, Ian pictured flames shooting into the air.

They'd set his truck on fire, or at least the newspapers. The heat intensified and he feared his skin would peel, but he managed to roll away.

Footsteps scurried away and then everything went dark. For how long Ian didn't know but eventually sirens split the night air. His last thought was *Maybe I don't want to work late night anymore.*

In the afternoon, Stephen Russell took charge of the Alliancde's executive board meeting.

The room in his expansive Brownstone apartment was dim, lit only by an old floor lamp in one corner and images on a wall from Russell's laptop computer. Drawn shades kept light from the street from filtering in.

The smell of incense was heavy, the smoke swirling in front of the television monitor with the image of the Boston newsroom of Truth Publishing.

Russell tapped a point in the screen with a laser pointer. "So, the second bomb mangled some computers, plus the floor and a couple of walls. Nothing more. Except for the first explosive taking out the satellite on the roof, we mucked up the assault!"

He looked around. Roger Clapp looked spaced, but the others were still with him.

Sitting cross-legged on the floor, Tanya Frizzell of the Citizens for Free Abortions was taking notes. She was secretary of the Alliance. Flanking her were Icky Coffman, president of Atheists for Full Removal of Non-private Theism (AFFRONT), and Clapp, head of the Society for All Lifestyles and editor of *MEAT* magazine. They passed a joint between them.

Angela Freeman and Buddy Joe Tatum, co-chairpersons of the Black Power League, lolled on an overstuffed couch against the back wall, Buddy Joe's hand resting possessively on Angela's thigh.

Peter Whitetree, chief of the Indian Lands Reclamation Federation, sat Sitting Bull-style in a chair on the opposite side of the room, ready to open the shades when Russell was done.

And the newest member of the coalition, Mosey Kreko, who led the Advocates for a Nuclear-Free World, stood board-still near the projection wall.

Russell pointed again at the image. "Well, at least the bomb caused quite a commotion. They're like a bunch of bees without a hive." He laughed ruefully. "And the queen bee, MacMillan ... he must be stewing now. Especially now his wife's blown to bits."

"Before you choke on your own guffaw, Stephen," Kreko broke in, "losing your wife is no laughing matter. Plus, you're wrong about MacMillan."

Kreko folded his arms and looked dully at the skinny young man before him. "Losing a satellite helps, but they'll overcome the problem. Wire-service stories ran before satellites; they ran before dishes; and they even ran before computers—though you'd have to ask my grandfather about that. No, MacMillan'll survive. He'll be standing after whatever you do."

Russell looked pointedly at Kreko, a handsome, dark-haired six-foot-tall man in his early thirties. "Kreko," he said, somehow dragging out the staccato name, "you talk like you're on *his* side."

Kreko began to protest, but Russell broke him off. "Because you're new on the board maybe I should orient you. It's *we* against the enemy. And in order for *we* to win, *we* have got to stick together. Now, MacMillan and the Truth empire are one of our last surviving enemies and *we* want to put him out of business. *We* want to make him hurt—real bad—*don't* we?"

Kreko held Russell's hard gaze for a long moment. The others in the room became obviously uneasy.

"Stephen," Kreko said finally, "you guys have won lots of battles. Abortions are as easy to get today as divorces. Homosexuality, sex changes in prison, man-child relations, prostitution, all that free love and pornography manifesto is out in the open on the streets. Icky's atheists drove the government to tax churches. People of color and other minorities have their at-large representatives in Congress to fill quotas. And Pete's folks have reclaimed a whole lot of land in all parts of the country, plus their casinos are draining the 'white man's' money."

Nods of agreement around the room added weight to Kreko's words.

"Ever since the Alliance was formed, you've been on a winning streak," Kreko continued. "It's been one donnybrook after another for your enemies. No guns were fired. Yeah, there were a few fist-fights and Antifa gangs beating up people. But not warfare. So, I gotta ask—what's your sudden obsession with violence?"

"Listen, friend," Russell said, "when you've got 'em on their knees, you don't let 'em up ... You kick 'em all the way down, right on their faces. When they're on their faces, you break their legs. The only way to do beat MacMillan is with force. We can't buy him off or shut him up."

"Then how about letting him be? That's just one television station, one radio network, one newspaper, one web site."

"But it's the Gibraltar for the people who believe such vain, deluded, outdated, self-aggrandizing crap. We take Truth down and we've broken their backs. The whole lot of 'em are spineless without that monolith."

"And the only way to take Truth down is with violence?" Kreko asked.

"The best way," Russell retorted.

Kreko looked at the others. "You all feel this way?"

Tatum leaned forward. "Hey, man, this fat cat MacMillan ain't just gonna disappear. He ain't gonna fold his tent and wander off into the desert. The white boy's been layin' heavy metal on us, trash-talkin' like he was a homey, and he's gonna keep sluggin' away 'less we take him down."

"And the way to 'take him down' is to clobber him right in the vitals," Clapp said. "With MacMillan, his vitals is the rag he puts out and the TV station and web site. Yeah, our next target."

Kreko looked at Whitetree, the one on the board he knew well. "You agree, Pete?"

Whitetree shrugged.

"Stephen's right, Mosey. We've got to stick together to keep making progress. MacMillan isn't against Indian rights, or against us getting our lands back, just as he hasn't attacked you on the nuclear issue. But he *has* slammed our gambling enterprises, and he **is** opposed to others here. We've got to stay united. Now's Musketeer time—all for one and one for all."

Kreko backed up to a chair and sat down. "Okay," he said. "Go on with your presentation, Stephen. But I'll tell you, MacMillan's going to somehow get his message out, no matter what you do to him."

Russell grinned. "Score one for our men on the road."

He pressed a key on his laptop and a new picture filled the screen—a road map of greater Boston with red dots marking a number of places.

"Those red marks," Russell said, "are where the *Truth* newspaper trucks drop off their papers. See the dots with the number '1' beside them? Those are where we hit 'em. There, and there, and there ..." He laser-pointed to more than a half dozen spots. "Same thing at major cities across the country. A couple more hits like that and MacMillan won't be able to find a man willing to deliver his papers—here, Ohio, California, or anywhere."

"Just *how bad* did we 'hit' them?" Kreko dragged out the last two words.

Stephen chuckled. "Seven of the eight here in Boston are still in the hospital."

Kreko leaped up. "Stephen, those guys're just drivers, man. What've they done to earn a beatdown?"

"Listen, Kreko," Russell snapped, "we voted to play the game this way. Matter of fact, Hisey Brinks from *Back Off!* is heading here to train some of our people on tactics. If you're lacking the stomach for what's comin' maybe you should cut and run."

"Hisey Brinks? As in Heist Brinks?" Kreko was incredulous. "The guy who thought *Earth First!* wasn't destructive enough?"

"One and the same," Russell said proudly, hooking his thumbs on his shirt as if he were wearing suspenders.

A disturbing thought flashed in Kreko's mind, and the words stumbled out of him: "Stephen, is the Alliance in any way involved in the crash of Jake MacMillan's airplane and the death of his wife?"

The question obviously caught Russell unawares. His face twitched and he stammered, "Uh, uh, wh-what makes you ask?"

"Answer me straight, dude. Is the Alliance responsible for Dawn MacMillan's death—Dawn MacMillan, whose family gave the state of Michigan thousands of acres of land for a state park and built all its infrastructure; Dawn MacMillan, who helped raise millions of dollars for the Holocaust Museum and championed finding a cure for HIV-AIDS; Dawn MacMillan, whose 'sin' was being married to Jake MacMillan?"

Stephen took a step back. Was guilt and self-defense lining his face?

Kreko pressed on, "Stephen, answer me."

"I can't answer you, Kreko. I can only say we do have a relationship with Hisey Brinks and others of his persuasion. But we never asked anyone to blow up that airplane."

Kreko peered long into Russell's face, didn't like what he read there, and took a step toward the door. Looking around the room, he said, "I'm going to meet with my people, then we'll see if we remain involved with the Alliance."

He strode out of the apartment without looking back.

Whitetree jumped up. "I'll talk to him," he said, and in a moment he was outdoors, taking the stairs two at a time up to the sidewalk.

Kreko had reached his car, and was walking around looking at the tires, when Whitetree caught up to him.

Kreko cursed.

"What's the matter?" Whitetree asked.

"They took my hub caps—all of them." Kreko stepped up to the sidewalk. "A couple of years ago, they would've stripped the car. Now, the hoods are locked and sealed, so they take whatever they can get at."

"I know."

"Pete, I *don't* know. I just don't." Kreko threw up his arms. "What kind of world are we creating? Kids are given everything they want through all the welfare programs and they're still burglarizing cars.

"You know, I look at those four wheels without any hub caps and I wonder—what's the difference between vandalism and those people in there?" Kreko nodded toward Russell's apartment.

"What? They're not thieves," Whitetree protested.

Kreko spoke in exasperation, "They're worse. A lot worse."

"Mosey, you've got to look at the big picture. Certain battles they've got to fight in different ways. MacMillan's influential as hell—particularly in one last bastion of power that supports the old society. He's a rallying point for a bunch of ministers and evangelists—Bible-thumping better-than-thous."

Peter raised an eyebrow and continued, "And don't forget, some of those evangelists, like Barry Clime, are still drawing big crowds. Get rid of MacMillan, and you eliminate one of the last obstacles in our way."

Kreko stuffed his hands in his pockets. "Maybe you're right. But I'm not so sure I want to be on the opposite side of religion. And I'm certain I don't want to go around bombing their buildings and knocking their airplanes out of the sky."

He shook his head. "I knew Dawn MacMillan."

"Yeah?"

"A wonderful lady. What's next? We gonna bomb their churches? We're acting like the Arab terrorists we've denounced since nine-eleven."

"Come on, Mosey. You know we're not going to start bombing churches."

"Oh? Why not? We've taken one, make that two, sizeable steps in that direction. Where do we draw the line, and who's got the ink? Russell? Yeah, right."

"We'll *all* draw the line. Tanya, Roger, Angela, me—and you if you'll hang in there with us."

"You and me, yes; Tanya, perhaps; but I'm not so sure about Roger. And the way Angela seems to be getting on with Buddy Joe, I'm far from sure about her." Kreko ran his fingers through his curly, black hair. "Look, I realize I'm the new guy, and this was my first board meeting, but the cards appear to be stacked against reason here.

"Rhetoric's been a powerful ally for the Alliance—that and all the groups sticking up for one another. Why change a winning formula? Public opinion will turn against this violence."

Whitetree laid a hand on Kreko's shoulder and, in a low voice, said, "Mosey, you're missing an important point. True, some of Stephen's operatives have bombed the Truth building. And, yes, some have beaten up delivery men. And maybe, just maybe, we had something to do with the MacMillan airplane. But the plan's to put that entire broadcasting company and web site out of business. And we're not laying claim to those actions. In fact, we're going to release a statement condemning the violence. Publicly we're against the attacks, and no one can't tie us to them."

Kreko shook his head. "'Publicly we're against brutality, sadism and carnage.' That's great, Pete. Just like the Palestinian

Authority denouncing the homicide bombings while naming streets after the bombers."

Kreko turned and walked to the car door. "I'll be in touch."

Whitetree stood watching him drive away, and remained staring after him, thinking deeply as his friend went out of sight. A minute later, he muttered, "Drat," and started back to the apartment.

Mosey drove through the Boston streets en route to the hotel he'd booked into the day before. He was unfamiliar with the city, so unlike his own New York, whose streets were orderly and you knew where you were going. Boston was a maze in which he felt like a baffled laboratory rat. But he had GPS.

The confusing spiderweb of streets seemed to parallel the mess he faced now. He'd come to Boston representing a non-violent organization opposing nuclear power, yet had discovered he'd joined a group apparently committed to a strategy of violence.

Had he joined unwittingly? Darn right.

But how innocent was he, really? The Alliance *had* shown signs of devolving into this reprobate behavior. Surely, he'd seen that. Marches in Washington, San Francisco, Chicago, and other cities had turned to ugly scenes—four-lettered signs and placards, yelled obscenities attacking opponents, nasty clashes with authorities. Surely, he'd been perceptive enough to foresee what was roaring around the bend.

Very disturbing. What was he going to do? He suddenly wished he were a child again. Kids didn't have to face things like this; your parents handled all the messes. No worries. Just go to school, eat, play ball. Repeat. So simple and uncomplicated.

But he wasn't a child any longer. Phillips-Andover Academy, Loyola University, his Rhodes Scholar studies at Oxford—they were all behind him. His job in physics for a progressive think tank—also in the past. He'd chosen a more noble cause.

His future was what confronted him now. But what was he to do? Mary—she'd have the answer.

Mosey parked the car in the hotel lot, the pastels of the early-evening sky enshrouding him. He didn't notice the doorman tipping his hat, couldn't muster a smile to match that of the lady at the reception desk, nearly walked smack-dab into the wall siding the elevators.

When he entered his seventh-floor room, he had to switch on the light. So, Mary was still shopping. Quiet as a dead man's tomb. That was a poor analogy, but his burden weighed on him as heavily as if the air were leaden.

Mosey walked to the window but could see only the lights of the city. Turning to the phone on the bedside table, he rang room service. "Room seven-o-seven, a bottle of your house claret, please."

"Right away, sir," a pleasant voice replied.

Mosey set the receiver down. "'Sir,'" he mimicked. "I wonder if she'd call me 'sir' if she knew I'd just made the Advocates for a Nuclear-Free World members of a murderous gang. She might rather say, 'Never, you murdering scum. Not on my life.'"

He sat on the bed, thinking. Nonchalantly, he opened the drawer of the end table. Three postcards, all showing a swan boat on a pond in Boston Commons. A pamphlet with a duck boat on the cover and welcoming visitors to "enjoy all Boston has to offer." And a Gideon Bible.

Wow! This must be a mistake.

The Supreme Court had ordered every Gideon Bible removed from every hotel room in the country, so as not to offend any unsuspecting hotel guests. They'd missed this one.

Taking the Bible from its place, Mosey slowly turned the book in his hands, then squeezed. He hadn't held a Bible for years; yet the feeling wasn't alien. In fact, the cover warmed to his touch. On impulse he rifled through the pages, then stopped. Proverbs 1, the upper left-hand corner told him. He scanned down the page, stopping on the words:

> My son, if sinners entice thee, consent thou not. Forsake the foolish, and live; and go in the way of understanding.

He flipped past a couple more the pages and stopped at Proverbs 13. Again, looking down the page, he focused on verse 20 and read:

> He that walketh with wise men shall be wise; but a companion of fools shall be destroyed.

Mosey shuddered.

Why would I open the Bible to those two verses?

Just then the door knob turned and in walked Mary.

"Oh, hi, honey." Her voice sparkled in surprise. "I didn't expect you back so soon. Quick meeting, huh?"

"Why don't you drop those packages on the chair over there and sit with me?" He tapped the bed by his side. "I need to talk over some things with you."

Mary obviously read the troubled look on his face and did as he asked, then ran her hand down his arm. "A problem with the Alliance?

"You could say."

"A falling out?"

"How do you know these things?" he asked, one eyebrow raising.

He recounted what had transpired. Mary was attentive, nodding agreement when he related what he'd said to Stephen Russell.

When he finished, Mary said, "Apparently these people just put their minds in neutral and go where Russell pushes them."

"Some of them, yes," Mosey replied. "I'd say Icky Coffman of AFFRONT does, and Roger Clapp. And Buddy Joe Tatum is pro-violence by nature, for sure. He'd have been right at home with the old Weathermen or Black Panthers. I'm sure he's been in the middle of some of the Antifa thuggery. And since he and Angela are getting it on ..."

"Mosey, I think maybe we should reassess belonging to this group," Mary said. "Remember when our board agreed to join. We talked about building on a dream, a world without nuclear warfare, so we could dare to have children. But we also want a world without violence, period—nuclear or otherwise."

Mary looked sharply into Mosey's eyes

He interpreted her look: "And so here we have the 'otherwise.'"

"Right."

"So, we drop out, huh?"

Mary thought for a few moments, curling a lock of her short, brown hair around a finger. "Maybe. Maybe not, sweetie. Maybe there's another way—a better move."

Mosey caught the glimmer in his wife's eyes. She'd formulated a solution.

Jake spent the morning on Boston's North Shore negotiating a satellite launch with a start-up company run by three recent MIT graduates The kids were brilliant, hungry for clients, and willing to absorb any heat they might get for dealing with Truth.

On his drive back to Boston he received a cell call from Ted McAnlis, head of distribution for the newspaper. Jake's next stop was no longer the office, but Massachusetts General Hospital.

"Eight of my men, both in Boston and the suburbs, were attacked while making paper drops early this morning," Ted said.

Jake turned his car into a parking lot. He wanted full attention on this conversation.

"How bad are they hurt?" he asked.

"Badly beaten. Five are in intensive care. Two are in surgery right now. If you can get to Mass General, one of my guys is awake and alert enough to fill you in. You should hear this."

Jake checked his watch. "I'll be there in a half hour."

"Jake?"

"Yeah?"

"They torched all the delivery trucks."

Ted met Jake inside the Mass General entrance.

"I'm getting calls from around the country—Dallas, Minneapolis, Phoenix, LA, Miami. These attacks were well rehearsed and coordinated. They all went down roughly the same, from the first punch to the light of the match."

Jake nodded. "The question is 'coordinated' by whom?"

Jake followed Ted to the third-floor room where Ian Ryan was stitched, bandaged and wrapped, and sitting up in bed. A young woman was seated beside him. They were holding hands.

Ted introduced Jake to Ian and his wife, Ellen, and they exchanged "hellos."

Jake scanned Ian from head to foot and asked, "Nothing broken?"

"Incredibly, no, sir. Must be my Irish good luck." He began to laugh but winced and by reflex put a hand to his ribs.

"Ian," Jake said, "tell us what happened, exactly?"

Ian touched his hand to the stitches on his cheek and flinched, then rubbed his left knee. "I feel like the Mummy with all the Ace bandage they wrapped around my knees and ribs."

He told the entire story up to rolling away from the heat of the fire when he lost consciousness.

"They told me I should leave my job or else next time—"

Jake shook his head in disgust, then asked, "Could you make out any of the faces if you were to see them again?"

Ian thought for a moment. "The cops asked me and I said 'No.' But then again I'm not sure. When they were holdin' me up and beatin' on me, a light from somewhere—a streetlight maybe—caught one of 'em in the face. Just for a second, but I think he had a pock-marked mug with a crooked scar down one cheek—right out of the movies. Like Béla Lugosi."

"Béla Lugosi?" Jake chuckled. "A fan of old movies, are you?"

"Lugosi, I love. There's a bit of Hungarian mixed in with my Irish blood." Ian laughed and again grabbed at his ribs.

"So, you could pick this guy out of a lineup?" Ted asked.

Ian groaned, then said, "Well, with all those night shadows twistin' around, I really couldn't swear to an ID, sir. I was spendin' more time prayin' I'd pass out than I was tryin' to see their faces, to tell ya' the truth."

Jake stepped forward and grabbed Ian's hand. "We'll take care of you and yours, young man. And if you want another job, we'll see to that as well."

Then Jake prayed for healing and against fear.

As he and Ted left the room Jake said, "I want a security guard accompanying every delivery truck in the country."

Ted's eyebrows rose. "But, Jake, the cost!"

"Cost be damned." Seldom before had Jake felt this kind of anger.

There was murder, arson, and assault. At this moment rioting and intimidation of advertisers seemed like small potatoes. What else did his enemies have in store?

CHAPTER EIGHT

Jake reveled in his decision to team up Darek and Jillian. The pair especially excelled covering the One World Government. The countries of the world had quasi-united under the global umbrella and Premier Clifford Sardis had coaxed a seven-year peace agreement out of the Israelis and Palestinians, while Mother Nature went berserk.

One day their story drove home one point:

WORLDWIDE CLAMOR FOR US TO "CLEAN UP" CALLED MISGUIDED

By Darek Fields and Jillian Down

Staff Writers

HONG KONG—The view was once spectacular from the shores here—the morning sun sparkling off the waters of the South China Sea, tempting sportsmen and sailors to partake in the then-British territory. Today, the sun struggles to glint through the haze of smog, and when successful, the sparkle is lost in the brackish waters of the sea. Yet, this is the land in which the majority of the nation-states of the One World Government are meeting and demanding the United States of America reduce its air and water pollution.

Since the Kyoto Accord III, many of the leaders of Eastern and Third World nation-states, claiming global climate change is not only a fact but mainly caused by mankind, have tried to politically strong-arm America into actions they themselves have not undertaken.

One World Premier Clifford Sardis has even threatened global sanctions if America does not relent. The standard-bearing cry is America uses more energy, burns more fossil fuels, produces more byproducts from manufacturing, than any other nation-state.

Of course this was no surprise given the United States' substantial portion of world production since the triumphal revival of US manufacturing starting in mid-2017.

The article continued on, explaining since the first Kyoto Accord in 1994, the US had become the whipping boy for these nations and the One World Government which continued wresting control of once-sovereign nations.

Having set itself up as the police force of the world, employing massive military might to enforce political correctness in all sorts of avenues, the One World Government—particularly the popular Sardis—stood ready and willing to assume physical as well as moral leadership around the shrinking globe.

But a free press was one thing the new global government had not seized from America, and Darek and Jillian continued to stick their finger in the eye of these efforts. Pointing out the shortfalls of the progressive and socialist governments and their societies, their stories were at times derisive and caustic, but perhaps never so much so as when the One World Government re-incorporated the International Criminal

Court under its control from the now-defunct United Nations and set up the tribunal in Italy.

INT'L CRIMINAL COURT A HAMMER OF JUSTICE OR REVENGE?

By Darek Fields and Jillian Down

Staff Writers

BRUSSELS — The persons on the wrong side of a war between nations, a civil war, or simply a fracas, have a new, international, nemesis.

World Premier Clifford Sardi and his International Criminal Court (ICC) are now self-empowered to determine which of two sides of an armed conflict is "right" and which is "wrong." And the people in the wrong may be headed for judgment outside their country's own court system.

There is speculation the recent peace between Israel and the Palestinian Authority was a result of the threat of Sardis using this court as a hammer.

Napoleon, Genghis Kahn, William the Conqueror, even US presidents who engaged the United States in wars, could have all faced judgment at the hands of this seven-member tribunal if this abomination had existed during their lifetimes.

Created to prosecute "crimes against humanity," the ICC takes center stage now fully ratified by the Americas (North, South, and Central) and all the other six world regional governments.

US President William Carver admitted the ICC could be viewed as a threat to sovereignty among the regions of the world, but added, "In the final analysis, this sort of global court was a foregone conclusion. I prefer to look at the situation much like the US judicial system has worked for 250 years. We have district courts, federal courts, appellate courts, and the US Supreme Court. With the advent of the ICC, we can take criminal cases directly to the final arbitrator."

So, final decision-making of right and wrong has been transferred outside America's borders to Brussels, the home of the One World Government, and Italy, home of the International Criminal Court.

World Premier Sardis bristled when asked about objections surrounding national sovereignty. He granted an audience because of the critical nature of the court's existence, but declared there is "no higher authority in these matters—on the earth or in the heavens—than me. Only I can overturn the World Court."

Asked about the pro-Arab bent of the One World Government and the possibility of former heads of states like Israeli prime ministers being brought before the ICC, Sardis said, "The Arabs are peace-loving people. They understand the past should be buried in the past. However, if they want to bring a prime minister before the Court, I will decide at the necessary time."

Darek and Jillian's coverage continued, but omitted one personal note. When Darek asked Sardis if he ever felt he had made a mistake, Sardis stood to his feet. "You dare suggest I am *not* infallible?"

"To be infallible would make you God," Darek said.

"Um-hm." Sardis stared woodenly at Darek.

"You're saying you're God?" Darek's eyes widened, and he chuckled.

"You dare laugh at me!" Sardis voice rose an octave. "Security!"

In an instant, two men in dark suits pushed through the wide door.

"Remove these people from my office, and from this building."

Jillian later told Darek she felt the air in the room drop to a chill at the moment of Darek's defiance.

Then there was the report on covering an Iranian oil tanker's spill of an enormous amount of oil:

CRUDE CURRENT FLOWS, BURNS OUT OF CONTROL

By Darek Fields and Jillian Fields

Staff Writers

HILO, Hawaii—Efforts to stem the flow of the giant oil spill, which has covered much of the eastern Pacific Ocean, continue to be fruitless on a long stretch of the ocean south of here.

The historic slick, nicknamed the "Crude Current," is flowing westward toward the Marshall Islands just over 2,000 miles away. The Hawaiian Islands apparently will survive the threat since the North Equatorial Current has the spill in its grip more than 100 miles offshore.

Other areas along the route are less fortunate. Since the world's four largest oil tankers—Iran's Al Quasa, Al Ahkba, Quin Disi and Ya Lima—mysteriously broke up off the coast of the southern leg of Alaska four months ago, the oil slick has slowly ruined beaches and untold numbers of aquatic and animal life for 4,000 miles.

Carried along first by the Subarctic Current and then the California Current before being pulled into the North Aquatic Current, the oil has wreaked havoc along the coastline from Alaska to Mexico's Baja Peninsula.

Homeland Security Secretary Barry Waters and American politicians question what four Iranian oil tankers were doing off the shores of Alaska, and have implied the multiple spills were an intentional Islamic attack on this country.

California Coastal Commission Executive Director Nel Babbot reported innumerable waterfowl, fish, and crustaceans along the Pacific Coast have perished.

US Travel Association spokesman Michael Deering said the tourist industry is devastated. The stock markets in America, Japan and the European Union have tumbled.

And still the worries continue as the Crude Current moves on—unabated.

In many areas, patches of oil have caught fire and are burning, uncontrolled, as dozens of firefighting boats battle in vain.

Officials from America's Sea and Shore Fisheries, the Department of Interior and the Coast Guard and Navy look hopelessly away when asked of their chances to stop the Crude Current.

People and industries the oil spills have affected are distraught—as witnessed last week when a young woman fired a shot at Iranian Ambassador Husseini when a mob of Columbia University students marched outside One World Government's American headquarters, the former United Nations building.

And those people living in areas in the path the Crude Current is expected to travel are frightened their livelihoods will be ruined.

"When will this end?" asked Ed Perez of San Juan, and his face went slack. Meanwhile, captains of the oil barges deny charges of sabotage, and Iran itself will share none of the blame, shrugging off claims the four simultaneous spills were intentional.

"The West is a ghastly, big thankless beast," said Ayatollah Akbah el Arobi. "For decades they asked for more and more oil and Arab nations obliged. They devoured with no thought of the future. Now they don't need our oil, they snub us. I say this is an act of Allah!"

Right, Allah, Jake thought. Insanity.

Militant Islam had continued waging a war globally against all non-Muslim countries—Premier Sardis be damned—and demanded numerous nations, including the United States, parcel out land for new "Islamic states within."

They insisted a swath of land from Southern California through New Mexico be given to them to be run under Sharia law.

Almost humorously, Mexican-Americans and illegal aliens followed suit, demanding roughly the same territory for a nation of *their* own. The whole thing was reminiscent of the Palestinian Authority demanding Jews cleave off large portions of Israel for a new Arab nation.

Premier Sardis, of course, was in the midst of the negotiations, wielding his charismatic magic to reconcile two wildly divergent adversaries.

Nearly everyone in the West, especially America, had been pierced by one disaster after another—on both physical and emotional levels.

Jake laughed ruefully. *Nearly everyone is pierced, period.* He thought of the ear-, nose- belly-button, eyebrow-, lip-, tongue-, and who-knows-what piercing that was an accepted practice since the late 1990s.

Piercing aside, a lot was ailing the country and the world, and had been for years. With gay marriage, homosexuality and prostitution now "Constitutional rights," the Pledge of Allegiance declared unconstitutional, the Ten Commandments barred from public places in America, especially courtrooms, and with the entire world awash in sensual indulgences, society was spiritually exactly what Pastor Bill Asbury had called it: "like a gangrenous carcass" covered with maggots devouring their prey.

CHAPTER NINE

THE FOLLOWING SPRING

Jake worked and slept—seemingly nothing else, though eating must have fit in there somewhere—fighting depression as seasons changed. A winter with more snow than any year in a century had turned the corner. The Red Sox were in spring training, having won yet another World Championship for Beantowners and beyond.

And he had given away the fatherless Jillian when she and Darek married. Immediately they had taken a two-week honeymoon, foiling the best efforts of paparazzi from *People, Us, In Touch, OK!, National Enquirer* and various other media to find them.

TMZ had offered $100,000 to anyone who could lead them to the Fields couple.

"America's most eligible man marries the most gorgeous damsel on television and no one knows where they are?" its on-air personalities asked. Incredulity poured from their lips.

Jillian's mother and Jake were the only people the couple had told they were going to a camp deep in the Maine woods and using the last name Sheldon, Jillian's favorite comic character from *The Big Bang Theory*.

Then, at nine o'clock one May morning, Darek and Jillian stepped into Jake's office to discuss their next assignment.

Jake's happy meter leaped. "You look great," he said and opened his arms to receive a hug from Jillian.

"Thanks ... Dad." She smiled brilliantly.

"The Church Universal," Jake said, speaking of the spiritual United Nations that had come into being.

"Antichrist in sheep's clothing," said Darek.

"True believers see through the disguise," Jake said, "but you have to look at the line-up of those involved. They include Catholics, Episcopalians and Universalist-Unitarians, Reform Jews, Muslims, Buddhists, Hindus, Bahá'í, Sikhs, Jains, Taoists—even Pantheists and Zoroasters and Wiccans."

"Well, they've been planning one world religion long enough," said Jillian. "I wrote a feature on them as a thesis for my master's degree. They began contriving Church Universal in the early 1990s. Two hundred delegates from around the world met at Stanford University. The whole idea was pooh-poohed by the general public, but I had this eerie chill.

"And as I investigated, my concerns soared. I'll never forget this quote at a conference in 1997 from Reverend William Swing, bishop of the Episcopal Diocese of California. He told delegates, 'You're deputized! Tell the people there is a United Religion, and somewhere in the world, it's beginning to happen—the religions are going to have an oasis where they can talk about peace.'"

"Peace," Darek said. "If you say that word alone sincerely enough, you'll sway the populace."

Jake groaned and thought of his wife's devotion to reading the Bible an hour a day.

"Especially if the populace doesn't know their Bible," he said.

"So Church Universal's our next assignment?" Jillian asked.

Jake toyed with his meerschaum. "You see this pipe? The bowl's been hot and cold, hot and cold, for years. Something like the earth. Since God created this little sphere, the earth has experienced Noah's flood, eight-point-0 earthquakes, volcanic eruptions, an ice age, tsunamis.

"Meanwhile, humans have experienced exhilarating heights, tumultuous times, victories, defeats, deceptions of great magnitude. I believe we've entered a dangerous age, and Church Universal is a signpost."

"A signpost?" Darek's brow furrowed.

"Read Revelation thirteen and ask yourself, who is the Second Beast?" Jake replied.

"I guess that'll be part of our preparation before we begin our assignment, eh?"

"Absolutely," Jake said. "I think you two are perfect for this one. I'm sending Ty Cole along with you, to get you up to speed as well as dig out the news while you two fashion the analysis."

Ty was the Truth Publishing religion editor, and Jake knew Ty and his wife, Bethany, had drawn close to Darek and Jillian. He'd chosen this team well.

"While you're there," Jake said, "I want you to check out the men Christians are saying are the 'two witnesses' in the Book of Revelation."

"But from Ty's account of his attempts to speak to them, he couldn't," Darek said.

"Right," Jillian said. "He said there was an aura, a force around them—that you don't dare even approach them."

"Yeah," Darek said. "Ty got within about thirty feet and watched them preach for a while. But when he took a couple of tentative steps closer, the big one, Elijah, peered at him. A look at those eyes and Ty froze. He literally couldn't move for minutes. By the time he could, they were gone."

"You may not be able to interview them, either," Jake said, "but it's important you see them, hear what they're saying, and at least attempt an interview."

"Okay, boss. Will do."

"Next up will be a feature on the One World Government. You already know many of the major players, and they all respect you, even if Sardis would rather not see *you* around his office again for a while." Jake nodded toward Darek. "But I think you'll discover the power lies in people, one man in particular, with whom you're not familiar."

"Sounds intriguing," Jillian said.

Darek rose and took Jillian's hand. "Let's go, partner. Work to do."

On their way out the door, Darek turned to Jake. "Thanks for all you've done for us. I wake up every day excited about going to work."

"My boy," Jake smiled, "I see myself twenty-five years ago when I look at you. Except you're better than I was, and I get a thrill out of seeing the end product of what you do—both of you."

Darek humbly returned the smile. "We'll try not to disappoint you."

The two walked out of the room, leaving Jake in contemplation.

"Dawn, my darling," he whispered, "perhaps you went Home at a good time—before all of this peace, peace, where there is no peace. I miss you terribly."

The phone rang and Jake picked up the receiver. His secretary appeared on the monitor.

"Jake, there's a man on the phone, and he won't identify himself. He insists it's imperative he speak to you."

"Put him on, Marcey."

The monitor was blank and voice on the other end of the line sounded vaguely familiar. "Mr. MacMillan?"

"Yes. Who's this?"

"I can't tell you. But I'm privy to life-or-death information you must hear."

"Really?" Jake said. "Can I see your face?"

"No, I don't dare reveal myself."

"Then how can I trust what you have to say?"

"Take the appropriate response, and you'll get your proof."

Five minutes later, Jake slumped in his chair, stunned.

That night, as Jake sat in his den reading a packet of information prepared for him on worldwide persecution of Christians, the doorbell rang. Bob Ward, who'd started work that afternoon as his personal bodyguard, answered the door.

After a few mumbled words, Bob appeared in the door. "Mr. MacMillan, Pastor Asbury's here to see you."

"Let him in. Thanks."

Bill Asbury strode in, tall, slim, confident—and with furrowed brow.

"I was in the neighborhood and thought I'd stop by," he said. "How're you doing, Jake? And what's that big fence they're installing around your property?"

"How am I doing?" Jake laughed, at ease with his best friend and pastor. "I'm in survival mode, Bill. I'm reconciled with Dawn's death. I figure she's in a much better place. But I miss her incredibly. I can't sleep. I'm mentally tired, spiritually exhausted. I'd love to get away to get out and visit Lisa, Ted, and the baby. But in these circumstances—" He tossed up his hands.

"You're going through a Job experience," Bill said, taking a seat in an overstuffed chair opposite Jake. "But at least you're better off than Job."

"How's that?"

"Well, for one, you don't have Job's wife telling you to curse the Lord. For another, you've got me instead of Job's buddies." Bill chuckled lightly.

"You're right there."

"Do you want some advice?"

"From you, yes. From Eliyahu, no." Jake grinned, referring to one of Job's companions.

"Fly out. Visit Lisa and her family. She needs your consolation now more than ever. I know her absence from the funeral was heart-wrenching for both of you."

"I've been speaking with her at least once a day."

"I know. But talk doesn't replace her daddy's arms wrapped around her, nor your daughter's hugging you."

"My new jet's taking some people to Israel."

"Imagine that, having to travel with the public." Bill spoke half-jokingly and Jake knew his friend wasn't going to let him escape with any excuses.

But he tried, just for fun. "I'd have to get used to traveling with a companion who's not my wife." He nodded toward the den door and Bob, who was sitting out in the entry hall.

"I think you can handle the challenge."

"M-hm."

"Listen, I know you're a strong person, a man of faith, and, despite smoking that darned pipe," Bill gestured toward the ever-present meerschaum lying on an end table, "you're determined to please God with your life."

Jake nodded and smiled. "Please leave my meerschaum out of this."

Bill waved off his comment. "But you need to take full advantage of your support system, including Lisa and Ted. Darlene and me. All the church family and those beyond the church. We're here for you and we love you."

"Okay, Bill," Jake said. "I didn't want to, but I'll share this with you and perhaps nobody else except Lisa and Ted. I've come by some, ahh, frightening information. Wherever I go, I may be endangering whoever's there. I may have to become a hermit, restrict my living between home and the office."

"Wh-What are you talking about?" Bill stammered.

Jake leaned forward and lowered his voice. "There's a hit out on me. The bomb that blew up my plane? They thought I'd be on board."

"How do you know this? The FBI?"

"Not the FBI, but I can't say who."

"Therefore, the fence they're constructing."

Jake nodded. "And we're installing the most sophisticated electronic surveillance and bulletproof windows. I feel like a Mafia boss, living in a fortress and surrounded by armed men. Ridiculous. I honestly sometimes wish I'd gone out with Dawn. Life without her hurts. Hurts right here." Jake tapped his chest, his eyes glistening.

"I know. You two were as close as any couple I've ever known. I can't imagine life without Darlene."

Jake rose from his chair. "Say, Bill, I'm going to fix some tea. Would you like some, or coffee, or soda?"

"You're my only friend with PG Tips tea. You think I'd turn down that offer?"

"PG Tips, then."

Jake left the room. Bill rose and wandered along the bookshelves covering three walls of the dark chestnut-wood room. He'd been in this den dozens of times, but never examined what books filled the walls.

He ran his finger along one shelf. The books ranged in variety from George MacDonald's *The North Side of the Wind* and *The Minister's Restoration* to C.S. Lewis's *God in the Dock* and *The Great Divorce*. Another shelf contained various Bibles from *The Complete Jewish Bible* to the *Aramaic Bible*, and a wide range of commentaries. Another shelf contained Christian fiction. Another was filled with biographies, autobiographies and nonfiction.

Bill's eyes stopped and froze when he came to a shelf holding *The Koran* and the Bible of Jesus Christ of Latter-day Saints.

Jake entered the room carrying a tray with a tea kettle and a dish laden with cookies.

"We've got tea steeping and some homemade oatmeal cookies from our neighbor, Sandy Oaks, a very nice lady and friend of Dawn's. You remember her from a couple of parties here."

"Lost her husband on September 11. I remember."

"Yes, she knows what I'm going through, spent a couple of hours here before the funeral. Afraid I cried up a storm." Jake hesitated. "She asked me, 'Why does God let good people die?' I'd just struggled with her same question for the hundredth time."

"What'd you tell her?"

"We live in a fallen world. Satan wants to kill all mankind. Better still if he can get some of them to kill others with them. Ever since sin entered the world through Adam and Eve's fall, the world has faced sickness, disease, and man's inhumanity to man. I haven't figured out yet why he saved my life several times, but allowed a bomb to blow up my jet with Dawn and the crew on board."

"There are questions we'll never know the answers to—not while we're on this earth, anyhow," Bill said. "And I'm not ashamed to say so. The Bible says faith is being sure of what you cannot see. I think faith's also trusting God in spite of what you don't understand.

"Speaking of what you don't understand," Bill motioned toward the bookshelves, "I noticed you have a copy of *The Koran*. Are you looking there for answers?"

"Oh, no," Jake blurted out. "First, I wanted to discover why so many people would want to worship this hateful god Allah when the God of the Bible wants to welcome them into his arms with mercy and grace."

Bill breathed a sigh of relief, then asked, "You get your answer?"

"As a matter of fact, no. What I did find out was they want to kill everyone—not just Jews, but everyone—who doesn't bow down and worship Allah. Premier Sardis, President Carver, all these politicians and apologists tell the world Islam means 'peace.' That's a lie. Islam is related to the Arabic word for peace, *salaam*, but has a militaristic connotation meaning 'to surrender, to submit—as a slave to his master, Allah.'"

Jake rose and walked to the bookshelf, snapping *The Koran* from its place.

"Islam," he said, "was born with the idea of ruling the world. Judaism focuses on national salvation; on the Jews having their own land, Israel; and being ruled by their own king as they serve Adonai. Christianity declares Jesus can save anyone, everyone from their sins."

Leafing through *The Koran*, he continued: "So, looking for why anyone would turn to Islam, I found, instead, that killing and violence have always been part and parcel of

Mohammed's teaching. While there are 114 verses about love, forgiveness and peace, they're all abrogated by Suda 9:5, known as 'The Verse of The Sword,' which came later in Mohammed's life."

Placing a finger on a page, Jake read: "Find and slay the pagans—that's us non-Muslims—wherever you find them, beleaguer them, and lie in wait for them, in every stratagem (of war); but if they repent—meaning 'convert to Islam'—and establish regular prayers and practice regular charity, then open up a way for them: for Allah is oft forgiving, most merciful."

Jake looked up at Bill. "Apparently, they believe by our mere existence, we're fighting against them, so killing us is all right. A number of verses in this book can be used for such a cause. Chapter two, verses two hundred and sixteen to two hundred and eighteen and back in chapter eight, Muslims are exhorted to fight and kill unbelievers in a jihad—a holy war. They declared, 'Allah sent Mohammed with the true religion so Islam should rule over all the religions.'"

Bill sipped his tea and nodded. "I remember Osama bin Laden, after September 11, saying the terrorism he practiced was of the commendable kind, directed at tyrants and the aggressors and enemies of Allah."

"We had one of our reporters call leading Muslim clerics around the United States asking for statements condemning Islamic terror," Jake said. "One imam—one—would do so."

Jake placed *The Koran* back on the shelf and sat down, his forehead wrinkling. "This is one reason I've been able to carry on after Dawn's death. I'm glad she doesn't have to live in this mess of a world."

"Well," Bill said, half-smiling, "at least we have peace in the Middle East."

"Seemingly."

"I'm going to preach on that Sunday. I think you'll find the sermon very interesting."

"I'd love to come. But I'm sequestering myself in this house and the Truth building. I don't want to endanger the congregation."

Bill began to protest, but Jake quieted him with his hand. "Don't argue, Bill."

Bill stroked his chin. "You're sure of this?"

"Yes."

"Then I'll have the entire congregation praying for you, Jake.

"What's your sermon about?" Jake asked.

"Be prepared for the End Times. We don't know when a rapture will happen, so repent of your sins and be ready.

"Well," Jake lowered his head, "without Dawn, the end can't come soon enough for me."

"Jake," Bill protested, "you can't let depression ..."

"I'm not thinking of ending my life, Bill," Jake interrupted. "I'm only saying so much is wrong in the world that when I confront a problem editorially I feel I'm simply putting a finger in the hole in the dike."

Bill leaned forward, "How do you think Christ felt? Here was this perfect Man surrounded by sin, decadence and degradation. But he approached each day one person at a time. He never flinched. Never gave up in the face of all kinds of evil.

"He had no rest, just like you feel you have none. Remember when Jesus learned John the Baptist had been beheaded?"

Jake nodded.

"He wanted to get away, to be alone, to mourn. But the crowds swarmed around him, he saw their needs, had pity on them, and stayed to minister to them. He wants you to do the same—pick up your cross daily."

Jake fiddled with his Meerschaum . "Bill, you've been in my office and seen the framed quote: 'I preach as never to preach again and as a dying man to dying men'?"

"Uh-huh."

"You're quoting Richard Baxter, who had a burning within him to reach lost souls. I've had such an unction. I know what the feeling to—as Elijah said—have 'fire shot up in my bones' so I couldn't help but speak the Word. But I don't feel the fire right now. I'm in a desert place. And now, with people blowing up airplanes and buildings trying to get me, I think I must feel like David hiding in caves when he wrote all those psalms asking where God was."

Bill placed a hand on Jake's arm. "I understand. But I do know this: David's psalms of anguish usually end with his acknowledgment of a trustworthy and loving God who would deliver him from his enemies, his sick bed, whatever afflictions or challenges he faced.

"In Psalm 60, after recalling God had rejected Israel and torn apart the land, David says: 'With God we will gain victory and he will trample down our enemies.' And in Psalm 140, where he talks about evil men who slander and set traps for him, David writes: 'I know the Lord secures justice for the poor and upholds the cause of the needy. Surely the righteous will praise Your name and the upright will live before You.'"

Later, as Jake was saw Bill to the door, he turned to his friend.

"I appreciate your coming by. I know you and Darlene and everyone are praying for me. I couldn't have survived the funeral without the Lord and your prayers. But I may have to forsake the assembling of the saints just to keep everyone safe."

"I understand. But let's not forsake our assembling— yours and mine—okay? I can get over here, or into the office, any time."

"And you know what else?" Bill said. "I still think you should steal away to visit Lisa and the family. Just be stealthy when you do."

"I'll consider the suggestion."

The men walked past Bob Ward in the entryway, hugged, and Bill walked out into the portico, shutting the door behind him.

Jake felt odd—somehow half-depressed yet half-expectant for the End Times.

CHAPTER TEN

Truth Publishing's newly purchased Gulfstream G650 jetliner was a beauty, Darek thought as he, Jillian, and Ty Cole took seats for their takeoff from Logan International Airport. The Jerusalem office would provide the cameramen.

As a precaution against another murderous assault, the plane had no Truth logo, no markings at all identifying the aircraft as Jake MacMillan's. As importantly, the jetliner contained a military-style jamming system to confuse surface-to-air missiles, making them miss their target.

As the trio stepped into the plane, biometric technology scanned them and their luggage for suspect patterns, such as sharp edges or bulges in luggage or beneath clothes. Security cameras were hooked into facial-recognition software able to identify known and suspected terrorists and criminals.

A biometric recognition system called Vein Sign, contained in a box about eight inches cubed, scanned the veins on the back of each person's hand and recognized them with a 0.0001 percent-of-error possibility.

The flight attendant, Marsha, welcomed them aboard and the pilot and co-pilot, twin brothers John and Paul LaFlamme, introduced themselves.

Although Darek, Jillian and Ty had been a little anxious about the flight. Marsha dispelled their fears. She explained the door to the cockpit was bulletproof Kevlar, and inside the cockpit, the LaFlammes had a cabin monitor in order to gain information about the state of the cabin without leaving the cockpit. Through additional broadband capabilities, the video from the monitor could be beamed to the ground, making the video easily retrievable.

Besides all this, panic buttons were in secretive places both inside the cabin and the cockpit. When pressed in the cabin, a buzzer would warn the pilots something was amiss in the cabin and vice versa.

"It even has a new-car smell," Darek observed.

Marsha smiled. "Call on me if you need anything, folks."

Soon they were airborne.

The flight to Jerusalem proved simply a long study session. They all sat in comfortable leather swivel chairs, each with a foldout desktop and with plenty of room between them so they could sit face to face.

Two large-screen televisions covered the wall at the front.

Marsha took their luggage to a compartment in the back of the plane.

Ty, who had spent three years after graduating from Howard University teaching English to inner-city high schoolers in Washington, DC, was putting his experience to good use, tutoring them about the principal players and philosophy of the Church Universal.

Jillian was familiar with many of the key figures because of the thesis she'd written. But the movement had advanced quite a bit in the past few years.

"It sounds so good," Darek said, reading Church Universal's mission statement: "'Our deepest yearnings are to live in a safe and peaceful world that reflects divine love for every being; a world where people honor and respect one another, help the needy, and are caretakers of the earth and all its life; a world where religion no longer leads to hatred and violence but to dialogue, the celebration of diversity, and cooperative action for global good.'"

"Peace and safety," Jillian said. "Peace and safety. Peace and safety. Their mantra."

Leaning forward, Ty said, "Of course. Who'd be against peace and safety—besides the Islamic terrorists, that is? A simple and easy message to win converts."

Ty ran his fingers through his hair. "In February 2019, Pope Francis and Islamic Sheikh Ahmed al-Tayeb, the grand imam of Al Azhar, signed a declaration calling for tolerance and peace among the nations of the world, as well as dialog between the world's religions and cultures. Their declaration claimed 'pluralism and the diversity of religions, color, sex, race and language are willed by God in His wisdom.'"

"No, no, no, no." Jill raised a hand in protest. "They think God's okay with more than one religion? The pope's okay with Islam denying Jesus's divinity?"

"Makes no sense," Darek said.

Ty shook his head. "The pope and grand imam claimed divine wisdom is the source of the right to freedom of belief and the freedom to be different. Therefore, they declared, we must reject the idea of people being forced to adhere to a certain religion or culture."

"This all sounds like the Antichrist," Jillian said.

"A religious Tower of Babel," Ty said. "Take a look in the Book of Revelation chapter 13."

"The same chapter Jake said to check—about a beast," Darek said.

"The first ten verses tell us the First Beast, the Antichrist, arrives on the scene and will exercise his authority for forty-two months—three and a half years," Ty said.

"So the First Beast is the Antichrist," Jillian said. "And the Second Beast?"

"Verse eleven says, 'And I beheld another beast coming up out of the earth; and he had two horns like a lamb, and he spake as a dragon. And he exerciseth all the power of the first beast before him, and causeth the earth and them which dwell therein to worship the first beast ...'

"Bible scholars have historically called this Second Beast the False Prophet," Ty continued. "And the False Prophet could very well be the head of Church Universal."

Looking at his watch, Darek said, "The person they are electing in about thirteen hours."

"Correct," Ty said, "a counterfeit Christian. Scripture says he has two horns 'like a lamb.' Well, Jesus Christ is consistently referred to as the Lamb of God, or 'the Lamb which taketh away the sins of the world.' And Satan often mirrors the work of God. He's going to do so again, sending a counterfeit lamb, a leader who claims to be Christian and who is accepted as such by the vast majority of the world."

"So, who's going to be the guy?" Darek asked. "Reverend Swing?"

"No, I don't think so," Ty replied. "He's not well known globally. Had you ever heard of him before yesterday?"

"Can't say I had."

"Has to be high-profile, known to a wide range of people around the world. Both the Antichrist and the False Prophet are indwelt by demonic entities which appeared to the Apostle John as green orbs, like frogs, when he received the Revelation. That's in Revelation 16, verses 13 and 14. We've seen this commonly in the New Age religion, so I'm not surprised New Agers are supporting Church Universal."

"This is amazing stuff." Darek squeezed Jillian's hand. "Does this scare you at all?"

She squirmed in her seat. "Yes. So bizarre it's surreal. I get fear-like tingles down my spine when I think about a global religion. We're actually living to see what Jesus revealed to John two thousand years ago."

Just then, Paul LaFlamme stepped out of the cockpit. "We're about to descend into Jerusalem," he said. "Better buckle up."

Thirty minutes later, the Truth Publishing jet taxied to a terminal.

Mosey Kreko felt relief. He, Mary, and their organization's vice president, Luke O'Neil, sat in a coffee shop, indulging in a mid-morning pick-me-up. The smell of newly ground coffee filled the place amid the quiet that followed the earlier rush of commuters grabbing cups of java.

Mosey had revealed everything to Mary and now to Luke. He'd shared the burden, the quandary of partnering with the Alliance. The notion was like wearing a hair shirt— uncomfortable at best.

The story of Truth Publishing delivery men being beaten up appeared the last straw for Mosey's close friend.

Luke eyed him and shook his head, then held up a hand as if to say *Please stop*.

"This is like The Mob, for heaven's sake," he said. "We don't need this. Listen."

Luke laid down his daily planner and opened to the current month of May. "For three months I've traveled around different countries. Membership and financial support are at an all-time high. Since Chernobyl-like meltdowns in Japan and Argentina, interest in Advocates is sky-high. We're getting more than a million hits a day on our web site, and headquarters telephones are ringing incessantly twenty-four hours a day.

"Our support is snowballing around the world. In the end, we may have more membership then all those groups combined—Citizens for Free Abortions, AFFRONT, the Society for All Lifestyles, the Black Power League, Indian Lands Reclamation Federation—the whole bunch of 'em."

"Besides all that," Mary said, "AFFRONT's behavior is—" she hesitated, "an *affront* to our philosophy."

Mosey put his hand on Luke's arm. "I agree—we agree," he said. "They've gone way over the edge. So much so that we think they have to be stopped. And we intend to help do so. But the only way we can succeed is by being on the inside."

"What will you do with that firsthand knowledge?" Luke asked.

Darek, Jillian, and Ty had unpacked at the King David Hotel in Jerusalem. Darek had called the Truth's offices, located across a little park from the Prime Minister's home, to let them know they had arrived. They probably wouldn't need the bureau's help, but would pay the office a visit.

After freshening up, Darek took Jillian's hand, they met Ty and walked the short distance to the Old City. History seeped out of the pores off the city's thirty-foot-high, white Jerusalem-stone walls off which the mid-afternoon sun glistened.

The cooler air came from being at a high point of land, the place King David ultimately had chosen as the bastion of his kingdom thousands of years before.

"Let's take the opportunity to check out the two witnesses," Darek said. "How about we walk over to Jaffa Gate and climb up the stairs to the walkway around the walls of the city, then go over to the Western Wall?"

"Great idea," Jillian said. She turned to Ty. "Do you think they're the real two witnesses of Revelation?"

"Very possibly. They first appeared and began prophesying when the peace agreement was reached. In Revelation chapter eleven, God says he will give power to his two witnesses and they will prophesy for twelve hundred and sixty days, clothed in sackcloth. Scripture says if anything tries to harm them, fire will come from their mouths and devour their enemies."

"Whoa!" Darek took a step back. "Would God really have two men do that?"

"You're asking a theological question we can discuss at length," Ty said. "But, simply, yes. God's caused a lot of destruction through the ages because of man's sinfulness. Two prophets spewing fire pales in comparison."

"Tells us again about why you couldn't speak to them," Jillian said.

"Well, to tell you the truth, I was very skeptical. I mean, Israel attracts some real fruit cakes. There's always someone or other walking the streets dressed like a prophet and claiming they're Samuel or Jeremiah or Elijah come to shake up the earth and bring down the heavens. In the end, they disappear, probably back from where they came.

"But I wanted to seriously check out these two. I got within about thirty feet and watched them preach for a while. Authoritative. Powerful. All truth. Then, I took a couple of tentative steps toward them, and Elijah looked at me, and—those eyes! Phew! I froze. I virtually could not move, for what felt like minutes. By the time I could, they were gone."

"Gone? Where to?"

"I don't know. They simply walked off, out of the courtyard, through the gate. A big dog walked up to them and licked Elijah's hand, and puff, they were gone ..."

"A big dog?"

"Yeah, a dog big as a lion."

"Did anyone follow them?" Jillian asked.

"No. There was a crowd of us, too. But I think we were *all* frozen in our tracks."

"Do you think they'll be there today?" Jillian asked.

"You never know," Ty said. "I came five different times, saw them twice."

"I read your piece," Darek said. "Their message seems to be 'repent and turn to the Lord.'"

"Pretty basic. But that was John the Baptist's message before the Messiah first came. He simply called people to repent and be baptized in the name of the Lord. There was no long theological soliloquy we know of, not even a Billy Graham-type turn-your-heart-to-tears, father-to-child talking-to."

"I can't wait to see them," Darek said. He fought off a shiver down his back and wondered if what he had so casually said was true. Was he hiding a fear—even just a little?

Then Jillian joined in. "Me too," she said.

My fearless wife.

"Let's go there via the wall," she said. She looked at Ty and added, "When Darek and I were here two years ago, we ended our trip there—walked the parapet. We were amazed to see a few Jewish families living in the midst of the Arab Quarter."

"Yeah, I've noticed," Ty said. "You can tell because they hang the Israeli flag off their apartment patios, putting their lives in their own hands. Unbelievable bravery."

Darek and Jillian had traveled to Israel almost immediately after Jillian led Darek to the Lord. Darek had been so excited about his born-again experience, he insisted they take time off from their jobs and go to "the land where our Savior walked."

The trip had transformed both their lives.

Walking where he had walked made them feel closer to Jesus in his humanity. Traveling to the Galilee, over rugged desert land, and the long trek along the Jordan River, made them appreciate his physical strength and dedication to saving his people.

Seeing how the Jewish people had turned a lackluster, lifeless land no one had wanted, "a home for jackals," into a Garden of Eden, made them appreciate how God had fulfilled his prophecies to return his people to their land and restore their inheritance from a wasteland.

Praying at the Western Wall, and realizing God's people had done so for thousands of years, filled them with a thankfulness to God for inclining His ears to their prayer.

Visiting the Garden Tomb and what many believed to be Golgotha nearby—the place of his crucifixion—they were awed again by Jesus's sacrifice and the fact he had overcome death.

Overcome death!

Dressed in sneakers and casual wear, the three friends set out for the Old City and entered Jaffa Gate on the southwest wall. They stepped past a One World Government guard who stood at the base of a stairway, red beret tipped to one side and military weapon strapped across his shoulder. When they reached the landing and looked around, Ty took a deep breath of exhilaration and quoted, "The Lord loves the gates of Zion more than all the dwellings of Jacob. Glorious things are spoken of you, O City of God!"

"A psalm?" Jillian asked.

"Eighty-seventh," Ty said.

Turning his gaze from the panorama of the Old City to the wall, Darek exclaimed, "Man, there are One World guards everywhere."

They looked left and right, spotting guards every two hundred feet or so along the walkway. From the Jaffa Gate, the wall traveled northwest to the New Gate, then turned northeast for some distance past the Christian Quarter to Herod's Gate in the Moslem Quarter. From Herod's Gate, it continued a short distance to a corner, then turned southeast and past St. Stephen's Gate and then to the Golden Gate, or East Gate, at the Temple Mount.

"Looks like the One World Government isn't very secure about Jerusalem's security," Jillian said.

"Especially not since Premier Sardis gave the Jews the go-ahead to rebuild their synagogue on the Temple Mount," Ty said. "Hopefully the guards will allow us to walk all the way around there. If so, we can see the construction."

"Nearly elbow to elbow with the Dome of the Rock," Jillian added.

"Never thought I'd see a Third Temple happen," Ty said. "The Temple Faithful had all the utensils ready, as well as musical instruments, back in 2002, 2003. They said all they needed was the go-ahead from the government. Of course, the timing was wrong. Jews put their lives in peril just venturing onto the Temple Mount except under very special circumstances."

They all stood still, surveying the view, breathing in the atmosphere of the most holy city. Darek envisioned Jesus walking the narrow streets, crowds trailing after him to touch his garments, hear his marvelous parables. The sight exuded a feeling of awe.

"I'll never get enough of this city," Jillian said. "And the view up here reminds you how very small its dimensions. It's only about a mile around the entire wall."

"Yeah, but the walk takes a couple hours," Darek said. "Let's head toward the East Gate and see what we can see."

Every few minutes, as they passed along the walkway skirting the north side of the Old City, they came to an abutment where they stopped for a minute to look outside the city walls to the bustling "new" city around them. Hydrogen-electro-cars, solar-cars and hybrids of electro-solar-hydrogen-and-gas combinations jostled on the four-lane highway circling the city.

What a contrast, Darek thought. Old and new—rather, ancient and modern. People outside bustling around unaware of God's presence at all, while others inside the gate were drawn by that very Presence. New immorality versus old morality. Darkness, light. Death, life everlasting. Was everything so simple? No. But absorbing the sights and sounds, and sense of God's Spirit within the Old City's walls, made one reconsider how consequential was the hum of progress on the outside.

An hour later, when they reached Herod's Gate, they had to walk down a stairway, pass the gate where people drove cars bumper-to-bumper to squeeze into the Muslim Quarter, and ascend another set of stairs to the walkway again.

At the bottom of the second set of stairs, Darek spotted a man who was scanning the crowds and stopped abruptly when he saw Darek. Darek could see a light of recognition in the man's eyes, but Darek was certain he had never seen this man before. When they made eye contact, the guy quickly turned away.

"Guess what. Don't look now," he said, "but we're being followed."

"What? Who?" Ty said.

"Let's head on up the stairs," Darek said. "I'll tell you when we get to the top."

Once they reached the walkway, Darek said, "Let's nonchalantly turn and scan the sights. We're looking for a swarthy man, French or Italian, I'd say, who's probably six foot tall, wearing a black suit and grey hat and sporting a dapper Van Dyke on his chin."

All three calmly turned and scanned the people in the court below them. Jillian nearly jumped off her feet and elbowed Darek. "Two o'clock, forty feet away from the gate, to the left of the plump woman wearing the red sundress."

Darek and Ty followed her directions. "That's him," Ty said. Just then, the man looked up at the wall, and there was no doubt, he knew he had been "made." He spun around and fast-walked directly away. They watched him as he took a cell phone out of his pocket and turned a corner around a street lined with shops.

Darek turned to Ty. "Now, who do you think is having us followed—and why?"

"I'd guess it's our friends at Church Universal," Ty said.

"Unless it's Sardis's gang," Jillian chimed in. "Remember, they didn't take kindly to our last interview with the premier." Jillian referred to a team of three One World security personnel who didn't try to hide the fact they were following Darek to the Brussels airport after the acrimonious interview that Sardis felt leaned too strongly against his plan to lessen the autonomy of the world's seven geopolitical regions.

Darek and Jillian had felt like unwanted strangers in a Western movie, being escorted to the outskirts of town by sheriff's deputies, with the not-so-subtle inference they were not welcome back.

"Menacing, but harmless," Darek now said as they stood looking down on the Muslim Quarter.

"Perhaps." Jillian shrugged. "But I don't trust them one little bit. They remind me of the Nazi SS."

Unlike along the Christian Quarter, only a handful of people walked the walls here in the Muslim Quarter. The threesome stopped to watch some young boys kick a soccer ball around in a beat-up old playground that, probably 50-by-100 yards, was worth a fortune in gold in this most priceless of cities. As they watched, a couple of the boys, around ten or twelve years of age, stopped and stared up at them. Their young eyes were steel, their faces turning from laughter to something approaching sinister.

Jillian shivered. "Oh, boy, I can feel the hate."

"It's a spiritual thing, straight from the pit," Ty said. "They're raised, taught in their schools to hate not just Jews, but Westerners as well."

"Let's get out of here," Darek urged. They all turned on their heels and walked briskly to the northeast corner of the wall and then to St. Stephen's Gate.

The Temple Mount spread out before them, a wide-open space punctuated at its center by the mammoth Dome of the Rock and Al-Aqsa Mosque, Islam's third-most holy site. To its south, no more than a couple of hundred feet away, scaffolding rose from the ground.

"The Third Temple's under construction," Ty said, pointing to the structure.

"There appear to be as many security guards as workmen," Jillian said. "Can we see if we can get close and take a look?"

They descended the steps and were met by a pair of burly One World Government security police. One of them, his right hand on his weapon, held his other hand up to stop them. "No one is allowed on the Temple Mount," the man said in Arabic-stilted English.

"We're reporters with Truth Publishing," said Darek, reaching for his pocket where he kept his credentials.

The other security guard snapped his rifle from his shoulder and pointed the barrel at Darek.

"Whoa!" Darek said. He, Jillian and Ty all took a step back. "I'm merely pulling out my press ID card."

The security guard who had spoken to them motioned his colleague to lower his weapon. "Press or not, you're not allowed here. You must arrange such a visit with the joint Palestinian Authority-One World Government security detail."

"Thanks," Darek said dully. "We'll check with them."

As they turned to walk away, Darek noticed the odd man at the top of the wall about fifty yards away.

"Our friend's still with us," he said. "Let's hustle out of here."

They hurried into the Muslim Quarter, down Sha'ar ha Arayot and the Via Dolorosa, until they got to a narrow alley leading to the Jewish Quarter and the Western Wall, near the southwestern corner of the Temple Mount.

Getting through an IDF security check, Ty turned to Darek and Jillian. "For some reason, I always feel less in danger from the Jewish soldiers."

A wide plaza spread out before them and, behind it, the great Western Wall, the one wall left standing from the Second Temple when the Romans leveled Jerusalem in 70 AD. Kippah-wearing men and boys milled around the left two-thirds of the wall and, on the other side of a partition, women and girls walked about.

Darek looked at Jillian. "See you by the Dung Gate in ten minutes?" he asked.

She nodded and strolled toward the women's portion of the Western Wall. The two men grabbed cardboard kippahs from a large basket and walked to the wall, where men of all ages and every faction of the Jewish and Christian religions stood facing the age-old edifice.

It's appropriately called the Wailing Wall. Darek reached up to touch the sacred stone and listened to a couple of old Hasidic Jews who rocked back and forth, bending at their hips, facing the wall and calling out in Hebrew to their God. He bowed his head and prayed for the salvation of God's chosen people and for their call to *aliyah,* return to Israel, the land the Lord had given them.

Hundreds of thousands of American Jews had returned in the last decade, even though jobs were scarce and terrorists had continued to rain hell down upon the people of the Book.

After a few minutes, Darek swiveled around and found Ty standing nearby, waiting reverently for him to finish.

He stepped toward Ty just as a voice boomed from the center of the courtyard, "Baruch atah, Adonai Eluhenu!"

All heads turned at the sound, but because the courtyard rose slightly away from the one hundred and eighty-seven-foot-long, sixty-two-foot high Western Wall, Darek could not see the speaker who may have been about thirty yards away.

"Blessed art thou, Lord God!"

Darek hurried to Ty's side and spotted the speaker. The man with the voice was big and burly. Dark-haired, about six-foot-four and two hundred and fifty pounds, apparently zero fat.

"*Baruch habbah b'ashem Adonia!*" Another voice rang from the top of the stairs rising up along the wall to the east by the Dung Gate. "Blessed is he who comes in the name of the Lord!"

People strained to see where the second voice came from—wide steps rising along the wall at the back of the courtyard. This man was perhaps five-foot-ten and lean. Both wore long, flowing pearl-white robes nearly touching the ground. Hoods hung from the robes to their shoulders. Were these the sackcloth clothes of which Revelation spoke?

The man on the stairway began descending the steps and called out: "Listen to Elijah and the words of the Lord God of Avraham, Yitzak and Yacob!"

The man on the stairs is Shlomo," Ty whispered.

"The prophets and governments are saying, 'Peace. Peace!' But there is no peace. They are hollow words, full of air and empty of meat … a promise made of meanness, meant to partition God's land from His people and to void His promises."

The man on the steps continued down, booming, "Pay heed to the words of Adonai, not the folly of men. Abandon the travesty of surrendering the land of the Jews to the hand of their enemies!"

Elijah was walking toward his comrade and met him at the bottom of the stairway.

Transfixed, Darek and Ty—indeed, everyone in the courtyard—could not move. *Is Jillian seeing this? She must be.*

As suddenly as they had appeared, the two men exited through the Dung Gate. A mammoth dog—or maybe a lion?—joined them. Several people entering the gate faltered and fell to the ground. Others stood motionless.

A few moments later, there was a global inhale in the courtyard. Shivers went down Darek's spine. Then, out of nowhere, a rain began to fall.

Confounded, Darek looked to the sky for a sign of a cloud. There was none. People throughout the courtyard simply exchanged perplexed expressions.

Darek scanned the ladies' side of the courtyard and spotted Jillian waving to him. He tugged at Ty's elbow to follow, then hurried to her.

"I know where to get an umbrella," Ty said. "Follow me."

They hustled after Ty, scrambling up the long flight of stairs down which Schlomo had descended and into an area with more modern shops.

They wound their way through the Jewish Quarter with its outdoor restaurants and tidy souks and Ty led them to one where they bought umbrellas.

Finally standing under the protection from the rain, Darek broke the silence. "Did you get tingles down your spine?"

"Tingles? The ground moved under my feet," Jillian said.

"I think you're literally correct," Ty said. "I felt that the last time I saw them, but thought the tremor must have just been an emotional reaction."

"I wonder if they truly are the two witnesses," Darek said.

"I've ten shekels saying they are," Ty replied.

"So you have enough to buy us all a coffee?" Jillian laughed.

A minute later, they sat in a cafe drinking strong, thick, Middle Eastern coffee and people-watching. The people obviously came from many nations. Tourists probably outnumbered natives two to one or more.

"Quite a change from ten years ago when people around the world were afraid to come to Israel," Ty said. "The tourist trade almost died."

"Fear," Darek said. Ty and Jillian nodded in agreement.

"Talking about trade," Jillian said, looking at Darek, "before we go, do you mind if we visit Rex Jewelers?"

"Great idea," he said.

When visiting Israel just before their marriage, they had discovered the jewelers off David Street in the Armenian Quarter. One of the two Christian brothers who had operated the shop for several decades, sized their fingers and hand-crafted their wedding bands, engraving in Hebrew the Scripture from Song of Solomon, *Ani la dodi va dodi le*—"I am my beloved's and my beloved is mine."

Jillian turned to Ty, "Do you mind?"

"Not at all. I've been thinking of buying myself a three-curl shofar. They probably have one there."

The threesome set off and walked through the narrow streets, skirting shop owners selling their wares. Ceramic "shalom" tiles and other souvenirs of all kinds. Scarves and other materials. Each was packed into tiny eight-or ten-foot-wide enclosures.

They found the two brothers manning Rex Jewelers. The scene was as if time had stood still since they were last there.

"Shalom!" Darek called out.

"Shalom Aleichem," replied the older of the two. "I remember you."

Darek and Jillian chatted with the owners while Ty found a three-curl shofar in the little shop. Darek noticed a photograph hanging on the wall showing the two brothers standing with Chuck Norris. The famous action movie star's signature stood out. On another wall was a photograph in which the two brothers had their arms around a famous

134

ballerina from the former Soviet Union and all three were nearly swallowed up by a world-renowned Irish tenor.

Saying their goodbyes, the three returned to the King David Hotel. One World Government security personnel were stationed all along the way. And once, after crossing the street fronting Jaffa Gate, Darek turned to look back and spotted the mystery man.

Over dinner in the King's Garden Restaurant at the hotel, Darek, Jillian and Ty discussed the two witnesses and strategized about their interview with Church Universal officials.

Darek turned to Ty. "Let's have a tennis match. I need to unwind. Winner gets to take on Jill."

Jillian laughed.

"Ha," said Ty. "You just don't want me to try to win."

Darek chuckled.

"Laugh all you want," Ty jibed. "Last time Jill and I played, I felt like an old Andre Agassi playing a young Sloane Stephens. Not funny."

A half-hour later, the three were out on the courts, Ty and Darek facing off and Jillian lounging in a chair, a book in her lap and Ty's shofar in her hands.

"How in the world *do* you blow this thing?" she asked.

Ty hesitated before serving the ball. "With intensity. Anything less won't work."

"God wouldn't accept any other way, right?"

"Just like him. Among other things, the shofar calls God's people to worship and to battle. Intensity's a good thing either way."

"You gonna play tennis or jabber over there?" Darek called. "I think you're running scared, my friend. I've got you right where I want you."

"Yeah, right, down two sets to one and love-thirty, your serve," Ty laughed.

"Watch out. He who laughs last laughs best," Darek said.

"Coin that phrase. It's a keeper," Ty said. "Hey, did you ever meet Yogi Berra? He was always coming up with those keepers, like 'the game ain't over 'til the fat lady sings,' or 'the game ain't over 'til it's over.'"

"No. But I'd wish I could have interviewed him. Say, what do you think about the two of us challenging Jill?"

Ty chortled. "Still wouldn't stand a chance. She'd just hit the ball between us and amuse herself as we stood waiting for each other to return it."

"I think you two boys ought to finish your match, or I'll start wailing on this ram's horn," Jillian said.

Smiling at Jillian, Darek noticed movement in a window two floors above them. Looking more closely, he noticed the swarthy, goateed man.

"Guess what. Our friend's back yet again."

Jillian turned to look up and the man hurried out of view.

"He must've been standing at a hall window near the elevators," Darek said. "What do you think about him, Ty?"

"Harmless."

"Jillian?"

"Probably a One World security person, making sure we're not up to no good."

"More like a One World spy," Darek said.

"I say we ignore him," Ty said. "Ready for your Waterloo, bud?"

Darek shrugged and walked to the back line, bouncing a tennis ball as he went.

Two hours later, Darek fell into bed and declared, "My, I'm glad we played. Released some of the tension."

"Me, too." Jillian slipped off her robe and slid between the sheets next to him.

"Someday, I'll get you to take up golf, and then, I might be able to win a match," Darek said.

"I'm not old enough for golf. Give me another ten years or so."

"Ha. Funny."

Lying next to each other, they locked fingers and said their nightly prayers.

CHAPTER ELEVEN

An odd sense of anxiety and excitement swirled around Jillian the next morning. After breakfast, she and Darek rounded up Ty and the trio hopped into their rented vehicle.

She sat in the front passenger seat and Darek sprawled in the back while Ty drove the short distance. They passed the Knesset, where Israel's Parliament met, and passed the Bible Lands Museum and Science Museum to the brand spanking new headquarters of the Church Universal.

His Excellency Howard Alphonse Bliss had refused to allow cameras into his interview, so they had arranged to meet their Truth cameramen at the next interviews at the Knesset and with the Chief Rabbi.

"That's a unique sight," Jillian said as Ty pulled into one of few empty spaces in the Church Universal parking lot.

The building was shaped like a spiral staircase, with two full swirls. At its apex was a gigantic sculpture of several hands, in different sizes and shapes, folded together in prayer so they pointed heavenward in the shape of a steeple.

"Remember the old song, 'Stairway to Heaven'? Put the lyrics together with the story of the Tower of Babel, and you get the picture," Ty said.

Jillian said, "Can we pray? I feel like David about to face Goliath."

"Good idea," Ty said. "Remember the outcome of that encounter."

Darek reached over the seatback and the three held hands.

"Clothe us with Your armor, Lord," Darek said.

"And cover us in the blood of the Lamb," Ty added.

"And grant us discernment and wisdom to face Your enemy and ours, Father," Jillian finished.

Moments later, as they got out of the car, Jillian said, "I love short prayers. It's not as if the Lord doesn't know what we need."

"Right," Ty said. "Plus, he sees situations from his own vantage point, not our distorted view. We can look at a Goliath from where we stand and it's huge and scary. When God looks on a Goliath, he sees a puny and weak foe."

Inside, the Church Universal headquarters appeared all glass and mirrors. In the middle of an expansive lobby stood a circular pedestal desk. Behind the desk sat an angular, beautiful, dark-haired woman in her thirties. An eyebrow raised when they approached her.

"We have an appointment with Mr. Bliss," Darek said as he approached the lady.

"His Excellence, General Secretary Bliss?" she asked.

"Howard Alphonse Bliss," Darek replied. "I suppose he did get a new title a few hours ago."

Jillian loved her man. He wasn't going to give in to a name game and entitle Bliss to some sort of theological kingship.

"His Excellency's offices," she replied, "are on the top floor. She pointed toward the fulcrum, the center of the spiral. "Elevators over there will take you up. I'll call ahead to alert them you're coming. Your names, please?"

"Darek and Jillian Fields of Truth Publishing and Broadcasting."

"Tyson Cole of Truth," Ty put in.

When the woman heard his name, Jillian noticed an eye twinge.

Hate. But she's hiding the feeling well.

"Man, this building has thirty floors," Darek said as they rode the elevator. "What is that, one floor for every 'former' religion joining this farce?"

"Oh, they've got offices here for outreaches of all sorts in the name of Church Universal," Ty replied. "All those branches we spoke about yesterday—clothing orphans, feeding the hungry, day-care for single parents, the VISTA-type outreach teaching Third-World peoples to farm. Then you have the offices for the church's real reason for existence—international affairs, economic development, One World Government liaisons pushing for further, ah, reapportioning of the wealth from the richer to the poorer nations."

"Right, appealing window dressing with a bonnet of communism on top," Jillian said. "A lot of things look really good, but their intent is evil. When will mankind realize taking earnings from entrepreneurs is a disincentive for people to even try to create jobs, run businesses, and create wealth?"

As they continued their ascent, Darek asked, "Do you recognize the smell?"

"Oil of myrrh," Jillian replied. "Sweet."

"Well, I like your perfume better, babe."

She smiled. "I think Church Universal wants all your senses to be pleasantly heightened."

"Yeah, check out the music," Ty said.

Jillian had barely noticed, but as she concentrated, she could discern the sound.

"New Age?" Darek asked.

"Snatam Kaur or Hauscka, I think," Ty confirmed.

Then the elevator doors opened, revealing glass walls and ceilings. While the steeple stood centered above them, everywhere else was a window to the sky.

A thin, swarthy man dressed in black robes walked toward them.

"You feel sometimes you can reach up and touch God," he announced, extending his hand. "Mr. and Mrs. Fields, Mr. Cole, my name is Ravi Chettri, personal assistant to His Excellence, General Secretary Bliss. Please follow me."

Wood was apparently verboten on this floor, Jillian noticed as they followed Chettri. All was glass. They were led to a huge office with glass walls and a glass door. Inside was Bliss.

Funny, no glass desk and glass chairs. I wonder if he's wearing glass slippers. Jill smiled inwardly.

"Impressive building, Mr. Chettri," she said.

"We're proud of her," he said. "We think we should all be transparent, and this is symbolic of Church Universal. The structure shows the world—and skeptics like yourselves I'm guessing—that we have nothing to hide. We're all-inclusive."

"'All-inclusive,'" Jillian quoted. "Sounds so nice."

"M-hm," the man said, oblivious to her innuendo.

Chettri went to Bliss's door, knocked, and opened it upon Bliss's motion to come in. "Your Excellence," he said, "Mr. and Mrs. Fields and Mr. Cole."

Bliss came out from behind his desk, smiling broadly, and shook hands.

"So glad you came, Mr. and Mrs. Fields. Nice to see you again, Mr. Cole. Please have a seat. Ravi," Bliss turned to his assistant, "would you have Owandu bring in a tray of coffee, tea and biscuits?"

Chettri bowed. "Yes, Your Excellence," and left the room.

"Well, this must be quite an assignment for me to get three of the world's foremost reporters," Bliss remarked, sitting down in one of a circle of overstuffed leather chairs.

Ty lowered himself onto a wide leather chair and Jillian took a seat with Darek on a leather love seat.

Jillian was impressed Bliss did not take the place of authority behind his desk. She measured the man before them. Taller than Darek by about two inches—probably six-foot-two. Narrow-shouldered. Definitely not athletic. Piercing blue eyes. A narrow mouth with thin lips.

And his cup runneth over with confidence.

Darek spoke first. "Jill and I want to look at the cultural impact of Church Universal.

Ty added, "And I'm here to unearth the religious perspective."

"Fine. What can I tell you?" Bliss asked. "Fire away." He sat back, looking comfortable and at ease.

A snake in lamb's clothing.

"Bottom line first," Darek said, setting down a digital recorder on the table in front of Bliss. "Why create Church Universal in the first place?"

Bliss ran his fingers through his blond locks, then interlocked them in front of him, alternately raising his fingers and curling them.

"Centuries of disharmony," Bliss said slowly, sounding hurt by the thought. "Millennia, actually." Then with a perky cadence, "Enough is enough. A major barrier between religions is each has thought, 'I'm right. Everyone else is wrong.' This is an old trick of Satan we first read about in the Garden of Eden. And killing each other in the name of God and what we think is right is absurd. I'm sure our Maker would have none of this.

"And we found there were a number of us—from all religions—who felt the same way. Peace is a universal word, a universal concept, and, we think, the basis for a universal religion."

"But," Ty said, "how do you get around the fact these various religions have, for millennia, worshipped very different gods?"

"Whatever gods they've worshipped are enshrouded in myths, fairy tales, and stories written by men and, thus, with man's errors," Bliss said. "We feel we can't truly know God, or the gods if there are more than one, because our minds are so limited compared to the great Mind that created the universe. And if we can't know him, how can we define him? It's best, we feel, to simply agree on the concept. There is a God, or gods, and he or she or they want peace for mankind."

Jillian sat forward. "How do you marry this concept with the Muslims' Allah ordering the destruction of people of all other religions unless they relent and worship him?"

"I don't have to reconcile anything," Bliss said. "I don't have to resolve anything to which any of the religions lays claim. Truly, I don't care to debate any point of any religion. My belief—and, yes, my life—are based solely on the idea of peaceful coexistence. A loving God would want nothing less."

"What of Jesus's remark," Jillian interjected, "that 'no one can get to the Father except through him'?"

Bliss shook his head slowly. "As I said, I care not to debate any particular scripture of any religion. What we've created here is a universal concept, one all mankind can believe in and follow without any of the trappings of existing belief systems."

Ty raised a finger. "I'm reminded of the old saying, 'If you stand for nothing you'll fall for anything.' The leaders of Church Universal are mere men. So how do you expect Christians and Jews to turn away from the teachings they believe came from the mouth of God—or Muslims, Hindus, and others who believe in their gods?"

"Mere men, yes. But, we believe, men who are ordained and anointed by God to the task at hand," Bliss said. "To your point, we believe in unity in cause even if there is not total unity in faith. Unity in cause is central to our duty as the Church Universal. And, again, our cause is peace. Ask any Christian if they want peace. Ask any Muslim."

"The Muslim might answer 'yes' with their lips while firing a bullet into a Jew with the rifle in their hand," Darek said.

That's my man. Straight and to the point.

Darek continued, "Isn't this 'cause in unity' too simple for such complex theological and political disagreements?"

Just then the door opened, and a dark-skinned woman entered, carrying a tray complete with tea kettle, coffee carafe, and a plate of biscuits. Behind her walked a blonde, blue-eyed Norwegian-looking young lady carrying a tray with cups and saucers, cream and sugar. Jillian was startled by the women's exceptional beauty. Setting down the trays, the two women poured what the four people requested.

"Thank you, Owandu, Kari," Bliss said as they finished. Settling back with cup and saucer in hand, he turned toward Darek. "You mentioned the simplicity of our cause in these complex times, Darek. May I call you 'Darek'?

Darek nodded assent.

"If our mission were too simple, would some of the great religious leaders of their time sign onto the concept as early on as 1996?"

"Like who?" Jillian asked, edging even further forward in the love seat, wondering if his response would confirm what she knew to be true.

Bliss did not lie. "From February through April 1996," he said, "Episcopal Bishop William Swing traveled through Europe, India and the Middle East, hoping for a Church

United—a sort of United Nations of Religion. He sought commitment from such leaders as the Dalai Lama, Islam's Grand Mufti in Cairo, the Sankaracharya of Kancheepuram, Mother Theresa, and the Archbishop of Canterbury. He also sought pledges from people active in interfaith work, including those at a conference at the International Interfaith Centre in Oxford. In July and August 1996, the bishop visited with religious leaders in Japan and Korea.

"In the end, he enlisted the commitment of many of the world's religions, as well as Mother Theresa." Bliss looked triumphant, his chest swelling.

"Amazing," was all Jillian could manage.

"Do you have records of this trip?" Ty asked.

"Yes," Bliss said. He leaned behind him, pushed a button on his desk. "Ravi, please put together a packet of information on Bishop Swing's 1996 travels enlisting collaboration for the Church United. We'll need the material before our friends leave."

"Yes, your Excellence," came the reply.

Bliss turned to his guests and, looking each in the eyes, continued, "In keeping with your question, Darek, the same God who made the hands of a Jew, made the feet of a Christian, the eyes of a Hindu, the heart of a Muslim, and the brain of a Buddhist.

"The Bible even says in God there is no male or female, Jew or Gentile. We in Church Universal believe we're all brothers and sisters in God, created by the same Father (or fathers, or even father and mother, if you prefer)."

Ty interjected, "The Koran declares God has no son and Mohammed is his prophet, directly contradicting the New Testament."

"As I said," Bliss responded, "I will not get entangled in scriptural arguments of the different faiths. My calling is peace and unity. Peace and unity. I'll go on with this refrain until my dying day."

Bliss's piercing blue eyes zeroed in on Ty. "We have to love each other as brothers in God the Creator. You and I. Jews and Muslims. Christians, Hindus, Buddhists and Bahá'í. Yes, and Mormons and Jehovah's Witnesses who, I'm sure you think, are cultists.

"We're all brothers and sisters in God just as two people born from the same parents are brothers and sisters. We all descend from Adam and Eve. Or, if one still believes in Darwinism—which I personally feel has been sufficiently debunked—we come from the parents of the first primate. Whatever we call ourselves today, we share a common ancestry."

Jillian began to ask a question, but Bliss held up a hand. "And I might add whatever the name of God may be in different languages—Yahweh, Allah, Dios, Dieu, Dio, Gott, Brahman—he is the same Being."

"How on earth, Mr. Bliss, can you have a religion without a specific theology?" Jillian asked.

"My answer, Jillian, is that I do have a personal theology to guide my own life. But Church Universal is just that— universal. We can't take sides and nit-pick about the particulars, or the semantics, of any single religion. Because of this, though I may have a personal belief on all sorts of topics, I won't get involved in debates on any of them.

"But I want to emphasize religious tolerance is not religious indifference. Tolerance values the right of another person to hold beliefs you think are wrong. We are, above all else, tolerant."

Jillian slumped back in the loveseat.

Slippery as slime. This guy could have been a politician of the highest order.

"Well, okay," Darek interjected. He sipped from his tea, then set the cup down. "I'd like to ask you about the extra-religious activities of the Church Universal."

"Please do," Bliss said. He crossed his legs, at ease.

"You have the support of the One World Government and Sardis. How much do you intend to get involved in government affairs?" Darek asked.

"As we've stated in an early white paper, we cannot escape, and indeed should embrace, the task history has imposed on us," Bliss said. Forming his hands as if holding a basketball in front of him, he added, "This is the duty of helping to shape a new world order in all its dimensions—spiritual, economic, political, social."

"What of Paul's admonition 'A good soldier does not get involved in civilian affairs'?" Ty asked.

"Obviously, I disagree," Bliss replied flatly.

"What are some of the specifics you refer to when you mention helping to shape spiritual, economic, political and social dimensions?" Jillian asked.

"We're establishing priorities right now," Bliss said. "How do we wrestle with population problems? Can we mediate in conflict resolution between religious groups in regional hot spots? How can we spearhead efforts to eradicate poverty? And climate change? In what ways can we help single mothers with daycare, or young women making the choice for or against abortion, or entire neighborhoods facing extinction because of massive job losses? There is a plethora of issues, of challenges Church Universal must discuss to determine the parameters of our role."

"So, at this point you have no specifics?" Jillian pushed.

"I'm afraid not. But those will come soon enough. You'll notice a lot of empty space in this building," Bliss said.

"Before long those spaces will be filled—occupied by people handling these issues."

"What happens," asked Darek, "if Church Universal is at odds with One World Government on a particular issue?"

"Compromise," Bliss said firmly. "It's a wonderful word, a marvelous concept, and a fruitful way of doing business. You're from America, a great country whose history is defined by compromise. Where would the nation be without compromise?"

"A whole lot better off, some would say," Jillian responded.

"Well, I don't believe so. The opposite of compromise is conflict, and the ultimate conflict is war. What has war ever proven?"

"Without America going to war, Hitler would have conquered the world, and then you'd have no chance to compromise," Jillian countered.

Bliss waved off her answer. "You may argue anecdotally, but compromise is the only answer to the great challenges facing mankind and Mother Earth. Premier Sardis is a master of compromise—he has to be. I believe I've displayed I'm also adept at conciliation. Working together, we'll show the world truly great leadership.

"Premier Sardis and the One World Government leadership have relentlessly distanced themselves from prejudice, intolerance, discrimination, oppression, and hate." A pained expression filled Bliss's face and he continued, "Those are five fruits the world has, too often, witnessed in connection with the various long-time religions. Church Universal has and will continue to distance itself from these characteristics—these fruits of bad religion and intolerant religious people.

"Yet, we've seen them among imams, pastors, rabbis, et cetera, et cetera, for thousands of years. God abhors hypocrites, and, my friends, we intend to avoid such a fault."

With that, Bliss thumped his clenched fist on the glass coffee table before him.

Darek turned to Jillian, gave her a half-smile as if saying, "Watch this," then faced Bliss. "Back to my question of what happens when Church Universal and One World Government are at odds. You say compromise, but will the two of you compromise on *all* issues? And, more fundamental to the question: What makes you think Church Universal should have any say at all in crucial matters facing the highly secular world?"

Bliss was unflustered. "The One World Government has the final say, of course. But we will be vocal. I have one example for you."

"Yes?" Ty responded.

"Cloning. Cloning has come a long way in the last couple decades, but no man has, or can, create a human being—or even one small part of a human being—from scratch.

"Because cloning is unnatural, I oppose the practice. We're playing God when we create clones to harvest their body parts. We're playing God by simply attempting this process. But Premier Sardis and others have decided we are out of our realm trying to stop this science. So—"

"But compromise is not compromise when it's one-sided."

"I disagree."

Jillian and the others waited for him to explain.

After several moments, clearly no explanation was coming. *Time for the leap.*

Jillian pointed toward Bliss. "How do you respond to the people—Christians, I should say—who are declaring Church Universal, and you in particular, are the embodiment of what was prophesied in Revelation? Who say Premier Sardis is Antichrist and you are his False Prophet?"

Bliss's face noticeably reddened. His nostrils flared. An eyebrow jerked skyward. Jillian wondered if he would reach across and slap her and envisioned Darek breaking his arm.

But, no, he remained seated and drew in a deep breath. There was an ominous silence. Jillian took a collective breath and wondered about the answer. She was certain they would be ushered out of the office once Bliss answered this question.

"I'll give you a short and a long answer," Bliss finally replied. "The short answer is, that is absurd. I cannot speak to the intent of such people. I can only forgive them for defaming Premier Sardis and me."

Sidestep number one.

"The long answer is these people should be looking forward to the coming of the Messiah, not trying to dredge up some sort of Antichrist or False Prophet. I, too, am looking forward to the coming of the Messiah. But I believe these people are hindering his coming.

"The Creator wants his great energies to flow to earth to produce the physical manifestation of the Messiah. But that flow can only happen when mankind raises its collective consciousness to be properly awakened receptors."

New Age, anyone? Jillian shook her head.

Bliss noticed her response and raised the middle three fingers on his right hand. "I believe there are three types of people on earth: Those whose consciousness has been properly raised so they can readily accept the Messiah; those whose consciousness has been raised somewhat but not so high they can readily and immediately accept him, but they might be able to accept him after further enlightenment; and those who will never accept him.

"Speak as they might about Jesus being their Savior, these Christians are deaf and dumb to what he said and stood for while living among us. He spoke of love, forgiveness, sanctification, and accountability.

"As for me, I'm at peace with who I am. Not the False Prophet, but the leader of a great movement to reconcile men—" he eyed Jillian, "—and women to each other. And if you want proof of the goodness of Premier Sardis and me, simply check with Owandu if you see her on your way out."

Jillian frowned a question as she looked toward the door.

"She had terminal cancer and was weeks, perhaps days, from death," Bliss said. "But we prayed over her, laid hands on her, and today, as you can see, she's healthy, restored, and happy. Would the Anti-Christ and the False Prophet actually heal someone?" He spit out the answer. "I think not."

In an instant, Bliss shot out of his chair. The redness began to retreat from his face, his blue eyes sparkled, smile lines wrinkled alongside his eyes, and his right hand shot out to offer firm handshakes to his three visitors.

"Thank you very much for coming all this way," he said. "Please feel free to come again, perhaps after we've finalized the cultural elements of our plans."

"We'll take you up on the invitation," Darek said. "Before we leave Israel, though, do we have your permission to speak with the leadership for these programs you mention?"

"Feel free. Ravi will connect you with Owandu and introduce you to our communications liaison who can make those connections for you."

Bliss motioned to Chettri, who was seated at a desk outside the office. Chettri stood and opened the door for the Truth team.

"Goodbye," Bliss called after them. "Go with God."

Jillian bit her tongue and offered a brief wave of her hand. Darek and Ty were silent and she could hardly wait to get their take on the interview.

Before showing them to the elevator, Chettri handed Darek a large packet. "The information you requested," he said. "I'll be happy to arrange interviews with whomever you would like to speak while you're here in Israel."

"We'll be here for a couple more days, and that would be a big help to us," Darek said. "We'll be in touch."

"Oh, but first," Chettri said, "His Excellence asked that I connect you with Owandu."

Chettri pushed a button on the desk beside him. Almost instantly, Owandu appeared through a nearby entryway.

"Yes?" she asked. Her voice was thick and sultry.

Jillian stepped forward. "We understand you had cancer."

Owandu nodded.

"Tell us what happened."

"I had cancer. Now I don't."

"But why not?"

"The prayers of many people around the world—to the Almighty, the one whom we all worship in one way or another. And then, the Premier and His Excellence came to the hospital to see me. I was a shell. I had no hair. I was very weak, dying. Last rites had been said over me, in fact.

"They laid hands on me, and I felt an amazing heat flow through my body, searing into my lungs where the cancer was. From then on, I felt better—then much better until I was totally restored. And—voilá—here I am!"

Her beautiful face sparkled. Jillian couldn't help smile along with her.

"To whom do you attribute the healing?" Ty interjected.

"Why, the Creator, of course," she smiled, "and to the Premier and His Excellence."

When they reached their car Jillian waved Darek to the front seat and sat in the back.

"Remember that old phrase, cool customer?" she asked.

"Formidable, too," Ty said.

"What else would we expect from the False Prophet?" Darek offered.

"I want his desk!" Jillian piped up and laughed.

"Me, too," Ty said.

"'We want to be transparent to the world,'" Jillian quoted Chettri.

"Opaque, maybe," Darek said. "I don't believe I've ever interviewed anyone so slippery."

"Like trying to get mercury to sit still on a glass," Ty said.

"Do you believe we just interviewed the False Prophet?" Jillian asked.

They went dead silent as the impact washed over them.

Finally, Darek spoke up, "Well, we came away alive."

"Must have been the prayer," Ty said.

"And the Holy Spirit," Jillian added.

Darek slipped into the driver's seat and started the vehicle. He looked around to see if any cars were coming. The parking lot was jammed full. But—

"Hey," he said, "our friend's back."

"Yeah, and he has a friend," Jillian said. The man who had followed them around the Old City was hunched forward behind the steering wheel of a car in the next aisle. Another man in a black suit and tie occupied the passenger seat.

"They know we spotted them," Ty said.

"Let's have some fun," Darek said. "Buckle up."

He backed out of the parking space, then jammed the accelerator to the floor.

"Oh!" Jillian shrieked as the force of velocity snapped her head back.

Darek tore down the parking lot and checked the sideview mirror. The two black suits bolted upright, the driver frantically turned the ignition and peeled out after them.

Darek whipped around the end of the aisle of parked cars, spun left, and sped up the next aisle. The suits barreled down the parking lot in pursuit.

Darek squealed right around the end of the aisle and accelerated down the next row. The suit ground gears in a frenzy to catch up.

Right again, and Darek gunned the car down the same aisle where they'd parked. Jamming on the breaks, he backed into the parking spot they originally occupied.

He turned and winked at Jillian in the back seat. Beyond her stunning face, he saw the suits tailspin around the turn. When the tires grabbed hold, the car fired down the aisle and past them. The vehicle slowed at the end of the aisle, then sped off, out of the parking lot.

Ty shook his head.

"Growing up as a black boy in New York City," he said, "I'm used to being watched closely, wearily—whenever I enter a store or walk down a dark street. But this, man, this is a cool way to deal with being stalked."

Darek smiled.

"Just call me Bond," he said, straightening his tie, "James Bond."

They all laughed, then Darek put the car in gear and drove at a moderate speed the short distance to the Knesset.

Pulling into the mammoth parking lot, he said, "So, Ty, you're taking the car and going to see Israel's Chief Rabbi, while Jillian visits with Foreign Minister Madod, and I interview Prime Minister Eckstein?"

Ty nodded agreement. "I'll meet you back here at one o'clock, say on the steps out front."

As Darek and Jillian walked up the steps to the Knesset building, they noticed two people standing at the top of the steps, television cameras sitting at their feet.

"Must be our guys," Darek said.

Moments later, they were shaking hands with cameramen Donnie Moore and Chris Boyle.

Donnie would accompany Darek while Chris teamed with Jillian.

Darek turned to Jillian, "I can't wait to compare notes when we're done. Good luck, darling."

"You, too," she said, and blew him a kiss. They smiled their good-byes.

Prime Minister Eckstein met Darek and Donnie at his office door, effusive in his welcome.

While Donnie set up the lighting, Eckstein said to Darek, "I try to never miss your show, young man."

"Thank you, sir."

"Loved your piece on the Chinese grip on some foreign countries. Comparing them to the internet conglomerate was brilliant."

Darek smiled.

"And your unveiling of the axis of Muslim terror groups was impressive. Not every Westerner understands Arab culture.

"You're well-versed in my work, Mr. Prime Minister."

"There are so few in the media, in the world, who are unbiased toward Israel," Eckstein said. "In the long years before this new peace, few cared to put into perspective that Israel's attacks against our enemies were always in response to murderous aggression. We never, ever began reprisals. But you, Mr. Fields, have been above reproach."

"Thank you, sir, but please call me Darek. I am so honored to see you privately. Thousands of journalists would kill for this opportunity."

"Well, just before you called my secretary, Jake MacMillan reached me on my personal phone at home. We've been acquaintances for years, and he smoothed the way, you might say, for your visit."

A surprise.

"Did you know," Eckstein said, "Jake was one of the first people involved when the World Jewish Congress teamed up with the Knesset's Christian Allies Caucus to foster the relationship between pro-Israel Christians and the state of Israel, back in 2009?"

Darek shook his head.

"It was, and is, an historical and unprecedented alliance between Christians and Jews," Eckstein said. "Israelis and Ministers from across the political spectrum finally realized the importance of this relationship. Jake's help, along with many others from a wide spectrum of Christian organizations, has been vital to its success."

Darek took in the Prime Minister before him. Eckstein was a big, burly man. Strong hands. A man of labor and war.

A bushy head of dark hair stood atop his rugged frame. Smile wrinkles framed his eyes.

A highly decorated IDF soldier, Eckstein had risen to the top of the military ranks and ridden his immense popularity to the position of Prime Minister at the age of sixty-seven. He was one of the last people Darek would have believed would "give in" to a peace agreement while knowing the Palestinians had never actually done anything they'd promised in numerous previous peace talks, road maps, or any other plan of coexistence. Never.

So what was up?

"Please take a seat." Eckstein pointed to an overstuffed chair. As Darek sat, Eckstein took his place across from him.

Looking at Donnie, he asked, "Will this do?"

"Tov," Donnie replied. "Excellent, sir. We can proceed when you're ready."

Darek jumped right in. "Mr. Prime Minister, why agree to this peace plan from Premier Sardis?"

"What else could we do? Now that the One World Government's in place, the entire world is against us. The United States no longer has veto power like in the United Nations. Certainly the UN was no friend of Israel's, but at least when the entire group of Arab nations pushed to slap us for some atrocity or other, the US could veto the action.

"The One World Government changes everything. The whole world not only *appears* to be against us, it *is*. When this peace proposal was presented, we felt we had to relent or perish."

"But why are you not dissuaded by the numerous times the Palestinian Authority has broken agreements, by continual failure to stop homicide bombers, by refusal, even today this spring a year after the peace agreement signing, to remove from founding documents the call for Israel's destruction?"

"We're weary of death and destruction, Darek. You have to walk a mile in our shoes to understand. Since May 28, 1948, when Israel was declared a state, we've been attacked by the Arab world. Every single Jew has lost a loved one. Every single Jew has feared leaving their home in the morning, feared their children stepping into a bus to go to school, feared holding a bar mitzvah in a public restaurant, feared venturing to certain parts of our own city, Jerusalem. We've had Arab bombs spray our businesses with blood and our streets with body parts.

"Imagine getting a call from the police telling you your child has died in a bomb attack, then going to the site of the carnage and discovering you can't even hold your child in your arms because he's not in one piece. The constant, unrelenting terror eventually wore down a majority of our little nation. And, as always, we saw we were outnumbered thousands to one. We felt the choice was for us to relent, or we'd all die."

"The Palestinian Authority was supposed to have been a democracy way back when Yasser Arafat was alive," Darek said. "Everyone thought Arafat alone prevented that from happening. But he's long dead and there's still no democracy. Will there ever be?"

Eckstein looked down to his hands and slowly shook his head. "The hope of peace resides in democracy. But do the Palestinian leaders, or any Arab country's leaders, truly want democracy? Perhaps their people do, but not their leaders. Democracies do not starve their citizens, torture political opponents, or threaten neighbors. By their nature, democracies neither enable terror nor instigate war. Do you see characteristics for democracy in any of our neighboring countries?"

After some thought Darek said, "Jordan."

159

"The one and only," Eckstein said. "Look at what happened after all America's good efforts in Iraq." He shrugged and lifted his hands in a symbol of acceptance, then continued, "So, we were in a state of terror for decades and decades. Then Premier Sardis arrived on his white horse, declaring he could deliver peace. 'The Jews must feel the One World Government is their home,' he said.

"I—we—never bought that idea," he added, "but, simply put, we were worn out and ready to accept the offer."

"Mr. Prime Minister, you're a practicing Jew, so you know God gave to the Hebrew people the land from the Red Sea to the Euphrates River."

Eckstein nodded.

"What do you say to Torah and Bible believers who declare the land of Israel is for no man to give away? And now Israel has even relinquished control of its own most holy city?"

Darek locked Eckstein's gaze with his own and noted a look of sadness.

"I respond there are many Jews, rabbis included, who argue if you must choose between a bad outcome and a deadly outcome, you pick the bad. For instance, if you must break the law against travel in order to save a life, saving a life is more important than the decree not to travel—so you do so. The land? It's the same."

Eckstein's eyes watered and he lowered them, adding with dejection, "Beyond that, I cannot respond."

A pregnant silence followed. Darek's eye caught movement outside the office window. Rain was falling—again. Rain was rare in Israel.

What timing, he thought. God's tears.

At one o'clock, Darek and Donnie emerged from the Knesset. The rain had stopped and Darek saw Jillian and Chris standing at the distant corner atop the wide stairs. Chris was chatting to Jillian as she typed into her notepad.

As Darek and Donnie strolled toward them, Darek took account of the love of his life. Winsome. Lithe. Luminant blonde hair. Then a feeling of fright struck him. Before him flashed a vision of Daniel Pearl, the *Wall Street Journal* reporter who was kidnapped and murdered by Pakistani terrorists in Karachi in 2002. Then, the knowledge of Arabs' fascination with blond women and the disappearance of some, who were rumored to be kept captive by wealthy sheiks pummeled his mind.

He felt like his heart leapt inside him, and he hurried to her.

"Hey, you," he called. "Let's have us a hug."

Jillian looked up and flashed a heart-winning smile. "What? You mean right here in front of the Knesset, before God and everyone, even Donnie and Chris?"

"Absolutely."

He held her tightly and long.

Jillian leaned back and searched his face. "What's wrong?" she asked.

"I just want to hold you, sweetie."

"Darek," she insisted, "what's the matter?"

"Listen, I know this sounds crazy, and Donnie and Chris here will probably agree I'm nuts. But I just looked over at you and had visions of an Arab sheik having you abducted and keeping you prisoner."

"A love slave?" Jillian giggled. "Oh, Darek—" She caught herself short when she noticed the concern etched on his face. She brushed the side of his face with her right hand. "I'm sorry, darling. Those kidnapping stories never occurred to me."

"Me, either. But we need to be ever vigilant." Darek turned to Donnie and asked, "Am I being over-protective?"

"Not at all. I knew two lady IDF soldiers who were kidnapped. One was raped, her body desecrated and left naked outside her barracks a week later. The other is still missing a year after she disappeared."

Chris cut in. "Remember when the Holy Spirit prevented the apostle Paul from entering Asia?"

"Yes," Darek said.

"We have to be that alert to God's leading—especially in the Middle East where Arabs outnumber Jews and Christians a thousand to one and *jihad* has been their middle name since 1948." Chris turned to Jillian. "Take extraordinary care. Please."

Just then Ty approached up the steps.

"How was your interview with the Prime Minister?" he asked.

"They're defeated," Darek said, turning his gaze back upon the Knesset building. Sun glistened off the white Jerusalem stone, making the structure appear bright, but Darek knew that inside, in the hearts of men and women, that was not the case.

"They're almost in a state of suspended animation," he said. "They're glad there's a sort of peace, but sad they've basically given up their land and control of their most holy city. So, they can neither feel complete joy nor overwhelming sadness. Any sigh of relief is caught in their chest by heart-felt grief."

"You know, guys, this building is standing on an earthquake fault line," Ty said. "And back in 2004, when the Cabinet was discussing unilaterally pulling all Jews out of the Gaza Strip and handing the land over to the Palestinians, a five-point quake hit Jerusalem and cracked the ceiling directly above the table at which cabinet ministers sit."

"Whoa!" Jillian said. "They didn't get the message, did they?"

"Nope." Ty held up a finger. "And since the deed is done, listen to this. Seismologists say Israel is due for the big one at any time.

Even a quake of six-point or over on the Richter scale could be catastrophic, flattening an untold number of buildings and leaving tens of thousands dead.

"Fault lines run throughout Israel due to the tectonic structure of the Dead Sea Rift running the full length of the country. And guess what is very susceptible to damage from a major quake?"

Ty waited for an answer. Darek and Jillian exchanged questioning looks.

Finally, Darek guessed. "The Western Wall?"

"Close," Ty said. "The Dome of the Rock and Al Aqsa Mosque are deemed most at risk."

"If not for the rest of the damage, I'd say 'great'!" Jillian said.

Taking one last, long look at the Knesset building, they turned and descended the steps.

CHAPTER TWELVE

Three days later, the Truth Publishing and Broadcasting team finished interviews on the political and cultural landscape of Church Universal and its relationship to the New World Order.

Drinking coffee over room service breakfasts, Jillian and Darek lounged with Ty in his spacious room.

Silence enveloped them. Jillian ran through her mind what they had witnessed. Overall, their time in God's normally exhilarating city had been depressing.

She loved Jerusalem. The Old City left her in awe, but she was ready to return home.

Finally, she said, "After talking to these social-type leaders of the church, I'd say they're brainwashed by the same person, at the same time, in the same room, under the same mantra."

"Yeah, seems like we're witnessing the end result of a multiple cloning," Darek said. "I'd laugh but this is not funny."

"What would you say the mantra is?" Ty asked.

Jillian spoke in slow, stilted, robot-like tones: "It mat-ters not what you be-lieve, or in whom you put your faith, we are noth-ing less than love-ly crea-tures of God, sweet bro-thers and sis-ters of the Lord, and we all de-serve every-thing the world can of-fer us. Give to the poor, the fee-ble, the na-ked and the hun-gry, but do not feed them spi-ri-tual nour-ish-ment for you might in-fringe on their be-lief struc-ture."

"You nailed it, sweetie." Darek smiled. "And I like the bride of Frankenstein touch."

"As a matter of fact, it *is* a monster," Ty said. "A monster created by a monster: Satan."

Jillian nodded agreement. "How would you sum up your interviews, Ty?"

Ty drank some tomato juice. "Intriguing. The chief rabbi and others in the hierarchy are pleased there's peace, but at the same time they're not unaware of the tension in the street. People are waiting for some terrorist to blow up a synagogue or school or hospital. They believe Sardis has charisma and power, but they don't entirely trust magnetism is enough to squelch all rebellion.

"Meanwhile, the state of Israel is happily building the Third Temple on the Temple Mount. The foundation is complete, the scaffolding is going up, and there's a fat-and-happy collective face on the Temple faithful. They feel this is the answer to their dreams."

"Isn't it?" Darek asked.

"Well, yes. But at what expense? Giving away rule of their Holy City to the world? Giving away a city to get a temple? I don't think God's happy with the exchange."

"Well, that puts a cap on things," Jillian said. "Troubling questions all around."

"I'd like to stay a couple more days," Ty said.

"Why?" Darek asked.

"I hate leaving Pascual and Cruz."

Darek and Jillian laughed. The three had taken to calling the two men trailing them names that fit their swarthy Spanish looks.

Darek tapped Ty on the shoulder. "Suppose we can get their real names and addresses so we can alert them the next time we come over"?

"I think they'd appreciate the help," Ty said.

Jillian asked, "Are you serious about staying?"

"Yeah. I'd like to put together a story on this massive influx of Jews from all around the world. The Chief Rabbi was ecstatic about the immigrants. He said the deluge we saw beginning at the turn of the century when there were so many pogroms around the former Soviet Union and France and Germany and elsewhere—is becoming a flood.

"Jews around the world are feeling safe coming home, and they're selling everything and moving here. Think of the implications."

"Talk about a brain drain," Jillian said.

"Talk about the logistical problems immigration is causing here," Darek added.

"Okay. What do you say we call Jake and ask for a couple of days to do this?" Ty asked. "We can talk to some of the new immigrants, the Israeli officials, the agencies in charge of handling them, the non-governmental groups helping the cause, like Bridges for Peace. Find out why they left, what they expected when they got here, what their hopes are for the future, what their reception has been."

"We can do a piece on one particular American family," Jillian said.

Darek turned to Donnie and Chris. "Are you guys available?"

The two photojournalists exchanged looks.

"It's a great story," Donnie said.

"We can handle the load," Chris added.

"I think Jake would buy the idea," Darek said. "Why don't you call him, Ty, since it's your concept? We'll have to give the LaFlamme brothers and Marsha a call and tell them they have more time to continue their tourist gig."

Jake took the call in San Francisco, where he was spending time with his daughter and her family. He agreed the story was an excellent idea. He asked them to buy a little shofar for his grandson and wished them well.

The next three days were a whirlwind, bustling from the Negev to the Golan Heights interviewing immigrants and others involved the surge in population.

Then they were in the air, flying home. Darek watched Jillian type away on her laptop and peeked at the monitor.

For Some Jews, Home Is on the Other Side of the Earth
JERUSALEM—Thousands of Jews from around the world are proving you can come home.

The Kravitz family believes as good as life was in Galloway Township, NJ, they are now living where they are meant to be—Israel, home to the Jewish people since the time of King David 3,000 years ago.

"Yes, we left behind a wonderful life," said Roy Kravitz, an investment banker. "My wife, Mardy, and I had terrific jobs. We lived in a secure, wealthy neighborhood. Our two sons were in good private schools. We played our golf at Pine Valley and Blue Heron Pines, held close friendships in a lovely conservative synagogue, and were basically living the American dream. But Mardy's and my true hope has long been to live here."

The Kravitzes are settling in after two months in Israel, diving headlong into learning Hebrew in ulpan, the language classes. Roy has even found a job, far more rapidly than normal for the 42,000 immigrants from around the world who have immigrated to their homeland in the last year.

Darek couldn't help himself, saying, "Hey, babe, I like your lead."

She smiled. "Thanks. I thought I'd start writing something down. This authorship by committee is difficult for me, as you know."

"Well, I think you should take the lead on this sidebar, for sure. Ty will take the lead on his overview feature. I'll sit in the background and stay out of the way, then add quotes and statements here and there when you're both done."

"Sounds like you got the snooze job, bud," she needled, then poked him with her elbow.

"You gotta play the angles."

Marsha stepped up and asked, "Would anyone like a snack?"

"Sure. Cranberry juice on ice would be perfect," Jillian said.

"Me, too," Darek said.

Ty held up his hand. "No, thanks. I'm waiting until we fly over England, then I'm going to request high tea—PG Tips, I'd say—and crumpets."

Marsha laughed. "I'm actually a step ahead of you, and I think three o'clock is upon us, so the timing will be perfect."

Later, over tea, they sat together and discussed the series of events set in motion by the One World Government. The thought of the magnitude and future of the global oversight was frightening.

Darek turned to Jillian. "I want to spend a long life with you."

She gripped his hand. "And I with you. I've decided against Pascual," she cracked.

When they landed at Logan International Airport, they hit the ground running, preparing written stories for Truth newspapers as well as the premier issue of the broadcast *Truth Be Told.*

CHAPTER THIRTEEN

IN THE FALL

This is contentment.

Lounging in their wharf-side apartment, Darek and Jillian sipped from glasses of cabernet and read weekly magazines. Several months had passed since their *Truth Be Told* debut. Jillian stretched out, her bare feet in Darek's lap. Every once in a while Darek stroked her feet, or reached over and squeezed his wife's hand.

A simmering fireplace crackled brightly before them.

A telephone rang on an end table, breaking the silence. Darek picked up the phone. No image appeared on the LCD. The caller was blocking the recognition. "Hello."

"Darek Fields?" The voice sounded distant, like at the bottom of a barrel. Also male and somewhat familiar.

"Yes. Who's this?"

"Mr. Fields, I'm calling to inform you the Alliance is going to start blowing up statues and public monuments that mention God. And they're going to start there in Boston."

Darek sat to attention. "Who is this?"

The telephone went dead. Darek looked at his caller identification readout. "Private Call."

"What the matter?" Jillian's face showed concern. He was certain she could read the same body language and perplexed look on his face.

"An anonymous call." He frowned. "A man. He said the Alliance is going to start blowing up statues and public monuments that mention God."

"Icky Coffman's Atheists." The words shot out of Jillian's mouth.

"I'll bet you're right. He said they'll start in Boston."

"Maybe he's a crank. I've gotten enough of those calls."

"Right. But they've all been just nasty, angry calls, or threats against you personally."

"This is different. I think I believe him." Darek hesitated. "Man, the voice sounded familiar. Vaguely, like someone I've interviewed or heard in the news."

"Young, old?"

"Young."

"Black, white?"

"White."

"Sophisticated?"

"Yes, educated."

"The president?"

Darek looked squarely at Jillian, not believing she said such a thing under such a serious circumstance. The flicker of a smile played on her mouth.

"Jillian, this is not a funny matter."

"I know. Just had to break the tension." She sat up. "What should we do?"

"First, call Homeland Security, then call Carlos Martinez," he said, mentioning the executive news director.

Jake took one last look into his daughter's brilliant, blue eyes. Those eyes, her face, the way she walked and held herself—elegant, the epitome of a lady. The mirror image of her mother but an inch or two taller.

He held his year-old grandson tight to his chest with his left arm, breathed in the baby smell, and reached with his right to cradle his daughter's face in his hand. He felt overwhelming love, and a deadening sadness Dawn could not, would never, be able to share the new life in their family.

A year since her death, and he still was often stopped short, missing her. He wished she were there to speak with concerning the new threat Carlos Martinez had just called about. The peril was dangerous enough to cut short his visit.

"I love you, princess. I'll try to get back out before long. But things are really heating up, so I'm not sure when."

Jake turned his eyes to the child. "And you, Isaac, your grandmama would love to have held you." The child smiled up at him. Jake started to tear up and gently handed the baby to Lisa.

"I love you, too, Dad, and I'll pray for you daily." She leaned up and kissed him on the cheek.

"Well, son," Jake turned to Andy, "are you ready to escort grandpapa to the airport?"

Andy grabbed a chain of keys from a hook beside the door. "Sure, Dad. All set to go."

As they drove to San Francisco International Airport, Jake thought back on these last three days visiting Lisa and Andy. The visit was at times joyous, at times tear-ridden, and at times surreal.

Until Dawn's death, he had never been to visit Andy and Lisa without her. Everyday life without her was a chore. Traveling alone, eating alone, sleeping alone, not being able to expect her brief, joyous phone calls during the work day— this Dawn-less life carried a heavy weight that was greater than the sum of those missing parts.

Jake thought wryly of the old saying, something like, "With love, in times of sorrow your pain is divided, and in times of happiness your joy is multiplied." He most often felt the missing of happiness—Dawn was not there to share a laugh. He and Dawn had been joined at the hip and united at the heart.

He wondered how Siamese twins must feel when they are separated by surgery.

Andy dropped Jake at the United Air wing of the airport. He was flying commercial since his plane had taken Darek, Jillian, and Ty to Israel, and a second company jet was not yet equipped with full security.

Bob Ward was waiting for him at the curb. His bodyguard had come to the airport a couple of hours earlier because he carried a gun, needed to go through the registering process, and wanted to see if an air marshal would be on board. Since Dawn's death, they were taking extra precautions—now especially so since hundreds of innocent people were traveling on the same plane.

Jake hugged Andy. "Take care of your lovely wife and child, son."

"Sure will."

Jake turned to Bob and walked into the terminal, wondering if he would ever again see his family. An anxiety gripped at his heart. He wasn't afraid of death, no. The cause was a matter of not holding his flesh and blood in his arms again, not watching his grandson grow up. His family might not have a lifetime ahead of them, and his grandson might never see the age of Boy Scouting and Little League.

Oh, how he wished Dawn were there at his side. "You—grandmama," he whispered as the memory of their last moments together flashed in his mind, and a sad smile touched his mouth.

Seven hours later, Jake and Bob entered the Truth Publishing front door.

"Jake. Jake!" Carlos Martinez called.

Carlos wasn't the type to get excitable, but Jake could see worry carved onto his executive editor's face. Jake's first guess was the first statue had been blown up.

"What is it, Carlos?"

Carlos motioned Jake and Bob to the elevator, closed the door, pushed the "Floor" button, then turned to Jake. "In just the last hour, the market has plummeted so much Wall Street was shut down. The Tokyo Stock Exchange and European Stock Market are free-falling, too."

Jake had kept the car radio off on his way from Logan to the office, so this was the first he had heard of the news. "What brought this on?"

"We don't know. Dan Cowan just called. He's been on the floor at Wall Street. Many of the key players are dumping stock, and no one's telling why."

Cowan was the Truth's business editor, a brilliant man with close contacts throughout the financial world. Jake trusted he could get to the bottom of the disaster. Something this big couldn't possibly be a mystery.

As they exited the elevator into the newsroom and headed for his office, Jake pulled his phone from his briefcase, punched a speed dial number, and seconds later, Dan's face appeared.

"Jake!"

"Dan, what's up?"

"Are you alone?"

"Carlos is with me. What's the cause of all this?"

Dan lowered his voice. He was obviously walking to a quiet place outside the massive brokerage building.

"The conspiracy theorists claim the Bilderbergers are the cause," he said, referring to the elite global secret society of power brokers.

"You sound skeptical." Jake opened the door to his office and waved Carlos and Bob to seats. "Hold on, Dan. I'm putting you on speaker." Jake pushed the speaker button. "All right. Go ahead."

"I think the Bilderbergers have been flummoxed—outflanked," Dan said. "I believe we'll discover this is a complicated, sinister plan—my guess is, a plot hatched by the Chinese."

Jake blew out a deep exhale. "What in the world do you mean?"

"Who did we sell all our debt to in 2009 and again last year? And watch who buys all the stocks when they hit bottom," Dan said. "I've been closely monitoring the stock-and-bond movements of the leaders of the Bilderbergers. If they planned to cause a plunge in the markets, they'd be positioning themselves for a takeover, building up their reserves for a massive buyout.

"But none of them has done so. No, today caught them unawares. I hear Lloyd Barclay is in a panic, even suicidal."

Barclay was a former US Treasury secretary and the Bilderbergers' current secretary general for the Americas. Jake knew him as a steady if headstrong individual, a Harvard man who'd tripled his father's fortune with takeovers, sometimes hostile, of multinational companies. If this rumor of suicidal thoughts were true, today's event must be earthshaking.

Jake took a moment to gather his thoughts. He'd never bought into conspiracy theories promulgated over the years about the Bilderbergers and its supposed "children," the

Trilateral Commission and the Council on Foreign Affairs. He figured the Bilderbergers was simply a broad cross section of the world's leading citizens, in and out of government, who met every year to discuss foreign affairs and the international economy.

Of course, each of them impacted the economy. Being powerful men and women was the reason they were chosen to join the Bilderbergers. But in the end Jake felt no harm, no foul.

He recalled Georgetown University Professor Carroll Quigley's magnum opus, *Tragedy and Hope*, in which Quigley acknowledged an international network with no aversion to cooperating with the Communists or any other group and frequently did so.

Quigley had studied the Bilderbergers for twenty years and said he had no distaste for the group or for most of its aims. As Jake recalled, Quigley objected only to a few Bilderberger policies and thought the group should drop any wishes to remain unknown.

"I believe their role in history is significant enough to be acknowledged," the professor had written.

Jake glanced at Carlos, who seemed to be studying him.

"Your thoughts, Carlos?"

"You know I *do* believe in the theories about the Bilderbergers."

"Yes. So what do you think about this market drop?"

"Not their style. L'Eminence Joseph Retinger, who created them, thought they could control the world economy through indirect political means. But he also believed countries with different ideologies could be brought into line by powerful multinational organizations dictating and applying economic and military policies. He thought this would create a union and a bond between the nations. If they want to control the world, how better than to bring everyone to their collective knees financially?"

Jake turned to the phone. "What do you think of that, Dan?"

"What Carlos says is true. But as I mentioned, I've seen no big movement in the markets from any of the Bilderberger leaders."

"What makes you name the Chinese?"

"China's economy has accelerated the global shift of wealth and power to East Asia. The shift began when President Nixon recognized them, then quickened when President Clinton gave China *Most Favored Nation* status, which opened the floodgates. The 2009 sellout to China to cover America's debts sent their economy into the stratosphere. And events in the region, or between China and its trading partners, have altered but not reversed the rate of growth."

Dan went quiet for a few seconds, and Jake heard a group of men pass by in frantic discussion, then continue in hushed tones, "The Chinese have long felt they belonged at the top of the heap in world politics and finances. They believe that, for most of recorded history, China has been the most prosperous, most advanced technologically, most powerful, and best governed of all societies. Their eclipse by the West in recent history, they think, is an anomaly that time and hard work will correct. And they've felt put aside from inclusion in global institutions and regulatory regimes. So they've lusted after the power they feel they deserve.'"

Carlos broke in. "But how can they cause such a violent oscillation in the American, Tokyo, and European stock markets?"

"Basically, because they've been excluded from the Group of Seven, the World Trade Organization, the New Forum and other global institutions, they don't need to adhere to global rules," Dan said. "Beijing is free to ignore complaints from any trading partners until they escalate into confrontation, and when that happens, the country with the most muscles wins. America alone stands a chance of prevailing.

"And subterfuge to turn any stock market upside down is well within China's abilities. They can use tens of thousands of people around the world—expatriates, real or imagined—to buy or sell limitless amounts of stock."

"But what about the One World Government?" Jake asked.

"What of it?" Dan shrugged. "The entire world, except China, has bowed its knee to Sardis. I wish the United States had China's guts. No, Jake, the Chinese have a cocky self-confidence they're destined to take their place as the preeminent society on the planet, regardless of any One World anything."

"But China owes its economic transformation to institutions like the International Monetary Fund, the International Bank for Reconstruction and Development, and the old United Nations," Jake said.

"Yes, but they're not looking to the past. Their mentality is the future and long-term," Dan replied. "They don't dump and run on anything. They're looking fifty, a hundred years down the road. Do any of us capitalists plan that far ahead?"

"No. Can't say we do." Jake hesitated. "Well, you're the expert. How do you think we should cover this?"

"I need to do some digging to confirm or deny my theory. Right now, I'll supply a story on … what's today? Tuesday? I'll provide a story on Black Tuesday."

"From our end, we can have our correspondents weigh in on reactions in various parts of the world," Jake said. "Anything else we should pursue?"

"I'd get whoever you can to interview the Bilderberger and Trilateral Commission leaders," Dan said. "I'll finish this up for deadline tonight, then give you a ring, Carlos, to set strategy. Can you get me any help here? Maybe Andrea Page. She's got an MBA, and we've worked well together."

"So I hear," Jake grinned. He'd seen the personal connection the two had made over the past couple of years. "Carlos, can you free Andrea?"

"Sure," Carlos said. "Okay, Dan, call as soon as you're done."

Jake hung up and turned to Carlos. "Napoleon once advised his fellow Europeans, 'Let China sleep. When it wakens, it will shake the world.' Knew what he was talking about, didn't he?"

"Right," Carlos said. "You ready for our next threat? The anonymous call to Darek Fields about the bombings of religious monuments?"

Jake sank to his chair, shaking his head.

CHAPTER FOURTEEN

Icky Coffman sat at his desk in his AFFRONT office. Across from him, Stephen Russell lounged on a plush sofa. The Alliance's board chairman sported a self-confident look.

Icky looked past Russell out the wide window. If he could only see around the building across the street, he could spot the Capitol. He loved the idea of sitting so close to the house of power. And to the Supreme Court Building which stood across the street behind the capitol.

Icky interlocked his fingers. "So you want us to wait on blasting the Supreme Court Building until Hisey and your people do a number up in Boston." A statement, not a question.

"That's our decision," Russell said. "The Tea Party, John Adams, Sam Adams, Paul Revere's ride, the tension and aggression fostering the American Revolution all started in Boston. So Beantown's where our Revolution should start, where we make our statement, where we can hold our heads high, draw the line in the sand, and put them on notice."

"You're so full of clichés, Stephen. Ever come up with an original?" Icky didn't like how Russell felt secure in making so many decisions unilaterally when their name was the Alliance. "Please sit up. If someone were to walk in here they might think you were striking a pose for an artist, for God's sake."

"God? You mention God?" Russell mocked. "But you don't believe in him."

"Stephen!"

The threat in Coffman's voice was enough to cut Russell short.

"Okay, okay." Russell swung his feet to the floor. "Icky, you'll get your chance. Real soon. What's your target?"

"Target?" Coffman repeated. "We have more targets than I can count on my fingers, but we'll start outside the Supreme Court Building with the sculpture of Moses holding the Ten Commandments."

"How tunnel visioned of our forefathers. How noxious," Russell said in fake effrontery. "How did they think they could get away with such a thing?"

"Don't mess with me, Stephen. God doesn't exist. He didn't call down from heaven the Ten Commandments, my father be damned. And we want every mention of him, and them, out—O. U. T.—out of public view. Here in Washington more so than anywhere else. This is where the American government rules. Imagine, one block away from Congress and the statue of Moses is still allowed to stand!"

"After you take out Moses, then what?"

"There are photos of Moses with the tablets in the rotunda of the Library of Congress, and the Ten Commandments are embedded in the floor of the National Archives. They'll get us started." Coffman wore a smug look. "I assure you, our campaign of God-removal will be longer—and more spectacular—than your puny effort in Boston."

With a "harrumph," Russell turned and faced the window.

Jake's secretary, Annie Stapleton, had called a task force into his office. *U.S. News* editor Todd Livingstone, *Boston Globe* city editor Nancy Blais, suburban editor Gloria Nesson, Darek and Jillian Fields, Ty, general reporters Jeff Warren and John Adams, and statehouse reporter Al Munson all sat around his office.

Jake sat on the corner of his desk, coat off, tie askew. He was running on adrenaline—the few days' rest with Lisa and Andy a distant memory.

Jake stood and looked at them all. "People, we have to move fast. I want us to be faster than Homeland Security, faster than the Coast Guard, faster than the National Guard, faster than the Boston Police Department and—if ever they're allowed on our shores—faster than the One World Army."

Carlos stepped forward. "As you all know, we've agreed with Homeland Security and the Boston PD to remain mum on this threat so they can stake out all the public places with Scriptures, or where God is mentioned, and capture the terrorists. In exchange, we get the scoop."

Darek spoke out. "I called them so they could warn people to stay away from those places, not so they could put them under surveillance."

"I know," Carlos said, "and I'm sure this decision was a tough call for them. They decided to try to catch these bombers to prevent future death and carnage as well. We just have to pray and trust they're equal to the challenge and can catch these creeps. Meantime, the team in this room is sworn to secrecy. Understood, everyone? Not even your husbands and wives. Well, I guess except for Darek and Jill."

Light laughter circled around the room.

"I want us in the back seats of the surveillance vehicles. I want us to have all the key local clergymen and legislators on our speed-dials. I want us able to turn around a story on the capture at the speed of light."

Thankfully, Jake thought, the targets in Boston were limited. The Old North Church might be the Alliance's prime target. The park across the street from the church, which had scripture around its fountain. The fountain in Christopher Columbus Park by the waterfront. Trinity Church in Copley Square. Boston College's Center for Ignatian Spirituality...

Mosey Kreko savored the mug of rich hot coffee that might be the last Columbian he'd ever taste. The battle for control of Columbia between the drug cartels of long standing and the Islamic terrorists who were vying to control all the drug traffic the world over, had brought carnage and death to South America. Countries were in shambles.

Premier Sardis and the One World Government may have brought "world peace" between the nations, but groups such as these accepted no rule from anyone. The higher the authorities at whom they could thumb their noses, the louder they proclaimed their own power.

Mosey turned to the back of the Bible on his kitchen table. At the end of a section called "How To Study the Bible" he read aloud,

> We do not know the Bible until we know it thus. The Book comes to us through natural channels, but with supernatural power. In origin it differs from all other books. It is like the Sabbath, made for man; but, like the Sabbath, it was made by God. The sacred Volume will never do for us what it can do unless we regard it as sacred, seeing in

it God's communication to His children. It took the form of a book, for what other form could it take? It has been marvelously safeguarded through the ages, for the Almighty would not commit His messages to blind chance. It proves its authenticity by its permanence and universality, and testifies its authority by its power over the souls of men.

Let us praise God for His Book. It is one of His best gifts to the world. Let us feed upon it, live with it, love it; and let us see that it does for us all God wishes to do for us through its blessed ministrations.

"Whoa, who wrote this?" he asked. Mary, sitting across from him, shrugged.

Mosey turned a few pages forward. "The late Amos R. Wells. Darn. Mary, I just want to talk to someone who knows this stuff, who can tell me exactly how Paul explained from Old Testament Scriptures how Jesus fulfilled all the Messianic prophecies. I mean, my folks have been anticipating the coming of the Messiah all their lives. It's why they moved to Israel."

"I know, darling." Mary took a bite of her bagel heaped with cream cheese. "Hey, you're going to Boston in a couple of days. How about the pastor who spoke at Dawn MacMillan's funeral?"

"Yeah, I liked that guy."

"I think I've still got the announcement. Hold on." Mary scrambled through her purse.

"Ah-ha!" she pulled out a slip of paper and looked closely. "The Reverend William Asbury. Messiah Evangelical Church, Boston."

"I'll call to see if I can speak with him," Mosey said.

"M-hm." Mary studied her husband. Dark, short-cut curly hair framed a face of rugged good looks. The stress of what he thought was the call on his life—to stop the spread of nuclear power and spent nuclear rods—the job had carved a few lines on his face ahead of their time. But they just added character, she thought.

"These past couple of years, I've been hauling you to church to no effect." She shook her head. "Then one day you pick up a Gideon Bible in a hotel room and everything changes. I don't understand."

"I left the Alliance meeting upset, confused, feeling betrayed. I got back to the hotel room hoping you'd be there to talk things out. My head was swirling, wondering what to do. I just felt compelled to open the Gideon."

Mosey locked his eyes onto Mary's and shrugged. "I simply opened the book to various places, and when I looked down onto the page, a verse spoke directly to my question. I was amazed. The experience was as though God was speaking directly to me, 'Mosey, he that walketh with wise men shall be wise; but a companion of fools shall be destroyed … My son, if sinners entice you, do not consent. Forsake the foolish, and live; and go in the way of understanding.' Boy, there was my answer."

Silently thanking God for answering her many hours of prayers, Mary reached her hand over to rest on his. "I'm so glad."

"Well, I'm convinced. And so here I am, ready to find out what other treasures are in these pages. But I need to get by the main obstacle first, the thing that divides my people, the Jews, and yours, the Christians.

"We Jews have grown up with a history of fear of the cross. To us, the cross wasn't a symbol of hope. Rather of hate and death. The Catholic Church used the cross to incite the

Crusaders. Hitler used the passion of the cross to urge people on to Kristallnacht and mass genocide. The Russians used the cross as a war cry for scores of pogroms. And the same is happening today."

Mosey wrapped his hands around hers and continued. "When many Jews see a cross hanging around a person's neck, we tend to cringe. The message we get is not of 'love your neighbor' but 'avenge the death of Jesus.' I wrestle with that. On the one hand, fundamental Christians are the biggest supporters of Israel in the world. On the other hand, anti-Semitism and atrocities against Jews are sometimes rooted in who killed Jesus."

CHAPTER FIFTEEN

"God killed Jesus." Bill Asbury peered intently at the young man sitting across from him, the head of Advocates for a Nuclear-Free World.

Bill had been praying for the moment he could say those words since Mosey Kreko had called two days before, asking for an audience. "Jesus said straight out to Pontius Pilate that the ruler wasn't taking his life, no man could. Jesus said he could call down a squadron of angels if he wanted protection.

"No, Mosey, the truth is Jesus—God incarnate—willingly laid down his life on the cross. He was the perfect Lamb, the sacrifice for the sins of all mankind. A blood sacrifice was required. And while the Jews for two thousand years have sacrificed with the blood of animals, which was a temporary sacrifice, the ultimate sacrifice of Jesus on the cross was sufficient for all time. He was without blemish, without sin.

"There was no way around his death on the cross, and he knew so. Anyone who says differently is lying, or they simply don't know the Bible, especially the New Testament."

Tears swelled in Mosey's eyes. "I feel torn to hear your explanation. On one hand, if you're right, Jesus going through such torture for mankind is wonderful. On the other hand, I feel horrible about feeling wonderful about his death. He died for us!"

"For you, Mosey. For you, personally—for me, personally."

"But how can I know for certain Jesus was who he said he was?"

"The wonderful thing about the Bible is the very words written there have proven God wrote the book. And the proof verifies the contents."

Leaning forward, intent on what he was about to say, Bill continued, "There is no other book filled with prophecies that later came true. No other religion or holy book can make such a claim. Mohammed, for instance, wrote one prophecy—a self-fulfilling one—he would go to Jerusalem, which he did. Hundreds and hundreds of prophecies were given in the Old Testament, and they've come true, right up to those foretelling the Last Days.

"Wow!" Mosey's jaw dropped. "Well, then. The New Testament says Paul reasoned with the Jews from the Scriptures, proving Jesus was the Messiah. What Scriptures was he using?"

"Glad you asked." Bill beamed. This was medicine to his own heart. "Let me first explain quickly God's plan of salvation for mankind. In the life of Abel, Adam and Eve's son, God provided atonement for one person. The story's in Genesis chapter four. On Passover, we see God's atonement for a family, told in Exodus. On Yom Kippur, the Day of Atonement, we read of God's provision for a nation. The story is in Leviticus chapter sixteen. And, in the Messiah, we see atonement for all who believe in him as their personal Passover lamb."

Bill reached for a Bible sitting atop his broad oak desk. "The prophets of old told us about the Messiah. Micah said he'd be born in Bethlehem. Isaiah said he'd be born of a virgin; be despised and rejected by men; live a sinless life. Zechariah prophesied he'd be betrayed for thirty pieces of silver and would die of crucifixion, which, by the way, was not heard of when Zechariah lived around 520 BC."

Bill drew a deep breath and continued, "Psalm twenty-two says Messiah would be crucified and his clothing gambled for at the time of his death. And Psalms 16 and 110 say he'd arise from the dead. Jesus's resurrection is one of the most attested to events in history since more than five hundred people saw him after his crucifixion and death.

"But, best of all," Bill caught Mosey's rapt attention, "and this is perhaps my favorite proof Jesus is the Messiah—Daniel prophesied the Messiah would come to earth before the destruction of the Second Temple. The Romans destroyed the Second Temple in 70 AD, after Jesus' death. So, your people who are looking for the Messiah's coming should scrutinize that Scripture—Daniel chapter nine, verses twenty-four to twenty-six. If they do, they'll conclude they missed him."

Bill breathed out deeply. He felt like he'd just preached a sermon.

"But it's not too late," he continued. "It's never too late until we die. In Revelations 3:20, the Lord says: 'Here I am. Behold, I stand at the door and knock. If anyone hears my voice and opens the door, I will come in and eat with him, and he with me.'"

"Pastor," Mosey said, "do you have any materials you can give me spelling this out? I have to share this with my parents in Israel."

Bill stood and walked to a floor-to-ceiling bookcase, his eyes wandering downward. "Ah-ha! Got ya'."

He handed a small pamphlet to Mosey. "From the Chosen People Ministries. Great stuff. There's plenty of proof in here."

Mosey took the booklet and rifled the pages. At the back of the manuscript, he locked onto a quote from Joel

3:5: "Whosoever shall call on the name of the Lord shall be delivered." A tear stung his right eye and worked its way down his cheek.

"This is too easy," Mosey said. "Far too easy. 'Whosoever shall call on the name of the Lord shall be delivered.' I mean, Jesus died a horrendous death, flogged to within an inch of his life, nailed to a cross, treated like a common criminal—or worse. How could he save my soul so easily by me saying a few words?"

"It *is* too easy," Bill agreed. "None of us deserve such an unbridled love. But God said that was the only way he could offer salvation. Jesus's sacrifice had to be a free gift, something we could not earn, so we would not be able to boast. We can't earn points for good works, looking for some magic total to buy us a place in heaven. Simply God's grace and mercy clear the way for us."

"So what do I do?" Mosey implored. "What do I say to God to be saved?"

"There's no formula. God's interested in your heart, what you believe. He wants you just to trust in him and believe on the One whom he sent—Jesus of Nazareth." Bill hesitated, waiting for Mosey to absorb his words. "Can you?"

"Can I not?"

"Then I'll lead you in a prayer to God. But, as I said, what makes a difference isn't the words you say but what's in your heart."

Bill began the prayer, and Mosey followed his lead—"Dear Heavenly Father, I know I've sinned against you and fallen short of your plan for my life, and I ask your forgiveness. Messiah Jesus, I believe you came to earth, died to atone for the sins of men, and were resurrected to sit at the right hand of the Father. Please come into my heart and life, cleanse me with your precious blood of atonement and transform me into a child of God."

Minutes later, Mosey stepped outside the church, waved a goodbye to Bill Asbury, closed the door behind him, and took a deep breath. Mm-m-m, he felt like a new man. He *was* a new man, with joy in his heart and lightness in his step.

The autumn sun, so delicious in New England, an almost tangible delight, warmed his bones. Life had just taken a beautiful turn. He felt giddy. He almost glided down the stone walkway, smelling the yellow- and blue-budded flowers lining the path.

Wait until I tell Mary. She'll be ecstatic!

Extracting his car keys from his pocket, Mosey pushed a button on the key fob to unlock the door. The car was parked at the end of the church walkway, and he reached for the door.

Then, bam! Out of nowhere, a strong arm slammed him into the side of the car face forward.

Agh-h! Was his nose broken?

His arms were forced behind him, and someone expertly slapped on handcuffs. Then, two sets of hands spun him around. Before him were two tall, athletic-looking men in suits and ties.

"Mosey Kreko," the taller and older of the two declared, "you are wanted for questioning."

"Questioning?" Mosey was flabbergasted. "Qu-questioning for what? Who are you guys?"

The tall one flashed a badge.

"Homeland Security. I'm agent Cusack. This is agent Downing."

Mosey's mind whirled. Homeland Security? What was happening? What could they think he did? Then a dark cloud descended on him.

They found out about the Alliance and the bombs. And they think I'm involved.

"What do you want with me?" he asked.

"We'll be asking the questions. Downtown. In the FBI offices," said Cusack. "For now, we'll take your key and look through this car."

"Don't you need a search warrant?"

Downing pulled a document out of his coat pocket and stuffed the paper into Mosey's jacket.

Downing and Mosey watched as Cusack opened the trunk. Finding nothing in sight, he pulled apart the top to the spare-tire compartment. Then, he thoroughly searched the car from back seat to engine. Nothing.

Cusack swore, took a phone from his coat and hit a button. Momentarily, a face appeared on the LCD. The person answering said, "Blake here."

"Buck," Cusack said, "find anything in the hotel room?"

"No. We tore the place apart, shredded the guy's luggage, everything. But there's nothing here. How about you?"

"We've got Kreko in hand, but found nothing in his car. I'll call HQ and have them send a team over to this church, cordon off the area, and check the building to see if he planted anything in the place."

Mosey was beside himself. "Plant something in the church? Listen up, you guys. The pastor in there is a friend. He just led me to Christ."

"Right, Kreko. I believe you." Cusack was standing in front of Mosey now, wearing a disgusted look. "I believe you're a real establishment guy. You belong to the Alliance only because you want to be well-rounded, to diversify your portfolio of friends.

"Right!" Cusack spat out. "Now come with us."

One on each side, the two men grabbed Mosey's elbows and pulled him along the sidewalk, then forced him into the back seat of a black Escalade.

Wish I had stock in Escalades. They've all got them.

"Do you mind if I call my board of advisers?" Mosey asked. "I'm supposed to meet with them in an hour."

"No calls," said Cusack.

"I just need to tell them I won't be there. They'll worry if I don't show and they don't hear from me."

"Let 'em worry," Cusack said with scorn.

Downing spoke in a low tone to Cusack, "Why not let him call?"

"We can't risk he'll somehow tip 'em off that we're onto 'em."

"How long are you going to keep me?" Mosey asked.

"Maybe forever, pal. You'd better pray nobody in this town gets hurt by any bombs, or I can almost guarantee your incarceration will be forever, or until your cell mates—" Cusack stopped himself.

"Bombs?" Mosey knew he needed to sound incredulous. "I don't have any bombs. I don't have any anything. One of the reasons I started Advocates for a Nuclear-Free World was because—"

"Why don't you hold your tongue until we get to headquarters?" Cusack said roughly.

"… was because I am opposed to bombs—of any sort, nuclear or otherwise." Mosey took a deep breath. His hands were trembling. He felt all jittery, like when he got in a heated argument with someone. Adrenaline.

"Gentlemen, there are a number of other people in the Alliance. My group must be the least likely to plant a bomb. Besides, plant a bomb where? Wouldn't the Alliance pick someplace like Washington, DC?"

Might as well plant a seed.

Cusack and Downing exchanged glances, but neither answered.

They maneuvered through the streets until they reached One Center Plaza in downtown. Cusack pulled the car past an armed checkpoint and into a parking garage. In a blistering minute, Mosey was in a room bare of anything but a table and metal chairs. On the table was a digital recorder. On one wall was a long mirror.

Obviously one-sided, just like in the movies. Oh Lord, you didn't make me wait long for my first test of faith, did you? Mosey chuckled to himself.

"Funny, is it?" There was no humor in Cusack's voice. "This all amusing to you, Kreko?"

Mosey straightened up. "No, sir. I was just talking to God."

"Allah, you mean? The god who wants his followers to blow up innocent people?" Cusack's sarcasm was palpable.

"No, it's the God of the Jews and Christians. The God of Abraham, Isaac, and Jacob."

"Kreko, I don't like being played. I don't tolerate crap from terrorists, and you're looking every inch a terrorist to me—right down to scoping out the church you're about to blow up."

"Church I'm about to blow up?"

"Yeah, Truth Evangelical Church."

Mosey envisioned Mary visiting him in prison, talking over a phone, plexiglass between them.

"Wha …. Y-you think I was there to scope it out? You th-think I want to blow the place up?"

"'God so love the world …' is carved in the granite out front. The statue of Jesus holding a lamb in his arms is in the foyer." Cusack got up out of his chair and pointed at Mosey. "And you, my friend, are looking at a bleak future—if you have a future at all."

"Wha-what do I have to do to prove I'm not involved?" Fear played down Mosey's spine. He shivered. "A lie-detector test? Truth serum?"

"How about telling us all you know about the bombings the Alliance is planning?"

"What makes you think I know anything about bombings?"

"Do you belong to the Alliance, or don't you?"

"I do."

"Don't you attend the board meetings?"

"Yeah."

"Don't they talk about their plans at those meetings?"

"Of course."

"Then, if they were planning bombings, wouldn't they discuss them at those meetings?"

Mosey knew he had to come clean. He looked at the mirror and then at Cusack. "Who's behind there?"

"Friends."

"L-listen, I know how you found out about the bombings."

"Sure you do."

"Darek Fields called you."

Cusack glared firmly at Mosey, then turned and peered at the mirror. He hesitated, collecting his thoughts, probably. "Just why would you think that?"

"Because I called him," Mosey whispered.

"You have a relationship with Fields?"

"No, I don't even know him. But I respect him. I don't respect many journalists, but I respect him."

"So you want me to believe you called this guy and said, 'Hey, Fields, this is Mosey Kreko. Guess what? We're going to blow up your city.'"

"N-no, I called anonymously," Mosey said, "and all I said was what I knew. They plan to blow up public places with Scriptures on them."

"What public places?"

"I don't know."

"When?"

"I don't know."

"You don't know much, do you?"

Mosey threw up his hands. "You're right. I don't. I wish I knew more. But I don't." A thought came to him and he added, "One thing I do know, though—"

"What?"

"If the Alliance finds out I called Fields, or I'm talking to you, my wife is a widow."

Cusack stood erect, arms folded, examining Mosey's face. Mosey felt naked, like this guy could read him.

Cusack stepped to the door and left without a word.

On the other side of the two-way mirror Darek pointed through the window at Mosey. He turned Jillian at his side and to Agent Downing.

"That's him—the man who called. I knew I'd heard his voice. I've just never met Kreko in person."

Mosey fidgeted. *Oh Lord. Oh Lord.* Then he realized he could pray. He might be locked up, but handcuffs didn't prevent him from praying. *Baruck atah, Adonai Elohenu, molech ha-olem.* The many nights with his parents on high holy days flashed back to him. *Blessed art Thou Lord God Almighty, king of the universe. I need Your help. I need favor with these people. I'm scared!*

The door flew open and Cusack walked through the threshold. "When did you say your board meeting is?"

Mosey looked at his watch. "Five minutes ago."

"Call and tell them you're on your way."

CHAPTER SIXTEEN

The Truth's reporters were spread around Boston when on duty, and were on call when off duty. The tension was exhausting.

Sitting at a small Italian restaurant on Salem Street in Boston's North End, Darek looked around the table at Jillian, Ty, and Bethany. The street was bustling, the narrow brick sidewalks packed with people. The smells of pasta sauce and garlic bread filled the air.

Darek recounted the state of the world, his right index finger tapping each finger of his left hand. "There are new reports of widespread famine in parts of Africa, India, and even Russia. Some weird new disease is destroying rice fields throughout Asia. Another virus has manifested in soybean crops across North America. A descendant of Mad Cow Disease, of all things, is running rampant through Argentina and, half world away, in Australia. And here we're waiting for Homeland Security to catch some creeps upset about, of all things, God being on view in public places." He shook his head.

"Nothing better to busy themselves with than hating the mere idea of a Creator," Ty said. "People never cease to amaze me."

"They exasperate me," Jillian said. "People think they know what the founding fathers thought better than the founding fathers themselves."

"They'd rather believe revisionist history than the truth," said Bethany. "Teachers are supposed to relate facts, not opinions. History books started to change in the early 1950s after John Dewey declared to his fellow humanists 'If we control the children's minds, we control society in the next generation.'

"Every series of textbooks since then has gradually removed any mention of God from the founding of the country. It's like the Nazi motto 'Say something often enough, and your words become accepted as truth.' Only in this case, the motto is 'Deny something often enough, and it becomes fallacy.'"

"Just like creation," Jillian said. "Declare evolution as fact, denounce creationism, and you establish your own validity, regardless of the science."

"Well," Bethany said, "my parents homeschooled me because they felt for a hundred and eighty days a year in public schools, students were being taught God is irrelevant to every area of life. They felt public schools were killing children morally and spiritually as well as academically, and my folks joked they would rather have me dead than alive."

They all laughed.

"I'm glad they didn't make that choice, babe," Ty said.

"Here-here," Darek said.

Jillian put her hand on Bethany's arm and squeezed.

"But it's really serious," Bethany said. "For instance, Mom was adamant about always seeking out the original manuscripts. Since we lived in Maryland, I researched and found out Maryland was officially declared a Christian state. The Declaration of Rights of the Maryland Constitution of 1776 said 'all persons professing the Christian religion, are equally entitled to protection in their religious liberty.' The legislature was even authorized to raise taxes to support the

Christian religion, and one article required all state officials to declare a belief in the Christian religion."

"Well," Ty interjected, "Congress authorized Bibles to be printed for use in the schools and mandated that new states teach religion and morality. One of the signers of the Declaration of Independence, Dr. Benjamin Rush, wrote all young people should be educated in the principles of Christianity."

"Rush must have butted heads with Thomas Jefferson," Darek said.

"Actually," Ty said, "as president, Jefferson became chairman of the District of Columbia school board and approved the use of the Bible and the Watts hymnal as textbooks."

"No way."

"Yeah, and Jefferson founded the University of Virginia, whose official motto is 'You shall know the truth and the truth shall set you free.' Jefferson had this Scripture inscribed on the walls inside the university rotunda, part of which he set aside for churches."

Jillian leaned forward. "I just read God is acknowledged in all fifty state constitutions."

"All fifty?" Darek asked.

"M-hmm."

"Hawaii, too, then. When was that—late nineteen-fifties? This means all of these acknowledgments aren't in the far-far distant past." Darek peevishly crossed his arms. "I feel a *Truth Be Told* segment coming on."

"The wheels are whirling." Jillian laughed. "I can almost hear them. Whir-r. Whir-r." She put her hands beside her ears and flickered her fingers.

"Hey, my wheels are well oiled. You can't hear them." Darek pinched her, playfully.

"Ouch!" She pointed at him. "Intolerance over here. Intolerance."

"William Penn," Ty declared, his mind obviously not hearing the playfulness. He was looking at the ceiling, recalling something.

"Excuse me, professor?" Bethany said, urging him to continue.

"William Penn," Ty repeated. "He once wrote people who will not be governed by God will be ruled by tyrants."

"You think we should go on the air and say we're being ruled by tyrants?" Darek asked.

"Prove otherwise," Ty said. "This country was founded as a republic. The government was formed to have checks and balances. Neither the Executive Branch nor Congress nor the courts could rule unabridged by the others. Right?"

They all nodded agreement.

"But what has happened over the past quarter century?"

"Actually, a lot longer, if you want to go back to *Roe versus Wade* and the Supreme Court ruling on a state issue," Bethany said.

"Okay. Since the Warren Court," Ty said.

"Add presidential fiat," Darek said.

"The only branch of government that can*not* make laws unfettered is Congress," Jillian added.

"Right," Ty said. "But the rule of law was not meant to be so lax. So, Darek and Jill, I give to you your next *Truth Be Told* investigation." He swept his hand upward with a flourish. "Ta-dah!"

Darek grimaced. "Thanks, pal."

"Actually," Jillian said, "we could go more global with the theme." She eyed Darek.

He read her mind.

"The One World Government." They spoke the words in unison.

"Whoa! That's scary. You haven't been married long enough to have morphed into each other." Ty hesitated. "Have you?"

They all laughed.

Boom! The windows beside them rattled. An explosion—nearby and powerful. Darek and the others jumped from their seats and looked out the window, down the street to the east in the direction of the blast.

Many of the wall-to-wall pedestrians were on their knees, which had buckled from the explosion.

Darek noticed that while the mass of people moved toward of the blast, one man in a dark sweatshirt, with its hood pulled over his head, was hurrying away, darting between people, coming in his direction.

The face. The face. I've seen that guy.

"Hey, do you see the dude coming our way?" Ty asked. He was talking about the same man. The guy had crossed to their side of the street, not running but obviously in haste. Then around the corner a block behind him a police officer raced, gun in hand, screaming something.

"I know that face," Ty said. "I saw him when I wrote a story about AFFRONT. He works with Icky Coffman in DC. Let's go!"

Darek and Ty hustled around the table, out the door, and began running toward the hooded man. The guy noticed them, read the intention in their faces, and turned left, fleeing down a narrow side street. The police officer was now more than a block behind, slowed by the gathering crowd.

Neither Darek nor Ty had to say a word. They were in pursuit and turned the corner.

This was going horribly wrong for Cabby O'Shaunessy. How had the cop spotted him anyhow? And now, who were these two boneheads? Somehow they knew he had something to do with the bomb. What the—?

He cursed at his bad luck.

He stumbled on the uneven brick sidewalk and bulled through a couple of kids walking with their parents.

Out of the way, brats!

Cabby turned into a restaurant façade below a sign with some Italian name, ripped open the door and bulled his way between people and tables. Half the customers were standing, or walking toward the front window. Others, eyes wide, glared at him, and mumbled to each other.

Clueless, but they'll find out.

There was not enough room between tables in this joint. He knocked one table ajar and plates crashed to the floor. Sidestepping a moron who stood up in front of him, he shoved an old lady off her feet and pushed her husband, forcing him onto the top of his table. Spaghetti flew, wine spilled, and bread rolled to the floor. People hollered at him.

He flipped them the finger.

Make that two middle fingers. Brain-warped creeps.

People were figuring out Darek and Ty were chasing the culprit and were parting like the Red Sea along the sidewalk.

Several pointed at a doorway to an Italian restaurant. Terra-something-or-other was the name. Darek reached the place first and smacked the door ajar with an open palm.

Inside, the restaurant was mayhem. Tables and chairs had tipped over. An old man was helping an elderly lady off the floor. In every corner, children were screaming and parents were hollering for them to keep the heck quiet or else.

A swinging door at the back of the seating area moved on its hinges. Darek pointed, and he and Ty raced through into the kitchen. Shouts greeted them there as well. Flames shot in the air where pots had spilled their contents. Hanging pans clanked into each other like heavy-duty wind chimes.

Someone swore at the back of the room. Darek looked and saw the hooded man hit the chef on the head with a skillet. The chef crumpled to the floor, and the other cooks in the room lurched away from the attack.

As the troublesome chef crumpled headfirst into the floor, Cabby spotted the two men in chase. Who are these guys, anyhow, he wondered. He felt like Sundance asking Butch who were those dudes in the posse chasing them, man.

He spun and thumped through the rear door of the restaurant into a dark alley.

Lose the jerks.

He wasn't made for foot races, with the help of adrenaline or not. Where was a good motorcycle when you needed one? Jason Bourne, James Bond, those guys always found one handy. He cursed again.

Ahead of Darek and Ty, the man pushed through a rear door. Ty was right on Darek's heels, and they were closing on this cretin.

Darek ran by the chef to the door, but Ty stopped and knelt down to see if the man was all right. He wasn't budging.

At the door Darek turned and hollered, "Ty, they can take care of him. Come on!"

Ty felt the man's carotid artery for a pulse. "He's alive. Someone call nine-one-one!"

Darek pushed through into the back alley. A dark figure was one block ahead, turning right onto North Street, heading west.

Smack! Cabby turned the corner and ran headfirst into a stroller. The stroller crashed onto its side, sending a pink-blanket-covered baby rolling over the edge of the sidewalk like a candlepin on its side. Screeching in horror, the mother hurried to her child.

Cabby's hand flew to his right knee which had met baby-carriage metal.

"Out of the way!" he hollered, cursing the woman.

A man who was apparently the baby's father bellowed an obscenity, and Cabby almost stopped to congratulate him on his choice of words. He hadn't heard that expression before.

Darek had seen the crash. When he rounded the corner, the father had apparently thought better of giving chase and decided to tend to his wife and child.

The woman was holding the child to her bosom, crying in great gasps.

Darek was thankful for his five-mile daily run and wondered how far behind Ty was. Just then, his friend called, "Right behind you, buddy!"

"He's right up ahead," Darek called. He turned the bend in the street and saw the figure trying to open a wooden gate in a yard. The man took just enough time figuring out the gate was locked for Darek to catch him. Diving shoulder-first, Darek drove the guy to the ground. He felt the air leave the man, then straddled him, one knee on each side of the man's waist. His left hand held the man's right wrist to the brick sidewalk, and he drove his right fist into the man's jaw.

"Just for good measure, pal," he said.

A particularly foul swear word nearly escaped Darek's lips, but he stopped himself. Ty came to a stop beside him, breathing heavily. The man beneath Darek groaned.

Ty looked down at the fellow. "I know you. Don't I?"

He was young. Twenty-five, maybe.

"No!" he spit out.

"Sure, I do. You work with AFFRONT. In DC. Your name's something to do with cars, or similar to a Boston sports writer."

The culprit locked his lips together and looked away toward the street.

Darek glanced up at the little home where the chase had ended. "Paul Revere's house," he said. "We're on North Square."

"Ha!" Ty said. "Ironic. Paul Revere's cry was 'The British are coming!' Today, at his house, the atheists are coming."

Ty scrutinized the young man. "What in the world makes you hate God so much, kid?"

A string of expletives gushed from his mouth.

"Vile cesspool, aren't you?" Darek said, and slapped him on the face. "Shut up, you pathetic worm. Jesus Christ died for you, and you do this stuff? I'm sorry, I can't love you like he does. So, you'd better keep a civil tongue, or I'll pummel you all the way to North Station."

A siren cut through the night air and a police cruiser barreled up the street from the west.

"Wonder where the heck Homeland Security is," Ty said.

A cell phone rang. Darek said, "Ty, my cell's in my left pocket. Can you answer for me?"

Ty pulled out the device.

"Darek's cell."

A moment later, he smiled. "It's Agent Cusack, for you. Says they're in pursuit of a bomber."

Darek and Ty cracked up.

Darek said, "Tell him we're aware."

CHAPTER SEVENTEEN

Concerned about mad bombers in the city, a government over-the-edge in Washington, and a One World Government in Brussels demanding America relinquish more sovereignty, Jake MacMillan forced himself to dissect the mechanisms of the world stock markets, money exchanges, and the dark side of corporate and government manipulation of global economies.

Was the turmoil of the world's stock markets caused by the Bilderbergers or China or someone else? Or was the event a massive correction out of everyone's hands?

Personally, he had years ago put most of his money in gold, silver, and real estate. He figured if he could touch his valuables and see them, whatever they were, they couldn't vaporize like fortunes seemed to do on Wall Street at the most unexpected times. He recalled nine-eleven and winced. What devastation to a country, both in terms of human lives and finances.

Then, two years ago, he'd sold most of his real estate and put the money into precious gems. The move came after Suffolk County in the Commonwealth of Massachusetts (the Peoples Republic of Massachusetts) grabbed twenty acres he and Dawn had owned, then sold the parcel to a mall developer.

The land was their personal property, Jake had argued. The Constitution gave the MacMillans the unfettered right to own property, their lawyer had argued. But the county declared its ownership of the land would be "for the greater good" of the community.

Bottom line—a mall would produce more taxes for the town and county than an undeveloped property. Game, set, match to the county and mall developer. The scenario was being played out all over the country since the turn of the 21st century when one court in one city overnight changed the law of the land. And, so, Jake and Dawn had taken the cue and retained only the parcels of land they owned in rural areas.

So, here he sat, meerschaum in hand, pondering evidence regarding the market crashes. He was far removed from his comfort zone. This was more like a war zone, and he'd actually fought in those.

Far greater financial minds than his were investigating, analyzing, and meticulously pouring over data to solve the mystery of this mega-downturn. The nation and the world were reeling. All except China. And perhaps also with the exception of the Bilderbergers, regardless of the reported suicidal actions of Lloyd Barclay.

Jake's angle was different than the others. He was researching the involvement, or lack thereof, of the Bilderberger Group, Trilateral Commission, and the Council on Foreign Affairs.

He'd long considered conspiracy theories inventions of dark subterfuge meant for movies and novels. Great reading, questionable reality. He dealt in facts. Just what he told his reporters "You can have your theories—show me the facts."

Dawn had loved digging into the conspiracy stuff and had cajoled him into reading some of the materials she'd compiled. Now, here he was, at Dawn's desk immersed in her files. Her interests were wide-ranging, and she'd kept meticulous files on subjects ranging from the Alaskan oil-drilling debate to the Middle East crisis to the slavery and murder of Christians by Muslims in Sudan. Alphabetical and either printed out or clipped, pasted and dated, Dawn had the files in perfect order.

Wish I were this organized, darlin'.

Jake was reading through Dawn's files on the Bilderbergers.

One paper caught his eye—interesting because the manuscript was a quote from a US president and also was spoken more than one hundred years before.

Writing his *The New Freedom* in 1913, prior to the passage of the Federal Reserve Act, President Woodrow Wilson revealed:

> Since I entered politics, I have chiefly had men's views confided to me privately. Some of the biggest men in the U.S., in the field of commerce and manufacturing, are afraid of somebody, are afraid of something. They know there is a power somewhere so organized, so subtle, so watchful, so interlocked, so complete, so pervasive, that they had better not speak above their breath when they speak in condemnation of it.

"Bob!" Jake called his bodyguard. Bob was in a small room off the front foyer that had been transformed into a central security office, with monitors for cameras scattered around the property outdoors.

A moment later, Bob came around the corner. "Yes, sir?"

"Jake," he corrected. "How about brewing some of the special Columbian coffee we just bought?"

"Love to, Jake."

"Then you can join me in here. Got some interesting information I'd like your opinion on."

"Right-o."

Jake dug back into Dawn's file. He had found members of the Bilderberger Group were challenged with the post-war takeover of the democratic process.

They were a conspiracy. They were given the mandate of controlling the world economy through indirect political means. While the constitutions of several Western European democratic monarchies banned members of their royal families from playing an active role in the political process, the Bilderberger meetings provided exactly this forum for them.

Key among the Bilderberger founders was Joseph H. Retinger, known as L'Eminence—His Grey Eminence. To Retinger, a country's economic ideology was insignificant; powerful multinational organizations could bring these differences into line by dictating and applying forceful economic and military policies. This would create a bond between nations.

Learn about the head, and you understand the body, Jake had always said. Dawn had taken his advice. She'd created a separate file on Retinger. A colorful, lifelong career had raised him to the top of the world power elites.

At his funeral in 1960, Sir Edward Bedington-Behrens said: "I remember Retinger in the United States picking up the telephone and immediately making an appointment with the president, and in Europe, he had complete entrée in every political circle as a kind of right acquired through the trust, devotion, and loyalty he inspired."

Retinger was who convinced the Mexican government to nationalize US oil interests.

How mighty one man can be. He chuckled thinking how the Alliance whined about his own supposed power.

Here was a group of few more than one hundred members—about eighty from Western Europe and the remainder from North America—and look how wide-ranging was its reach—into government and politics, finance and industry, education and communications.

Jake spotted a wrinkled page in the file. He pulled the paper out and read a quote from President Franklin Delano Roosevelt, written in a letter on November 21, 1933, to Colonel Edward Mandell House, President Woodrow Wilson's close advisor. "The real truth of the matter is, as you and I know, a financial element in the larger centers has owned the Government ever since the days of Andrew Jackson ..."

"Owned the government," Jake repeated.

"What was that, Jake?"

Bob had entered the room with a tray filled with a coffee pot, two mugs, cream, sugar, and Tollhouse cookies. When Jake had discovered Tollhouse cookies were Bob's favorite, he'd bought several bags of them. Now they were a constant with coffee between the two.

Jake was growing to enjoy this man's company and to trust him. A fellow congregant of Bill Asbury's church, Bob was known to Jake as only a big, strong, athletic man with a permanent smile and a strong handshake. Then Jake needed a bodyguard, and Bill mentioned Bob, a former CIA agent whose wife had forced his hand into leaving the agency after he was nearly fatally wounded.

Their two children, she reasoned, needed a father alive, not six feet underground. Her husband, she felt, should seek his adrenaline rush in some other way than putting his life on the line every day.

A bodyguard? Well, the job was a compromise.

Jake looked up at Bob. "I was just reading this quote from a letter FDR wrote to Woodrow Wilson: 'A financial element in the larger centers has owned the Government ever since the days of Andrew Jackson.'"

He motioned Bob to a chair. "What do you think?"

Bob set the tray on a coffee table. "I'm startled this thought goes that far back in history, but not surprised such an organization controls governments behind the scenes. Supports the old saying, 'Follow the money.'"

Jake poured steaming coffee into the two mugs. "Apparently the One World Government is the culmination of a group called 'the State of the World Forum,' which began annual meetings in 1995. I vaguely recall this, but I think the Forum kept pretty much under the radar even though members included Mikhail Gorbachev, George Schultz, Maurice Strong, and Ted Turner among more than five hundred leaders from fifty countries."

"Who are these five hundred people?" Bob asked, stirring cream and sugar into his mug and crossing his lanky legs.

"Heads of state, Nobel laureates, senior military officers, scientists, politicians and policy-makers, business executives, social activists, academicians, even spiritual leaders."

"Spiritual leaders?"

"Yep."

"Can't be very spiritual." Bob harrumphed.

"Nope."

Jake brought his black coffee to his lips, but at this moment just wanted to enjoy the aroma. He smiled grimly at Bob. "If only you and I could have been flies on the wall when the Fields and Ty interviewed His Excellency Howard Bliss, the head of the Church Universal." He shook his head. "Spiritual has a whole new meaning today."

"Yeah. Can one be secularly spiritual?"

They shared a rueful laugh.

"Can I use that in one of my columns?" Jake asked.

"Permission granted." Bob leaned forward. "What do they talk about, these world shakers?"

"That's very secretive. Apparently human and animal welfare, science, politics. Hold on." Jake pulled out a single sheet of paper. "This says the Forum topics range from 'the most controversially political to the most personally transformative.' We've got to remember this stuff is what they want us to read. We don't know for sure what they're discussing. The meetings are behind closed doors."

Just then, a sound came from the security room. "P-ting, p-ting, p-ting."

Bob jumped from his chair and ran to the little alcove, Jake on his heels. When Jake stuck his head into the room Bob had shut off the alarm and was sitting down, looking over a bank of monitors.

"An intruder," Bob said, "along the Amherst Street gate."

Jake stepped up beside Bob, who was calling the police, and peered at the monitor. Sure enough, a figure dressed in a long coat stood next to a big SUV like an Escalade, surveying the eight-foot-high wooden fence. A second person stepped out of the driver's side door holding a crowbar and hustled to the fence where he proceeded to start prying off a strip of fencing.

Bob reached for his holster and gave the address as Jake watched these two and wondered to himself about being a hunted man, hated enough people would want him dead.

Just then another alarm went off, with a different sound. "Dong, dong, dong."

Jake looked up at the monitor. The man had pried off one strip of wooden fence and had started on a second. A second piece removed would give a person enough space to squeeze through. Bob and Jake then noticed the man in the long coat was pulling out a rifle.

"An AR-15 sniper rifle." Bob's voice rose a level. He was revealing the information to the police and Jake at the same time. "Or maybe an AR-10. Better knockdown power. Probably has night vision."

Jake looked at Bob. "I admire your knowledge, Bob, but that person is about to enter our property with evil intent."

Bob hurried to a rifle case on the wall and grabbed an Uzi-SMG.

"I prefer shock and awe to sniper 'ping-pings.' Stay here," he said and headed for the door.

"Bob, no!" Jake called.

"Don't worry. Police are on their way. I'm on my way. And angels are watching over us, I promise. My wife said so." He smiled.

"No, I'm serious," Jake said and motioned for Bob to join him. "I've got an idea."

Jake sat down at the security console. He'd toyed with the equipment after installation and had a handle on its capabilities. "Watch this."

Bob returned to Jake's side, hefting his Uzi-SMG, and watched as Jake flicked a switch. On the Amherst Street monitor, they both saw the effects. The rifle bearer was squeezing through the fence when a blinding light hit him in the face. The light was mounted on a pole about twelve feet high and could be moved and switched on from the control panel.

Then Jake snapped on another switch and spoke into the microphone. "Mister sniper. Beware the hand of God!"

The man held his hand in front of his face. Temporarily blinded, he fell back on his feet, then tried to get back out of the fence. But the hole was such a tight fit, and he was in such a panic, he was finding escape difficult.

Jake then turned a knob and the light began to strobe. He again leaned toward the microphone. "Mister sniper. I say to you, repent before God!"

Now the second person tugged on the sniper's arm.

"I'm going out there, boss," Bob said and headed for the door. Jake didn't stop him. Everything should be safe now, he thought. The monitor was picking up flashing blue lights. Must be an approaching police cruiser.

The sniper and his driver were running to their vehicle, now they were jumping in, and now they were speeding off. Five seconds later, the cruiser sped by in hot pursuit.

Jake breathed deeply and leaned back. *I've got a target painted on my chest.*

Then he considered the many Christians from China to Sudan to the Philippines and Indonesia—numerous places— who were being crucified, decapitated, hanged, tortured, imprisoned, or enslaved for their beliefs. Suddenly, he didn't feel so beleaguered.

He checked the monitor. Bob came into view, reached the fence, and peered out. Then he slung the strap of his Uzi over his shoulder and bent to pick up the fence boards. Turning toward the camera, he put a hand over his eyes and with his other hand made a motion across his throat. Jake flicked off the switch to the strobe light but kept the area bathed in the spotlight. Bob waved a thank-you, then turned back to the fence.

A moment later, a telephone rang next to Jake. He picked up. Bob.

"I'll put a hammer to these boards," Bob said. "Looks like you might consider installing a chain-link inside the outer fence, after all. Let's hope they caught those guys, sir."

"Again, I'm 'Jake.' And let's *pray* they catch the culprits."

7:55 p.m. was the time on the set of *Truth Be Told*. Ty joined Darek and Jillian.

They had all covered people, places, and events. They had watched from the sidelines during peace negotiations and wars; during rallies for free drugs, free medicine, free love, and free abortions; during congressional hearings concerning the homeless, the wealthy, the prim and proper, and the poor and destitute; in the aftermath of house fires and bus bombings. In their three young lives, they had seen enough for ten lives.

Darek and Jillian had actually *been* the news. But they had never actually been news*makers*. Not until two hours ago when Darek and Ty had captured the bomber.

Now, they had beaten the world to this story and were wasting no time telling the tale. The timing of *Truth Be Told* was perfect.

"Five, four, three ..." the director counted down to airtime. Catchy-but-serious theme music played. Darek, Jillian and Ty all turned in their stools behind the anchor desk to look at anchorman Dan Gooden to their left. "Two, one ..."

"Good evening," Gooden said to the center camera. "Is the world spinning out of control? What happens to a society where some support bombing public places, endangering lives and destroying property, simply because those places, in some fashion, contain the word of God?"

Gooden gave the question a moment to sink in, then continued: "The state of America today is such that just two hours ago our own reporters, Darek Fields and Ty Cole, captured a bomber moments after he'd set off an explosive device here in Boston. Darek and Ty are here to tell us the story."

He turned toward them. "Well, heroes—"

Darek laughed. "Thank you, Dan, but I wouldn't call us heroes. We just happened to be in the right place at the right time."

"Divine guidance?" Gooden asked with a smile.

"Both divine guidance and divine lasagna," Darek said with a chuckle. "We were in an Italian restaurant." He turned to Ty. "You're our theologian-in-chief, Ty. Was this divine guidance?"

"Without doubt," Ty said.

"Gentlemen," Jillian cut in seriously, "bombings of public places—at least in other countries—have become all too commonplace since September 11th, 2001. More and more so since Israel and the Palestinian Authority signed their peace agreement."

Darek stepped in: "Yet Muslim believers, following the lead of the Koran to kill Jews and, quote-unquote, infidels around the globe, are not the only ones lethally armed against the people of the Bible."

"Or *countries* of the Bible," Ty interjected. "Today's attack was not against any one individual or individuals, but against America."

"An old menace," Jillian said, "has become a menace with teeth—deadly sharp. Two hours ago, in the heart of Old Boston, a man who works for the atheist group AFFRONT allegedly bombed the statue in the park across the street from the Old North Church.

"No one was killed, but at least fifteen were injured, three of them seriously. As Ty said, the man—whether this alleged perpetrator, Peter 'Cabby' O'Shaunessy, or someone else—was not targeting the people, but the country. He wanted to blast apart a monument containing the word of God. Whether this was sanctioned by AFFRONT, we don't know. If so, such an attack steps up the group's assault on God to another level.

"The Chinese government for a century has imprisoned Christians, and a dozen years ago began burning down non-government-certified churches. Sudanese have long tortured and killed Christians—even crucified them. In Southeast Asia, the same report. But, here in America—once Judeo-Christian America—the closest we've seen to terror attacks have been a few cases of arson and shooting at synagogues, desecration of Jewish cemeteries, and the numbers 6, 6, 6 painted on churches."

Ty asked, "What drives these atheists? Why don't they simply not believe? Why go to the extreme of *hating* God? And do they plan to attack again?"

"Those are questions we'll explore tonight," Darek said. "But I want to editorialize for a moment here. We should not ask these questions with the motive of begging these atheist terrorists not to hate Jews and Christians. We don't want to reward them for their actions. In the aftermath of nine-eleven, many people questioned, 'Why do the Muslims hate America? What can we do to make them like us? How can we change?'

"In some quarters, this self-loathing was palpable. One president actually went on an apology tour of the Middle East. But those were the wrong questions. We've witnessed the viciousness of these Islamists cannot be appeased. When you do yield and offer them a hand of friendship, their culture sees the move as weakness, as capitulation, and an indication their tactics have succeeded.

"In Osama ben Laden's declaration of war on America, he said President Clinton's threats in 1998, followed by inaction, showed America's weakness. They saw President Obama's 'red line' as proof America was a paper tiger."

Observing out his study window, Jake watched Bob finish his work on the fence. He'd had to get a ladder out of the garage in order to reach the top of the fence with a hammer.

Put in a chain-link fence? What insanity.

Jake's phone rang. No picture. The voice on the other end sounded harried, excitable. As he listened, Jake's jaw dropped.

Atlantic Avenue was well-lit. Plus, Boston Aquarium was only a block or so to the south, and popular restaurants dotted the street on its harbor side.

Two people, one behind the other, scurried southward along the street's innermost sidewalk, satchels on their backs, trying to stay in whatever shadows they could find. They didn't say a word.

They were dressed in black, from the woolen caps on their heads to their sneakers. Past North Street they hustled. Two minutes later, past Fleet Street. Suddenly the man in front, Campy, motioned the other to stop.

Truth Publishing and Broadcasting rose up before them, a building dressed in brick and glass. A noble structure? Pshaw! Campy considered the place a pit, exemplifying everything uncompromising and evil, the epitome of people who thought themselves better than him.

Religion. A load of superstitious drivel that shouldn't be taught without a health warning.

The place was run by delusional, self-important mudslingers who'd force him, and those like him, to pray in school, to sing "God Bless America," to put up with "In God We Trust" on their money, to even consider human life divine, as if there were a divinity in the first place. Where was this God when his mom died of cancer? When his big brother died in the war? Yeah, "In God We Trust" was the one reason he stopped using cash fourteen years before.

Truth? What is truth?

Religion and the idea of truth had held back human progress for centuries. People would be living in outer space by now if not for religion. Good thing the Age of Enlightenment freed men so they could make some progress, or they'd still be stuck in the Dark Ages.

No. This building rising up seven floors above them was filled with evil people, malicious ideas, and bad karma. Truth deserved to be taken down and he was the man to do so.

Campy's plan was simple. He'd move around to the far rear corner of the building and set his charges. Norine would set hers on this side of the building as far forward as she could safely stay out of the light. Easy-peasy, baby.

Campy gave Norine the go-ahead signal, turned and ran down along the edge of the building's parking lot.

"So, in this broadcast," Jillian said to the camera stage-left, "we deal with a fact and a question. The fact—my colleagues caught a bomber tonight. The question—shall we expect more bombs from atheists? What are the government's security forces doing to root out the terrorists among us?"

"And as a sidebar to the issue," Ty said, "other countries have called themselves Christian, but America is the only country in the world that has called itself Judeo-Christian. We'll explore what that means."

The camera zoomed in on Dan Gooden. "All this when we come back after these messages," he said.

The production crew began a series of commercials.

Campy shrugged off the satchel, set the pack on the ground, then knelt down to open the bag. His palms were moist, which made pulling on the plastic gloves difficult. He liked to think he had nerves of steel, but his hands were shaking.

Hisey Brinks had taught him and several colleagues how to make and detonate bombs, but Campy had never done so before in a live situation. His training—a couple of practice sessions in the apartment of the AFFRONT Boston chapter president.

The enormity of what he was about to do suddenly engulfed him.

You may not just blow up a building; you might kill somebody. Mays and mights, mays and mights. If someone gets hurt, it's their own fault, working for this company.

But no one deserves to die simply because they believe in God. Well, you might be right if they'd just keep their beliefs to themselves and not cram them down my throat.

When was religion crammed down your throat? My mother did, every day until she died. Drove me nuts. Then my dad became a drunk and his liver croaked on him.

A car horn sounded out on the street, jerking Campy out of his internal debate. He didn't have time for this.

Set the charge, get to a safe spot and blow her up!

Ted Anderson, promoted to head of security for the night shift, bit down on a pickle. Yecht! What kind of a diet was this, anyhow? A small snack eight times a day?

"Right down your alley," his wife, Helen, had teased him. "You never have to wait long before your next meal."

Meal? A pickle and eight almonds?

The phone rang and Ted picked up on the first ring. "Security. Ted And—

"Ted! Its Jake MacMillan."

"Mr. MacMillan?" Ted sat up straight, intent. "Yes, sir. How are you, sir?"

"Ted, you need to send your men out to secure the perimeter of the building. Right now!"

"Sir?"

Jake MacMillan seldom called the security office, and Jake MacMillan never sounded afraid. Here, on his shift Ted thought, Jake MacMillan had called and sounded frightened. Hairs rose down Ted's spine.

"I just got a call saying someone is going to bomb our building. Call in the police as well as our off-duty security. PA the entire building to get them out. I'm coming in."

The line went dead. Ted stared blankly at the phone for a moment, then the foreboding of the message kicked him into action.

The C-4 explosive weighed only about five pounds, but Hisey said this was plenty when combined with Norine's bomb.

Suddenly, Campy heard noises around the other side of the building, where Norine was preparing her charge. Then a dark figure appeared around the front of his side of the building, and a high-powered flashlight hit his eyes. He swore, then stood to run. He got two steps before remembering the cell phone to detonate the bomb. He spun around, came back and picked up his satchel. The person with the flashlight was running toward him now.

"You! Stop!" It was man's voice but high-pitched, like a girl's. Campy stopped for a moment. Perhaps he could take down this girly-guy. Stomp on his face, then still blow up this abomination.

"Freeze!" came a command and this time, Campy noticed the guard had a gun in one hand.

Campy gambled the guy wouldn't shoot and took off at a sprint. No gunfire, but he heard feet pounding the pavement in pursuit. Then someone else called out, "I've spotted him! This way."

No! There're others? Norine, you better be runnin'.

Campy sprinted through a dark, empty back lot, then down Lewis Street, cutting over to Fulton, among the narrow inner streets of the North End.

On the other side of the building, Ted Anderson raced behind one of his security men, chasing what appeared to be a girl. Then he spotted a package on the ground halfway along the structure and hurried there. He'd finished a course on disengaging bombs just yesterday. Thank God. So, the class was fresh in his mind.

Tell my nerves.

Then he deduced the bomber being pursued might be able to set this thing off any moment.

Oh, my!

The faces of his wife and three teenaged children flashed before him.

He shone his flashlight on the package. One of his guards ran up and stopped beside him.

"Shine your light down here," Ted said. "We've got to disarm this thing—fast."

As Campy emerged onto Richmond Street, he thought he heard a muffled gunshot.

Dang. These guys are serious!

He flinched and turned to search for a place where he could quickly dig into his satchel and get the cell phone to detonate the C-4. He reasoned Norine had been caught, or had escaped, but was unable to detonate her explosive.

But he could still extract some damage of his own. He darted down the sidewalk and looked for an open entryway to one of the six- and seven-story apartment buildings. Finding one, he slid in and pressed his back against the wall.

His breathing was heavy. He swore he could hear his heart thumping. He felt dizzy.

Lack of oxygen to the brain.

He fumbled with the satchel, reached in and pulled out the cell phone. With a satisfied smile, he pressed the button … Silence.

Silence!

He swore out loud.

His peripheral vision caught a motion to his left. A gun. A big gun. A cop! An expletive escaped his lips.

Campy lowered his head. Dark visions of prison jumbled his mind. Weird, black-robed figures swirled before his mind's eye, flashing gap-toothed smiles in his direction. He was sure he felt spiders run down his spine. Then the body connected to the arm holding the big gun moved around the corner of the entryway.

Campy cringed and closed his eyes.

"Pow!" the person said loudly.

Campy's heart leaped. Then a familiar voice said, "Loose lips sink ships. And I thought you were my 'A' student, Camp-man."

Campy opened his eyes and focused on the dark figure before him. Hisey Brinks!

Campy swore. "I thought you were the guard," he breathed.

"Guard? Don't worry about him."

Brinks put the gun in his pocket and grabbed Campy's elbow. "Come with me. Guess I've got to train you better, eh? But let's get out of here first."

"Norine!" Campy said. "What about Norine?"

"I think she got away. Hurry up!" Brinks pulled Campy along and when they turned the corner they melted into the crowd of unsuspecting people on bustling Hanover Street.

A half hour later, police cruisers with their lights flashing lined the street in front of Truth Publishing and Broadcasting.

Experts from a crime unit were dusting two bombs for prints and had cordoned off those areas. They would make molds of shoe prints and look for the most minute clue to identify the perpetrators.

At the front of the building, four policemen stood watch. Pedestrians stopped to peer at the goings-on, pushing the envelope of how close they could get to the scene.

Inside the building's first-floor entryway, two officers spoke to Jake. Carlos Martinez and Lauren Ireland, the director of *Truth Be Told*, were at his side. And Darek, Jillian, Ty, and Dan Gooden stood to the side and listened in on the conversation along with Bob Ward. Jake could feel the tension sizzling around him.

"The girl on the south side of the building maced your guard and got away, but left behind her backpack," said the sergeant in charge. "We've got officers combing the area in the direction your guard was chasing the other bomber. Looks like between the two bombs, they could have brought down a good part of this building."

Ted Anderson burst through the front door. Seeing the look on Ted's face, an alarm went off in Jake. Something was wrong.

"Jake," Ted nearly shouted. "Barry Goetz—"

The name was familiar to Jake. He'd made knowing every new hire standard operating procedure. Each one was brought to his office to meet him and be personally welcomed to the company. Barry Goetz was hired about a week before. He was a Jewish believer. Young. Engaged to be married.

Jake hesitated. "Y-Yes?"

"Barry's the one who gave chase to the bomber on the south side of the building."

"Yes. And?"

"Well, we just found him." Ted's mouth quaked and he could barely muster a whisper.

"Spit it out, man," Jake said.

"Dead, Jake. Took a bullet to the chest."

Silence struck like an anvil—heavy with dread. Jake leaned his weight on a counter at the reception desk and drew a breath.

My God. My God. This is too much.

The sergeant was quickly on his radio, asking for homicide detectives.

Jake felt all the air had been sucked out of him. He looked up at Ted.

"Get me Barry's fiancée's and parents' telephone numbers, will you? I'll call them personally."

At midnight Jake and Bob arrived back at the MacMillan house. The heavy steel gate at the end of the driveway opened to allow them entrance, along with a police cruiser close behind them.

"Is the battle worthwhile, Bob?" Jake asked as Bob drove up the driveway.

"What exactly do you mean?" Bob asked.

"Is getting the news into people's hands worth the struggle? If we have to sacrifice people's lives?"

Bob stopped the car, turned off the key, and turned to Jake.

"Shouldn't the question be, Would God want you to stop informing the people of the truth? Did he tell Paul, 'Stop right now, son. My people are dying. Enough's enough.'?"

Jake considered Bob's response for a few moments, then reached over and patted him on the shoulder. "You've got to be the wisest bodyguard around, my friend."

Bob smiled somberly. "Thank you."

Jake and Bob stepped out of the car and waved the police officers into the house.

Jake led them to his study, then asked, "So do you know who broke through our fencing?"

One of the officers, a corporal—a stout man in his fifties—explained they had caught up to the suspect's SUV at a mall parking lot.

"But we lost them," he said. "They disappeared in the mob inside the mall. The SUV'd been stolen. The crime unit's checking over the vehicle for fingerprints and other evidence."

Jake and Bob related all they'd seen at the house earlier.

"Any idea who they are?"

Jake chuckled ruefully

"The list isn't a short one," he said. "Heck, the list of people who hate me is endless, from president to pauper, Supreme Court Associate Chief Justice to our state representative. If I listed them all, you'd be here all night and then some."

The officers shrugged.

Bob spoke up. "You could compare notes with the officers who responded to the murder and attempted bombing at The Truth building tonight."

"Could this be tied to the man from AFFONT who was captured earlier in Boston by Homeland Security?" the corporal asked.

"I wouldn't be surprised," Bob said.

"Could the Alliance be involved?"

Jake answered, "I don't know, but I wouldn't be surprised. I wouldn't be shocked if the Alliance were behind my wife's death and the bomb attempt at The Truth building. I'm beyond surprise at this time.

"But for all I know, the source could be advocates for gay rights, abortion rights, man-boy rights, animal rights—whatever rights," Jake added. "Man, you'd think I was against all 'rights.' What's a right, anyhow? And what's the difference between a right and a privilege?"

Again, the police officers shrugged.

The corporal said, "We'll let you know what we find out, Mr. MacMillan. Sorry we didn't catch those guys. Maybe we will."

He turned to leave. "We'll show ourselves out."

"Thanks, officers," Jake said.

Bob followed them to the door and gave the corporal his business card. "Call *me* when you get any information, will you?" he said.

"Sure."

Jake looked at Bob. "Thanks for your help. For your protection."

"Honored to do so."

"Why don't you go home? No one will try anything else tonight. I'll sleep here, then go back to the office early in the morning."

Bob checked over the security system to make sure everything was in proper order, opened the gate for the police cruiser, then said his good nights. On his way out the door, he turned to Jake. "I was impressed with your control-room skills, especially the strobe lights. Ha! What a great idea having them installed."

"Came from my *Dance Fever* days." Jake laughed. Then the pain of what had transpired in the last several hours struck him, and a sudden weight pressed upon him, squashing a smile.

CHAPTER EIGHTEEN

The next day, Truth security forces were increased, and construction began on a new perimeter system around the Atlantic Avenue headquarters. Lights behind bullet-proof glass would shine brightly along all sides of the building now. Security cameras would keep vigil.

"More and more like a fortress," Darek said to Jillian as they entered the front door.

"Hmm. I know God will protect us here, anyhow," she said, "but still I'm happy we're leaving on this assignment."

"Yeah. Famine and locusts. A plum assignment," Darek said wryly.

They nodded to Marcey, whose new desk was centered in the foyer. To her right, two security men flanked a metal detector. Darek and Jillian exchanged glances.

"Jake must be beside himself," Jillian said. "He's had an open-door policy since forever. And now, having to do all this—"

They walked through the metal screener. No bells or whistles, but they snapped to attention. Ten feet in front of them stood a three-foot-tall photograph of Barry Goetz, framed and on a tripod.

A small sign above the photograph read "In Memory of Barry Goetz of the Truth Publishing and Broadcasting Family."

Below the photograph, in script, was written, "Precious in the sight of the Lord is the death of His saints—Psalm 116:15."

"He was a Christian. That helps mellow the sting," Jillian said.

"We'll miss the funeral." Darek spoke offhandedly, but knew if they were in town they'd attend along with everyone else at Truth. Whether you were a family member for a day or a decade, time didn't matter.

And Jake wouldn't lose touch with Barry Goetz's survivors, either.

"I heard he was getting married in a couple of months," Jillian said. She shook her head. "What a waste."

Darek nodded and grabbed his wife's hand to pull her toward the elevator. They rode to the third floor and stepped out into the newsroom.

From his office across the vast room, Jake spotted them and waved them in. The newsroom was half full with staffers and empty of cheer. Darek and Jillian exchanged nods and waves with several of them.

Bob Ward, arms folded, stood outside Jake's office and nodded a "hello" to them. Sitting inside were Executive Editor Carlos Martinez and U.S. News editor Todd Livingstone.

"Darek, Jillian," Jake said, "we're pulling you off the famine and locust story and sending John and Hank."

Darek and Jillian flashed questioning looks.

"We need you here," Jake said. "Devoted to this bombing story. Who knows how many places and where this will happen again?"

"Besides," Carlos said, "the police and Homeland Security may want to question you more about the bomb across from the Old North Church and your chasing down the bomber."

Jake rolled the meerschaum in his right hand and turned to look out the window. "I've bought two more high-security jets." He spoke to no one and everyone. "As much as possible, I want our staff to use them when traveling."

He turned and faced Carlos Martinez. "Make the announcement, will you? If possible, our people on the move should be in our own planes."

"Sure, boss." Carlos looked intensely at Jake. "What's up?"

For the first time, Jake shared about the incident at his home. Listening quietly, Darek wondered what would happen to Truth if someone assassinated Jake MacMillan. *Kill the head and the body will die. Evil. But good strategy.*

"I'll be spending more nights in the apartment up on the top floor," Jake said, pointing upward. "If you're trying to reach me, and I'm not in the office, I might just be upstairs."

In the past, everyone knew Jake only used the apartment in emergency situations or at times like Election Night when he wanted to stay near the action but needed to catch a few winks. Since Dawn's death, he had spent more time there, but not a significant amount.

He continued, "I also wanted to talk to you about personal protection—at least for the higher-profile folks who're recognizable on the streets. You, for instance." He pointed at Darek and Jillian. "And Dan Gooden and others on our newscasts. Columnists whose faces appear in their articles."

A moment of silence set in as everyone considered the import of Jake's statement.

Finally, Darek said, "The head."

"What's that?" Jake asked, not catching the words.

"The head," Darek repeated. "I don't think the rest us are in danger. Not now, anyhow. I believe they're going for the head of what they see as the viper—you. They believe if they take down the head, the body will die."

The others nodded agreement.

"I appreciate your thoughtfulness, Jake. But you've got enough on your mind without being concerned with us people in the streets."

"Besides," Jillian said, "it would be rather cumbersome for us—and maybe make doing our jobs impossible—with bodyguards at all our sides."

Jake again turned the bowl of the pipe around in his palm, and rubbing his chin with his other hand.

"I'm new at this faith thing," Darek said, "but don't we have to exhibit a degree of belief in this circumstance? What about the psalm about God's angels protecting you?"

"Psalm ninety-one," Jake said. "'And He will give His angels charge over you, to watch you in all of your ways, to keep you in the palm of their hand so you will not strike your foot against a stone.'"

Darek laughed. "Yeah, that one."

Jake smiled and turned to Carlos. "Your thoughts?"

"Darek's right, Jake. You're the one in danger. We have to keep you protected, more so than broadcasters and reporters. Maybe you want to add security at the house. Continue to keep Bob at your side but have someone else at home while you're gone to guard against intruders."

Todd spoke up. "I agree. But I do think our reporters, and others traveling, should use our jets if they're available rather than flying commercial. That is, now that we've got all the safety measures, and the planes are essentially anonymous."

Icky Coffman wandered along the National Mall. The Reflection Pool lay ahead. Beyond the pool, the US Capitol Building rose up Capitol Hill.

Staying in the shade of the trees lining the mall, he passed the National Museums of American History and Natural History across Madison Drive to his left. He was deep in thought. Anxiety, really.

Cabby O'Shaunessy was caught. *Moron! Idiot!* Icky had told him to get someone else to bomb the statue. Icky needed to be distanced from any perpetrator of crime in case they were captured. And now what happened? Cabby was behind bars. *Stupid, stupid, stupid!*

Icky wondered if his aide would crack under questioning. Despite his athletic build and gym workouts, he was such a wimp. The sight of a flannel shirt would probably scare the daylights out of him. He'd probably fess up to every cold-case crime in Boston, including the condoms he stole from a drug store when he was fifteen.

Icky debated if he dared return to his office just a couple of blocks distant. But Homeland Security thugs were probably waiting for him. And what about his apartment? They'd be there, too.

Get to the bank, he told himself. *Withdraw all your money and hide out in some mountain cabin in West Virginia.*

Icky uttered an epithet against cops and cowboys—cops like the ones investigating the Boston bombing and cowboys like Darek Cutey-boy Fields who thought they could posse up and chase outlaws.

He fired another epithet at himself. He surely deserved the reprimand. He should have hired Hisey to do the bombings himself, not train a group of inexperienced pagans (proud-to-be-pagans, actually, he told himself—hey, a catchier name than AFFRONT. Let's change our name—no, too late, I'm on the run).

Anyhow, Hisey could blow up half the Western Hemisphere blindfolded.

Icky extracted a burner phone from his trousers. *Gotta avoid being traced.* He took a slip of paper from a shirt pocket, then punched its numbers.

Two bleeps and Hisey Brinks' face appeared. "What!"

What? Who speaks to people like that?

"Hisey, where you at and what's happening?"

"Whattaya mean?"

"I saw *Truth Be Told* last night about Cabby being caught. And I heard the news this morning about the botched bombing at The Truth building." He swore. "What's going on?"

"Well, the Cab Man better keep his trap shut. Meanwhile, I've got Campy and Norine with me."

"Where?"

"Icks, my man, do you think I'm going to tell you on this phone? You think this line's secure? I don't trust nothin' no more."

"Okay. Okay." Icky scratched the back of his head. *Think, man, think.* "Listen, remember your Plan Cyclops?"

"Yeah."

"I want to buy in."

"How soon?"

"Today. Right now. As quickly as you can."

"Target numbers?"

Icky pulled another tiny slip of paper from his wallet, then read off his wish list. "Letters *R, S, W, L, J, T, D* and *A*—all of 'em. But those first four right away."

"Hold on, hold on," Brinks said. "Let me write these down."

A moment later, he read back the letters, and Icky ran them through his mind. He loved these targets. *R* stood for the Rotunda of the Capitol. At the heart of the American government, called the Sanctum Sanctorum or Holy of Holies, a reference to the most sacred part of the Jewish temple in the Old Testament. Depicted in the enormous frescoes along the Rotunda's walls were, among other things, Pilgrims in prayer, the baptism of Pocahontas, and George Washington praying at Valley Forge.

S stood for the statue of Moses holding the Ten Commandments which stood outside the Supreme Court building just a block behind the Capitol.

W meant the Washington Monument. The tall, slender sentinel standing above the city had the Latin phrase "Laus Deo" ("Praise be to God") inscribed on the capstone at its highest point. Some of its memorial stones along the stairway, given by every state and numerous foreign countries to honor George Washington, boasted Scripture, such as "Holiness to the Lord" and "The memory of the just is blessed."

On the south wall of the Lincoln Monument, *L* on Icky's list, the Gettysburg Address was engraved, including the president's declaration that "this nation under God shall have a new birth of freedom …"

And so the list went. The Jefferson Monument, the Ten Commandments Monument, the Department of State and National Archives—all paid homage to God in some way or other.

Of course, Brinks didn't give one whit if these edifices stood or fell. He'd told Icky he didn't care for God one way or the other—if weaklings needed some fairy tale to hold onto to get them through the night, so what? But Brinks's own operatives were capable of bringing these structures down, and the money these assaults would put into his coffers could fund *Back Off!* for quite some time.

In his hiding place Hisey Brinks was salivating. Icky was a weasel, but a weasel with deep pockets. Amazing some people hated the idea of God so much they'd give boat loads of money to these twitty atheists.

What did it matter? This assignment meant money for the real war, Brinks's war, the crusade to protect Mother Earth against worldwide corporate greed. Brinks agreed with Greenpeace co-founder Paul Watson, who'd left the group after forty years of sinking fishing boats, destroying whale-processing facilities and ramming whaling ships. When Watson departed, he declared Greenpeace "Avon ladies of the environmental movement" and established the Sea Shepherd Conservation Society.

A maverick all his young life, Brinks loved the idea of a vigilante band of high-seas pirates, flying the flag of the skull and crossbones on their ships. Brinks's own logo incorporated a grisly pen-and-ink sketch of a hooded executioner, from the times when beheadings were popular in England and France, standing over a smoking smokestack surrounded by forest. His artist's first drawing included a guillotine, but Brinks had read Dr. Joseph Guillotine invented the guillotine as a *humane* way to execute criminals.

And his thoughts of people who wasted the environment were opposite far distant from humane. How dare they think themselves and their wallets more important than Mother Earth? Money is the root of all …

The thought of the money brought Brinks back to the moment. Speaking into the phone, he eyed Icky's image. "Okay, pal. You know my account. Wire the payment, half now and half later, and I'll level every one of your monuments into dust."

"Pronto?" Icky's face was a mixture of pleading and demand.

Pathetic.

"Yeah … pronto."

Brinks turned in his seat. He was driving Campy and Norine to an Alliance board meeting at a hotel in Milton, on the south side of Boston. Norine sat beside him. He checked her over, a smile curling his lips.

"Whattaya say, No-No. Since you've escaped the grip of the beast and your adrenaline's hit the lid, you wanna see some real action? Wanna freak out the cholesterol-and-cellulite crowd in DC?"

<hr/>

Tall, leggy, and beautiful, Norine looked askance at the bold, handsome guy beside her. Though he was famous in the underground, she knew very little of him personally, except what she'd learned when he taught the bomb-making group.

He wasted few words, felt no need to debate, was devoted to his cause, and coupled his beliefs with action. She liked the whole package. His broad-shouldered six-foot frame and rugged, square-jawed face weren't bad to look at, either.

He was about thirty years old, so he had a few years on her. But she could envision a Bonnie-and-Clyde-type relationship. Sure.

She gave him a sultry look. "Sounds exciting."

"You'd only be there as an observer—at first."

She overemphasized a pout.

"Kid, you've had one try and almost ended up in prison. Let me show you how my guys work. Those wasters at *Mother First!* gotta grow out of their knickers and watch how the big boys play. Phuf! Nails in trees. Wrecking sprinklers on golf courses. Spraying Roundup in little green spaces here and there." Brinks spit out the words in disgust. "Puny minds. Wasted efforts."

He pulled the car into the hotel parking lot and braked to a stop. "You in?" he asked, eyes keen on her.

"I'm in."

"What about me, your best student?" Campy asked from the back seat.

"Yeah, you, too. Best you get out of town anyhow. We'll put you on a plane to DC after the Alliance meeting. No-No and I will take a train after we make her a blonde and cut her hair short."

"Cut and color my hair?" Norine complained.

"Hey, No-No," Brinks said, looking her up and down, "don't you worry. Your hair's not what flutters the heart."

Oh-h, she liked his tone—a lot. When he looked away she undid the top button of her blouse.

Let the games begin.

Icky hung up the phone and glanced around anxiously. Tingles flickered down his spine. Had someone overheard and deciphered his conversation? Was he being watched? A couple walked nonchalantly across the mall. Several businesspeople, briefcases in hand, hurried up the sidewalk.

A group of schoolchildren followed three adults into the Natural History Museum. Nearby, several older people sat around the Sculpture Garden. Everything seemed normal.

He looked up the incline to the Capitol Building and sneered.

His mood hung a one-eighty. "Wake-up call, America," he sang under his breath and issued a guttural, nasty laugh.

Turning aside to hurry to his bank on 7th Street, Icky's thoughts moved on to how and where he could hide out for a while. And, of course, wiring the four million bucks to Brinks's Swiss bank account—two million now and two million later.

That night, Jake decided to go home. The new security guards had reported all was well. One patrolled the house outside. Another sat at the control panels, with monitors showing camera views around the entire property. They'd reported no attempted breaches, no action at all.

When they arrived, Bob Ward remained at Jake's side and sent the security detail to their own homes.

"I'm going to do a thorough check of the house," Bob said, and stepped off toward the stairway.

"Thanks, but then go home to your wife, okay?"

"After a bit," Bob said.

Jake walked into the study. Pulling off his jacket and undoing his necktie, he went to the phone on his desk and punched replay button on the answering machine. Pastor Bill, his daughter Lisa, several other friends and colleagues, his chief nemesis among the Associate Chief Justices. *Really? The old bugger, kissing up to me.* They were all calling, concerned about yet another attempt to harm him and Truth.

He made brief calls to Lisa, Bill, and a couple others and decided to leave the rest for tomorrow. The hour was too late to bother people.

Taking a seat behind Dawn's desk, he replaced the Bilderberger file he'd left out the night before, then scanned the tabs on the other file folders. "Profiting from War" jumped out at him.

"Hmm."

The next hour, Jake poured over newspaper articles, transcripts of Congressional hearings, and Dawn's hand-written notes. The Bush-Cheney Administration had hired Bechtel and Halliburton for contracts worth more than six billion dollars to help rebuild Iraq's infrastructure and oil fields back in Bush 43's tenure. President Clinton's secretary of defense, William S. Cohen, had worked with his consulting firm, The Cohen Group, to maneuver an eighty-million-dollar contract for a client, Nour USA, to provide security services for Iraq's oil pipelines and related infrastructure.

Clinton's bombing of then-Yugoslavia had opened up doors for tens of billions of dollars of revenue for some of the world's largest infrastructure and construction companies.

Oh, this is interesting. Some of these companies are owned by Bilderberger members.

Was the old saw true—the same people finance both sides of wars?

Evidence pointed to politicians of all persuasions looking the other way when mammoth contracts were handed out. After all, candidates could always use more green for their reelection campaigns. And at some point, they'd be trading in their Congressional license plates for lobbyist credentials to sway former colleagues into releasing lucrative contracts to their clients despite legislative attempts to prevent such profiteering.

Again, proof of another age-old maxim, "Follow the money."

But who caused this worldwide financial chaos? Surely not these war profiteers. Perhaps the Bilderbergers. After all, some made billions by toppling governments. Or what about China?

Jake returned the "Profiting from War" folder to its place and hauled out Dawn's folder on China. *Oh, boy, this night is going to be even longer.* He hefted the materials.

Bob entered the room, carrying a tray filled with a coffee pot, two mugs, cream, sugar, and a plate of cookies.

"Thought you might like a little snack with your coffee."

Jake stood and walked to a chair as Bob set the tray on the coffee table.

Jake reached to pour two mugs of black coffee.

"Gotta get to the bottom of this economic collapse," he said.

"Not enough on your plate?" Bob said with a chuckle. "Bombings and attempted bombings, attacks on your life, all the heavy news around the world from famines to crucifixions, and you have to figure out the economy?"

Jake nodded in agreement with the incongruity.

"Well, I've got reporters covering those things around the world. But I feel compelled to tackle one thing at a time here at home. Must be the old newspaperman in me. And if the world economies collapse, a quantum shift in power is coming.

"I started looking into theories of economic subterfuge the other night, and I feel I should see the thing through. Dan Cowan and Andrea Page will get the ultimate answer, probably, but I should be educated enough to join the discussion, debate their findings, be the devil's advocate if necessary. Ultimately, what goes into Truth's newspapers, broadcasts, podcasts, and the web site is my responsibility."

Jake bit into a cookie. "If we blame the Bilderbergers, we'd darn well better have proof positive. Same with the Chinese."

Bob nodded. "Maybe the downfall's nobody's fault, just one of those infamous market corrections."

Jake smiled. "Should I put you on retainer as a news advisor?"

Bob chuckled. "My degree's in criminal justice. How about I be your advisor on criminology?"

A few minutes later, Jake was back at Dawn's desk. The aroma of cherry wafted into the air from his meerschaum as he scrutinized the China file. Not only was China's increasingly decentralized economy the fastest growing in the world, but the money the leaders were pouring into the defense budget in recent years was staggering and yet, put little strain on the economy.

Experts felt China sought to join, not overthrow, the international order. But how many times had *experts* been duped? These experts had advised European and North American leaders to welcome China in a way that would ensure its rise in this new millennium. Indeed, China's economy would be buttressed rather than eroded in the new international system and One World Government.

But what if China saw itself as the head and not the tail? And what if China decided to take its considerable muscle and make an economic gambit of global proportions?

Dawn had kept reports on China's purchase of US nuclear-reactor technology starting several years before. American companies selling and installing the technology reveled in the bonanza.

American government officials, salivating over booming profits and jobs, overlooked China's imprisoning and torture of Christians; its help in arming Iran over the years; its support of North Korean tyrants; their heavy-handed dealings with Tibet and Taiwan; the assistance Chinese gave to Pakistan and other countries in building reactors capable of producing plutonium. The list went on.

China's officials had promised America getting this new reactor technology would not pose a risk of proliferation. And naïve America politicians had taken them at their word.

Amazing how we shoot ourselves in the foot so often. We think with a Western mind set and just don't care to learn about other cultures.

Normally that inclination was most obvious with the way America had dealt with Arab countries, but here the philosophy meant the continued rise of China.

"Are we blind?" Jake said aloud.

Bob looked up from an *Inside Baseball* edition. "What's that, Jake?"

"The Asia-Pacific region has displaced the Atlantic community as the center of world economic affairs, and China's rise to wealth and power has fueled the change."

Jake massaged the bowl of his meerschaum and inhaled deeply as he thought through the process.

"There are Chinese nationals and emigrants all over the world, many of them wealthy. How'd they get their starts?"

Bob could only shrug an "I-don't-know."

"How did so many of them, since say 2005, get the wherewithal to start multimillion- and multibillion-dollar businesses in Canada, America, South America, Europe, and so on? And, if they have a source of funding—say, the Chinese government—wouldn't they be able to put millions, even billions of dollars into the world's stock markets?"

Bob put down the magazine and sat up. Jake had his attention.

"Yes, and ..." he answered, and Jake almost expected him to say what would come next.

"And," Jake said, "being beholden, even controlled by the Chinese government they could have been ordered to pull all their stock on Black Tuesday."

"Just a bunch of wealthy Chinese pulling their stock at the same time could cause such a disaster?"

Jake gnawed on his lip. "I don't know. It's one theory. I'd think many billions being withdrawn could be the cause. Hopefully, Dan Cowan and Andrea Page are finding the answer."

Jake stood and walked to his own desk a few steps away. He picked up a photo of Dawn and him in front of a castle in Adair, Ireland. He touched her face. "You knew Dawn, Bob." Jake sat against the edge of his desk. "She always harped at me, 'Think the best of people, Jake. The Lord says to think on things that are lovely, pure and of good report.' Of course, as a newsman I was always thinking the worst—or at least suspecting the worst—of everyone. Everyone in the news at least."

Jake looked down at the photo and remembered the words carved high along the top of the walls of Adair Castle.

"All around the top of the wall of this castle, Bob, was carved the Scripture 'If the Lord does not build the house, they labor in vain that build it.' I guess one way to look at this stock market collapse is with that word in mind. If the Lord is not causing the collapse, those who are doing so are working in vain."

CHAPTER NINETEEN

The next morning, Mosey Kreko stuffed the airline ticket in his jacket pocket. His stomach was churning. He was nervous. He didn't think he'd ever been this nervous, even his first public speaking effor when he ran for president of the student body at Loyola.

If he hadn't overcome his fears and dared to run, his whole life would be different, probably unhinged. He'd needed something to hold onto, to believe in. Direction.

If he hadn't screwed up the courage to run, he would have lost so much confidence he'd never have had the courage to take charge of any demonstrations, never have dared to run for office for Advocates for a Nuclear-Free World, never have been so bold as to take over leadership.

Maybe this this trip to see his parents in Israel wasn't such a good idea. Perhaps he should leave things alone. He'd broken his parents' heart when he married Mary, a gentile.

"Moshe, you're forsaking the command of Adonai," his father had said, barely containing his anger. "He told us not to marry outside our faith. Look what happened to King Solomon, the wisest man on earth. Once he started marrying women of other religions, he was in a downward spiral."

Defeat and pain were etched on his father's face. "As our young men and women marry outside the faith," he'd said, "the Jewish race is assimilated into the world."

Mosey's mother had simply wept.

How in the world would they react now—when Mosey told them he believed Jesus was the long-awaited Messiah? Would they even allow him to point out the many prophecies Jesus fulfilled? Daniel's timetable foretelling the Messiah would come before the destruction of the Temple, which happened in 70 AD, thirty-seven years after Jesus' death? To the horrific way Isaiah said the Messiah would die, long before crucifixion had ever been dreamed up?

Moshe prayed for the best, prepared for the worst.

A warm hand squeezed his shoulder. He turned. Mary looked up at him, offering a sympathetic smile. "You're concerned, darling. I understand. But don't worry. Your parents love you very much."

"You remember their reaction to our engagement?"

"Hey, they eventually came around. In the end, they attended the wedding."

"Not without diplomatic meetings on par with a Middle East peace agreement." Mosey chuckled.

"Well, they did." She put her hand to his face. "And I'll be praying for you. And I'll have the congregation praying for you. Most of them have gone through what you'll be experiencing."

Mosey thought of the Messianic congregation they attended. Most members were Jewish believers.

"Yes, and many of them have been disowned by their families."

"But your parents are seekers. Learners. They're always going to those senior citizen university workshops around the world, always studying different subjects. I think they'll be open minded and dig into their scriptures for the truth." Mary held up her hand. "Just a moment."

She disappeared into the bedroom, then returned with a book in hand. "I think this might help. Something for you to read on the flight."

"*Betrayed!*," Mosey read the title. The book was the true story of Stan Telchin, a Jew whose daughter came to faith in Jesus. Telchin set out to prove her wrong and, after months of research, was converted himself.

"Thank you, sweetie." Mosey set the book on his suitcase and wrapped Mary's hands in his. Looking into her blue eyes, he said softly, "I love you. You're the best support system I could ever have."

She hugged him. "I'll miss you."

"Ibid."

"Call and fill me in about what's happening."

"Of course."

A horn blew outside.

"There's my taxi," Mosey said. He kissed her deeply, then, with reluctance, released her. He handed her a slip of paper. "You've got Mom and Dad's number. Here's the hotel's phone in case I end up staying there, which I think is probable, to tell you the truth."

Mary bit her lip. "I hope not."

A final kiss and Mosey hefted his suitcase and the book, straightened his back, and walked out the door.

Mary said a prayer for him. She knew his parents well. His father, Levi, was the son of a Holocaust-surviving father. His mother, Sarah, was a sabra, a woman born in Israel. Moving to Israel was a return home for her, a country she'd left to attend graduate school in America.

Levi had earned a bachelor's degree in mathematics from Yeshiva University in New York, a master's degree in business administration from Brandeis University in Boston, then, "for the sake of diversity," returned to New York City to obtain a law degree from Columbia University.

It was during Levi's law studies when he attended a concert at his alma mater, Yeshiva, and felt his jaw hit the floor at the sight of the concertmistress, the lead violinist, whose curly black hair fell around the sweetest face he'd ever laid his eyes upon. Screwing up his courage after the concert, he approached her, struck up a conversation about her homeland, Israel, and they had never been apart since.

Sarah completed her studies at Yeshiva University's Stern College for Women, and they were married in Manhattan.

Levi, who'd begun tinkering with finances when he joined the Max Investment Club at Yeshiva University, set about conquering the risky world of commodity speculation and managed futures, devising a trading model shrewd enough to launch him and the firm he created to the stratosphere of the business world.

Meanwhile, Sarah earned a place with the New York Philharmonic, working her way to the honored corner seat of the violinists. She played under Zubin Mehta, Kurt Masur, and Lorin Maazel before retiring, fulfilled that she had toured on five continents and performed with such virtuoso violinists as Itzhak Perlman and such extraordinary pianists as Arturo Benedetti Michelangeli, just before his death in 1995, and Vladimir Ashkenazy, not long before he became principal conductor of the Czech Philharmonic Orchestra in 1998.

Since Levi's offices were on Wall Street and the New York Philharmonic's home was at Lincoln Center on Broadway, the couple resided in a massive apartment overlooking Central

Park in Manhattan, where they raised Mosey. Living among the illustrious, they held intimate parties with fascinating and famous people.

But despite temptations toward decadence, they remained humble and devoted to their God. They'd instilled the quality of humility in Moshe, and he was extremely bright. But his disinterest in Judaism disappointed them. He faithfully attended synagogue, anxiously accompanied them on vacations to Israel to visit his mother's family, but never aspired to become a cantor or, better still, a rabbi.

When they urged Mosey to attend Yeshiva University, he eschewed their choice for Loyola University in Chicago, wanting to be more his own person. When he took a junior year abroad at Hebrew University in Jerusalem, they had hoped his decision was a sign of drawing closer to God. But that turned out to be far from the truth.

As Orthodox Jews, they kept a kosher house. But they'd heard that during Pesach (Passover) in Israel, when observant Jews avoid leavened bread, Mosey simply walked into the Arab Quarter for a falafel. He was indifferent, which concerned them.

Then, the bombshell: his engagement to Mary, a goyim, a gentile. Oy-veh!

Mary smiled wryly to herself. *Boy, I'm glad I wasn't there for* that *Armageddon.* But she was glad Mosey had stood fast. She loved him so dearly.

Thankful he had an aisle seat, Mosey shifted about to try to get comfortable. Restless, he kept tumbling the upcoming visit about in his mind.

He'd known his parents had always loved Israel, but to move there? When terrorists could blow you up in the mall, in a bus, while strolling along a busy street? He'd lost three cousins and an aunt and uncle to Palestinian terrorists. Two other cousins, one of them a girl, had died fighting Hezbollah in southern Lebanon. He'd attended more funerals in Israel than in America! And his parents had moved there?

"Yes, son," his father had answered him when questioned about the move. "Adonai tells us time and again in the Torah to *aliyah*, to return home. Your mother and I have been rebellious in not doing so years and years ago."

"But, Dad, the danger—"

"Moshe, Jeremiah the prophet said: '"However, the days are coming," declares the Lord, "when men will no longer say, "As surely as the Lord lives, who brought the Israelites up out of Egypt," but they will say, "As surely as the Lord lives, who brought the Israelites up out of the land of the north and out of all the countries where he had banished them. For I will restore them to the land I gave their forefathers. But now I will send for many fishermen," declares the Lord, "and they will catch them. After that, I will send for many hunters, and they will hunt them down on every mountain and hill and from the crevices of the rocks."'

Mosey recalled the sincerity in his father's deep brown eyes as he continued, "I believe the hunters are about to come for us Jews. Who they will be this time, I don't know. Since Adonai gave us Eretz Israel, there have been those who would drive us into the sea, expel us from their lands, or simply kill us. The Turks, the Spaniards, the Crusaders, Hitler, the Muslims—

"This time? More likely, they'll be a legion. The whole world condemns Israel for killing Islamic terrorist monsters in Israel while they themselves attack terrorists in their own countries. The World Court even condemned Israel and ordered her to pay restitution for building a fence to protect herself. There seems to be no end to hypocrisy and double standards when the topic is killing Jews. Even America is no longer safe for Jews walking a street wearing a kippah. Remember Josef?"

Mosey recalled Josef Kidelman, a business associate of his father. He'd been found in an alley in Manhattan, stabbed to death with the word *Jew* carved into his forehead. A light-skinned man, the kippah he wore was the only sign he was Hebrew.

Levi Kreko had continued, "Mosey, Jews around the world are coming to the conclusion another holocaust is on the horizon. Where will we be safer—New York City or Israel, where our own people control the government and care to protect us?"

Mosey had felt powerless to argue.

"Your mother and I feel the Lord was speaking to us through Jeremiah and others, telling us to return to our land. We're helping prepare the land for future generations. By this time next month, the American government will forbid people to emigrate and take their money with them. By going now, we can use our finances to strengthen Israel.

Mosey had hung his head. He had not seen eye to eye with his parents on a number of things. But he loved them dearly, and he knew their love for him was unconditional, even if strained at times.

"Moshe, don't be sad. This is our dream, not yours. You can visit—you and Mary both. We'd love to see you move there too. Your cousin Jonathan would absolutely do flips, and Uncle Theodore would hire you in a minute."

Levi Kreko had smiled, then turned deadly serious, "Son, in the nineteen-forties some Jews aliyahed to Israel in fear of their lives, but at least six million waited too long to be rescued. Please don't you wait too long."

Sitting in the Boeing 747, Mosey determined his father had been right. About a month after they moved, the American government capped how much of their wealth emigrants could take with them.

He recalled a headline in the morning's *New York Times*. He glanced at the paper he'd stuffed in the netting in the seat in front of him and pulled it out. Just above the fold, in thirty-six-point type, the headline read: "Some Blame Jews for Economic Conspiracy." The subhead added: "Omar: 'Greed Their Creed.'"

Indeed, the Jews had a target on their chest whenever a government just about anywhere in the world needed a scapegoat to take the blame for an economic upheaval. After all, they became business leaders wherever they settled.

Reflecting on the headline, Mosey wondered if those who blamed Jews for economic woes were among the hunters his Dad had mentioned.

Mosey rummaged under his seat, where he had stuffed a small carryon containing his Bible and some writing materials. He pulled out the Bible and searched for the Book of Amos.

"A theologian, huh?" The question came in a British accent, from the older man sitting next to him. Lost in thought, Mosey hadn't paid much attention to the man. Casually dressed, he was in his fifties, balding, and sporting a well-kept van Dyke.

Mosey smiled. "Hardly."

The man extended his hand. "Trevor Mann."

"Moshe Kreko." Mosey shook his hand. "Friends call me Mosey."

"You look familiar. Should I recognize you?"

Mosey told him about his work with Advocates for a Nuclear-Free World.

"Oh, well, that's how I know you," Mann said. "I'm a supporter. A member. My wife and I just became—oh, what is it—Swans? Doves? Something of the sort."

"Eagles?"

"Right," Mann said, and Mosey knew he was wealthy. Gifts of $25,000 or more were necessary to attain Eagle status.

"Then you'll be coming to our international convention in Paris in July?"

"Actually, I refuse to travel to France. Ever since the French pulled out of Iraq on us Brits and you Americans back in 2004. I'm a man of honor, Mr. Kreko. Honor and common sense. What else is there? When we go to our graves, we're worm food. What people remember of our character is all that remains."

"Worm food?" Mosey looked quizzically at him. "I admire your stand for honor and common sense. I'm a quasi-optimist, quasi-pragmatist, and I try to live by honor, too. But I believe we were created to be of far better use than worm food when we die."

"I assumed so when I saw the Bible," Mann said. "But, Mosey, I have a difficult time dealing with absolutes. The Bible sets out a number of absolutes. Yet, I'm sure there are no absolutes."

"Are you absolutely sure?" Mosey asked.

"Absolut—" Mann caught himself. "Ha!"

For the next four hours, right through dinner, Mosey shared his new-found faith with Mann. Praying internally all the time—because he was aware he knew so little of the Bible—Mosey told of the sinless life of the Messiah, of the point resurrection was not even a debatable fact of history, of the many prophecies foretold thousands of years before Jesus was born, that he fulfilled.

"What other religion contains prophecies that were fulfilled?" he asked.

Mann shrugged.

"The answer is none," Mosey said. "Mohammed prophesied he would return to Mecca, but this was self-fulfilling. Otherwise, nothing."

He reached for his Bible. "I'm going to visit my parents, who are examples of another series of prophecies having come to pass."

Mann's look asked the question, *What?*

Mosey found the Book of Amos and started reading from chapter nine, verses 24 and 25. "'I will bring back my exiled people Israel; they will rebuild the ruined cities and live in them. They will plant vineyards and drink their wine; they will make gardens and eat their fruit. I will plant Israel in their own land, never again to be uprooted from the land I have given them,' says the Lord your God."

"Well, they're certainly planting vineyards," Mann said. "The reason I'm going there is to cut deals with a couple of vineyards."

"Really? Which ones?" Mosey didn't want to stray from the focus of the conversation, but felt he should give Mann a break from the profound topic of theology.

"I'm negotiating with wineries up in the Galilee and down in the Negev."

"The Shomron and Samson regions have been the primary wine growing areas, haven't they?" Mosey asked.

"True. My favorite has been in the Golan Heights, where they rewrote the book on making wine. There's no disputing the real turning point in Israeli winemaking in terms of quality is largely due to the Golan Heights Winery. But we're very interested in these new wines."

Mosey pointed at Mann. "You see? Another example of God's prophecies fulfilled. The pharaohs of Egypt favored Canaanite wine in the Bronze Age and when the Egyptians ruled the area."

Mann nodded. "Thousands of years later, the whole world is buying from Israel. For the past twenty-five years, it's been a leading exporter of fruits and flowers."

"All coming from a tiny little country the size of Delaware," Mosey said, "and surrounded by people who yearn to destroy it."

Mann's brow furrowed and he asked, "Mosey, you're Jewish, and you believe in Jesus. I wonder, how has your family reacted?"

The question stung. After a moment, Mosey replied, "I haven't told them yet. That's why I'm going—to tell them."

"They're Orthodox?"

"Yes."

"Oh."

A dread silence followed. A memory flashed through Mosey's mind of a summer day in Central Park when he and his Dad kicked around a soccer ball. Then came a premonition of his father slamming a door in his face.

Mann obviously didn't dare continue the conversation. Neither did Mosey.

After a few minutes, Mosey broke the silence. *Now I've met my Messiah, I can't remain silent.*

He turned again to Mann. "Jesus said the only way to the Father is through Him. If I believe so, then I have to tell people, especially those in my family, those I love the most."

Mosey knew his face revealed earnestness that spoke volumes of the anguish and concern he felt. And he could read the questions swirling in Mann's mind. Was this fellow correct? Is there a God? Did Jesus die for my sins? What if he's right and I die without acknowledging it?

As the airplane touched down at Ben Gurion Airport on the outskirts Tel Aviv, Mann tapped Mosey's arm. "What do I do?" he asked.

Perplexed, Mosey looked at him. They'd both sat silent for the past hour as they flew over the Mediterranean Sea, lost in their own thoughts. "What do you mean?"

"To get saved? What do I do?"

"You're asking me? I hardly know myself."

"But you know," Mann said matter-of-factly.

Then the fact struck Mosey. *He's right. I do know.*

The aircraft was taxiing to a stop by the main gate of the small airport as Mosey led his new friend in a sinner's prayer.

The plane stopped and all around them people hustled to grab their carry-on luggage and coats from the overhead carriers. But Mosey sat with Mann, whose hands covered his bowed head and swiped at tears trickling down his cheeks.

Solemnity filled Mosey's spirit, yet a thrill sent a charge through him. He was a baby Christian himself, and the Lord had already allowed him to lead a person to the Messiah. Oh, if he would just do the same with his parents.

Ten minutes later, the plane empty of passengers and just the flight crew waiting for them, Mosey and Mann walked down the stairs to the tarmac.

Both their faces were washed in tears of gladness. A flight attendant and co-pilot looked at them, wondering what was the story. But, hey, this was Israel. Emotions ran high.

The lead flight attendant, a lanky dark-skinned girl with long black hair, looked at her watch—seven a.m.—and then out the door at the sky.

"A sunny, fall day!" she said in Hebrew.

"Yeah, but I hear a storm's brewing," the copilot deadpanned.

Darek loved this apartment, the verandah and closeness to Boston Harbor, to the ever-changing tides. And close proximity to The Truth building didn't hurt. He sat in a deck chair and inhaled the salty air, lost in thought. Then he felt a presence. *Ahh*, and his favorite reason for loving this place stood behind him, he was sure.

"Hay-lo," he said.

"Can't sleep?" Jillian asked.

"Can't get some things out of my head. We must get to Brussels and speak to His Mighty Highness. I can't but wonder who exactly is orchestrating all this—stuff—and I'd like to know who were those dudes in Jerusalem following us."

"Three wide-ranging questions to consume your mind at midnight." Jillian took a seat next to him and wrapped her nightgown tightly around her. "And his name isn't Mighty Highness. It's Premier Sardis to you, mister."

They exchanged sardonic smiles in the dim light from the living room.

"I'm looking forward to that interview," Jillian said. She swiped away a stray strand of hair from her magnificent eyes—a signature move for Jillian, one that always got his attention. "But sitting out here at all hours of the night won't keep us in peak mental condition, right?"

"You sound like my mother, God bless her soul."

"*I* miss your mom," Jillian said and reached for his hand. "Miss your dad too."

"Um-hm. I miss Dad calling me up and saying, 'Why didn't you ask that rascal this?' Or 'Why not ask that question yet again so they'd have to answer?'" Darek chuckled. "I'll probably do the same when our son becomes a globe-trotting superstar reporter."

"Yeah, right. Hey, superstar, let's go off to bed. I'll ply you with an anti-coffee drug to get you to sleep. As a matter of fact, I know just the thing." She hesitated. "Our son, huh?"

Was that a twinkle in his wife's eyes? Darek sprang to his feet with a spryness that even startled him. "No more persuasion needed."

Midnight in Washington, DC, and the near-empty streets glistened in a mist brightened by streetlights the length of Jefferson Drive.

Corporal Bert Stevens and his partner, Patrolman Ernie Stokes, rode slowly up the broad street, Stevens at the wheel. The Washington Monument behind them rose toward the stars. A young couple held hands and looked up at the obelisk.

"Somewhat like the other couple holding hands and admiring the Lincoln Memorial," Stevens said.

"Nothing really suspicious," Stokes said, "except perhaps this is an odd time for sightseeing."

Stevens considered the point. Then he ruminated over how well this partnership was working out. "Yeahs" and "buts" were part of their relationship, not just "yeah, I agree."

They'd become a true team, everyone agreed. The SOS team. Stevens or Stokes.

On this night shift, they were the cops any good citizen would want answering their call. Either Stevens or Stokes, SOS. They could handle themselves and any malcontent stupid enough to be their collar. Stevens was the Metropolitan Police middleweight boxing champion. Stokes, two years out of an Army Ranger unit, had won last year's World Judo Championships in Munich.

"So, this couple returns home to Falls Church from a weeklong vacation, tired from jetlag and too much partying, and they find a guy asleep in their bed," Stevens said.

Stokes laughed as Stevens held forth.

"Leaving the guy there asleep, they quietly call the police and stealthily check out their house. They'd left the place in a bit of a mess but they find the dishes have been washed, the laundry done—including the guy's underwear, apparently— and he'd even bought some groceries.

More laughter.

"So the cops arrive, cuff the intruder and take a statement from the couple." Stevens hesitated. There was more to come and Stokes pushed his jaw forward, waiting in anticipation.

"Did this man steal anything?" the sergeant asks.

"Well," says the woman, and she lowers her voice, "he *did* burn an old saucepan. But that happens!"

Stokes burst out laughing. Stevens simply wore a satisfied grin, his job complete.

Levity was necessary during long nights breaking up brawls in DC's fine drinking establishments, as they called them. A little light entertainment when dealing with drunk wife-beaters and wrestling homeless people off the sidewalk grates just two or three blocks from the Capitol. After all, for all DC's time in the world's spotlight, the city basically went to sleep at night.

Beddy-bye. Sleep tight. Stevens smiled at the thought of saying these words to his two-year-old son. *Don't let the bed bugs bite.*

"Say," he asked, "who in the world first thought of saying to your kid, who you're trying to put to sleep, 'Don't let the bed bugs bite'? We're probably giving the poor kids nightmares."

"Or at least keeping them awake in fear." Stokes laughed.

"Yeah, but I'm serious," Stevens said. "There's enough real danger today without make-believe stuff. You never know what kind of images you put in your kid's mind."

"Well, I've got an image of a thick Philly and cheese right now. Let's head over to Independence Deli before they close."

"Independence," Stevens spit the word out. "What's that anymore?"

"Yeah, right."

They'd been down this road before. Just four months ago, America had agreed to One World Government security forces working in tandem with the Metropolitan Police.

It all sounded good. "Working together to ferret out terrorists, to foil plots of enemies of the world."

But these One World guys had moved right into Metro's Joint Operations Command Center, an amphitheater-style room boasting the latest version of Clarity Lion—a twenty-two by one-hundred-foot digital wall filled with sixty-seven-inch high-resolution displays from camera links around the city.

Major streets, parks, the subway system—many public areas under surveillance to help various law-enforcement agencies take public-safety and homeland-security measures.

All this technology developed by Americans, now being made available to this One World Government crowd. Both men felt America had handed over too much of its sovereignty to One World. This was one more step in the wrong direction.

"One more turn around the Capitol and we'll head over to Independence," Stevens promised.

They'd reached First Street and turned left to pass by the Thomas Jefferson Building and Supreme Court. The statue of Moses and the Ten Commandments loomed up ahead.

Out of the blue, a blast blistered the thin night air in the distance. Stevens looked left. The boom was beyond the Capitol, perhaps a half mile away, perhaps the far end of the mall.

"What the—" The words had barely left his mouth when another explosion, no more than forty feet in front of them, blasted the statue of Moses to smithereens. The cruiser's windshield imploded and the vehicle lifted off the ground straight up three feet, then landed sideways—a twisted, mangled heap of metal, its headlights shining at the spot once occupied by Moses.

Windows shattered all around the Capitol and inside the Command Center alarms blared, lights flashed, and women and men monitoring the city jumped from their seats.

The captain in charge called out, "Where?"

"Somewhere around the Mall," shouted a reply.

"Get on the horn to SOS!"

Inside the crumpled cruiser the police radio crackled to life. "Five-niner. Five-niner. Come in, five-niner ... We have a report of an explosion near the Capitol. Five-niner? SOS! You guys okay?"

Deaf ears were dead ears in Stevens' and Stokes's cruiser. Both men hung upside down in their shoulder straps, dead from the concussion.

Were they alive, they could have heard other explosions in the distance and the unending yelps and squawks of sirens in surround sound.

Twelve midnight in Washington, DC, and the near-empty streets glistened in a mist brightened by streetlights the length of Jefferson Drive.

The entire Western Wall was in shadow in the early-morning sun. Three or four dozen people ambled around the expansive plaza, most of them men on the left side of a six-foot-high partition and a bit fewer women on the right side. All the men wore yarmulkes, either their own or black cardboard ones available in a straw basket on a stand.

"Baruch habah b'ashem Adonai!" The voice caromed off the courtyard walls from the nearby city gate. "Blessed is he who comes in the name of the Lord!"

Seemingly out of nowhere, Elijah appeared in front of the partition between the men and women.

"The Lord speaks righteousness, but his enemies preach hatred and destruction," he declared. "The Lord offers salvation, but his enemies seethe with the taste for death. We bring a message of freedom in Messiah. His enemies hold deceived masses in bondage."

Shlomo, next to Elijah, spoke up. "But in the end, know God's justice will reign supreme, and all those who call on his name and the name of his Son will be saved, for now and eternity."

As if shot by bullets, the two witnesses sank to their knees and pulled prayer shawls over their heads.

In Tel Aviv, Mosey and Mann stepped out of a cab at the Crowne Plaza on Hayarkon Street. The Mediterranean Sea across the four-lane highway sparkled in the morning sun.

Mosey put his hand over his eyes to shade them and looked up. Boy, this was going to be a scorcher of a fall day. Must be seventy-five degrees already.

The cab driver popped open the trunk and pulled out the suitcases. Mosey was going to call and tell his parents in Jerusalem he'd arrived. They'd drive the hour to Tel Aviv and pick him up. Enough time for Mosey and Trevor to enjoy a casual breakfast at the Crowne Plaza, where Trevor was staying.

Mosey pulled a phone from his pocket. "You go ahead, Trevor. I'll catch up to you inside after I call my folks and give Mary a ring to tell her I arrived safely."

"I'll check in, send my luggage to my room, and meet you at the restaurant." Trevor beamed and patted a hanky to the sweat beading on his forehead. "Can't wait to ask you some more questions."

Mosey smiled. They'd become friends in such a short time despite their distance in age. During the taxi ride from the airport, they'd even planned to meet in London the next spring and get the grand tour from native Brits.

Trevor's wife, Molly, sounded like a real hoot who could keep them entertained all by herself. And Trevor Jr., a teen-ager, played the electronic fiddle in a band. Mosey, who couldn't strum a chord on a guitar but loved all strains of music, looked forward to the experience.

Mosey took hold of his suitcase and walked a few steps from the entrance of the hotel to get a little privacy and quiet. He punched in his parents' phone number. On the third ring, his mother picked up. When she saw his face on the monitor she lit up like a lantern. "Moshe!"

"Mom."

"You're at the airport. We'll head right out to pick you up."

"No, Mom. I'm with a friend at the Crowne Plaza by the Mediterranean and we're going to have breakfast together. Then I'll—"

Suddenly, a loud explosion from inside the hotel tore into the front wall and blew Mosey to the ground. Shrapnel blew through the front windows, sending shards of glass everywhere.

Mosey crawled a couple of feet and hunkered down on the brick sidewalk as glass sprayed around and upon him. The ground quaked. Alarms blared around him but he felt deaf, the sounds dull and distant. Pain shivered along his arms. He looked and saw blood seeping from both elbows where he'd landed on the pavement.

On his knees in the courtyard of the Western Wall, Elijah looked up to the heavens.

"Adonai," he called, "they hear not. Listen to the bombs as they explode here in Jerusalem, in Bethlehem, in Tel Aviv and Washington! Their hearts are darkness, and they see no light except the deceit from their god, the father of lies!"

All of a sudden, the earth-shaking thud of explosives reached the courtyard. All eyes swept eastward from where the sound came. A plume of dark smoke billowed above the buildings around them.

"Behold, the Church of the Holy Sepulcher," Elijah bellowed, pointing toward the nearby massive, monolithic structure that had stood in the Christian Quarter for centuries and housed several Christian religions from its basement to the rooftop. "The church's knees are buckling today so she will drop to her knees in prayer and supplication."

"Bombs away!" Hisey Brinks smiled at Norine and looked out the window of the room high atop the 5th Street hotel where they were staying in Washington, DC.

Plumes of smoke rose to the south where the Washington Memorial had stood sentinel for so long. Stones flew into the air like so many pebbles where the Supreme Court building stood, just a few blocks to the north of their room.

Then beyond the Washington Memorial and out of their sight, another explosion blew apart the Lincoln Memorial, where the Gettysburg Address was quoted declaring, "This nation under God shall have a new birth of freedom …"

At almost the same instant, across the Tidal Basin, the Jefferson Memorial, which contained quotations declaring homage to God, shook from its belly as an explosive charge set beyond the statue of Jefferson went off.

Hustling down East Basin Drive, away from the Jefferson Memorial and toward Maine Avenue, a couple grinned at each other and turned to watch, knowing they should be escaping but drawn like a magnet to the carnage. The Jefferson Memorial swayed as if shaken by an earthquake, then settled for a moment.

Several seconds later, one its seven marble columns in front began to quiver, then wobble. Then an adjacent column shivered. Seconds more elapsed, and a crack appeared, running up Jefferson's left leg, through his chest and across his face. A crack in a bronze statue!

After a few more moment's hesitation, the two columns dislodged and plunged to the steps. Quickly others followed suit and huge chunks of the stone ceiling plummeted to the ground. Then a cascade, smashing into Jefferson's statue.

In another thirty seconds, Jefferson's semblance was obliterated, along with any mention of God.

The couple turned and disappeared into the night at the same time another couple crossed 15th Street in front of the US Holocaust Memorial Museum. They high-fived, fist-bumped and laughed as they hurried toward their rendezvous.

In the hotel room, Brinks gloated, "Big payday coming! No-No, we've started to gut your enemies. Now your boss is giving us all the money we need to cause some real damage to *our* mortal enemies. Ha!" He threw up his head.

Norine smiled back at him. "Yeah, bombs away. In more ways than one."

"Here and in Israel."

"Israel, too? You didn't tell me."

"Oh, there are lots of things to teach you, sweet No-No. Among them, we have *muchos amigos* with other agendas in other parts of the world. We scratch their backs, they scratch ours. And, sometimes, we can synchronize efforts. Synchronization—a wonderful thing to behold."

He cupped his hand around the nape of her neck. "This we've witnessed tonight—" He swept his other hand in the direction of the Capitol Mall, "is just the beginning, baby. We have an entire alphabet of targets just here in the good old capitol of America. And that's simply for your friends at AFFRONT and our buddy Icky On-the-Run Coffman."

Norine looked up at him, and he could read admiration in her eyes. A good time to spring his next line. "And, in response to us helping you, you can kindly lend us a hand in our mission. Right, No-No?"

She looked puzzled.

"No matter," Brinks said. "I'll share my plan with Icky— when he surfaces."

As if in a surreal dream, Mosey watched as tragedy unfolded around him. Ambulances and Humvees with canopied backs arrived from different directions, screaming to stops in front of and beside the hotel. Israeli Defense Forces soldiers jumped from the vehicles as emergency personnel pulled stretchers from their mobilized emergency rooms. Others who appeared to be doctors ran into the hotel.

An American-made Jeep slammed to a stop across the street and a soldier, obviously with authority, stepped out.

Organized mayhem. Nails, bolts, and assorted chunks of metal and pieces of glass had ripped into dozens of people in the registration area, the front lounge, and outside the entry doors.

Dazed, Mosey stepped over broken glass and peered inside the hotel. Rubble. A cloud of white dust. Toppled furniture. Body parts! He twisted away from the scene and felt bile rise from his stomach.

He heard someone call out in Hebrew that no one was alive in the reception area. Falling to his knees, oblivious to the people scrambling around him, Mosey covered his face with his hands.

"How could you allow this to happen?" he asked God as sobs racked his body. Some amount of time transpired, and Mosey quieted. Then he seemed to hear a small, distant voice, "My children are safe with me."

Then the realization struck Mosey that Trevor Mann was dead. But he had accepted the Lord an hour ago in the airplane. Accepted the Lord unabashedly, with tears of joy streaming down his cheeks. Mosey pulled a handkerchief from his pocket and wiped his face dry. Even as some stubborn tears continued to dribble from his eyes, he thanked God for Trevor's salvation—and his small role in the miracle.

And yet, the carnage, the destruction, the death. Among the dead were the unsaved. Jewish people who did not know their Savior. Another wave of tears gushed forth. Deep moans erupted.

Mosey wished he were a child again and his parents were there, so he could lay his head on his mother's breast and hear comforting words.

To be precise, he wanted to be five again. The world at five was filled with friends who played ball with you, parents who sheltered you and read you to sleep at night. Five was an uncomplicated time without worries.

CHAPTER TWENTY

Jake's telephone blasted to life, interrupting his first good sleep since Dawn's death.

Sue Haynes, *the Truth*'s night wire desk editor, was breathless.

"There've been bombings, Jake. Lots of them! Correspondents in DC and Israel just called in."

Jake pushed the bedsheets aside and sat up. "Where?"

"The Washington Memorial, Supreme Court building, Lincoln and Jefferson Memorials in DC; a hotel and nightclub in Tel Aviv; the Church of the Nativity in Bethlehem, and the Church of the Holy Sepulcher in the Old City; and, oddly enough, a small theater in the town of Tiberias on the Sea of Galilee.

All he could muster as he tried to wake up fully was "What's the deal?"

"I don't know. The Tel Aviv bombs look like Palestinians terrorizing tourists at the hotel and frightening Israelis to do even the mundane things like dancing in a nightclub. The DC explosions were at sites where the Bible is quoted. Otherwise, I've got no clue."

"Rouse the task force and have them meet in my office at—" Jake rubbed his eyes and focused on the clock at his bedside. 12:15 a.m. "At my office at one o'clock. Are you coordinating with the TV folks?"

"Sure am. SOP."

Good woman. Standard Operating Procedure.

"Good. I'll be in ASAP."

Jake hustled into some khakis, a polo shirt and button-up sweater, stuffed his feet into a pair of loafers, grabbed his meerschaum off the end table and headed down the wide stairway to the main floor. He nodded to the man in the security control room. "I'm off to The Truth, Tank."

Tank, the size of an NFL defensive lineman, nearly leaped from his chair. "I'll get your security detail, sir."

"Nah. I'll be all right. But around six o'clock, give Bob a call, will you? Tell him I'm at the office?"

"Will do."

Jake hustled to the garage, climbed into his automobile, pushed the button to open the garage door, laid rubber on the cement floor, hit a button to open the outside gate, and drove like a NASCAR racer to Boston's North End.

All the time, he considered the facts as he knew them. What sense did these bombings make? They seemed disconnected. Them blowing at the same time was no happenstance.

As he approached The Truth building, the question creeped out before him, like a slinking, dark creature in a foreboding alleyway. An atheist had been caught in a bombing just a few blocks away. All the DC monuments and the Supreme Court contained Scripture, as did the churches in Israel.

Suppose the atheists are continuing their campaign here in the States and collaborating with terrorists in Israel. No. Didn't make sense. What did they have in common? Perhaps this was coincidence.

Jake pulled into The Truth parking lot. The area was well lit, encompassed around by a high chain-link fence, and a security guard was stationed at an entry gate.

"Mr. MacMillan." The guard nodded. "Sammy will escort you inside, sir."

Sam White, another guard, approached from the building. "Fine, Todd. Thanks."

A few minutes later, ahead of the one o'clock meeting, the entire team was gathered in Jake's office.

Jake pushed the intercom button. "Can we have some coffee and pastries in here please, Annie?"

"Certainly, sir." Ann Stapleton sounded half asleep.

Jake looked around, "You all look alert, but you all look tired, too."

Nods were the consensus.

"I could use a double coffee, double black," said Jeff Warren. "I'd just landed at Logan, coming back from LA, when Sue texted. By the way, Jake, that is some plane."

"Safety," Jake said. "My first and foremost concern nowadays. Kind of constraining, but look what just happened." He took a seat behind his desk and continued by listing all the bombings.

"Actually, Jake, to be more precise," Sue said, "the bomb was outside the Supreme Court building. They took down the statue of Moses and the Ten Commandments."

"Oh? Well, that clarifies the message." Jake turned the bowl of his meerschaum in his hand. All eyes were on him. "Tell me, are the bombings overseas connected to these at home?"

"Jake," Darek broke in, "we've been to the theater in Tiberias. Christians operate the place. Every Jewish child in Israeli schools for the last thirty years has been taken there to see a popular film about the rise of the Jews in Galilee. Snuggled in the middle of the presentation is a message about a young man named Yeshua who changed the world."

"Yes," Ty said. "And the other places are Christian. They didn't bomb any Jewish synagogues. Why not?"

"Perhaps they're sending the same message in Israel as they are in the US, directed at our Judeo-Christian heritage." Jake looked at Jillian. "Any information from the young man Darek and Ty caught in the bombing?"

"He's not talking."

"Even as a Christian, sometimes I think we're too humane with people charged with high crimes," said Todd Livingstone.

"We simply take civil to the nth degree," said Boston city editor Nancy Blais.

"Well, we might not be able to force him to talk," Ty said, "but they identified him as Peter 'Cabby' O'Shaunessy, a volunteer for AFFRONT, living in Falls Church, Virginia, outside DC. So Homeland Security is surveilling the Atheists' headquarters there. My guess is we'll see Icky Coffman arrested, if they can find him."

"He's afraid of his shadow and probably running for his life," Jake said.

"But," Warren said, "he has a ton of money in the bank. He could fund this."

"And pay who to carry it out?" Jake looked around for an answer. None came. "A guess, anyone?"

"The Black Power League," offered Nancy. "Buddy Joe Tatum is one of the meanest men on the outside of a jail cell."

"When he *is* on the outside," Jillian cracked.

"How about Society for All Lifestyles?" asked statehouse reporter Al McAnlus. "They've secretly done some violence. Roger Clapp's *MEAT* magazine certainly doesn't back off."

Heads nodded in agreement.

"Back off," Darek said, slapping his forehead as if he was late remembering a birthday. "The group *Back Off!*—Hisey Brinks' gang?"

"But *Back Off!* doesn't belong to the Alliance," Jillian said.

"As far as we *know*," Darek responded.

Jake motioned for quiet. His hand raised, he asked "What if we're facing a weird, loose alliance between atheists and Arab terrorists. Who's to say who is and isn't cooperating at this point?"

Jake started tapping the fingers of his left hand, one at a time. "Muslim terrorists, atheists … Atheists, gay rights … Gay rights, Citizens for Free Abortions … Citizens for Free Abortions, Black Power League …Who's dancing with whom, and what's next?"

"Choke and croak," said Darek.

"Choke and croak?" Jake shot him a questioning look. There was nervous laughter.

"Euthanasia. The new big thing."

"Choke and croak," Jake said again. "Hmm. We've come to this … You know, at one point I would've said the odds were fifty-fifty as to whether euthanasia or cryogenics would win over. But I guess we'd rather, uh—"

"Choke and croak," Darek answered for him.

"Right." Jake straightened his shoulders. "Okay, people. We digress. Let's all get to our sources and start digging to get some answers on who is doing what for whom, when and where."

He reached for his humidor of special cherry blend and dipped his meerschaum bowl into the moist concoction. At that, everyone knew the meeting was over.

Somewhere south of Richmond, Virginia, driving a car—rented under a false name—on Route 95 headed toward his cousin's house in Florida, Icky Coffman gave a victory shout and pumped his fist into the air. News on the radio reported a plethora of bombings.

"DC Metropolitan Police and Homeland Security are pursuing theories but have no solid leads at this time," the news announcer said. "Some speculate the bombs were set off by an anarchist group, attacking monuments of the United States republic, but no one has yet publicly taken credit for the destruction."

Maybe we should take credit, Icky thought. Maybe the publicity would spur people to jump on our bandwagon, make these Christians the outlaws instead of us. This craziness about a God and his rules is the cause of half the world's problems.

"Yeah," he said aloud. "Maybe I'll call the cops and take credit."

Life on the lam wasn't as appealing as movies made out. He thought over the consequences of fessing up. Social media would eat up his story. Splash his name and face everywhere.

A smile washed from his face and his chest stuck out noticeably more than before he heard the broadcast.

"Right, I'll call the cops."

Mosey's phone was ringing somewhere. He went to his knees seeking the source of the frisky piano chords and found the instrument beneath a black Volkswagen sedan.

His father's worried face filled the monitor.

"Son! What happened?" his father said and his face turned to the side. "Sarah, Moshe's all right!"

Then he looked back at Mosey. "You *are* all right, right?"

"Yeah, Dad. I am."

"First the phone went dead, then we heard explosions in the distance here in Yerushelayim, then the television reported about several bombings. So we hopped in the car to come find you."

Mosey's father wiped a tear of joy from his eyes.

Sarah Kreko took the phone from her husband. Relief filled her pretty face. Satisfied that Mosey was not injured, she turned to her husband. "Levi, slow down! You don't have to beat the devil to Sheol. Moshe looks shaky but he's alive."

She looked back at Mosey. "We're about fifty minutes away, Moshe. Your father's been flying down out of the hills of Yerushelayim at a hundred miles an hour. The hair on the back of my neck is standing up. I think I saw my life pass by, but we're going too fast for me to be sure."

Mosey chuckled.

"He forgets," his mother said, "he let his pilot's license lapse four years ago. *Oi Gevalt!*"

Despite the misery unfolding around him, Mosey couldn't prevent a laugh. His mother had always been the comic relief as well as the glue holding the family together. Super-glue actually, balancing her own philharmonic career with a husband absorbed in high finance, a renegade son, and all the peculiarities of maintaining reality in Manhattan's high society.

If the world appeared giddy, Sarah Kreko slapped it to attention with common sense. If the world seemed too somber, she'd tickle it with wit.

"Your father wants to know where we'll find you."

Moshe told her to meet him at the round glass building by the entry gate to the Tel Aviv Marina down the street from the destroyed hotel. That would get him away from the carnage.

"Okay. Look for a large, black mausoleum driving down the street."

Mosey smiled. "Mausoleum?"

"Well, you could call this monstrosity the Queen Elizabeth Three. Your father wanted transportation better than the prime minister's. It's longer than Pavarotti's limousine. Do you remember riding in Pavarotti's limousine?"

"Yes, Mom. I do."

"Our new car operates on hydrogen, solar power, a mixture of soy oil and gasoline, and, I think, camel urine. *Oi vay*!"

Spotting another victim on a stretcher being loaded into an ambulance, Mosey managed to shake his head. "I miss you, Mom." He ran his fingers across his mother's face on the monitor.

"I miss you, too, dear. Can't wait to see you." She put her fingers to her monitor as well—finger to finger, their way of touching a good-bye.

"Can't wait to see you, either," he said. He ended the call. *Or not.*

He normally was excited about seeing his parents, but this visit—this visit.

"Oh, boy," Mosey said aloud, then picked up his suitcase. Taking one last look back at the blackened hotel lobby where Trevor and so many others had died, he crossed Hayarkon, which had been shut down to traffic by the soldiers. A couple of the soldiers were girls, just teenagers by appearance, and yet they had rifles strapped across their shoulders.

Look what I missed by not growing up here. He shook his head.

On his way to the marina, Mosey thought of Trevor's wife, Molly. Should he try to call her? Yes, a good idea.

284

CHAPTER TWENTY-ONE

The Boston waterfront slept. Darek Fields caught a glimpse of his watch in the light from a street lamp. Three o'clock. He and Jillian were walking along Atlantic Avenue back to their apartment. Her hands were wrapped around his arm. They had rushed to the office in slacks and shirts, no jackets, without much thought of the temperature on this cool fall night.

"We've about four hours to sleep, then we've got get to work on the *Truth Be Told* piece on the bombings for tonight's broadcast," Darek said.

Jillian yawned. "Don't let the looks fool you. I'm asleep already. I'm a walking, talking zombie."

He smiled down at her.

A movement in the water startled them. Around a pier came a Coast Guard patrol boat. They'd not even heard the vessel approach. A searchlight flashed around the docks. Most were empty, but here and there floated a luxury sailing yacht or a large power boat. In low gear, the helmsman quietly maneuvered along the contours of the pier.

"Looks like they may have heightened guard of the waterways. There's something we didn't know," Darek whispered.

"Why are you whispering?" Jillian whispered back, her smile mischievous.

"In case there's a satellite monitoring our conversation, beaming our words straight to the home of Neil Bennett, head of Homeland Security." Darek chuckled.

"Those transmissions are actually beamed to the home of Premier Sardis, your good and lasting friend," Jillian teased.

Darek harrumphed, then a moment later said, "Speaking of Sardis, did you hear? Carlos Martinez said Monica at the Jerusalem office believes their phones have been tapped. They think the culprit is One World."

"Oh my gosh!" Jillian said. "This is no longer funny."

"No. Those Gestapo wannabes following us in Jerusalem could actually be dangerous."

"No, not them. But some other guys could be." Jillian shivered and drew closer to Darek.

"There they go." Darek pointed toward the Coast Guard boat, which was stealthily heading south, making its way around to the next pier, Commercial Wharf.

Darek put his arm around Jillian's shoulders. "Almost home."

Just as "home" escaped his lips, a tall figure stepped out from behind a tree in little Christopher Columbus Park. A man dressed in black and wearing a black ski mask stepped in front of them and wielded a knife.

"Wallet and purse. Now!"

Darek angled in front of Jillian. The man was broad-shouldered and a couple of inches taller than Darek.

"You serious, pal?" Darek asked.

Pointing his knife at Darek's stomach, he declared, "I'll seriously gut ya' out, man, if'n ya' don't hand over yer money." He hesitated. "Hey, I know you. You're the news guy."

"Right. How about I give you an autograph, and we call this a night?"

"Ha! Sign yer own death warrant if ya' don't give me yer valuables, too, since now I know you've got 'em."

"I should warn you," Darek took a half-step toward the man, now no more than a foot away, "very few people know this, but I have a license to kill."

The guy gutter-laughed. "Yeah, well, I don't need a license to kill."

He menacingly circled the knife, pointing the tip at Darek's face.

"Okay, okay," Darek replied and reached into his front right pocket. He pulled out an object and—Flash!—a powerful beam of blinding light struck the robber in the eyes. He screamed and threw his hands in front of his face.

Darek reached up and grabbed the wrist with the knife, twisted hard and, with a spin move, bent the man's arm forcefully behind his back. The man shrieked in pain.

Darek tripped him to the ground face-first and drove his knee into the middle of the guy's back. Grasping the knife, Darek looked up at Jillian, flashed a smile, and said, calmly, "Call nine-one-one, will you, babe? This guy's in need of some serious medical attention."

Jillian fumbled for her phone. In a few seconds, she was informing police of the attempted robbery.

Clicking the phone shut, she turned to Darek. "You know, we're going to have to put you on police department payroll if you keep up with this stuff."

The man on the ground groaned. "You blinded me, man."

"You rather I killed you—man? Remember, I said I had a license to do so."

The man swore.

Darek slapped him on the back of the head. "Watch your tongue, bud. You're in the presence of a lady. My lady."

Darek put a little more weight on his knee and the guy groaned a "sorry."

Jake closed the Venetian shades in the windows looking in on the newsroom, then turned off the lights in his office. A few moments before, meerschaum in hand, he had looked out his window onto Atlantic Avenue and watched Darek and Jillian disappear down the sidewalk.

Then Jake himself disappeared—into an old memory of Dawn and him walking arm in arm down the same sidewalk to one of their favorite restaurants, Joe's All-American Grille right on the water and next to Christopher Columbus Park.

A table on the bay, holding hands with his best friend and lover, discussing what had happened in each other's day. It was bliss. A cry, sudden and unexpected, heaved from his chest, and tears erupted from the corners of his eyes. This told him he was overly tired and needed to sleep.

He settled onto the plush leather couch, shut his eyes, and reflected on all the concerns bombarding him. Assassins at his house. Bombs at his business. Explosions at religious sites. The worldwide economy being sucked in a downward spiral to Hades. Advertisers running scared from the One World Government and the Alliance because of his editorial stances. The Church Universal winning over or neutering leaders of mainstream Christian religions.

When he was a child he had taught himself to juggle. Four balls, maybe five, was his limit. Here he was, juggling myriad matters of a global magnitude, operating a major newspaper, television station, web site, and on and on.

His personal lifeline, his wife, was dead. A zillion people wished he were dead as well. At home, in bed, alone, he sometimes agreed with them. No wonder his emotions were on edge—as if he had to be emotional to cry about Dawn.

The verse from the 59th chapter of Isaiah came to mind: "… when the enemy rises against you like a flood … the Lord will raise up a standard and deliver you."

He remembered driving over a bridge across the Androscoggin River in Lisbon Falls, Maine, during a flood, and noticing a small tree rising out of a ledge of rock in the middle of the dam. The tree was no more than eight or ten feet tall but stood unmoved as floodwaters crashed into and over its branches.

By the tree's height, he knew the stalwart little specimen had withstood many storms, and the torrents of powerfully moving waters coming from them, defying the odds against survival. Yet, how?

Because, he answered himself, the roots were deep in the rock. For hours and days on end, the little guy stands unmoved.

Jake looked at his watch. 3 a.m. Too late to call Bill Asbury. Shrugging himself off the sofa, he went to his knees and perched his elbows on the couch.

He began, "I'm utterly exhausted, mentally and physically, but I want to always stand against the storms the enemy batters me with, Father. Please give me strength to fight on."

Mosey phoned Mary, then made a difficult call to Trevor's wife. What do you say to a person you don't know, about a man you hardly knew, who has died a death you nearly died yourself? How do you console an agnostic about the death of her husband? What hope do non-believers have?

Mosey recalled how he'd felt when his Uncle Hiram and cousin Yosef were shot dead point blank as they waited in his uncle's car at a stoplight in Haifa. He remembered the funeral of his cousin, Miryam, who died in a bomb blast at a friend's bat mitzvah. He remembered a young man, Zev, who had befriended him on one of the Kreko family's visits to Israel. An IDF soldier, Zev was later kidnapped and his mutilated body unceremoniously dumped outside his settlement.

These whom Mosey remembered all belonged to religious families who had expectations of seeing them again in the after-life.

Mosey struggled with the idea of not calling Molly Mann. After all, who was he? Not an official of the state of Israel, or the British embassy who would probably give the official notification.

In the end, Mosey thought, but at least I knew Trevor. With that, he dialed the home phone number on Trevor's business card.

Mosey fumbled over the words when he broke the news. Then thoughts he had not considered poured out. Molly should know Trevor had recognized the existence of God before he died. He'd given his life to the Messiah on the airplane. He had a joy and expectation of seeing the Lord after his death. At this very moment, Trevor was experiencing this joy firsthand.

And, at this very moment, Molly could possess the same expectation of eternal life with her Creator—and with her husband.

In tears and mourning, interspersed with anguish and anger that her husband should die, Molly resisted his message—at first. But, finally, she asked him to call her again later. She said she had to have time to grieve, to bury her husband's remains, to get her bearings on her life and her emotions. She couldn't deal with this God thing right now. He promised to call her again.

Talk about tests! I get saved and You immediately allow me to be arrested, put me in a situation to lead a man to you, then, two hours later, inform his wife of his death. Thanks a lot.

Just then, Mosey spotted a large black car cruising slowly up the street.

Dad's mausoleum. As big as a barge. Fitting we should meet at a marina.

He noticed his mother nudging her father and pointing at him. Picking up his suitcase, he stepped from the shade of the circular glass building to the curb.

Levi Kreko bear-hugged his son as if Mosey were a teenager. His mother patted his cheek like he was a preteen and offered him the front passenger's seat.

Mosey preferred to spread out in the back for the ride to Jerusalem.

As they exited the city, his father asked, "So, Son, what brings you to Israel?"

"I'd like to wait until we're back at your place before we get into that, Dad."

"A mystery, then?" his mother said.

"Things can get dangerous when your mother dons her Miss Marple hat, son," his father joked.

Mosey smiled, but he wasn't about to get into such turbulent atmosphere right out of the chute.

Instead he deflected. "Hey, Dad, why didn't you find a home in Tel Aviv or Haifa? Some place on the Mediterranean?"

"Very decadent, Tel Aviv," his father replied. "Yerushelayim? It's holy. People there live with more respect for God."

"Besides," his mother said, "most of the American immigrants live in Yerushelayim. We've met several we know who've moved there."

"Seems like half of Manhattan is planning to move here, what with all the anti-Semitism," Levi Kreko said. "Several of your mom's philharmonic friends say they're coming."

"What about your Wall Street colleagues?" Mosey asked.

"Oh, well, persuading people to leave their source of wealth is like prying open the closed fist of a dead man."

"But *you* left."

"I'm me. This is my story. Our story. Others write their own stories, son. Like you."

Mosey shrugged. "I'd think they might be making a beeline here soon, if not yesterday," he said, "what with everyone blaming the collapse of the stock markets on Jews."

"Plain foolishness," his mother said.

"So were Hitler's claims," Levi reminded his wife. He looked in the rearview mirror at Mosey. "You may be right, Moshe. The hatred alone might drive some of the Wall Street crowd here."

"Well, many others, too," said Sarah. "Haman doesn't discriminate between a rich Jew and a poor Jew."

Mosey recognized his mother was referring to Haman, who had wanted to have all the Jews killed in King Artexerxes's kingdom in the time of Esther, a heroine of Israel.

CHAPTER TWENTY-TWO

Jillian sat beside Darek and across the table from Ty and Bethany at the coffee shop. They had finished the night's broadcast of *Truth Be Told*, delving into the bombings in Boston and Washington, DC, and were trying to relax before a grueling schedule ahead.

She was recalling "our flirtation with death."

"Honey, the guy was just a mugger," Darek said, taking a bite out of a cinnamon scone.

"Well, he's going down in my autobiography as 'a huge devil of a man, brandishing a broad sword and threatening to pluck out our hearts.'" Jillian winked at Bethany.

"Right," Bethany added, "and he was on the One World Government's Ten Most Dastardly List, wanted on five continents for multiple homicides, wasn't he?"

"Darek will be the one on the One World Government's Most Dastardly List if he continues on his path of rebellion," Ty said with a chuckle.

"Now, hold on," Darek objected. "We're getting far astray here. We were talking the lack of safety on the streets."

"True," Bethany said, "but I *do* want to hear about what you're doing to poor Mr. Sardis."

"Call him mister at your own risk, Jess," Darek said. "Pretty soon citizens of the world will be called to genuflect and kiss his ring when in his presence."

"Now, that attitude gets you into trouble with the premier," Ty said. "Have no doubt, those were his goons who followed us everywhere in Jerusalem."

"We'll be all right as long as we don't do anything illegal," Darek said.

"What's legal today may be illegal tomorrow," Ty replied. "At the whim of Caesar. Don't forget Nazi Germany."

"Okay. Okay."

Jillian interjected, "Jess, if the boys will stay on track"— she looked out the corner of her eye first at Darek, and then, Ty—"I want to hear about what happened to you and your car."

Ty changed subjects. "So, Jess, who always scoffs at my concerns for safety, suddenly is rethinking possessing a firearm."

Jillian sucked in air at the revelation and noticed Darek did the same.

"Calamity Jess!" Jillian finally declared.

Bethany laughed. "Well, you can have your fun teasing me, but I've been checking out handguns the last couple of days and I'm leaning toward the latest mini-Glock."

"You *are* serious," Jillian said.

"Sure am. Weighs twelve ounces, has a three and a quarter-inch barrel. Simple to disassemble and clean. And," Bethany's mouth widened, "you know how much I hate cleaning."

Everyone laughed.

"Plus," she added, "I found out the Glock's the weapon of choice of the Washington, DC, Metropolitan Police Department. If Glock's good enough for them, she's good enough for me."

"Guns scare me," Jillian said.

"Me, too. But my friend Mandy was carjacked a couple days ago, so—"

Jillian took Darek's hand. "I can understand. I don't know what I would've done if I'd been alone last night."

"You would've given him your money and your jewelry," Darek said.

"Yes. And what if he had demanded more?"

The idea stopped him short. He hesitated, considering her implications.

"Well, I've got a thought," Ty said. "As Christians, we're opposed to killing people. But a deterrent can be a powerful thing. The mere possession by the United States of nuclear weapons deterred the Soviet Union from attacking us. As a matter of fact, the arms race drove them right into oblivion."

"Right, and there's a town in Texas where everyone is allowed to carry a gun—in fact, they're encouraged to—and the crime rate there is zero," Darek said.

"But," Jillian said, "everyone knows people carry guns there. Russia knew we had nuclear weapons. How is a thief or rapist to know Jess or I have a gun?"

"People, people. I'm not considering this as a deterrent before the fact," Bethany said. She folded her arms. "If Mandy had had a gun in the glove compartment before they robbed her, they still would've stopped the car. But then she could have pulled out her girl"—she folded her arms together like holding a baby—"and scared them off."

"Unless one of them had a gun of their own and shot her," Ty said.

Bethany pursed her lips in thought. "Well, as I said, I'm still considering. I haven't made the purchase yet."

"Well, time's running out for you to make a decision," Darek said. "Sardis wants to ban all sales of weapons to all private citizens in all countries. The Grand Committee is voting on the issue next week."

"Right," Ty said and drank his coffee. "So much for the Second Amendment. I wonder how many other rights we'll relinquish before this is all over."

Mosey looked out at the panoramic view from his parents' plush living room high in the Golden Tower on Rabbi Akiva Street. The Old City loomed beyond the wall of windows before him.

Levi and Sarah Kreko had found their ideal location. Near the Great Synagogue. Near the Old City. In the Holy City and far from "shameful and decadent" Tel Aviv, many of whose residents prided themselves on their hedonism.

The apartment had four bedrooms, four baths, a living room to die for, a dining room that could seat twenty people or serve cocktails to fifty.

How many million did this set them back? Mosey wondered.

Well, the money's theirs to spend. They can't take their fortune with them.

"What are you thinking, dear?" His mother had walked up behind him and placed her hand on his shoulder.

He turned to her. She'd been a beautiful young lady. And still is, especially as I know her heart. His mother would give her life for anyone she cared for, without a second thought. Love bubbled out of her.

Mosey glanced across the room to where a violin stand held her Stradivarius. He knew when Antonio Stradivarius died, he took with him his secrets of making the finest violins.

Mosey didn't want to leave any secrets from his parents as far as salvation was concerned.

"I—I see you're keeping up your, um, music," he stammered.

"Of course, dear. How could I not do so?" She peered at him with the look he knew well from his rebellious teenage years, the stare that said "I'll find out whatever you're hiding."

"But that's not what's on your mind," she said. "You've been distant since we picked you up. There's more than your new friend who died."

"I've got a lot on my mind, Mom." Mosey turned back to look out the window, afraid he'd be lost for words, concerned he'd stumble all over his good intentions, scared, most of all, of rejection.

"Care to share?" she pushed on. Mosey knew his mother. She was relentless. All through his growing up, if something was bothering him, concerning him, troubling him, she'd notice. And when she did, she would not, probably could not, let the problem slide. She would not allow him to hold any crisis, any predicament within himself.

Her motto was: Get the matter out in the open and deal with it.

Finally, Mosey answered, "The question is, do I *dare* to share."

"Dare? Moshe, you've been so secretive about your visit. Is everything all right?"

"Except for my friend and all those other people being killed yesterday."

Sarah Kreko wrapped her arms around him. To the world, he might have seemed like a strong, broad-shouldered young man who never lacked an opinion, whether about finances, psychology, art, or sports—a man to be reckoned with in politics. But to his Mom, he was still her boy. Always would be. The child she bore, breast-fed and raised.

All those times flashed before him. His mother soothing hurt feelings, explaining youthful follies, bandaging banged knees, cooling his fevered face, prepping him for school tests and his bar mitzvah. She had hugged and kissed, encouraged and cajoled, disciplined and fretted over, wept with him in his sorrows, and laughed with him in his joys. Through all the years her love had been unconditional.

But that was about to be tested. Mosey pictured a rag doll tossed in boiling water, thrown into a bowl of ice, withdrawn and filleted. What were the odds of the doll's survival?

His mother stepped back and asked, "Is everything okay between you and Mary? "

"Yes, Mom. I love her more than life."

"Because I want you to know, dear, although we first opposed the marriage, your father and I have grown to love that girl very much. She's a *tokhter*, a daughter, to us."

"I know, Mom."

Sarah pushed on. "Is your health good?"

"Yes, Mom. I'm healthier than ever. Working out at the gym three times a week."

"Your anti-nuclear group?"

"Listen, Mom, there's something I have to talk to you and Dad about together. Once will be enough."

Phew. Once would be more than enough.

Sarah Kreko was puzzled. Her one and only son had always been a complex person. In his youth, he was forever at the top of his class, president of the student body, captain of the soccer team. But golf was his love. And he approached the game as something more than a sport. To him, golf meant personal exchanges, not shooting par. He was fascinated by, and focused on, the fact he gained insights about a person, learned about their character, their integrity in just one round of golf.

After Phillips-Andover Academy, Moshe had chosen Loyola instead of her and Levi's alma mater, Yeshiva University. Levi had rolled out the red carpet for him at his Wall Street business after Moshe finished studies at Oxford, but, no, he'd chosen a confounded "think tank."

In the midst of all this, Moshe had fallen in love with a gentile, despite their best efforts to connect him with some of the most attractive Jewish girls in New York City and beyond. They wanted so much to stop the Jewish assimilation into the world—at least in their own family.

And now this anti-nuclear group. No, Sarah had long ago decided, although he was flesh of her flesh and bone of her bone, she would never understand her own son, completely. Not absolutely.

She heard a door open and Levi call out.

"In the living room," she said.

When his father entered the room, Mosey said a silent prayer, then motioned to the sofa across from him.

He kept his voice solemn, quiet. "I have some news to break to you."

They nodded and sat forward, brows furrowed, eyes full of concern.

It suddenly struck him just how momentous was this moment. Like dropping a nuclear bomb on them—a spiritual one, but nevertheless. Maybe this was a bad idea.

"Go ahead, son," his father urged.

Would the citizens of Nagasaki have asked the bombers to "go ahead?"

Mosey hesitated, breathed deeply, then spotted a copy of the Talmud sitting on an end table.

He reached for the book and said, "I want to read to you from Isaiah, the end of chapter fifty-two through chapter fifty-three."

His father held up a hand. "Son, we know Torah. Just tell us what you want us to know."

"No, Dad, I need to read you this one section." Mosey rifled through the pages of the well-worn holy book, found his place, then started reading.

> See, my servant will act wisely; he will be raised and lifted up and highly exalted. Just as there were many who were appalled at him—his appearance was so disfigured beyond that of any man and his form marred beyond human likeness—so will he sprinkle many nations, and kings will shut their mouths because of him. For what they were told, they will see, and what they have not heard, they will understand.

> Who has believed our message and to whom has the arm of the Lord been revealed? He grew up before him like a tender shoot, and like a root out of dry ground. He had no beauty or majesty to attract us to him, nothing in his appearance that we should desire him. He was despised and rejected by men, a man of sorrows, and familiar with suffering.

Like one from whom men hide their faces he was despised, and we esteemed him not.

Surely he took up our infirmities and carried our sorrows, yet we considered him stricken by God, smitten by him, and afflicted. But he was pierced for our transgressions. He was crushed for our iniquities; the punishment that brought us peace was upon him, and by his wounds we are healed.

We all, like sheep, have gone astray, each of us has turned to his own way; and the Lord has laid on him the iniquity of us all. He was oppressed and afflicted, yet he did not open his mouth; he was led like a lamb to the slaughter, and as a sheep before her shearers is silent, so he did not open his mouth. By oppression and judgment, he was taken away. And who can speak of his descendants? For he was cut off from the land of the living; for the transgression of my people he was stricken.

Mosey glanced up. He had his parents' utter attention. He grabbed a breath and continued.

He was assigned a grave with the wicked, and with the rich in his death, though he had done no violence, nor was any deceit in his mouth. Yet it was the Lord's will to crush him and cause him to suffer, and though the Lord makes his life a guilt offering, he will see his offspring and prolong his days, and the will of the Lord will prosper in his hand.

After the suffering of his soul, he will see the light of life, and be satisfied; by his knowledge my righteous servant will justify many, and he will bear their iniquities. Therefore, I will give him a portion among the great, and he will divide the spoils with the strong, because he poured out his life unto death, and was numbered with the transgressors. For he bore the sin of many and made intercession for the transgressors.

Mosey discerned the shift in his parents' countenances. His father was edgy, his mother apprehensive.

He shut the Torah and set the volume down.

"I don't recall that Scripture, son," his father said.

"It's the only passage the rabbis skip in the daily Haftorah reading," Mosey replied.

"Why would they do such a thing?" his mother asked.

"Well, Mom, do these verses describe someone in particular?"

A moment passed, then Levi Kreko nearly leaped from his chair. A dangerous look came into his eye.

Mosey was startled.

"What are you saying, Moshe?" his father asked, accusation resonating in his voice.

"I'm simply asking, Dad, who does this sound like to you?"

"Like a Messiah who has yet to come!"

"Levi," his mother pleaded, "no reason to raise your voice. Now, please sit down."

Reluctantly, Mosey's father took his seat.

Turning to Mosey, his mother asked, "Tell us, dear, what are you getting at?"

Mosey reached for a satchel beside his chair and pulled out a sheath of pages filled with type.

"Mom, I love you and Dad very, very much, and I am so glad how you brought me up, the values you instilled, the knowledge of the God of Avraham, Yitzak, and Yacob. I would never purposefully do anything to harm you. In fact, I came to share with you good news. But this is good news you probably will not consider good."

"Moshe—" His father had figured out where the conversation was going and wanted to stop Mosey in his tracks.

"Dad, I must continue—"

"Moshe," his father cut him off and leaned forward at the edge of his chair, "do not dishonor—"

"Father, I'd be dishonoring Adonai if I did not accept his sacrifice for me. I'd be spitting in his face if, on the one hand, I knew what he forfeited for me, how he bore my sins and suffered for my transgressions, and yet did not acknowledge his sacrifice."

"Moshe!" his father's voice rose as he took hold of the Torah.

"Go ahead and read the passage, Father. And read what Daniel said about the Messiah. He was to come before the destruction of the Temple. That happened in 70 AD."

"No son of mine—" Mosey's father faltered. "No son of mine will turn his back on his Creator."

"I'm not, Father. I'm embracing him. Receiving my Messiah is the ultimate in Judaism." Mosey felt desperate.

This is not working. This is going terribly wrong, Lord!

His father stood and pointed toward the door. "You've been listening to the father of lies, Moshe. Leave this home until—until you come to your senses!"

There was fire in his father's eyes, crimson in his face, something dangerous in his eyes.

Shaking, Mosey stood up.

His mother jumped to her feet. "No, Levi. No!" she exclaimed.

"Our relatives died in the Holocaust." His father now looked at Mosey's mother. "Our ancestors died in the Crusades. What does this Jesus say to those atrocities?"

She stuttered. Mosey guessed his mother had never needed to search for such an answer. All her life, the cross of Christ had been an abomination to her.

Mosey picked up his satchel and, hand trembling, offered his father the sheath of papers.

"I simply ask you, Father, to read this article by Simon Greenleaf, one of the founders of Harvard Law School."

"And why should I?" His father drew his hand away.

Mosey offered the manuscript again. "Simon Greenleaf was a Jew and the foremost authority on judicial evidence in the 1800s. He set out to disprove Jesus's resurrection—"

"I don't want to hear this. I want you out," his father said. Disgust was on his face as he pointed toward the door.

"But after investigating all the evidence, Simon Greenleaf was converted to Christianity. This is his account of his findings."

"I'll read no such thing." His father stepped out of arm's length from the document.

Mosey set the papers down on the end table. His head hanging, he mumbled, "I'll grab my things from the bedroom and be on my way."

"Moshe!" Pleading, his mother held out her hand toward him. "Levi," she turned to her husband in despair, "do something."

Levi Kreko stood like a rock, his face stern, his lips quivering.

His mother grabbed Mosey's arm. "Moshe, don't go. Let's talk this over."

"Mom, I expected this. I truly did. I've already booked a room—at the Jerusalem Caesar Hotel up the street."

He looked at her tenderly. "I love you." He looked at his father, who had turned back to. "And I love Dad too. But I have to follow the truth. And the truth led me to Yeshua HaMashiach, Jesus the Messiah."

"Oh, no!" his mother's hands flew to her face. She tried to stifle the wailing, but failed.

"Just think on this one point, Mom," Mosey pleaded. "Thousands and millions of people have died for causes they believed were true. But how many have died for causes they knew to be false?"

Her eyes wet with tears, his mother searched blindly for a chair. Her legs were wobbly, and she appeared to feel faint.

Mosey pressed on. "If Jesus had not been raised from the dead, his disciples would have known. And yet all of them died, most in horrific deaths, proclaiming him as Messiah. Why?"

She did not respond.

Mosey grabbed his suitcase from the floor in front of the guest bedroom and, voice cracking, whispered, "Goodbye."

There was no reply, simply a stunned silence from two parents looking noticeably older than thirty minutes earlier. They looked, Mosey thought as he closed the door behind him, as though they were at a funeral.

Mosey decided to walk to his accommodations. His suitcase had wheels, so he could simply walked along, and the satchel was noticeably lighter without the Simon Greenleaf material. He prayed his parents would read Greenleaf's treatise, which was stunning in its clarity.

He would also send them the book, *Betrayed*, when he got back to the States. His parents had to know accepting Yeshua as Messiah wasn't anti-Judaism—rather the most Jewish thing a Jew could do.

His nerves still jittery from adrenaline, his mind churning, Mosey walked slowly along Rabbi Akiva Street to Hillel Street and stepped into Aroma Coffee Shop.

Well-named. He inhaled the pungent tang of coffee grounds. He ordered a steaming cup of java, with a shot of espresso, and dropped into a seat to contemplate his future, and the future of his relationship, or lack thereof, with his parents. His parents, who until now had always supported him in whatever he'd decided to do, even when his choices clashed with their wishes.

Watching young couples walk in hand in hand, take seats and gaze into each other's eyes, Mosey searched for his phone and punched "1."

Two rings later, Mary picked up.

"Darling!" she said when she saw his face. Then "Oh" escaped her lips when she read his expression.

"Operation Messiah?" he said. "The mission was impossible. I'm heading for the Caesar Hotel."

"Oh, Mosey, I'm so sorry. I was praying for you. I was!" Mary shook her head. "Did they listen at all? Even perfunctorily?"

"Partially." Mosey hesitated, depression like an ominous cloud in his mind, an anvil leaden on his shoulders. A half-smile of resignation tugged at the corner of his mouth. "Boy, this trip really stinks."

"Your parents love you beyond belief, Mosey. They'll come around."

"We'll see. I feel like I've been shot out of a cannon, and there was no net to catch me." His mouth wrinkled into a hurt smile.

"What are you going to do?"

"I'll stay tonight, and maybe through tomorrow night at the Caesar, then head home. I'll call you."

"I love you, Mosey, and I miss you."

"Me, too."

He planted a kiss on his index and middle fingers and placed them on the monitor. Mary did the same.

When he finished his coffee, Mosey walked to Jerusalem Caesar, a modest hostel-style business on Jaffa Street. The accommodations certainly weren't like his parents' digs, but, luckily, he was on the top floor of the seven-floor building. He set his suitcase on the king-sized bed and went to the window, discovering a view of the Old City. The sight comforted him to a point. But he ached—dull and relentless—nonetheless.

The next day, Mosey slept late. No calls came from his parents, his watch read 11:13 local time, and when his stomach grumbled, his first thought was of falafels, not breakfast. He gazed out his window at the parapets of the ancient city. Like a magnet, the city of David was drawing him. Tugging. Tugging.

Pulling on an LL Bean windbreaker, he headed out for the Old City and thought through a priority list. At the top was praying for his parents and what better place than at the Western Wall? Plus, he was sure just touching the wall would carry much more impact now he knew the Lord. If he were lucky, the guys who some thought might be the two witnesses would be there.

A pair of IDF soldiers stopped him at a checkpoint on Jaffa Street near Mea Shearim. The stop made sense since the neighborhood was home to the ultra-Orthodox, and a homicide bomber had successfully blown up a score of school children there just a month ago.

Soldiers at a checkpoint on Ben Yehuda Street stopped him again. Again the stop made sense, since homicide bombers had killed so many people on that shop-laden street through the years.

He was stopped yet again, this time by One World Government forces, as he entered the Jaffa Gate to the Old City.

Now, this is ridiculous. I'm wearing a thin jacket, no backpack, nothing bulky to hide a weapon.

Then he thought of the fear and apprehension these people lived in, day in and day out, decade upon decade—ever since their fight for freedom in 1948. Killings piled upon killings, compounded over the years. Palestinian terrorists killed women and children, so the Israel Defense Forces blew up a Palestinian radio station. In response, Palestinian terrorists blew up buses, killing dozens of innocents so the IDF rockets pounded a Palestinian Authority office building into dust.

Each time Palestinian terrorists detonated another flesh-splitting arsenal of nails and bolts, they proclaimed the attack was in revenge for the last Israeli response to terror, usually on Palestinian Authority offices or buildings containing known terrorists.

Now One World Government troops could witness firsthand what Israelis knew intimately.

Ironic in a way.

Soldiers from Norway and Argentina and the Philippines and New Zealand and America—from nations home to all sorts of religions—could see the absurdity of their leaders' claims Israel overreacted to the Arabs' deadly assaults.

If they had eyes to see, they couldn't mistake the imbecility of tiptoeing around mosques that were certainly storehouses of weapons, yet hardly raising an eyebrow when Hamas desecrated the Church of the Nativity; the apostasy of using Jesus Christ's name as a swear word but putting out fatwahs on anyone who impugned the Koran; the bias of a world that didn't protest when Western workers were burned to a crisp, mutilated, hung by their genitals from a bridge, and then displayed in a public square in Iran, yet went ballistic when captured Islamic terrorists were stripped to their underwear in prison and photographed; the dark irony of railing against America for doing security checks on Arabs, yet doing all within their power to emigrate to America.

Mosey thought of his own country's leaders who had screamed at Israel for blowing up buildings housing terrorists—and in Israel's own homeland—yet itself had stormed an entire country and blown up the government to rid the place of terrorists—and that across the world.

Oh, well, who was he to stew about this? He possessed enough concerns in his own little life. He could tackle the issue of the salvation of his parents, the love of his wife, and in his job, derailing nuclear proliferation around the world. Beyond this, he was a powerless peon filled with pointless, weak words and impotent grievances.

Mosey's stomach rumbled, and he headed up King David Street, past the little Christ Church complex in search of a falafel. His hunt ended in a side alley in the Jewish Quarter. The crowds were thick. He realized they must be gathering for the upcoming Feast of Tabernacles.

Christians from around the world came to celebrate, along with Jews whom the Christ-followers considered family. A pain of grief stabbed Mosey. Family. Would his parents truly disown him? Would they hold a funeral or say shiva for him? Would he be able to see them again, to hold them and show his love for them? More important, would they examine the evidence for Messiah themselves?

Mosey munched on his falafel and walked smackdab into a crowd. They were four and five deep, all peering at a huge pile of smoldering rubble. Mosey turned in a circle, getting his bearings.

This—this was where the Church of the Holy Sepulcher stood.

Mosey tugged at the elbow of an older man wearing a Houston Astros baseball cap, figuring he was, well, American.

"What happened?" he asked the guy.

The man tossed his hands in the air. "Blown up!"

"When?"

"Yesterday. Seven o'clock. Same time everything else was blown up."

Mosey took a step back. "Everything else?"

"Where you been, son?" The man shook his head. "All my favorite places in DC. Puff!" He threw up his hands again.

Mosey realized he had been so caught up in Trevor's death and his own life that he hadn't read a newspaper nor watched news reports. He moved away and found a bench to sit down. Contemplating these things, he took a final mouthful of the most delicious falafel he had ever tasted.

Then a commotion arose in the distance, grabbing people's attention all around him. In no time a stream of humanity, with Mosey in the middle, was heading in the direction of the excitement.

Ten minutes later, he and scores of others squeezed past an unmanned security checkpoint—unheard of—and into the courtyard at the Western Wall. There was hardly room to move your arms but Mosey, taller than most, rose up on his toes and got a glimpse of what was causing the tumult.

One World Government troops, rifles held across their chests, formed a line and held back the crowd, creating room for a group of people wearing odd outfits and a couple of tall, bearded men in long robes. Mosey recognized the outfits as those belonging to the hierarchy of the new Church Universal.

How silly. They look like the Nehru suits in old 1960s footage.

The larger of two men dressed in robes looked directly at the Nehru gang and boomed, "The Lord reigns. Let the nations tremble!"

One of the Nehrus said, "By what authority do—"

"By the authority of the Lord of Zion, the only true God, the One who fashioned the universe, the One who knew you, Theodore, in your mother's womb."

"How do you know my name?"

"*Ruach HaKodesh*, the Holy Spirit, knows your name and, more importantly, your heart, Theodore. And yours, Terrance." He looked at another Nehru. "And yours, Paula." He stared at another. "And yours, Henri."

The person who, apparently, was Theodore pointed at him. "You blaspheme the Church Universal and expect to continue unimpeded?"

The second of the two men in robes, whom Mosey figured were the supposed "two witnesses," stepped forward.

"We say nothing in secret, but always here at the site of the ancient Temple. We blaspheme no man's religion. If you question me, where are your witnesses? Bring them forth. We simply state the only way to the Father is through his

311

Son, the Messiah Yeshua. Believe what you want to believe. We speak the truth from him who is the Truth."

Her face turning red, the female Nehru pointed a finger at him and declared in a high-pitched whine, "We have One World Government authority to arrest and jail you."

"You would have no authority at all unless such were granted to you by our Father who is in heaven," replied the smaller of the two witnesses. "And if we wanted, we could call down a legion of angels in our defense."

"Oh, Yerushelayim, Yerushelayim, you who kill the prophets and stone those sent to you!" the first witness called out. The pang of anguish filled his words.

He looked around at the crowd, "Children of God, soon you will see our dead bodies in this Holy City, just as your ancestors saw the Messiah crucified two thousand years ago. When this happens, do not weep for us. Weep for yourselves and for your children. At that time, you will say, 'Blessed are the women who are barren, the breasts that never nursed.'"

The din of the crowd rose an octave. More and more people crowded their way through the alleyway into the courtyard, tightening the grip on everyone. Mosey was astonished the voices of two—*were they ordinary?*—men could amplify over such a distance.

The second witness took over. "Yochanan the Beloved foretold through his vision what those living in the Last Days would experience. Like a witch's cauldron teeming with fetid animal parts, this world is overflowing with hatred, hypocrisy, lewdness, debauchery, persecution, and spiritual filth. And billions who believe the lie die in a fantasy filled with promises of paradise. The men dream of devouring seventy-two virgins. The women expect luxury on clouds of peace.

"Look around the world and you see the signs—a One World Government promising peace. But evil men—in groups of highwaymen and armies of terrorists—prove this dream a lie. In some places, a quart of wheat consumes a day's wages. On nearly every continent, crops die in the fields, either scorched by heat and drought, flooded by monsoons, withered by disease, or devoured by pests."

He waved a hand in the direction of the Nehrus, then continued, "Men create something called Church Universal, supposedly dedicated to peace, and yet here are their representatives, threatening to jail two prophets of the God they claim to honor. Remember, judgment begins in the house of the Lord. Beware if you think you are that house!"

Theodore, face red and eyes blazing, bellowed, "Guards! Guards, take these men!"

A handful of guards standing behind the Nehrus stepped toward the two witnesses, but the witnesses moved toward the Dung Gate. Like a swinging door, the crowd split, allowing them passage. Some appeared to fall over backward at their approach.

The guards strove to catch up to them, but the crowd closed its ranks. In moments, the two witnesses disappeared out the gate, a big shepherd dog joining them.

Left behind, in the midst of the crowd, were the guards and the contingent of flummoxed Nehrus from One World Religion.

What must they be thinking? Mosey wondered. Their eyes were wide, their brows furrowed, their hands peevishly on hips.

Ha! Two guys looking like they came out of the first century had handled twenty-first-century *moderns* with such ease, then vanished like vapor.

In the crowd, murmurs took on a tone of anxiety.

313

Mosey heard fractured sentences all around him.

"Did you … them mention … End Times?"

"They … called the … Universal the modern-day Pharisees … Jesus' time."

"Judgment … house of the Lord."

"Killing prophets?"

"Are they … witnesses?"

The guards formed a wedge in front of the Nehrus and escorted them in the direction of Dung Gate, farther and farther from where Mosey stood.

Insults were hurled in their direction. Calls of "Antichrist!" and "Apostates!" reverberated in the courtyard.

Then those calls were answered by shouts of "Apostates wouldn't want peace!" and "You're the evil ones!"

A sudden tussling broke out. People pushed people and less-than-Christian epithets were exchanged.

"God will condemn you."

"He'll condemn you first!"

"Heretic."

"Liar and thief!"

"What did you call me?"

"You deaf as well as stupid?"

Mosey was stunned, watching two women scream in each other's face. One slapped the other, knocking her hat off her head. The now hatless woman looked at the other, stuck out her jaw, and turned her cheek. Her adversary slapped her other cheek. Then the hatless one swung a haymaker at her.

Nearer by, two men began punching one another while a woman tried to break them up.

Mosey angled his way toward the back of the courtyard opposite the Western Wall. He wanted no part of any altercation. He was attempting to recall what the two witnesses had said. This was one of those moments he wished he carried a tape recorder around with him. He scanned the crowd looking or a cameraman.

Scores of people held their cell phones over their heads, recording the scene. The episode certainly would make the evening news.

High atop the Western Wall, two cameras were fastened to the Jerusalem stone, but they weren't news cameras. Their operator could scan the scene below, zoom in on any area to get a closer image, and pick up conversations with a boom microphone.

Standing behind him in a dark control room, on the second floor of the Church Universal headquarters several miles away from the Western Wall, His Excellence, Church Universal General Secretary Howard Alphonse Bliss stood behind the camera controller. His six-foot-two frame was knotted in a ball of anger. He ran his fingers through his blond hair and gritted his teeth.

He turned, stormed out the door and rode the elevator to his office. Ignoring greetings from Owandu and Ravi Chettri, his secretary and his personal assistant, Bliss burst through his office door and went to a red phone—a high-security instrument. He punched a button, and the person he was calling picked up almost immediately.

"Our problem just got worse," he said.

Sitting in his office in Brussels, Premier Sardis scrutinized the agonized face of his comrade. "Let's talk, my friend."

Most of the stifling crowd had left the courtyard. Mosey had studied their faces and, best as he could, listened to their conversations as they departed. English and Spanish he understood. The others—gibberish. A few wondered out loud if the two outspoken men had caused the destruction of the Church of the Holy Sepulcher.

One man said to another in low tones, "What's so great about those guys? Anyone could stand up there and spout off."

Another man who looked Middle Eastern groused to a companion, "Where's a good sharpshooter when you need one? They could take out both those guys with two swift shots."

A group of very Western-looking women—very churchy-looking, Mosey thought—mumbled excitedly among themselves about personally seeing prophets of God. What a wonderful experience this whole tour had been, and what a way to end it!

One elderly lady said to a man who appeared to be her husband, "That wasn't very Christian of the Church Universal people. Why, they wanted to arrest those men."

Her husband replied, "They're *not* Christian, Mildred. They're living proof if you stand for nothing you'll fall for anything."

Mildred looked at him questioningly.

Mosey chuckled, and the man looked at him and smiled. Then the idea struck Mosey. This all occurred in what remained of the Jewish people's most holy place. A confrontation between good and evil, wicked intent versus God's truth.

He gazed up at the Western Wall and knew why the structure was also called the Wailing Wall. If you had God's heart, you'd be compelled to wail and weep over what lay within men's hearts.

Starting with my own heart, so dark and bitter against so many people.

Mosey walked slowly to the Wall, pulled his yarmulke out from his rear pocket and placed the covering atop his head. At the Wall, he reached a hand out and touched the rough stone. Stuffed between its many stones were myriad little slips of rolled-up paper containing prayers and supplications from around the world.

Mosey pondered the bitterness he held for Stephen Russell and the other Alliance board members, how much he disliked those who developed nuclear bombs and spread potentially dangerous technology just to make a buck, and how simple things upset him.

How frail was his Christianity? Weak as overcooked spaghetti. What sort of witness was he? A poor one. What had he done to deserve salvation? Nothing. Nothing? Right, nothing.

Mosey pressed his body against the Wall, his face lifted high, and raised his arms toward the sky.

Oh, Lord, such a sinner am I!

Suddenly, as if watching a film on fast-forward, Mosey saw snippets from his life, sins committed from childhood to adulthood. Fast-frame forward: stealing swim trunks from a store, worn under his jeans. Fast-frame forward: peeking a look at a classmate's math exam. Fast-frame forward: taking a stoke. Fast-frame forward: sleeping with this girl and that one out of wedlock. Fast-frame forward: Lying to a Congressional hearing—a white lie, but a lie nonetheless, for a "good cause." Fast-frame after fast-frame, he saw sins, big and little; sins he'd long forgotten; sins he'd not even considered sins at the time he'd committed them.

He realized the Holy Spirit was showing him although he thought he was a good person deserving of salvation, he was nothing of the sort. Tears pouring down his face, Mosey opened his eyes and called out, "How great a salvation, Lord!"

At that moment he saw the vision. The face of Jesus Christ, Yeshua HaMachiach, bigger than life, hovered before him. Smiled at him. Love filled his eyes.

Oh, such love!

Though Jesus' mouth did not move, Mosey heard him say, "Moshe. Moshe. I love you. You stand sinless before me. Your sins were washed away at Golgotha, cast away as far as the east is from the west. You are set free. Simply go and share the Good News. Beware evil and persecution, but my angels are watching over you."

As quickly as he had appeared, Jesus vanished.

Mosey, his eyesight clouded by tears, looked around to see if others had seen Jesus. Obviously, the apparition was his alone.

Was his mind playing tricks? He looked back up at the stones rising above him. No. No tricks. Phew! The import of what had just happened took his breath away and he placed his hands against the Wall, trying to grasp what he had seen and heard, to embrace his Savior.

CHAPTER TWENTY-THREE

Within two weeks after the initial bombings, Hisey Brinks, with Norine at his side, had finished the mayhem in DC, completing the alphabet of targets—*J, T, D* and *A*— the Jefferson Monument, Ten Commandments Monument, Department of State, and National Archives. All had paid homage to God in some way or other, a sign of God's hand on America throughout the country's history. Now the monuments were history themselves.

At the National Archives, the Ten Commandments had been embedded in the building's entryway. No more entryway.

At the Department of State building, the Seal of the United States had been emblazoned on one side with the bald eagle holding an olive branch and thirteen arrows; and on the reverse side the words "Annuit coatis," meaning "He has favored our undertakings." No more.

On the Jefferson Memorial, quotations had declared thanksgiving to God. No more.

And the Ten Commandments Monument? Well, enough said.

Ha!

Brinks's self-satisfaction was almost palpable.

As he and Norine stepped out of a cab at Dulles International Airport to catch an airplane headed to Paris, he rubbed his hands together in anticipation of spending four million bucks on his own cause for a change. "Well, No-No, onward and upward. Sure you're with me?"

Sliding out of the back seat, Norine looked at him, and with a tantalizing grin, replied, "Oh, yeah. All the way."

Taking their luggage from the cabby, Brinks turned to Norine. "No more ramming whaling ships or sinking fishing boats, No-No. We're going big-time."

Hisey's head swirled with visions of oil-drilling rigs, meat-packing factories, logging-company headquarters, large retail and housing developments, and power projects— all being blown to smithereens, of course. None were beyond the bounds for Hisey's operatives. They were trained at the hand of al-Qaida in Niger and Chad. While their co-trainees were financed, trained, and indoctrinated by religious authorities from Saudi Arabia and Pakistan—and looked askance at them as outsiders—they'd proven they were good, very competent indeed, at their job.

And now his troops had marching orders for the next round of mayhem, forcing mankind to get right with Mother Nature.

CHAPTER TWENTY-FOUR

TWO MONTHS LATER

Holding high-level meetings at the Washington, DC, Metropolitan Police's Joint Operations Command Center, the Homeland Security terrorist experts were confounded. They'd been unable to prevent any of the bombings. No organization had taken credit for any of them. They felt certain Icky Coffman was behind the destruction in America, although they'd been unable to capture him. And they'd been unsuccessful connecting the bombings in the US to those elsewhere, which now included two at the Vatican that leveled much of the Sistine Chapel and the adjoining St. Peter's Basilica.

Homeland Security's Clarity Lion had been proven to be a lamb in this circumstance.

In fact, the entire crime-fighting community around the world—from One World Government's high-technology International Security Agency to the seven regions' individual intelligence-gathering units—were proven inept at tracking Hisey Brinks, let alone arresting him. Driven by hatred and underpinned by high finances transferred from one numbered Swiss bank account to another, his meetings with comrades were wrapped in utter darkness.

Like this meeting tonight in Hamburg, Germany. The two figures were silhouettes, really, in the shadows of a park. They had come to this spot in the middle of the green space, away from prying streetlamp cameras and boom mike listening devices.

Hisey sauntered there from one direction. He looked at a towering clock on the street about fifty yards away. One o'clock in the morning—the appointed time. An insomniac, he was used to late-night strolls like this. This was a great time to formulate plans. Few people, little noise, and no bleepin' kids running around.

He spotted a figure approaching from the opposite direction. This must be the guy. A short, thin man dressed in black, wearing a fedora and a black raincoat with collar upturned.

"Hot night," the man said.

"Not where I come from."

"You here on vacation?"

"No. I'm here to make heat hotter, darkness darker."

"Then you've come to the right place," the man said. "I can help you make that happen."

Hisey looked about. They were the only people in the park. Where they stood was so dark neither man could very well see the other's face, but from what Hisey could discern, the man resembled a skeleton. No matter. Words were what counted.

"We understand you've been trained on weaponry to take down airplanes," the man said.

"Top of my class." A mixture of pride and swagger dripped from Hisey's lips.

"Five million dollars, my friend. Half now, half when the job's done."

"What, exactly, is 'the job'?"

"You've heard of Darek and Jillian Fields?"

Jake MacMillan read the account of a massacre of Christians in a Sudanese village in a *Voice of the Martyrs* newsletter and threw the pages angrily onto his desk in his study.

Islam, a religion of peace! He screamed in his head. American president after American president since September 11, 2001 had drum-beaten this statement into people's heads, even hosting Ramadan dinners. World heads of state, United Nation's leaders, and now One World Government and Church Universal spokesmen had hammered home this message.

And now, how could anyone believe this propaganda? Despite the evidence, the beheadings, the assassinations, the scores of bombings, the kidnappings and slavery of non-Muslims, the crucifixions. Despite the hate-mongering rhetoric from imams in mosques even inside democratic countries like America, England, and France calling for the overthrow of those countries.

And when had the Islamists ever once offered apologies for the extremist elements of their religion or condolences to the untold thousands of murdered, maimed, and tortured victims?

Now was the time to not simply report these atrocities one at a time as news stories, but to expose the black heart of the beast with a hammer of Jake's own—his newspaper, cable network and web site.

Jake picked up his phone and called Darek and Jillian Fields.

Darek's face appeared. "Jake," he said, "how you doing, sir?"

"Darek, my boy ..."

"Uh-oh," Darek responded.

"Uh-oh?"

"Whenever you start a conversation with 'Darek, my boy,' I know the second shoe is already falling."

Jake laughed. "Well, I guess you're right. "Son, I seem to recall the Pulitzer you won was for a series about Islamic terrorists."

"True."

"Well, then, do I have a story for you."

Two days later, Darek and Jillian were on a flight to Brussels. From there they'd fly to Rome to interview One World Government and Vatican officials about persecution of Christians around the world, including crucifixions from Sudan to Malaysia and points in between. Afterwards, they'd visit survivors of attacks in Nigeria and Sudan.

Darek had asked Jillian to return to the States when they were to travel on to Africa. The request was for her own safety, he said, but she refused.

No surprise there.

Except for the flight crew, they were flying alone until they reached Africa because neither Premier Sardis nor the Vatican's Secretariat of State would allow cameras into their interviews. Ty and a cameraman were on another plane to South America and Asia, and their itinerary would include interviews with Christian and Jewish leaders as well as victims of terror.

Flying over the Atlantic Ocean and surfing the internet, Darek let out a gasp.

Across from him, Jillian looked up from notes she was pouring over and tossed a strand of hair from her eyes. "What's the matter?"

"The latest from our friendly American government. At the, ah, urging of our other friends—the ones we're about to visit at One World Government—the Alliance now basically has a place at the table at US Congressional hearings."

"Oh, my." Jillian sat up straight. After a moment's reflection, she said, "Well, I guess we shouldn't be surprised. Can anything really astonish us anymore?"

"Listen to this," Darek said. "Stephen Russell of Gay Rights Resolve will be called as an expert witness on legislation dealing with LGBTQ-plus issues, including marriages the courts have commanded every state to make lawful. Mosey Kreko of Advocates for a Nuclear-Free World will testify about all nuclear issues. And Tanya Frizzell of Citizens for Free Abortions has been named to an ad hoc committee on late-term abortions, a committee on which Right-to-Life groups are not allowed to serve."

"Talk about going places!" Jillian said. "A few years ago these people would beg for a hearing. Now it's being handed to them."

"Right. Let's go through the rest of the Alliance board," Darek said, ticking them off on his fingers. "Peter Whitetree, chief of the Indian Lands Reclamation Federation, will be called to testify in Native American Indian matters. Heck, he's already the go-to guy for all the networks whenever a news story deals with Indians. Buddy Joe Tatum and Angela Freeman are the Jesse Jacksons of the 21st century. Did you hear Buddy Joe rhyming his declarations for black rights at the Black Power March the other day?"

Jillian nodded and Darek continued, mentioning the head of the Society for All Lifestyles and editor of *MEAT* magazine,

"Even Roger Clapp is seen on the Public Broadcasting System, being interviewed as an expert on all the new types of families and relationships. Gay-and-gay, bisexual-and-gay, bisexual-and-bisexual, transgender-and-bisexual, transgender-and-transgender, man-child, woman-child."

"Hey, you missed sadomasochist-dominatrix," Jillian deadpanned.

"Don't laugh. That's on next week's agenda," Darek said.

Jillian laughed ruefully, then turned serious. "Darek, I know you have no anxiety about meeting with Sardis. But I'm afraid. I remember the darkness in his eyes, and the chill in the room, when he unceremoniously dismissed us in Rome. I was shocked he agreed to interview with us again, frankly.

"Me, too.

"But the more power he gets, the more he appears untouchable. We know he hates Truth Publishing, but he has to deal with us. What happens when he feels above and beyond demands for media appearances?"

"I don't think Sardis has ever seen a camera he didn't like," Darek replied. "Just think. He's a master manipulator and he uses the media—all of us—to do his manipulation."

Darek interlocked his fingers and pushed his palms together, forming a ball. "He and the media are like a snug little group of co-enablers. He allows us all into his space, and we allow him access to, basically, the entire world."

He held up his interlocked hands. "Here's Sardis in the middle." He lifted the middle finger of his right hand. "And he is surrounded by CNN, MSNBC, Fox, the AP, Reuters, Truth, the New York Times, London Times, Tokyo Shimbun, Pravda ..." One by one, Darek had lifted all his fingers and thumbs as he named the news outlets. He looked at Jillian. "Remove your audience and you lose your power ..."

"... Especially when your charisma somehow impresses and confounds most of the world," Jillian finished his thought.

"Right."

"So, tell me, why have us surveilled?"

"If the guys following us were Sardis's goons, and not Bliss's, the tail could have simply been to keep tabs on us. Hey, they have all these people working for them, they might as well give the guys something to do." Darek smiled. "How else would they earn a wage?"

Jake finished his editorial with a flourish, looking like Liberace at his piano. He read the last two paragraphs out loud.

> Displaying the Ten Commandments ostensibly offends those who are otherwise un-offensible. The sight of aborted children doesn't offend them. They run over each other to get into the latest slice-and-dice horror movie. They snap up the newest songs filled with trash-talking, rape-inducing, Jew-killer-inciting lyrics. They cheer the Set-Free Parades as the sexually fluid, strut half-naked down Lexington Avenue and Market Street, Dykes on Bikes bare their breasts, and grown men tug along boys on dog leashes. They are unfazed by lewdness, crudeness, and assorted uncouthness. Immersed in filth, they are—excuse me—nevertheless offended by the Ten Commandments?

> Oh, yes, America and, indeed, the world should accede to Premier Sardis's wishes and get those

confounded *suggestions* entirely out of public view
... before something good happens.

Jake grabbed his meerschaum and stood to look out the
window at the harbor and the people walking by on the wharf
across the street. He snapped a match alive and lit the bowl of
cherry blend. He felt like the Boston Celtics' Red Auerbach
lighting a cigar at the end of an especially satisfying victory.

Blowing the sweet aroma into the air, he noticed Dan
Cowan, his business editor, driving into the Truth Publishing
parking lot, with Andrea Page at his side.

Ah, here is where we put the evidence to the test.

After more than six months of investigation, Dan and
Andrea had compiled an avalanche of documentation, they
said, incontrovertibly proving the Chinese had caused the
worldwide economic down-spike. Now China was in a
position to cash in her chips, so to speak, and take a dominant
role in every single stock market around the world. China
was the one country that hadn't kowtowed to the One World
Government. China was the one thorn in the flesh of Premier
Sardis.

Odd, an evil country opposing an evil world government.
Hmm.

This was a huge story as much for what the facts revealed
as false as for what they unveiled as true. First, for all the
conspiracy theories swirling around the Bilderbergers—and
many of them were indeed true—concerning manipulations
of economies and governments and social movements, the
secret organization had not caused this specific Black Tuesday.
Their members themselves were, in fact, reeling, many losing
massive fortunes.

Second, from pundits to hate mongers, many headline-grabbers around the world had declared "without doubt" Jews were at fault. In countries at the four corners of the earth and in between, more and more voices—even many who normally were even-handed and above reproach—joined the chorus, proclaiming Jews were at fault for bringing the world's stock markets to their knees.

After all, wherever Jews lived, they were in leadership positions in the financial world. How did one explain such a phenomenon? A fraction of one percent of the world's population, and they controlled financial institutions of all sorts and even headed government and quasi-government agencies dealing with money. How such a minute number of people could wield such great power seemed impossible to fathom.

Synagogues the world over had been fire-bombed, rabbis and their families beaten and tortured. Just the week before, several wealthy businessmen and financiers in Argentina had been dragged out of their homes and into a city park, where they were summarily hanged on adjacent trees by hooded men who dressed shockingly like the Ku Klux Klan members of America's dark times.

Jake cringed just thinking about the hatred. Even in the United States three days before, senators from Minnesota, Wisconsin, Vermont, Michigan, and North Dakota had coauthored a proclamation laying the blame at the feet of Jews. The decree had not yet passed but had gained momentum, with several senators from both parties joining as co-signatories.

Jake thought of the verse in Genesis 12:3: "I will bless those who bless My people, but those who curse them I shall curse."

A few minutes later, Dan and Andrea walked across the newsroom floor. Jake saw them coming and smiled at the satisfied looks on their faces. Dan was in his forties and had never been married. With an MBA and a lot of money in his pocket, he had left a promising Wall Street career to do what he loved—write.

Andrea was in her late-30s and was widowed with a teenage son, having lost her husband in the war on terrorism in Iraq. She had found raising a boy on her own difficult, especially when he reached puberty.

Dan had become a part of their lives—and a wonderful influence on the boy—in this last year.

Jake waved them in, and they all sat down in chairs around the massive coffee table. Dan set down and opened a large briefcase filled with notebooks and stacks of Excel-looking readouts.

He looked at Jake with a half-smile and declared, "Evidence."

"Ah-ha!" Jake answered. "Tell me everything."

The unmarked Truth Publishing and Broadcasting jet settled down at Brussels Airport and taxied to an area reserved for private aircraft.

After two hours in customs limbo, Darek and Jillian said their goodbyes to Marsha and the LaFlamme brothers and took a taxi to Hotel Le Plaza in the center of Brussels' Rue Neuve shopping district just a few blocks from the One World Government headquarters.

An hour later, bushed, hungry, and realizing they had to catch up the six-hour time difference, they arrived in front of their hotel. Waving aside the bellman, Darek hauled their two carry-on-size suitcases from the trunk of the taxi, and he and Jillian stepped into the hotel lobby. Spying the registration desk, they made their way past couches in a conversation area and through a jumble of people in small groups speaking various languages.

"Monsieur and Madam Fields!" The strong French accent belonged to a tall, nattily dressed man stepped up to them. He tipped his hat to Jillian and addressed them both: "My name is Henri Sebastian. I am a friend of Jake MacMillan's."

He shook hands with Darek, then bent to kiss Jillian's hand before raising himself back up. "Jake and I were speaking on the phone just a few moments ago, and he mentioned you two were arriving about now," he said. "I was in my branch office and heading out to dinner, so I thought I'd meet you here and invite you to be my guests. There is a wonderful restaurant in my hotel and it's just a three- or four-minute walk."

Darek and Jillian exchanged glances, agreeing this could be an interesting tête-à-tête.

"We'd enjoy dining with you, sir," Darek said. "But this may be a quick evening for us. We're both pretty tired."

"It's Henri, please, and I understand."

Darek glanced at the registration desk behind which stood three clerks, and in front one guest. "Good. I'll just get us registered, have our things sent to our room, and be right with you."

"We'll take a seat on the couch here," Jillian said, and she and Henri sat down together.

Walking to the registration desk, Darek pulled out his phone and punched Jake's number. Jake's face appeared after one ring.

Darek spoke first, "Henri Sebastian."

331

"My good friend," Jake said.

"All I need to know," Darek said.

"Remember," Jake said, "if you need any help at all, ring up Deke Brewster at our bureau there. But, if it's anything cultural or social, Henri will be a useful acquaintance."

Darek had ceased to be amazed at the wide variety, and proximity, of friends Jake had around the world. Whether he and Jillian were in Jakarta, Tokyo, Melbourne, or Johannesburg, Jake often called ahead to a friend to be on the alert and available if help were needed.

Darek checked in and walked back to the lounge area. Jillian was obviously enjoying herself, a wide grin playing on her pretty face. *A suave Frenchman and my girl. I oughta be jealous.*

Henri was about Jake's age, Darek guessed, and appeared very much like the sophisticated Charles Boyer of filmdom.

Jillian looked up, eyes sparkling. "Henri was telling me about his grandchildren. Five of them."

"Enough for a team of, ah, basquetball," Henri laughed.

"Basquetball?" Darek smiled at the pronunciation.

"Oui!"

Jillian and Henri stood, and the three of them walked out of the hotel and along the boulevard.

"The city is breathtaking," Jillian gasped.

The Rue Neuvre shopping area was modern, all-glass. But all around were buildings that were sometimes splendid, sometimes homely. Medieval and futuristic huddled elbow to elbow. Magnificent fifteenth-century structures with little statues scattered about. Stunning seventeenth-century buildings with golden inlays. All monuments to their architects' creativity or lack thereof.

"The sights are many here," Henri agreed in his excellent but heavily accented English, "never boring—whether you speak of architecture, people, business, or, and especially, politics."

"I've been here only once, and this is Jillian's first time," Darek said. "It's amazing to us Americans, I think, to see so much activity in a foreign city. If these were skyscrapers all around us, this could be New York City with all the hustle and bustle."

"A New York City with class, eh?" Henri smiled. "Oui. Brussels is the second international city in the world, if you gauge it by the number of headquarters of international organizations. And about one-third of its one million inhabitants are foreigners, like me—mostly expatriate business people and diplomats."

"Yes," Darek said, "I'll bet with NATO and the European Union headquartered here—"

"As well as your friends at One World, eh?" Henri added with a twisted smile.

"Yes. Them, too."

"Flexing their muscles." Henri hesitated. "When were you here last, Darek?"

"Two thousand-sixteen."

"Then you haven't seen the new One World Government headquarters?"

"No."

"Oh-oh-oh!" Henri said, his voice rising mischievously. "Premier Sardis actually wanted to take over the Palais Royal, the Royal Palace. To move right in." Henri swept his hand upward in a flourish. "When the king bristled at the thought, Sardis appeared shocked, then came up with a better idea."

"Right," Jillian joined in, "build in the park across the street."

Henri smiled remorsefully. "Correct, Jillian, in Le Parc de Bruxelles, Brussels Central Park. What once was a huge and beautiful park is now half-consumed by this, this—" he gave his hands a dramatic upward wave—"modern monster of darkness."

Henri's voice had risen and he stopped abruptly, obviously checking to see if anyone had heard him. Putting a finger to his lips, he said, "Mustn't speak in any way against the world premier around here, eh?"

Darek spotted someone across the street and stopped in his tracks. Jillian and Henri pulled up short.

"What is it?" Jillian asked.

"Speak of being watched and listened to. Look! Our friends, Pascual and Cruz."

They followed Darek's direction. Two men, medium-sized, one shorter than the other, dressed in black suits with black ties, one wearing a fedora, pretended an intense discussion, one pointing at a statue of a little boy peeing.

"This is not coincidence," Jillian said.

"Well, their appearance seems to answer our question of whether they work for Sardis or Bliss," Darek said.

"Who are these men?" Henri asked.

"Let's walk on, and we'll tell you all about them," Darek replied. They turned and proceeded on their way.

A minute later, as they entered the Métropole Hotel, Henri smiled and said, "Perhaps Pascual and Cruz would like to join us for dinner."

"Yeah, but they can take another table," Darek deadpanned.

"And they can pay their own bill," Jillian exhaled as she examined the splendor around her. The main entrance where they stood was all French Renaissance frivolity. Before them was an Empire-style reception hall replete with gold stained glass windows. Huge, glittering chandeliers sparkled with reflected light above the lobby.

Jillian turned to Henri. "This is where you stay?"

"Oui."

"It's stunning."

"And perfectly located," Henri said. "Very near where I work, in the midst of Brussels' historical center, just steps from the Grand Palace and the Bourse. And if you enjoy plays, very near the Theatre de la Monnaie. But come, let's dine."

Henri directed them to follow him.

Moments later, they found themselves at the hotel's restaurant, Alban Chambon, very old European—more chandeliers and mirrors galore. As the maître d' seated them at a corner table, soft piano music filtered in from a bar next door.

Five minutes later, glasses of Pinot Noir before them, they settled into conversation.

"Very busy here," Darek noted.

"Dining out is a national pastime in Belgium," Henri said with a laugh. "Wonderful food is everywhere. Some say the best is in restaurants with rickety furniture, tiled floors and globe lights. Much like your New Orleans, eh? At least before the hurricane.

"Wonderful food whether you pay a fortune or a modest price. But, here, I enjoy Alban Chambon. And because I live here when I'm in Brussels, they are always nice enough to pass me to the front if there are lines and waiting. Their ravioli of langoustine with wild mushrooms and white sauce is fabulous, and, if you like lamb—" Henri smacked a kiss to his fingertips—"Chef Dominique's fried lamb fillet with mint tabbouleh is marvelous."

Over dinner, Henri revealed he was an importer-exporter of wines and lived in the town of Montpeyroux, in the foothills of the Pyrenees south of Paris. "A mere speck on the map, near Gignac, a little larger speck on the map," he said. "But our wine is the lifeblood of the earth."

He had met Jake and Dawn MacMillan many years ago when they were traveling through France.

"They came to visit an old Roman fort near our town. In the village, they stopped and asked directions. I invited them to the warm and welcoming home of some current inhabitants—my wife, Christine, and me—rather than visit the crumbled fort of former conquerors." Henri's smile was wistful, mixed with melancholy and sadness. "I introduced them to Christine, and we together introduced them to some excellent Bordeaux. We've been friends ever since. We were so sad to hear of Dawn's death. At the time, my own Christine was in hospital dying of cancer, and so we couldn't travel to the funeral."

He hung his head. "Wonderful woman. Two wonderful women. So sad."

"We're sorry to hear of your loss, Henri," Darek said. *How could this man be so jubilant, so lively, even though the love of his life had died?*

Jillian put her hand on Henri's arm. "A difficult time."

"Difficult, oui." Henri looked Jillian in the eye. "But we will have a glorious future, eh? In heaven with our Lord, eh?"

"Eh," she agreed, and they exchanged smiles. And the answer to Darek's question was like a neon sign.

Over dinner, Darek asked Henri his thoughts on the One World Government's lack of action to protect Christians, Jews, and Hindus around the world from Muslim attacks.

Henri glanced around the room. "You see the people in here? They're indicative of Brussels as a whole. One-third are foreigners, and most of those foreigners are either Islamic immigrants or diplomats—some Islamic diplomats. This situation is not just Brussels, but everywhere Muslims have moved.

"We French, we have small families, eh? One child, two perhaps. You Americans—one child, maybe two—if you make a mistake. Ha! But they ... they have five, six, seven children."

Henri raised an arm at elbow length above his head as if trying to hold down a balloon intent on floating to the ceiling.

"Now, the premier," he said, "he knows this and he's aware most of the imams are preaching worldwide conquest. En route to their goal, they'll kill Christians, Jews, and Hindus. This is not opinion but fact. Here's the intriguing point. From the Premier's viewpoint, why stop them? The fewer religious people, the better for a One World Government that prefers secularism to reign."

Darek interrupted. "Are you saying Sardis is simply allowing one of his enemies to destroy others of his enemies?"

"Ah-ha!" Henri said. "You're ahead of me, eh?"

"No, just trying to keep up."

"Just think," Henri continued. "Once Christians, Jews, and Hindus are depleted in numbers, the premier can more easily handle the rascally problem of the Muslims."

"But what about Church Universal and Sardis's connection to Bliss and his people?" Jillian asked.

"Sardis holds only one thing sacred—himself," Henri replied. "He'll use Church Universal for his purposes, then drain its power. And Bliss might well stand with him."

"I get the idea," Darek said. "Say you had a backyard full of ticks. You send out a few guinea hens to gobble them up, then you can roast the guinea hens."

"Exactly," Henri said. "Or, like gathering all your prey in one thicket rather than scattering them throughout the forest."

"I don't particularly care to be compared to a tick or prey," Jillian said with a laugh, "but I understand your point. Let the Muslims do your dirty work, then take care of them. At the same time, let Church Universal absorb the mainline religions, then you can take out just one group—Church Universal—instead of a dozen."

"Much less convoluted," Darek said.

Henri nodded and popped the last mushroom on his plate into his mouth.

The next morning was drenched in sunlight, so Jillian and Darek decided to walk to One World Government headquarters. Amid streams of people, many speaking French or Dutch but various other languages sprinkled about, they absorbed the Gothic architecture; the ornate, columned front of La Bourse, the stock exchange; and the grounds of the Royal Palace, bordered only by a low fence.

"Ah, here we are," Darek said.

Jillian followed his eyes and was impressed by what she saw. Across the street, a shining sphere of pewter seemed to shoot out of a low, curving, bronze-colored structure. The bronze building, two stories high, wound back into what was left of Brussels Central Park. The pewter sphere was a dozen stories high.

"From the air this looks like a very fat serpent, slithering along the ground like a snake—lots of curves," Darek said.

"It certainly overshadows the king's little place of business," Jillian said, nodding toward the Royal Palace. She pointed to the sphere. "And the viper's probably ensconced in the tippity-top floor of that thing, right?"

"No doubt. Let's find out."

At a traffic light, Jillian grabbed his hand, and they crossed the Place des Palais, then strolled across a wide walkway centered with a huge fountain spurting a high spiral of water in the middle and numerous tiny plumes all around. A slight breeze carried the fountain water in a spray cooling the area.

Circling the fountain and walking toward the building before them, Jillian squeezed Darek's hand as they stepped inside the One World Government headquarters.

The word *foyer* did not describe the room before them. One word that did define the circular space about eighty feet across—*sterile*. In the center, a young woman sat behind a large semicircular desk with three monitors.

Beyond her desk, a metal detector and image screener fronted a glass elevator, bracketed by two men on each side. No furniture or plants spoiled the room's pristine character.

There was no ceiling or was there? No second, third, or fourth floor. No fifth, sixth or seventh floor. The space above them seemed to ascend all the way to the top floor. Darek turned to Jillian and said quietly, with a touch of awe, "Sardis's office must be the only thing in this entire rotunda."

Jillian nodded. She looked up. "What's that?" She pointed.

High above, several objects hung in the air. She looked more closely, and identified the flags of the nations—each one suspended by itself and moving counterclockwise.

What were the flags doing? she wondered.

Then she got her answer. In the middle of the rotunda, stationary and much larger than the country flags, was the One World Government flag. A dragon shot flames out of its mouth and held an olive branch in one talon-fingered paw and a scroll in the other. The country flags rotated around the dragon, like a model of the solar system with planets circling the sun.

"So this is the center of the solar system," Jillian noted.

"Always wondered about that," Darek said. "And I thought it was St. Andrews, Scotland, the home of golf."

She elbowed him.

A sudden influx of people from the street jostled them. They stepped to the reception desk. Nodding to the receptionist, Darek said, "We have an appointment with the premier. Darek and Jillian Fields."

The girl smiled, oh-so-calmly pushed a key on a keyboard in front of her, and, on the flat-screen monitor before her, followed a manicured finger to the time of day. She turned to another monitor to her right and typed in the name "Darek Fields."

A photograph of Darek popped up on the monitor. She fingered arrows on the extended portion of the keyboard and the face before her turned to profile. She looked at Darek and smiled.

"I know you from television," she said. "Welcome."

Then she turned again to the keyboard, typed "Jillian Fields," and repeated the procedure.

She smiled at Jillian and said, "I recognize you too, beautiful lady."

Jillian was taken aback but smiled her response. *What can you say?*

The receptionist opened a drawer, pulled out two already-prepared name tags, and handed them to Darek and Jillian, then turned to a tall black man in a dark suit who had approached and now stood behind her. "Mr. and Mrs. Fields have an appointment with the premier."

The man gestured for them to follow him. They all walked to the scanning equipment, and Jillian and Darek passed through the metal detector. Beyond the detector, their fingerprints were scanned.

The burliest two men ushered them to the glass elevator and waved them inside. As they rose up the sphere, the two escorts remained mute. The feeling of lifting off the ground in a glass elevator was surreal and made Jillian feel a bit light-headed.

Darek whispered to Jillian, "Wonder where Pascual and Cruz are."

She smiled at his ability to ease tense moments for her.

"Still driving circles around the Knesset parking lot?" she said. Darek harrumphed.

The elevator came to a gentle stop and the door opened. The two men stepped out ahead and motioned them off the elevator. Before them was small reception area with a red Persian carpet spread over a waxed wooden floor and beautifully polished wood on the walls. A gorgeous woman sat at an oak desk. She noticed Jillian's wonderment at the room's beauty.

"Acacia wood," she said, "like the First Temple built by King Solomon in Jerusalem."

She stood and offered her hand. "Mr. and Mrs. Fields, I'm Lucinda Lucerne, the premier's personal secretary."

Jillian couldn't pinpoint her exotic accent, but her aura of authority was unmistakable. Dressed in an expensive business suit, she was tall, blonde, blue-eyed and cover-girl striking. Jillian wondered if she was more than Sardis's secretary.

"Stop thinking that," Darek whispered, and extended his hand to Miss Lucerne.

"Nice to meet you," he said aloud. Jillian also shook her hand.

Like the First Temple, hmm? I wonder what's inside.

Jillian didn't like the way this Lucerne woman eyed her husband, but she had to admit this secretary was an improvement over her predecessor. Sardis's assistant when Jillian and Darek first interviewed him was a man who had disappeared and never been found after disconnecting Sardis during an interview with *CNN News*.

Miss Lucerne escorted them to a large oak door dominated by the carving of a dragon in flight. She led them inside and announced in a soft, sultry voice, "Premier, Mr. and Mrs. Fields."

Darek strode into the office bold as brass. Jillian, remembering the impolite dispatching from Sardis's former offices in Rome, was more tentative. She took in the scene.

Sardis stood behind a large teak desk at the far side of the room. A very tall black man dressed in a dark suit and white shirt, with a dazzling red silk tie, stood at attention to the far right—obviously Sardis's bodyguard.

Between Sardis and Jillian was an expanse of wooden floor. An inlaid design in oak rimmed the entire room. The whole inlay was about eight feet in diameter. A medallion in the middle dominated the layout. Narrow boards of teak flared out in all directions from the medallion until they reached the oak rim.

Jillian looked more closely. A maple-and-oak dragon centered within appeared to leap out of a teak background.

Furniture was sparse—all Corinthian leather, including the throne-like chair from which Sardis had risen.

Where the semicircular outer wall met the inner wall of the room, a small waterfall gurgled lightly over shimmering gold- and copper-colored stones. The cascade was shaped like a brook sloping down to a tiny holding pond. The water recirculated to the top of the waterfall for another bubbly run through the stones.

The entire ceiling glittered gold, and gold edged everything from chandelier-type lighting to a letter opener sticking out of a porcelain mug on Sardis's desk.

Sardis extended his hand to Darek, who was already at his desk. "Mr. Fields."

"Premier."

"Mrs. Fields, are you joining us?" Sardis beckoned Jillian to a chair near his desk. As she crossed the room, she noted the chairs where she and Darek would be seated were lower than Sardis's seat.

Darek hesitated, remained standing, and looked out the floor-to-ceiling windows along the rounded outside wall of the office.

"Far from your old offices, Premier."

"Yes, in Rome, the last time we met. An unfortunate ending to our interview, Mr. Fields."

Jillian couldn't read the meaning behind those words, nor the thoughts of the man before her. His face seemed at once handsome and yet non-descript. His looks swarthy and yet Norwegian. His build powerful and yet slim. His eyes dark and now blue, or green?

Darek responded simply, "Yes. Unfortunate."

Jillian could tell her husband was seething below the surface and was glad he was controlling his temper.

"Happier surrounds, perhaps a cheerier interview."

"Perhaps."

Jillian had to break the tension.

"Your office is stunning, Premier Sardis," she interjected.

"Yes," he responded. "Designed with Feng Shui, Reiki and Vastu."

"I'm aware of Feng Shui," she said. "But Reiki and Vastu?"

"Well, you know Feng Shui has long been considered the universal language of the divine, and is used for the construction of temples and holy spaces. Its use is what makes a house—and in this case, my office—a sanctuary." Sardis swept his arm in a semicircle around the room. "Reiki is Feng Shui for the soul. Vastu is the ancient predecessor of Feng Shui and is more directly rooted in sacred geometry than Feng Shui."

"Strategic placement of objects is the key, right?"

"Yes," Sardis said. "Representing the elements of fire, earth, metal, water, and wood as either color or material, Feng Shui transforms negative or benign energy into positive energy. You can feel it, can't you?"

"Can't say I can."

Sardis spoke to Jillian as a teacher would to a pupil, "Any room you live in—as I do to a large degree here—is really a metaphor for your life. Balance, harmony, and geometric proportion are symbolic—representative of being in right relationship to creation and the Creator. Think of the impact on your life of religion, philosophy, and mythology."

•••••

While Jillian and Sardis spoke, Darek took stock of the tall dark man in the corner opposite the fountain. He stood straight as a rod, his arms folded, paying close attention to those in the room and, on occasion, scanning out the windows—*for what, low-flying aircraft?*

The man was obviously athletic, although not intimidating. A coffee-colored black. Jamaican, perhaps. From the look of the One World Government staff on the first floor and here, Sardis was employing people from many different regions and cultures. Since Sardis had declared English the world's operative language two years before, communication wouldn't be a problem for long.

Sardis interrupted Darek's thoughts. "Please," he said, "have a seat."

Grudgingly, Darek sat in plush leather chairs before Sardis's desk, Jillian at his side.

Boy, aren't we symmetrical?

He and Jillian exchanged glances, and he knew she was thinking the same thing. A smile worked at the corner of her lips.

Darek pulled a small digital recorder from his pocket, asked Sardis if he minded, received an approving nod, and placed the device upon the desk. Jillian removed a pen and narrow notebook from her purse.

"As we indicated to your chief of staff," Darek said, "our interview is singularly focused. We want to find out what the One World Government intends to do about the worldwide terrorism by Muslims against people of other faiths."

Sardis folded his hands and toyed with a huge ring on the index finger of his left hand, obviously weighing his words. Finally, he said, "As you know, I declared peace in Israel, and we have peace in Israel."

Darek nodded. Jillian scribbled in her notebook.

"In Israel, we basically have the good people of Islam and the good people of the Jews. They are living in harmony. Indeed, the construction of the Temple on the Temple Mount itself declares that, yes, our Muslim friends are tolerant. They will allow others their place on this earth."

Darek started to interrupt, but Sardis lifted a hand to cut him off. "Yes, indeed, there are rebels, there are Muslims of evil intent, bad seeds among Ishmael's descendants. Also, there are bad seeds among Isaac's descendants, among Jesus's followers, among Buddha's? What of the Crusades? What of the Spanish Inquisition? What of the Holocaust?"

"You're speaking of the distant past," Darek said. "The bad seed among Jesus's and Buddha's followers are not killing and maiming others today."

"Things take time, Darek. I promise we will root out the evil among us."

"You seem to be taking your time," Jillian said. "Do you have a plan?"

Sardis looked at Jillian with hooded eyes, his jaw set tight. "Our Department of World Security is intensely investigating, coordinating intelligence efforts around the globe. They're doing all the operative things that mankind, in his limited wisdom, has done for millennia to handle man's own inhumanity toward man."

Sardis shifted in his seat, appearing uncomfortable, then continued, "Our species, Jillian, has been such an oddity among all the beasts of creation. We possess reasoning power, creative artistry, innovative ability, communicative skills, adaptability to the elements from the North and South Poles to the Equator. All this and men employ such a puny amount of their mind's power that they have to stoop to murder rather than persuasion, violence rather than peaceable dialogue. If one's beliefs are superior to another's, then win them over by conversion, I say. Prove you're right and they're wrong—with words, not bullets."

"More like shrapnel—and nails through the wrists—than bullets," Darek interjected.

Sardis nodded. "I know the stories. I receive daily intelligence reports. I read the news. In fact, I read the *Truth* daily. Someday, I want to meet your Mr. MacMillan."

"I'm sure he'd like to meet you, too," Darek said, pokerfaced.

"And strangle me." Sardis laughed.

"No, I think he'd use those persuasive words of which you speak."

Darek could sense Jillian's impatience before she even spoke up.

"You were suggesting you have a plan," she said.

"Yes." Sardis settled back in his chair, like a cowboy preparing to ride a bull, and his eyes were just as wide in anticipation.

Oh-oh. What do we have here? Then, he and Jillian got their answer.

"I have called for all countries to disarm," Sardis said. "A giant step forward. Beyond that, we have reconnaissance from the heavens, surveillance at the streets of the world's major cities and many of the minor ones, all fed into a computer here in Brussels with imaging technology to identify known terrorists and even people whose composure and facial traits suggest they are to be watched.

He waved a hand. "The technology China so deftly created and used to sift out its ne'er-do-wells. If a person of evil intent is spotted, off go our security forces to capture them. And I promise we will root them out."

Sardis hesitated as if pondering if he should continue his next thought. Then he pushed on. "But to be more basic, Jillian, I do have a plan."

"Yes?"

"I *am* the plan."

"Pardon?" Jillian peered at him, her eyes questioning.

"*I* am the plan," he repeated.

"You … are … the … plan?"

"*I am* the plan." He leaned forward and pointed an index finger at Jillian. Darek prepared to break the cretin's digit if it stayed there much longer.

"The world," Sardis said, "believes in me, trusts in me, understands I have their best interests at heart." He folded his offending finger into a fist and patted his chest, then added, "They believe I am unbiased toward all mankind, that whatever I do is for the good of the whole.

"In my State of the World Address, I will direct them to lay down their arms, to put aside their hatred—for the greater global good. I will offer amnesty. Once they hear me out—even these terrorists—they will leap out of hiding. They will discard their weapons. Indeed, they will repent and change their ways."

"So you, the premier, are the ultimate bringer of peace?" Darek asked.

"My image and likeness, my character, and, yes, charisma are my weapons of mass destruction—destructive to the enemies of peace."

Sardis stiffened his back, then nearly leaped to his feet and spun around, facing the windows. He took two steps toward the portals and opened his arms wide as if embracing the city. "Do you see hurting mankind?"

How dramatic, Darek thought, knowing Jillian, too, was on the edge of going ballistic on this narcissist. She'd done well restraining herself.

But the two of them were silent.

Sardis turned back toward them and shrugged. "Not necessarily the hurting here in this city. Here in Brussels, the sickness is in men's hearts and minds." Sardis's voice rose a half-octave. "Greed. Power. Outside this office, of course. No. I mean, beyond our view, around the world. I am well aware of the droughts and floods. I'm conscious of the earthquakes and hailstorms. I know there is famine and pestilence, that armies of locusts are ravaging crops on various continents.

"Do you think those Muslims who are torching churches and synagogues full of people, the ones who set fire to Notre Dame Cathedral, are killing more than who died in the floods that carried two hundred thousand people to their deaths in the Dominican Republic?" His voice rose another half-octave. "Are these Muslims killing more than are dying of malnutrition in Africa?!"

Darek restrained himself from burning Sardis's straw man to the ground.

"Afflictions, friends. Afflictions are everywhere!" Sardis exclaimed. His eyes—now not blue or green but black, jet black—were piercing, his jaw stiff. "I promised peace to the world. I will overcome these miseries, no matter their source, no matter the power behind them. No army can accomplish this. Nothing manmade can be mankind's deliverer. Nothing created by the hand of man can be man's salvation. As I said, *I am* the plan."

The words struck Darek, and he noticed Jillian flinch as well. *I am.* The words Jesus spoke to convey he was the Lord. He exchanged looks with Jillian, then searched Sardis's face. "Do you mean to say—"

"What I am saying," Sardis cut him off, "is I am the answer. I am all things to all people. Why think one-dimensionally, Darek? Yes, I will work with His Excellency Mr. Bliss. We've spoken of this. The Muslims, as a religion, are under his domain. But the Muslims, as a people on this earth, are under my authority as well. We will handle this together. But we all know he," Sardis pointed in the vague direction of Jerusalem and Bliss, "is not me."

He put an index finger to his chest. "I can't say any more for now." He looked at his watch. "And I see we're out of time. I have an important teleconference with the regional leaders in sixty seconds."

Sardis pointed to the door, through which Lucinda came even as he spoke. "Miss Lucerne will see you out and help you in whatever way she can."

"Mr. Sardis," Darek said as he rose and grabbed his digital recorder from the desk, "when you say 'I am,' are you saying you are God?"

Sardis took a step forward. "Isn't this where we ended our last interview, Darek?"

"Yes, and I didn't get an answer then, either." Darek straightened his shoulders, not intimidated.

"Just observe, Darek," Sardis said. "Just monitor what I do and what I accomplish, then make your own judgment as to who I am. Again, I'm glad I could oblige you this time, but I really must end our interview." He gestured toward the door. "Ciao, Darek. Ciao, Jillian."

Two minutes later, walking toward the outer door of the building, Darek gripped Jillian's hand. "What does God say about two being better than one?"

"It is good to have a companion. If one falls, the other can lift him up."

"I'm glad there were two of us in there."

Jillian stopped, looked up at him, reached up on her toes and planted a lingering kiss on his lips. "I'm glad there are two of us wherever we go. Remember our wedding ceremony?"

"The part about 'Love makes two one, and one two'?"

"Yes, and 'a cord of three strands is not easily broken,' the third strand being the Lord."

Darek smiled. "And what about the rib?"

"Is this a test?" Jillian giggled, then deepened her voice. "Jillian, do you remember our wedding, word for word?"

He laughed at her attempt to copy his speech. "A bit more baritone, please," he said.

"Okay. You're on, *Mr.* Fields," she continued, quoting from memory and a smidgeon deeper: "God made Eve out of Adam's rib so she would be beneath his arm for him to love her and at his side to walk in full equality with him."

Darek picked up the recollection: "As an ancient rabbi put it—'In the wisdom of God, He did not take a bone from Adam's hand, lest Adam use her as a tool. He did not take a bone from Adam's foot, lest he tread upon her. He did not take a bone from Adam's head, lest she try to dominate him. But out of his side, a rib was taken, so together they might be covenant partners, side by side for life.'"

He shot Jillian a look of pride at his recollective abilities. She smiled back, "And I thought you were too dazed to be paying attention."

He lifted his head back and laughed, then gave her a gentle nudge through the revolving outer door. As they emerged outdoors, a gentle rain began to fall.

"I remember one more thing from the ceremony," he said.

"What's that, Mr. Fields"

"Okay, okay." Darek shook his head and chuckled. "I remember one more thing Pastor Banks said. 'May your love and commitment continue to grow, so in times of sorrow, your pain will be divided, and in times of happiness, your joy will be multiplied.'"

"Very good, Mr. Fields. Very, very well done." She swung her arms into the air. "I'm into the joy thing right now."

"Even after that interview?" he nodded at the building behind them.

"Especially after the interview." She looked up at him and held her hands apart like holding a basketball. "It's over."

Darek laughed with her, then looked at his watch. "Think we could ring up the flight crew and take off earlier than planned?"

"Oh, give them this afternoon. They've planned their schedule. Besides," she flashed an intimate smile, "we have our room until three o'clock. Let's make use of the place, companion."

"No, pronounced com-pag-ñon," he corrected. "Think of yourself as Cyrano de Bergerac, French soldier, satirist, and dramatist, and say, 'De-tañ-yon.'"

Jillian played along. "De-tañ-yon."

"Now say 'com-pag-ñon!'"

"Com-pag-ñon!" she said.

"But with a flourish," Darek said, waving a hand.

"But with a flourish." She smiled craftily.

"No, say 'com-pag-ñon' with a flourish." He faked frustration.

Jillian laughed and pulled him along. "Come on, we're wasting time, com-pag-ñon."

Darek's face lit up and his stride quickened with hers.

CHAPTER TWENTY-FIVE

The phone rang in the Kreko apartment. Mosey turned to Mary, on whose side of the bed the phone stood. He squinted into the early-morning light. *What's the time, anyway? Six?* A second ring.

The alarm clock next to the phone was a blur.

"What's the time?" he asked.

"Six fifteen," Mary said.

At the third ring, Mosey mumbled, "Pass the phone to me, babe."

Clearing his throat, he took the receiver from Mary.

"Hello." Knowing how he must look, he did not turn on the video transmitter, but on his LCD screen, he could see his father. Mosey sat up straight. Months had passed. How many? Five? Six? Yes, six. Six months since he'd heard from his parents. Six months since he'd told them of his decision. Six months since he'd left Israel with not a goodbye from them.

Something must be wrong for his father to call. His mother, perhaps? Had something happened to Mom? Another death in the family? One of his cousins? Mosey's heart raced.

"Dad!" By the look on his father's face, Mosey realized the unbelief in his own voice was evident.

"Shalom, son." Levi Kreko smiled faintly.

Are those tears welling up in his eyes?

"What is it, Dad? What's the matter?"

"Tears of happiness, son. And tears of regret at how I treated you."

"We. That's we," Mosey's mother spoke in the background.

Mary sat up next to Mosey to hear the conversation.

"Is everyone okay?"

"Why, yes, son. More than okay. Wonderful. Fabulous. There are no words to express the feeling."

"Dad, please," Mosey pleaded. "What's going on?"

"Son, we must see you."

"Okay. When?"

"How about one hour? We're at Kennedy International."

"Kennedy International! We'll come pick you up."

"No. It's early. We're taking a taxi and will be there before you know."

"All right," replied Mosey, all he could think to say.

"We love you, Son. Shalom." His father's face, now with tears surely slipping down his cheeks, disappeared from the screen.

Mosey turned to Mary and put his arm around her. "I'm afraid to hope."

"We've been praying," she said. "Morning and night. Expect a miracle."

"This would be a miracle on steroids."

The hour gave Mosey and Mary time to shower, dress, and put on a pot of coffee for the elder Krekos. "I'm making your Dad's favorite—potato pancakes, latkes," Mary said when Mosey stepped into the kitchen. "And for your Mom, popovers with real butter and strawberry jam."

"You're ambitious." Mosey grinned. "I hope everyone's hungry. I must say, darlin', you've done everything a girl could do to gain my parents' affections."

"Short of becoming Jewish, you mean?" One eyebrow rose.

"Well, that—" he hesitated. "Actually, you're grafted in now, right? Spiritually?"

Her smile was all the answer he needed.

At that moment, the security buzzer came to life, and Levi and Sarah practically sang a hello.

Mosey pressed the button unlocking the downstairs door to his parents, and two minutes later, they were at the apartment door.

Mosey let them in. His father immediately bear-hugged him. "Wonderful to see you, Son." He looked for Mary and squeezed her. "Both of you, in fact."

Sarah Kreko, always graceful, followed her husband's bear hugs with gentle squeezes of her own.

"No luggage?" Mary asked.

"All with the bellman at our hotel," Levi said.

"You stopped at your hotel and still got here this quickly?" Amazed, Mosey checked his watch.

"Astounding, right?" Levi said. "I felt like Moshe at the Red Sea. The traffic simply parted before us. And there was quite a bit for six-thirty in the morning, too. The traffic lights were all in sync, the stars were aligned—"

"I had to search your father to see if he was holding a shepherd's crook like Moshe." Sarah chuckled. "Imagine. All the years we lived in Manhattan, I never hit more than two lights in a row. We must be on a divine mission."

"We *are* on a divine mission, Sarah," Levi said. "Two divine missions."

"You know, you're welcome to stay with us," Moshe said. "We have two spare bedrooms."

Levi waved him off. "Son, we're going to be in and out, in and out. Staying here would be too disrupting to you and obstructive to our schedule. But thanks for the offer."

355

"I'm curious," Mosey said. "What are your 'divine missions'?"

"First of all, please come and sit in the dining room," Mary said. "Dad, I've got potato pancakes for you and Mosey, and, Mom, popovers are in the oven for you and me."

Sarah smiled and put her arm around Mary's shoulder. "You're getting to know me well, daughter-in-law."

"These latkes are from heaven," Levi said, smacking his lips as they sat around the dining table.

"Thank you," Mary said.

"I'm sorry to surprise you both like this," he said. "But our most important mission is to speak with you two."

There was a long pause as Levi gathered his thoughts. He turned to Moshe.

"When you came to see us in Yerushelayim, Son, and dropped your bombshell on us, I was in shock. I was devastated. I— I couldn't think straight. I reacted. I blew up. And I'm sorry." His eyes pleaded with Mosey.

Mosey reached for his father's arm. "Dad, it's all right. I understand."

Levi held up a hand to stop him. "But after you left, I picked up the paper you left me by that Jewish law professor. And I read the essay. Then I read the Scriptures you mentioned from Torah."

"And me, too, Moshe," Sarah joined in. "Your father would read something and pass the Bible to me, and we would talk over the issue. Then on to the next thing."

"I have to admit," Levi said, "my intent was to prove you wrong, then to confront you with evidence and change your mind."

"But the world's foremost expert on evidence wrote the article," Mosey objected.

Levi laughed. "That, I found out. Once he proved to me all the evidence confirmed the Scriptures had been held in custody and were genuine, the foundation was firm. The burden of impeaching a witness's credibility lies with the objector, and I could find no evidence against any of the four gospel writers."

Levi read the growing joy in his son's face and noticed Mosey had grabbed Mary's hand.

He continued: "What Simon Greenleaf wrote struck home. 'The great truths the apostles declared were Yeshua had risen from the dead, and only through repentance from sin, and faith in him, could men hope for salvation. This doctrine they asserted with one voice, everywhere, not only under the greatest discouragements, but in the face of the most appalling terrors that can be presented to the mind of man."

Sarah picked up the quote: "'His religion sought to overthrow the religions of the whole world ... The interests and passions of all the rulers and great men in the world were against them ...'"

Levi stepped in. "'Propagating this new faith, even in the most inoffensive and peaceful manner, they could expect nothing but contempt, opposition, revilings, bitter persecutions, stripes, imprisonments, torments, and cruel deaths. Yet this faith they zealously did propagate; and all these miseries they endured undismayed, no, rejoicing. As one after another was put to a miserable death, the survivors only prosecuted their work with increased vigor and resolution.

The annals of military warfare afford scarcely an example of heroic constancy, patience and unshrinking courage.'"

Levi rubbed his eyes to prevent tears from flowing.

"I can't get your father to remember our own anniversary," Sarah chuckled, "and he memorizes this dissertation."

Levi laughed with his wife and went on. "Not one single remnant of antiquity has been found that impeaches the credibility of the gospel writers. On the contrary, every finding has tended to confirm them."

"Your father has even taken to reading the magazine *Biblical Archaeology*," Sarah said. "My husband, the *Fortune* magazine reader, the *Worth* magazine junkie. Always reading about himself and his friends."

"Now my friends are in here," Levi said, pulling a hand-sized Bible from his trouser pocket. "Ha!"

Mosey and Mary were clearly engrossed. Levi realized Mosey knew the coming punch line, but it was so exciting getting there.

"We searched the Torah for the prophecies of our prophets about HaMashiach, the Messiah," Sarah said, "and, guess what? As you said, Moshe, Yeshua fulfilled them all."

"But the sale was made to me," Levi nearly whispered the words, "when I considered what you said to us in Yerushelayim: 'Men do not die for something they know to be a lie.'

"Besides the signs and wonders, Christianity all hinges on the resurrection," Sarah said. "If Yeshua did not come back to life, then his claim of Messiah wasn't true. Well, the disciples knew if his claim was true or not. They were alive to see him! If Yeshua hadn't been resurrected, the disciples wouldn't have all died for a falsehood."

"They weren't *mashuga*," Levi said. "That's obvious from their writings. And when your mother and I considered that one point, it was like Saul Goldman coming to us with a million-dollar diamond and asking if we'd buy the gem for a buck. No, better still, if we'd accept the diamond as a gift."

"Why, of course we would," Sarah finished.

Tears were now pouring from everyone's eyes around the table. Mosey jumped from his chair and hugged Levi, while Mary and Sarah embraced across the table.

After celebrating their newfound faith and discussing the growth in Messianic Jewish congregations in New York City to determine where they'd worship on Shabbat, Mosey asked his Levi, "You said you had two missions for coming to New York. What's the second?"

Levi felt flush with joy. "Aliyah, son. Aliyah."

"You know the history of our people, Moshe," Sarah said. "God warned us for years, through Zionist prophets, to leave Europe in the nineteen-thirties. But only ten percent went home to Israel. All the rest refused until everything shut down. They wouldn't believe their neighbors, their government would harm them. Zechariah chapter twelve, verse eight says two-thirds of the Jews in the world would be killed. One-third of them, six million, were killed in the Holocaust. We believe six million more could be murdered in America unless they return soon."

"True," Levi said, "many have moved to Israel the last fifteen, twenty years. But most of them were from other countries, where the pogroms were most fierce, where hatred against us spilled over into violence. Here in America, Jews feel such a thing will not happen to them."

He looked at Mosey. "You, for instance, son. Do you feel afraid here?"

"I admit to some fear, Dad, but not debilitating fear. I try to push apprehension to the back of my mind," Mosey said.

"Well," Levi said, "if more than ten percent of the Jews in America leave the country before pogroms begin here, such would be the first time in history."

"We're here to make the shofar call home," Sarah said. "Your father, Moshe, has even brought his four-curl shofar."

"And I'm going to sound the horn from ocean to ocean," he declared. "We've made a lot of contacts and even have an itinerary of synagogues from New York to Florida to Chicago to Phoenix to Los Angeles where we'll speak."

Sarah's face lit up. "And you know Jonathan Sekulow, the tenor?" Mosey and Mary nodded. "We've known him since he sang with the symphony and he's going to travel with us."

"Amazing," Mosey said.

"Incredible you could get him," Mary added.

"Well, he's our neighbor now," Levi said, "and he sure can sing better than I."

"*Oi gevalt.*" Sarah laughed. "So true."

"But how will you persuade people to leave?" Mosey asked. "Even with the stock markets plummeting and the economy in a whirl, they have homes, businesses, wealth."

"Yes, yes, and yes, they do," Levi replied. He frowned. "But we have the truths of history, and you know the saying about what happens to those who refuse to learn from the past."

"They're doomed to repeat it," Mosey said.

"Yes. We'll be telling our fellow Jews the fishers came, years ago, to call them home—to aliyah to Israel. Few listened. In parts of the world, the hunters have been driving them home for a decade now. But listen," Levi lowered his voice, "we've heard from a source with contacts within the One World Government that Premier Sardis is about to stop all immigration of Jews to Israel. Only gentiles will be allowed to move there."

Mosey and Mary sat up, shock on their faces.

"You're kidding!" Mosey said.

"It's not to kid about, Moshe," Levi said. "You see, it's all about demographics. Always has been. Why in the 1940s did Great Britain stop all those ships full of Jews trying to get to the Holy Land and send them back to be incinerated in the concentration camps?"

Mosey and Mary looked puzzled.

"The Arab world believes, and always has thought, they can win this struggle if they can out-populate the Jews. Their pressure on England is what kept our people out."

"Demographics," Mosey intoned.

"If this report is true, Jews everywhere must aliyah now, or—" Levi's voice trailed off. He felt a chill akin to what his ancestors in Poland must have felt when the Nazi SS officers knocked on their doors.

"So," Sarah said, "we pray that combining this upcoming declaration by the premier and the violence of the hunters, the Jews in America will listen, will act, will follow us back home."

Levi matched his wife's intent look at Mosey and Mary. "Will you consider *aliyah*, too, Moshe? Mary?" he asked. "The hunters may be at your very door."

Sarah turned and looked at the door to the hallway. "They're on every continent where a single Jew lives. And they're armed and loaded and set on violence to our people."

"Even with this One World Government's supposed peace in Israel," Levi said, "the signs of neo-Nazi anti-Semitism are everywhere. Remember, Jews were dismissed from civil service jobs and university faculty. The practice is happening again—in Asia, in South America."

"In Brazil," Sarah said, "Jewish-owned bonds and stocks can be transferred only to the national government. Already they can't take their fortunes with them."

"And the European Union just yesterday declared a curfew to keep Jews off the streets between nine in the evening and five in the morning," Levi said, "the law stating 'for their own safety,' of course."

Holding Mary's hand, Mosey listened warily. He was thrilled they'd accepted Messiah and yet was afraid for their lives more so than his own.

Yes, he'd seen distaste in the eyes of some people passing him on the street. Maybe he and Mary should accompany his parents on this tour. But what about his work with Advocates for a Nuclear-Free World? He could take some time off, for sure. And Luke O'Neil could carry the ball. Heck, Luke could run the entire show.

Advocates was a worldwide organization, so why not operate out of Israel? Heck, maybe God was calling them to a whole new work.

Todd Winter slammed the phone down. Disgust hardened his jaw. Gutless! he thought. These people were invertebrates, jellyfish, slugs.

Yet another major advertiser, this one a software developer, had told him they were not renewing their contract with Truth Publishing for the upcoming fiscal year.

Todd felt like a bank with a run on. Only instead of a line of people at the clerk's counter anxious to take money from the vault, his line was advertisers putting a lock on their own bank accounts—at least when the spending came to Truth.

Todd was Truth's vice president for advertising and marketing. He'd been with Jake MacMillan since the beginning and had stayed the storm in previous ups and downs of the economy. God knew, this certainly ranked at the top. But this time, the economic crunch was exacerbated by subterfuge. Truth's advertisers faced blackmail from powerful forces—people who threatened kidnappings, bombings, arson, all sorts of ill—unless they pulled advertising from Truth.

He picked up a large ledger mirroring the Excel program on his computer and hammered its mass onto his desk. He was about to kick something, hit something, throw something, scream, or something. Then Jake stepped through his office door.

"Bad news," Todd greeted him. "Bad upon bad, heaped and piled upon us. I feel like Job. Give me some good news, will you?"

"Good news, eh?" Jake smiled and walked to the front of Todd's desk. "Let not your heart be troubled, Todd. Trust in the Lord always and he shall supply all your needs according to his riches and glory by Christ Jesus. He shall supply all our needs."

The words convicted Todd, a little. But he still fumed. "You know what I mean, Jake. This is extraordinary. Three more hits this morning—Sunglow, Cornerstone, and Blitz. All three run by Christians. All three running like scared little mice."

"Well, they *are* scared, Todd. We have to see their point of view. They probably have to answer to boards of directors.

And they're afraid the blackmailers will carry out their threats." Jake sighed deeply. "And who's to say they won't?"

"But people can't just let roughnecks control their lives." Todd threw up his hands in exasperation.

"No, you'd hope not. But look, Americans are still not used to terror on our own shores. Since the Civil War, conflicts have always been overseas, or on the seas. Never here. If someone told you they'd kidnap your wife if you, say, paid a bill from a creditor, would you give in to their demand?"

"N—" Todd stopped mid-word and looked Jake in the eyes. "Okay, I see what you mean. But I don't know how much longer this bleeding can go on. I surely would like to know who's the instigator."

"We could make a pretty good guess," Jake said, then added, "but it may actually be more than one."

"Besides the Alliance?"

"Yep. Another source far away." Jake moved to the windows. The corner office was two stories above Jake's—the windows on the east, similarly facing Boston Harbor. Old Ironsides stood proud and unmovable on Boston Harbor's north shore. "I've been spending some time looking out my window at the people, Todd. They move about differently today than they did a couple of years ago. You don't see many stop and talk. You don't see a lot of joviality. When people are concerned, or afraid, or anxious, they tend to keep to themselves, throw up barriers and hunker down."

"Well, they do have plenty of reason to be anxious." Todd stepped beside Jake and looked out the window. "They're being told 'peace, peace,' but they don't feel peace in their soul, in their spirit."

"Peace, peace. I guess it all rests on who you are, right?" Jake said. "Your point of view. Obviously, peace in Sardis's mind is not peace in mine. I don't call the situation peace when one religion terrorizes another, or when a government of bureaucrats ordains a godless mindset to rule over the masses."

"Or when thugs bring retribution against you for your beliefs," Todd added.

CHAPTER TWENTY-SIX

As the Truth jet taxied along a runway at Leonardo Da Vinci International Airport, Jillian unstrapped her seat belt and looked out the window. They were passing an Alitalia jetliner, the mid-afternoon sun glinting off its green-and-red insignia and, next to the logo, the circular SkyTeam emblem designating the airline was in allegiance with airlines in America, France, Mexico, Korea, Czechoslovakia.

Jillian recalled Premier Sardis had encouraged airlines to form one all-inclusive alliance, sort of a union, to suggest people worldwide were one in spirit.

"Hey," Darek said, "people getting off the plane over there are on their knees kissing the ground."

"Whoa! I've seen such a response in Tel Aviv, but that was in the Holy Land," Jillian said.

"These people obviously consider Rome the holy land."

Jillian and Darek made their way through customs and jumped aboard a train for the twenty-mile ride to Termini Station. Their destination was Hotel Valadier on Via Fontanella in the heart of Rome, between the Spanish steps and Piazza del Popolo.

Since this was to be another quick in-and-out visit, they decided to hail a taxi rather than secure a rental.

"Besides, the people here drive like madmen," Darek reasoned. "They're all Mario Andretti wannabes. We'd get ourselves killed."

Jillian thought Darek was joking until they were about five minutes into the cab ride. Their taxi driver appeared to be one of those Formula One wannabes. But he got them to the hotel in one piece and was particularly attentive to her, if not Darek.

A bellhop grabbed their two small suitcases from the trunk of the taxi and escorted them into the hotel lobby. Intimate, refined. Tipping the porter and saying, "I'll take them from here," Darek took hold of the luggage and turned to Jillian. "*Italian* men are the ones who scare me."

"What do you mean?" she asked.

"Well, the French can cook, Germans are better organized, Jews are the most intelligent, Dutch have the tastiest chocolate, Asians are the most courteous, but the Italians?" He raised an eyebrow. "They'll take your woman."

Jillian laughed and slapped his shoulder. "Talk about stereotyping people."

He shrugged.

She said, "I half-expect another of Jake's friends to step up out of nowhere and invite us to a late dinner."

But none arrived.

Minutes later, they were in their fifth-floor suite, ordering room service.

The next morning, they surveyed the glorious green of the Villa Borghese out their window and plotted their day. Darek insisted on lunch at Giggetto al Portico D'Ottavia in the city's Jewish section.

"It's tucked behind the Portico d'Ottavia and has fabulous Jewish cooking," he said. "Besides, if I have you on my arm in Rome for only a few hours, I figure I'd impress you with how well I know my way around."

Sipping a cup of espresso, she said, "Being married to you is like living with Mr. Foder." She flashed the enchanting smile that captured him when they first met.

Darek look at her, bemused. "Foder?"

"You know—Foder travel guides. Would you rather I call you Guiseppi the Guide?"

Darek played along. "Why Guiseppi?"

"You didn't check the name tag of our taxi driver?"

"Guiseppi." Darek nodded. "I see."

Jillian shot out of her chair and peered out the window. "Speaking of tour guides—"

Darek stood and followed her eyes. Two men were crossing the boulevard, walking toward their hotel. "Pascual and Cruz!"

"Two and the same," Jillian agreed. "From Jerusalem to Brussels to Rome. Then we *don't* have a better clue as to who they work for."

"Perhaps. Perhaps not. Let's see if we can give them a treat." Darek had a mischievous look as he tugged Jillian along. "Let's grab our stuff and go."

A few minutes later, making sure he caught the eye of Pascual and Cruz as they emerged into the hotel's downstairs lobby, Darek loudly asked the doorman to hail them a taxi.

The bellman motioned a taxi driver to pull forward for the fare. Following Jillian into the rear seat, Darek leaned forward and handed the driver Euros worth about fifty American dollars. He looked out the back window in time to see Pascual and Cruz step into the taxi behind them. He noticed the driver's name tag on the dashboard.

"I'll double the tip if you can lose the taxi behind us, Antonius, my friend." Darek turned and winked at Jillian.

Antonius returned a swarthy grin. "You betcha, cowboy!" Without hesitation, he slammed the little Italian-made vehicle into gear. G-forces pushed Darek and Jillian to the back seat as the car peeled into the street, leaving a trail of smoke and rubber skid marks.

They looked out the rear window. Pascual and Cruz must have flashed some cash to their driver as well because he left the curb with engine revving.

Down Via del Corso they flew, weaving through heavy traffic. Blaring his horn, Antonius shifted, then double-clutched onto Piazza Venezia.

Darek and Jillian were jostled from side to side. They looked out the window. The ride was a rush past Renaissance and Baroque buildings, a blur past Etruscan and classical Roman architecture, past arches and pillars and columns.

The oddest thought passed Darek's mind: *Doric, Ionic, and Corinthian*—types of columns he'd learned about in a college architecture class.

He shook his head in amusement at what one's mind would conjure when blazing past automobiles like they were stationary. At least he wasn't seeing his own life passing before him—that would be ominous.

He looked behind them. Pascual and Cruz were losing ground.

Antonius downshifted, pulled around another car and upshifted to cut across another lane and pull onto Via dei Fori Imperiali. He laughed as he pulled into faster traffic and glanced in his rearview mirror. No Pascual and Cruz. He held out his right palm and Darek slapped down another wad of bills.

"Now you can take us to our destination," Darek said. "Giggetto al Portico D'Ottavi."

Antonius nodded and a couple of blocks further, exited Via dei Fori Imperiali with a squeal of brakes and gear shifts.

Darek turned to Jillian. "What did I say? In his mind, Antonius is driving a Lamborghini or Ferrari."

"And this is the Grand Prix," Jillian added.

"You must be a reporter," he smiled.

Soon they arrived in Rome's Jewish section and pulled to the side of the street in front of Giggetto al Portico D'Ottavia. Darek gave Antonius a hefty tip on top of the fare. "It's been a pleasure, my friend."

"For me as well, cowboy!" Antonius again flashed a smile Mario Andretti's paparazzi would appreciate. "And all this to get to a restaurant alone?"

Darek simply nodded and shrugged.

"Well, my dear," Darek said and extended his hand to Jillian to step out of the taxi, "a savory meal awaits us. A place for friends and lovers. A place for Jewish-style artichokes, fried salt-cod filets, and stuffed zucchini flowers." He smacked his lips to his fingertips.

"I've spun around so much, I can barely stand up." Jillian laughed, grabbing for her pocketbook which had fallen to the floor of the taxi.

Darek had been to Vatican City a couple of times, but Jillian had not. She was not prepared for the sheer size of the Vatican.

As they walked the grounds en route to their interview with the Vatican's Secretariat of State, she turned to Darek and said, "I thought there would be a few buildings and a church surrounding one big structure, where the Pope lives."

All around were gardens and churches and museums— each one immaculate, each beautifully designed with intricate reliefs.

"We're actually in another country now," Darek said. "The wall surrounding the city serves as an international boundary."

St. Peter's Basilica dominated the small city. They entered from St. Peter's Square, and with an hour to while away before the interview, they did a Jericho walk. Holding hands, they prayed as they passed St. Martha's Palace, St. Charles's Palace, the Palace of Justice, the Church of St. Stephen. The circuit was awe-inspiring.

"I thought Rome was like a whole other world," Jillian said. "This is another world within the other."

"We'll have to ask Ty about all those carvings of flies everywhere," Darek said.

"Right."

"Ah, here we are."

They stepped into the edifice in which they were to meet the Secretariat of State and their footsteps echoed in the great hall before them. They exchanged glances. This was magnificent. Resplendent stained windows, massive paintings.

"How'd you like to get their heating bill?" Darek asked.

"A mite bigger than ours." Jillian grinned.

A man in priest's robes walked toward them. "Mr. and Mrs. Fields?" He extended a hand. Darek and Jillian took it in turn. "I'm Father Leon. His Excellency the Secretariat is expecting you. Follow me, please."

They followed the priest up a long staircase.

"You sound American," Darek said.

"San Francisco. How're those Giants looking?"

"Just traded Driscoll to Cincinnati for a left-hander named Paige."

"Any relation to Satchel Paige?"

Darek laughed, although the comment was lost on Jillian.

"Not unless Satchel was married to a very white Norwegian."

"Oh. Well, possibly a good move for both teams. Giants always need pitching."

"And the Reds always need hitting."

"See, a trade everyone can live with. I'd love to see the Giants win another World Series before I go home to the Lord."

"You're young yet," Darek said with a chuckle. "Don't lose faith. Remember, Red Sox fans waited eighty-six years."

"That's right. You're from Boston."

"Am now."

Jillian simply shook her head. Darek could read her mind. Boys and baseball, she'd be thinking. Boys and baseball.

Here they were, in the midst of papal splendor, on holy ground in the eyes of Catholics everywhere, halfway around the world—well, one-third of the way—and he and this priest were talking baseball.

Darek winked at her and patted her hand. "It's a genetic thing, hon."

"Hey, I played soccer, but I couldn't recite the players for Manchester United." She shrugged.

They reached the top of the staircase and turned down a very wide hallway. Each step rang out, sounding like a column of soldiers marching with hobnailed boots.

"Here we are." Father Leon gestured to a large oak door with a window in the upper half. "Secretariat of State" was painted in Roman serif font on the glass.

Appropriate, Darek thought.

Father Leon opened the door and waved them into a spacious area apparently serving as the anteroom for the Secretariat of State.

A minute later, they were seated in luxurious chairs before a very tall, very thin man dressed to the nines, with black cassock trimmed in red with gold buttons, a similar shoulder cape and white collar, and topped with red yarmulke atop his head. The early-afternoon sun shone brilliantly through large windows behind him.

Not a cloud appeared in the sky. Odd, since the topic of the moment was a dark and cloudy one.

The Secretariat assented to Darek's recording the interview, and Darek jumped right in. "Murders of Christians and Jews from one corner of the world to another. Crucifixions and torture—"

"Yes," the Secretariat interjected, "once again, Cain has pounced on Abel." The Secretariat was Hungarian and spoke with a throaty accent, but his English appeared good.

"Well, sir, in this case it's Ishmael who's pouncing on Isaac."

As he contradicted the Secretariat, Darek noticed Jillian flinch.

The Secretariat tilted his head as if he were not disagreeing.

"The Pope and the Vatican have been in dialog with Muslim leaders for more than a decade," Darek continued. "Are you making any headway in getting them to stop these murders?"

"First, let me say, Mr. Fields, dialog is the only way to establish ongoing understanding and harmony with our friends of the Muslim faith. There's no way to save our world except through dialog, consultation, and the definitive rejection of murder and assassinations."

"Mr. Secretariat, you've been dialoging with these people for many years, and we still haven't heard a wave of apologies for any murders, whether for nine-eleven or anything else."

"Dear Mr. Fields," the Secretariat said, leaning forward, "at the last World Day of Prayer for Peace, right here in St. Peter's Basilica, the Holy Father spoke of the need for Christians to serve as witnesses of the Gospel of Christ, the Gospel of peace. Do you think we should call the righteous to bear arms?"

"No, I'm simply asking what you might do differently in your dialog to get results?"

The Secretariat flipped a pencil between fingers like a baton.

Finally, he said, "The Pontiff said in his latest Post-Synodal Apostolic Exhortation—a feeling he repeated at the Synod of Bishops just last week—we all need forgiveness. Christians do. Jews do. Muslims do, especially the terrorists among them. We must proceed, every step of the way, with forgiveness in our hearts, not a rifle in our hands."

"So," Jillian said, "your response to the violence is to look inward at self-improvement, at your ability to forgive, and not to scrutinize your supposed partners in this hope for peace?"

The Secretariat twisted the pencil back and forth. "I think we have to look inward, yes. And ask ourselves how we would respond if we were in the shoes of these misguided people. In many areas, Muslims find themselves in situations of suffering, with no hope because of poverty and lack of jobs, restricted human rights. In Palestine, for instance, Muslims live in sometimes squalid conditions."

"Mr. Secretariat," Darek said, "let's be honest. In Israel, the Palestinians have the right to own land and to vote—something they don't even have in the surrounding Arab countries. The reason they're in poverty is because Arafat, Abbas, and other leaders have stolen billions of dollars in aid from America and other countries, squirreling a fortune away in personal accounts in Swiss and French banks and building mansions for themselves."

The Secretariat brushed aside Darek's comments with a flick of the hand. "Even if what you say is correct, the facts of the lives of the masses remain as I say. And their unresolved conflicts, from the nineteen-forties until today, have provoked this death and destruction. Muslims have deep wounds in body and spirit driving them to these horrible actions."

"Sir," Darek steeled himself for his follow-up, "your plan for peace seems to lack action. Do you have no proceedings in the works, no Muslim-Jew-Christian conference, no meeting with Mr. Bliss or Premier Sardis?"

The pencil snapped in two in the Secretariat's hands. His jaw rigid, he replied in a measured tone, "Our action at this point, Mr. Fields ..." and here he measured a distance between each word, "... is to forgive and act like Christ. Crusades are a thing of the past, an immeasurable mistake. Our Savior turned the other cheek. In fact, he gave his life willingly so we might have eternal life."

"Did he turn his cheek and did he die, so *we* might be murdered?" Jillian asked.

The Secretariat sighed loudly and turned his gaze to her. "Mrs. Fields, there are open wounds between Muslim and Christian and between Muslim and Jew—indeed, between Christian and Jew. We are deeply divided by culture, and to a great degree, by nationality.

"The Pontiff feels, and I agree, that religious fundamentalism occasionally arises as the enemy of dialog and peace. We, today, on this Earth where God created us all, must take the high road of peace and love, whatever another group does in our midst. Even if our goodwill means our death."

"Do you see *any* movement from your Muslim colleagues toward trying to stop these murders?" Darek asked.

The Secretariat simply looked down at his hands, which held the two halves of the broken pencil.

"Inane platitudes!' Darek spat out as they left the building a half hour later, having talked in circles with the Secretariat. "There must be a dictionary of banalities or a class in clichés studied by all these people in the One World Government and the Church Universal and in places like the Vatican."

"Platitudes 101," Jillian said. A smile curled her lips.

"How can you be carefree after that, that—" Darek fumbled for the right words.

"Because, my darling, God is in charge. You can't change things. I can't. But God can. And at this moment, he's allowing all this to happen. He's allowing the Pope and the Secretariat and the Muslim leaders and you-name-them to be blind to reason."

She took hold of Darek's hand. "Remember the Scripture, 'Why, oh man, do you worry? By worrying you cannot change one hair on your head.'"

"Yeah, yeah, yeah." Darek checked his watch. "Hey, we can't dally too long. We've got to catch up to the flight crew for dinner. Then, tomorrow morning, bright and early—" He put his free hand to his mouth as if creating a microphone. "Ladies and gentlemen, next stop on The Fields's Wild Mystery Tour: Nigeria. Get your tickets here."

Midnight had come and gone without a whimper. Jake sat in his den, relaxing with a late night pipe and Psalms. He had decided he'd simply start reading at the beginning of the Psalms and continue until, well, he felt released to go to bed. Bob was in the surveillance room.

When Jake got to the second verse of the second psalm, he stopped and glanced back at the first psalm. The verses drew a harsh distinction between the man who walks in the counsel of the wicked and the one who delights in the law of the Lord.

And here, Psalm 2 read, "Why do the nations rage and the peoples plot in vain? The kings of the earth take their stand and the rulers gather together against the Lord and against his Anointed One."

He reread the words and reflected. This is exactly what he was observing around the world—people plotting against God's family.

The phone rang on Jake's desk in his den, interrupting his thoughts.

He answered, "Hello."

"Mr. MacMillan." Jake knew the voice. He nearly jumped out of his chair and looked at the monitor. No face appeared.

"Yes." Jake's voice was guarded, husky.

"Warn Darek and Jillian Fields. They're in danger."

"Danger? How? Where?"

"On their trip. That's all I know." The line went dead.

Jake stared at the phone. The hairs on the back of his neck stood up. He rubbed his hand on his forehead. Darek and Jill. Where were they now? He looked at his watch: 12:05 a.m. Rome. Or were they? No, they were flying out with the sunrise for Nigeria. And, indeed, the sun was rising there right now.

The plane!

Jake speed-dialed Darek.

CHAPTER TWENTY-SEVEN

The red light had just blinked on, informing Darek and Jillian takeoff was imminent and to turn off their cell phones. Darek held her hand, knowing she always felt ill at ease until they were airborne.

Marsha sat down across the aisle from them, smiled, and buckled her seat belt.

"Just thought I'd listen in on you folks. You know, Strawberry Fields," she said mischievously.

"Strawberry Fields?" Jillian repeated.

"Yes, that's what the *Enquirer* tabloid called you two, and I quote, 'since they are both so tasty to the opposite sex.'"

"Geez. Embarrassing," Darek said.

"At least they didn't call us Poison Ivy Fields," Jillian nudged him with an elbow.

"There's no song, "Poison Ivy Fields," Darek deadpanned.

"Well, the song they used says 'strawberry fields *forever*,' so that's a good omen," Marsha said. "Obviously you two are made for each other—forever."

Darek and Jillian went silent and exchanged smiles. Darek grasped her hand. He'd never quite believe he was lucky enough to marry this beautiful woman. He loved her more than himself. What did Bill Asbury preach a couple of weeks ago? "Husbands, you must love your wives like Christ loves the church and gave his life for it."

He'd die for her. And he knew she'd die for him, if ever the need be.

She squeezed his hand as if she knew his thoughts. Well, she probably did.

"Someday, maybe we'll be able to take a long vacation and visit and stay for a while at these places instead of buzzing through them like bees on a honey run," Darek said.

"Or like Mario Andretti," Jillian added.

"Yeah. Hey, Pascual and Cruz. I wonder where they are now? Can you see them in the terminal waving at us?"

Jillian peered out the window. "Nope. No goodbyes from anyone, Mr. Fields. Even for you, whose face the world loves."

"Or loves to hate," he chuckled. "It's your face they love, Mrs. Fields. Or, to quote *People* magazine: 'Super Reporterette.'"

"Hmm. A little over the top, don't you think?"

"I think noth-ing. I say noth-ing." Darek did his best impression of Sergeant Schultz on *Hogan's Heroes* and squeezed shut his lips.

Marsha laughed.

"You've got to stop watching those old comedy shows on TV," Jillian joshed.

"Seriously," Darek said, "how can we both report the same story and yet everyone always loves you and not me? The polls are the proof."

Jillian shrugged. "Polls, shmolls. *I* love you, which should be all that counts."

Darek leaned over and planted a kiss on her lips. "Your love *is* all that counts."

"Don't believe the polls," Marsha said. "A lot of people do love you, Darek."

"Tell Premier Sardis. I'm sure he'd love me—if I were six feet under."

The jet's wheels had just left the ground and the hydraulic lift cranked the wheels into the belly of the aircraft. They pulled smoothly into the air.

Jillian sighed and looked out the window. The jet lifted one hundred, two hundred, three hundred, four hundred feet. A steady climb. Suddenly, she saw a flash from the midst of a clump of trees on the ground just outside the runway fence.

As twins, John and Paul LaFlamme were closer than two peas in a pod. Actually, the twenty-eight-year-olds were like identical halves of one pea. They finished each other's sentences as well as the peas off each other's plate. They'd grown up together; played ball as battery mates; went to the state championships in tennis as doubles partners; were named co-valedictorians in high school; started and finished flight school together; gotten saved at the same Franklin Graham crusade; and both jumped at the chance to work for Truth Publishing and Broadcasting.

They swapped off being pilot and co-pilot because when they flipped a coin for the duty—well, for anything—John always won. So if there were any difference between the two, the distinction was John was luckier.

And so today was John's turn to pilot the Gulfstream G650. When a red light flashed brilliantly on his instrument panel, and a warning sound beeped furiously at the same moment, his response was instinctive. In practice runs, they'd prepared for catastrophes, calamities, misfortunes.

Paul had no time to speak before John cut the plane sharply to the right and sideways and called out, "Heat deflectors!"

Paul switched on the deflectors.

Another warning light flickered, accompanied by a long fifty-decibel blare. The plane didn't have the speed or height for this kind of maneuver unless the engine went max throttle. John pushed forward pressure on the yoke to level off altitude.

Paul prayed out loud and flicked a switch for the speaker to the cabin. "Heads down to your knees!"

John screamed as a rocket whooshed past the window, missing the right wing by a couple of feet.

The jet hesitated as the engine caught thrust. More lights and a warning buzzer went off. John realized he must level off altitude. He pushed forward more on the yoke to put the nose over.

Paul was on the radio. "Tower. Tower. This is flight T-Zero-Seven. Flight T-Zero-Seven. We're being fired upon! I repeat, we are being fired upon from the ground!"

The air controller in the tower was all too calm for Paul. "T-Zero-Seven. This is tower. You say you're being fired upon? You mean you have a gunman on board?"

"No! Not a gunman! A missile!"

"By a missile from the ground?"

"Yes, a missile from the ground! Listen, we're coming back toward the airstrip. Warn planes away. I repeat, warn other aircraft away!"

In the cabin, Paul's caution came too late.

The three passengers were flipped to their sides, held only by seatbelts. But Jillian, in a window seat, was wrenched so vehemently her head cracked against the window.

Her cry grabbed Darek's eye. He looked and cringed. Her forehead was bleeding, but she seemed too stunned to realize the injury.

Held in place at a ninety-degree angle, he pulled a handkerchief from a pocket and reached for Jillian. What was happening? All he knew was his wife was injured and they were in serious danger.

"Lord, give your angels charge over us!" he called. "Have them keep this airplane in the air."

Jillian gripped his hand so tightly his nerve center registered the pain as a seven on a scale of ten.

He glanced toward Marsha and noticed the belt strap was cutting into her skin and she was frantically gripping the arm of her seat.

At the controls, John had flattened out the plane's flight path. He glanced at his brother, "Heat deflectors didn't work?"

Paul shook his head. "Not a heat-seeking missile, that one."

The red warning light flashed again, along with the frantic beep. Another missile!

John pushed forward pressure on the yoke to push the nose over and put the aircraft into a dive. But the jet was only four hundred or five hundred feet above the ground.

"Bank left," Paul cried. "Left!"

"Another missile?"

"The sun glinted off something."

John cut left even as he dived, thanking God this jet was the finest and toughest of its size ever constructed.

In the cabin, the maneuver tossed Darek, Jillian and Marsha the opposite way.

"Look out!" Marsha screamed as her shoulder struck the side of the plane.

Jillian prayed aloud for God's deliverance. Darek repeated, "Amen! Amen! Amen!" And Marsha simply cringed in pain and the repulsive thought she was going to throw up her breakfast.

"It's by," Paul shouted as he heard the missile whiz past. "It missed."

The jet was diving at sixty degrees and the ground was coming up at them at a frightening speed. They were going to crash.

Jake shot to the floor, face down. The voice message had told him Darek and Jillian's phones were unreachable. He'd tried to call Leonardo Da Vinci International Airport but found it impossible to speak with someone who could connect him to security or the control tower.

"Dear God," he called, "guard your children!"

Bob ran into the room and bent down on his knees beside Jake, agreeing with his boss's call to the Almighty.

They remained there for, how long? Time groaned on. There was no release from the prayer. The Spirit of God was heavy, like a force present in the room.

Beside John, Paul grabbed his copilot's yoke, and in unison with John, put his considerable muscle into a pull-up. Two hundred feet. One hundred feet. A crash was inescapable!

Worse still, they were heading directly at an emergency EMT vehicle parked on the tarmac. John could see the whites of the eyes of the two men in the vehicle nearly pop out of their frightened faces just before they dove out onto the ground.

A final tug at the yoke like a two-hundred-pound weightlifting bar and then, as if lifted on angels' wings, the plane pulled out of the dive. Flying by in a blur, the underbelly of the cockpit scraped the paint off the roof of the ambulance.

Could this be?

Then a firetruck appeared in front of them. Was the vehicle there before?

"John!" Paul pointed at the vehicle and John maneuvered the rudder controls to bank the plane leeward.

John's eyes bulged as the right wing of the plane missed the roof of the firetruck by millimeters. He glanced to his left in wonder the plane's left wing was not clipping the asphalt and flipping them head-over-tail into oblivion.

He turned the yoke to level off the jet. Beside him, Paul had turned white. John figured he was whiter still. But just as he caught his breath, a Cessna appeared out of nowhere a hundred yards ahead and to their left.

The Cessna's wheels were down and the plane was heading directly in their path toward a landing strip for small aircraft perpendicular to their own.

John lowered the jet toward the tarmac. The Gulfstream's wheels were up, thank God. With wheels up, the jet was sixty-three feet high to the tip of the fin. John figured the Cessna was about at that altitude.

In a millisecond the two aircraft converged. John cringed. The belly of the plane skimmed the tarmac. The Cessna's wheels flashed by the cockpit by how much? A foot? And a millisecond later, the two aircraft were past each other.

And that is when a row of a half-dozen Alitalia Airlines Airbus A330s loomed directly before them, lined up on the ground like a band of Texas line dancers.

"Twelve o'clock!" Paul declared.

"I see 'em."

At three hundred miles an hour, which is the cruise speed John figured the Gulfstream was flying right now, two hundred yards—the distance to the Airbuses—is covered in about three blinks of an eye, maybe two. In other words, a pilot would need the instincts and reflexes of an F-4 Phantom or an F-14 Tomcat pilot.

Did John LaFlamme have those instincts and reflexes?

In a split second, he yanked the yoke back, the Gulfstream's sleek body responded and screeched over the Airbuses, so close they shook in its turbulence.

Putting the plane into a steady climb, John turned to Paul. He figured his own look of astonishment mirrored his brother's. They both glanced heavenward and gave silent thanks.

In the cabin, the three passengers released a collective breath of relief.

Jillian tentatively touched her forehead and felt a bump and something slippery. She checked her hand and found a dab of blood. Her stomach ached from the trauma of the seatbelt holding her rigidly through the plane's twists and turns.

Over the intercom, John, or maybe Paul, said in an urgent voice, "Sorry, folks. Two missiles! And a whole lot more."

A moment later Paul stepped through the cockpit door. "Are you all right back here?" he asked.

"Fine," Jillian said.

"No, you're not," Darek said. "We need a first-aid kit."

Marsha clicked open her seat belt and stood, her knees wobbly. "I've got one up front. We'll patch you up, Jillian. You must need some pain relief, too. I know I do."

Jillian nodded.

Paul related the attack.

Astonishing, Jillian thought, then, "Who'd want to kill us?"

On the ground, in a clump of trees off the side of the runway, a string of swear words erupted. Hisey Brinks angrily tossed a rocket launcher onto the ground and strode out of the tree cover. He jumped into a waiting vehicle and sped off.

Five minutes later, when airport security arrived at the scene, they discovered the rocket launcher but found the weapon untraceable.

CHAPTER TWENTY-EIGHT

OCTOBER, SIX MONTHS LATER

Since their near-death experience, Darek and Jillian had worked a nonstop schedule. They couldn't even get refreshed by sitting out on the terrace and breathing in the saltwater aroma of the ocean.

Islamic terrorists had used some type of biological weapon to destroy ocean life from Georges Bank to Long Island. The result—untold millions of fishes and crustaceans floating atop the water, washing ashore and decaying in the sun.

"Now I know what the term run *ragged* means," Jillian said, gently lifting her legs and settling them in Darek's lap. She expected a leg rub and got one while sipping tea in her favorite spot—a new Canadian rocker couch.

"When was the last time we had more than a day here at home?" she asked.

"Can't remember." Darek massaged her calves and added, "Ty just said today he and Bethany really need a vacation."

"So do we."

"Then we're in agreement," Darek said. "Ty and Jess are thinking about a hiking vacation in Maine. Made me envious."

"Sounds deliriously simple." Jillian sighed. "If only we could."

"Why not?"

Jillian shrugged. "I, I guess I don't know why."

Five minutes later, Darek had called Carlos Martinez, who confirmed through Jake that a vacation was fine as long as, as Carlos put it, "We can reach you if the sky falls."

Five minutes later, Darek confirmed with Ty and Bethany that a two-couple hike in the Maine wilderness was just what the doctor ordered.

"We can reminisce about the last time you and I hiked Mount Katahdin," Ty said.

"Okay, pal. This time I'll remember to bring the Deep-Woods Off!"

"We've lost every last smidgen of decency in this country. It's like someone's pulled the stopper on the drain and decency has seeped out," Jake said to Carlos Martinez. Carlos had returned to Jake's office after speaking with Darek.

"No argument here," Carlos said.

Jake leaned back from his computer. "Sit down, will you, Carlos? Be my guinea pig. I want your opinion of my editorial."

Carlos sat in his favorite of Jake's leather chairs and nodded. "Read on, McDuff. And don't say I'm the first guinea pig you've heard speak."

Jake laughed, then began to read from his monitor.

> The slope is slippery and the fall is fast when a sovereign nation allows another entity to rule its internal matters.
>
> The current case in point is the One World Government's (OWG) edict that businesses, big and small, around the world must hire LGBTQs into

their work forces. Treating sexual proclivity as the American government treated African-Americans in the 1960s, OWG has set a timetable. Companies must employ certain percentages of LGBTQs until they reach fifteen percent of their work force.

Equating sexual rights to civil rights overlooks a number of facts, and indeed, other people's rights.

Fact number one: the color of a person's skin cannot be compared to his or her sexual lifestyle. Skin color is something you're born with. The proclivity for homosexuality and other abnormal behavior is a choice.

As black evangelist Star Parker said years ago— the main reason the black community was unsympathetic to the case of the gay community was the civil-rights movement depended on objective moral truth. Homosexual marriage, on the contrary, depends on a rejection of objective moral truth.

Jake looked at Carlos. "It's a simple choice to oppose God's law as set out in Leviticus 18:22 and First Corinthians 6:9."

"Leviticus," Carlos said. "Yeah, God says it's detestable to lie with a man as one lies with a woman, right?

Jake nodded and added: "And he says in Corinthians, 'Neither the sexually immoral nor idolaters nor adulterers nor male prostitutes nor homosexual offenders .... will inherit the kingdom of God.'"

He turned again to Carlos and added, "Believing this perversity is in their genes is to buy into Satan's lie."

Carlos stopped Jake with an upraised hand. "You know, Jake, I sympathize with practicing homosexuals. They're deceived, deluded. They believe their lifestyle is simply fine, even privileged.

"Abnormal acts? Not in their vocabulary. And look, entire Christian denominations have deviated from the Word of God. They somehow believe feeling compassion for these unfortunate people overrules God's commandments."

"Yes," Jake said, "but by that reasoning, all laws would fall apart—from theft to murder—be it homicide, abortion, or euthanasia. Once you start coloring life in shades of gray, with no firm right and wrong, you begin a perilous downward spiral."

"But I've heard plenty of gay men and women say, 'I believe in God. I'm a committed Christian. And I know God embraces me for who I am. No one can tell me otherwise!'" Carlos turned a questioning gaze at Jake.

"I feel compassion for that person, too," Jake said. "But compassion without truth is spiritual, and often literal, death. Look at the stratospheric suicide rates. Look at AIDS and this Super Gonorrhea. God's Word tells us to flee from temptation, right?"

Carlos nodded agreement.

"So I say, 'Dear homosexual, flee! Because the truth is God does indeed love you. However, his love cannot embrace what his holiness cannot endure.'"

Carlos sat mulling over Jake's last statement and repeated, "God's love cannot embrace what his holiness cannot endure. Hmm. I think you're right."

Carlos slowly rose from his chair. "The slope certainly is slippery. And once the countries of the world allow the One World Government to rule in a matter like this, they'll give implicit approval for its control of all kinds of things. The first nail in the coffin was probably acknowledging the One World Court had any authority at all outside its courtroom."

Jake nodded. "I think you're right as far as the One World Government is concerned. But we both know the foundations of the country began unraveling at least a generation ago."

"Yeah," Carlos said, "couldn't you see the celebrations in the ACLU offices? 'Boy, good thing we threw God out of the schools. With all the craziness in classrooms, the last thing we need is prayer.'"

"And according to one of our new gods, the oldest industry on earth, agriculture, is perceived as the most dangerous to the environment. Heck, common table pepper is more toxic than the most toxic chemical used in agriculture."

Jake shook his head in disbelief at the loss of common sense.

"And, as your editorial implies, gay religious leaders are in, Boy Scouts are out. Heterosexuality is an afterthought and sodomy has become a civil right, protected both by the US Constitution—somewhere, supposedly—and by the One World Government."

CHAPTER TWENTY-NINE

A week later, Mosey and Mary were packing their suitcases, all six of them, all the clothes they would take with them on their move to Israel. Everything else had been carted away to Goodwill. The Salvation Army was sending a couple of men over later in the morning to pick up the furniture. They'd catch a late-afternoon El Al flight.

"Imagine," Mosey said, "here it is, October. We'll get to Israel just in time for the Feast of Tabernacles."

"I can't wait." Mary looked up and smiled—the sweet smile Mosey had fallen in love with when they first met. She was folding blouses into a suitcase. "I love Israel this time of year. I love Israel every time of year. It'll be nice *not* to be going for a *shiva.*"

Mosey shivered. "Right. I've had enough funerals. Though I imagine that part of the equation won't get any better."

Mary laughed caustically. "Hey, life might be safer in Israel than New York City right now."

Mosey considered the notion.

His phone rang. Stephen Russell's face appeared on the screen.

Mosey muttered to himself, his tone flat, "Stephen."

"Kreko." Russell looked serious. "We need you at an emergency meeting."

"Stephen, I'm packing to move. We're leaving this afternoon."

"I know. I know. We've been through this move of yours. But it's crucial you be here. The board will all be here. In one hour at our Manhattan office."

"Yeah. Okay. But I can't spend all day."

"Believe me, this won't take more than a few minutes." The words were clipped. Russell was upset. Anger obviously seethed inside him.

Mosey mused over the thought Russell's head might pop off. Oh, that's not Christian, he scolded himself.

The monitor went dead and Mosey signed off.

"Sounds like Stephen's not a happy camper," Mary said.

"He's never a happy camper. Ha! As a matter of fact, if he saw a camp he'd probably burn the building down."

"Not being too harsh on him, are you?"

"Harsh?" Mosey mulled over the word for a moment. "Once Stephen told me he'd urinated on a bed in a hotel room because the maid, for three days, had made the sheets too tight even though he left her a note not to. Heck, the girl probably couldn't even read English."

"Nasty."

"Nasty is Stephen's middle name. Stephen Nasty Russell."

"He acted like a spoiled ten-year-old," Mary said. "Amazing he's head of the Alliance."

"No one ever checked our IQs when we joined the Alliance, and they never took them when we voted for chairman of the board," Mosey said. "Good thing."

"Well, I know *you* would have passed, honey." That smile again.

Mosey laughed. "Yeah, thanks."

He checked his watch. "I'd better get scooting. My stuff's all packed. I'll be back as soon as I can, babe. You can handle what remains, right?"

"Sure."

Mosey leaned forward and kissed her. "Bye."

As he left the room, Mary called after him, "God go with you."

He turned and smiled. "I'm counting on him."

Mosey decided to walk to the Gay Rights Resolve office. He needed to stretch and get some fresh air. And this might be his last day in New York City for a long time. Heck, the way the world was going, this might be his last time, ever.

Was he glad to be leaving? Ambivalent, really. He'd lived here much of his life. He loved the throngs of people, the excitement, the idea he could get up and go get a pizza any time of the day or night. The fact a famous actor or actress might stroll by at any moment. That many of the people who moved entire governments and industries walked these streets right alongside him. The fact great museums graced Manhattan and any time he wanted to see a Broadway show, all he need do is take a few steps.

The streets were oftentimes electric with energy. No one walked slowly here. They had purpose. Drive. Determination. And, every once in a while, someone would stop him on the street and shake his hand; they'd seen him on the news, or followed his career, or were glad he was on their side of the nuclear issue.

On the other hand, he felt strongly his parents were correct. The hunters were not coming, they were here. Even here in Manhattan—where Jewish people were leaders in the economy, had helped the business world flourish in the good times, and suffered with everyone else in the bad—yes, even here, threats had turned to violence.

The head of the Federal Reserve, a Jew, was shot on Wall Street just three days before and was recovering in Beth Israel Medical Center. A Conservative synagogue was fire-bombed a month ago. The outside of a Messianic synagogue full of

Russian immigrants, few if any of whom had much influence in the city, was spray-painted with the numbers 666 and with warnings of impending death.

Not long ago, you'd notice many men wearing yarmulkes on Fridays, Shabbat. Today, many of those men dared not do so.

Yes, he'd miss New York City, but not the evil that lurked in its dark alleys. He'd pine for his friends, but he had family in Israel and would gain acquaintances. He'd miss brothers and sisters from their church; but he'd see them again—in heaven if not here.

He'd miss singing "The Star Spangled Banner," but he loved Israeli music, even some of the funky modern stuff. He'd miss New York Harbor, but Israel had Jerusalem, the Dead Sea, the Sea of Galilee, the Golan Heights, the desert in the south, the wine country in the north, the ocean at Tel Aviv and Haifa. He'd miss the New York Symphony, but Israel's symphony was the best in the world.

He could go on and on comparing the two countries.

But in the end, above all else, Mary would be at his side. He and she had agreed, they wanted to make Israel their new home. They'd even shed tears when they hugged in agreement.

The moment of decision was a curious mixture. They were lifting a burden off their shoulders while facing the excitement of a new beginning. Mosey would continue to run Nuclear-Free World, but hoped to phase in Luke O'Neil to take over in a span of a few months.

What lay beyond the horizon? He didn't know, but change had never frightened him. Interestingly, although he'd kicked against the goads with his father for years, this very day he would come home.

Suddenly, he stood at the door to the Gay Rights Resolve office. He stepped inside. The place was neat-freak tidy. A rainbow was painted on the wall facing the entryway. Beneath the rainbow, in script, were the words: "Tell the children the truth."

How cute. Whose truth?

Roger Clapp, wearing a *MEAT* magazine T-shirt that begged to be burned, stuck his head out a door to the right. "Here's Kreko," he announced to others inside the room. He waved Mosey through the threshold.

A long, oblong mahogany table dominated the fourteen-by-fourteen-foot room. Sitting around the table were Russell, Tanya Frizzell of Citizens for Free Abortions; Buddy Joe Tatum and Angela Freeman of the Black Power League; Peter Whitetree of the Indian Lands Reclamation Federation; and, oh-my, Hisey Brinks of *Back Off!*

Mosey nodded to them and deadpanned, "Icky's still in hiding, I understand."

"Out of the loop, out of mind," Clapp said as he sat down.

Russell, seated at one point of the table, motioned for Mosey to take the empty chair opposite him. "We've just been talking about loyalty and the price of success, Kreko."

"Well, Stephen, I'd say you all can relate to that, with all the recent triumphs."

"Success, yes. Hmm. Loyalty's the question."

Mosey felt an ominous darkness surround him. He hurried past the sensation.

"So, what's the emergency about." He looked at his watch. "I have five hours until my flight."

Russell disregarded the comment. "In various cultures over the years, traitors have been stoned, beheaded, drawn-and-quartered— all sorts of beastly things."

Mosey didn't like where this was going. His cheek twitched. He stirred uncomfortably in his seat.

"Since you stormed out of our board meeting, we've kept a close eye on you, my friend."

"'We'? Who's 'we'?"

"The Alliance has eyes everywhere."

"And why would you keep an eye on me?"

"You recall your comments and your disagreement over our, ah, aggressive behavior."

"Attitude, boy!" Buddy Joe broke in, pointing a middle finger at Mosey. "It's your at-ti-tude." He spit out each syllable separately and distinctly.

Mosey locked Buddy Joe's eyes with a steely gaze that neutralized him.

"Ever since then," Russell continued, "you've attended our meetings, but your mind's been elsewhere. And your contributions?"

"Non-existent," Tanya Frizzell put in matter-of-factly. "Where were you for our Freedom of Choice walks? Our Supreme Court demonstration? Our call to arms where we all showed up soaked in blood to show what happens when a woman tries to abort herself with a coat-hanger?"

Mosey grimaced. "I disagree with infanticide, and your distortions of the fallout from laws forbidding partial-birth abortions. You need another reason?"

Tanya harrumphed, displaying her amazement at his narrow-minded stupidity.

Mosey decided to fill the silence. "Look, we all disagree on some things. We formed the Alliance so we'd have strength in numbers, not so we'd walk in each other's marches. Tanya, where were you at the protest we had at the One World Government meeting promoting nuclear power?"

She looked down.

"I know you have other places you'd rather be," Mosey continued. "We're all busy people with full agendas. Mostly those agendas agree. Sometimes they don't. So—," Mosey looked Russell in the eye, "I was opposed to beating up and terrorizing poor, defenseless newspaper deliverymen— far removed from Jake MacMillan and just trying to earn a buck." He shrugged. "Sue me."

"We'll do more than sue, buddy, if you've been back-stabbing us!" Hisey Brinks half-rose from his chair.

Only Peter Whitetree sat between Brinks and Mosey, and Mosey knew Brinks's proclivity towards violence, so he started to stand up in self-defense.

"Whoa!" Peter said, and pulled Brinks' arm down. "Easy, friend."

Brinks glared at Whitetree, then reluctantly took his seat.

Mosey also leaned back into his chair, but kept his eyes on Brinks. "What do you mean 'back-stabbing'?"

"You've been warning people about our attacks, bro. And we know it," Buddy Joe cut in, raising a fisted hand, then aiming his middle finger at him again. "We've got proof."

"Proof?" Mosey was amazed.

"We know the Homeland Security slime pigeon-holed you in Boston. We know they had you in custody, and— just like that," he snapped his fingers, "they let you go."

"Yeah," Russell interjected, "what about that, Kreko? You never told us any of this, did you?"

Mosey glanced from one man to the other. "There was nothing to tell. They grilled me, concluded I knew nothing, then let me go."

Mosey took a deep breath and looked around the table. "Besides that, Buddy Joe," he emphasized the name and glared at the man, "I didn't know anything about any attacks, so how could I tip anyone off about them?"

Buddy Joe clamped his lips shut, but Russell wasn't about to let the subject go. "Somehow, Kreko, you found out. Somehow you warned MacMillan about the attack on his home. Somehow you contacted him about the bombs at the Truth offices. And you tossed your loyalty in the toilet. For what? Thirty pieces of silver? What'd they give you? Immunity?"

Mosey threw up his hands. "What can I say? This is all bogus. And," he looked at his watch, "I've got to go. Soon enough you won't have me to deal with any more. So you can wind your conspiracy theories, like a noose, around someone else's neck."

He stood up to go.

Just then, two men appeared at the door. Shaved heads, menacing glares, and tattooed with skulls, chain link, lightning bolts and, Mosey was sure, various other intimidating engravings.

"I'm afraid you'll be going nowhere, Kreko," Russell said, "except with our friends here."

"What's this?" Mosey asked. Now this was getting scary.

"We'll be saying our goodbyes to you now, Kreko." Russell stood up and spoke to the two men while pointing at Mosey. "This is the one. He's all yours."

Fear ran down Mosey's spine and he turned to face the two men who approached him. They were an intimidating pair.

These guys could go on Wrestlemania. The Boston Maulers.

No time to be funny, Mosey squared his feet to defend himself. One of them pulled a gun and said, "Don't be stupid."

"No!" Peter Whitetree jumped to his feet. "Hold on."

Peter turned to Russell. "What's this, Stephen?"

"We're disposing of a problem," Russell said, too softly.

"No, you can't take Mosey."

"Peter," Roger Clapp said, "we all just had this conversation about how to deal with traitors. You were here and agreed with the rest of us."

"That was theory," Peter objected.

"We're moving from theory to fact, Petey," Buddy Joe breathed.

Peter looked frantically around the table. "B-but, this isn't right. Mosey's one of us."

Mosey looked from Peter to Russell to the two men dangerously close to him. "Listen," he pleaded, "you can't be serious about this. We're a law-abiding alliance. At least we're supposed to be. You talk about loyalty, Stephen. Where's yours?"

"Kreko, we're not murdering anyone here today."

Mosey breathed a sigh of relief because murder is exactly what he thought the two goons were going to do.

"No, we're simply combining the Muslim faith with some good old-fashioned revenge," Russell said. "When a Muslim steals, they cut off his hand. Well, here we're talking about a disloyal tongue."

Mosey's hand instinctively went to his mouth.

"No." Peter was determined. "No, you can't touch Mosey. It's me. It's me!"

"What do you mean, Peter?" Russell asked, incredulous.

"I mean, I'm the one who called in the warnings," Peter said.

Buddy Joe stood up behind Peter and put a full Nelson wrestling hold around his neck. "I'll kill you myself," he grumbled.

"Buddy Joe, let him go!" Russell snapped. Hands raised in question, mouth open in disbelief, he added, "Peter, I don't believe you."

405

Mosey doubted, too. He stood, frozen, just as others around the table watched in disbelief. Peter was giving himself up for Mosey. He didn't have to. He was putting, well, his tongue, if not his life, on the line for Mosey's.

Mosey stammered, "Peter, you don't have to do this." He and Peter were no more than a foot apart and Mosey could read the determination in Peter's eyes. He turned to Russell. "Stephen, this is insane."

He glared at Buddy Joe. "Let him go, or I'll inflict some serious pain on you—bro."

Suddenly, there was a flash of steel, and Buddy Joe displayed a long-bladed switchblade in his right hand. "I'm so seriously not afraid of you, white boy," he spat out.

Mosey appealed to Russell with his eyes. "Stephen, stop this."

Russell waved toward Buddy Joe and Peter. "As you can see, Kreko, it's out of my hands. Justice. Retribution. An eye for an eye and all that. In this case, a tongue will do. And if not yours, Peter's. I just can't believe Peter's guilty. Do you, Buddy Joe?"

Buddy Joe turned sideways to look at Russell, and when he did, Peter grabbed his wrist and drove his thumb into a pressure point that forced Buddy Joe to drop the knife. Bending beneath Buddy Joe's arms and spinning, Peter took control of the knife and held its razor-sharp tip to Buddy Joe's throat.

One of the two goons pointed a gun at Peter, but Russell sputtered, "Don't!"

Reluctantly, he pointed the gun downward.

Keeping the knife in place, Peter looked at Russell. "Stephen, I simply think we've gone overboard. Hisey here is destroying buildings and boats and who-knows-what all over the world. He tried to blow Darek and Jillian Fields out of the sky in Rome, man. We're strong-arming and threatening companies, big companies, trying to put Truth out of business."

"We are?" Mosey blurted out. Russell merely shrugged.

"We've gone from a group of the socially conscious to—to—well, I don't know. Hitler's brown shirts would be proud of us."

"Hey, they did it right, man, no matter what you think of their politics," Brinks barked. "Spread out the wealth. Get rid of the Jews."

"Hey, I'm a Jew!" Mosey objected. "You wanna get rid of me?"

Peter pushed the tip of the knife into Buddy Joe's chin. A drop of blood beaded on the steel.

Brinks held up a hand. "No-no-no. You know what I mean."

"Well, what *I* mean," Peter said, "is I'm getting outta here. I think you can withdraw the Indian Lands Reclamation Federation from the Alliance, Stephen."

He held onto the knife and, tugging Buddy Joe along with him, backed toward the door and the two bruisers who, moments before, were going to handle the problem of Mosey Kreko.

"You comin' with me, Mosey?" Peter asked.

"Right behind you."

Outside, moving hastily, Peter hailed a taxi and pushed Buddy Joe to the ground.

Sliding into the back seat beside Peter, Mosey said, "Hey, thank you, man. You put your life on the line for me."

Peter shook his hand. "You would've done the same for me."

"Would I?"

"'course. You're a Christian now, right?"

407

"Well, a Messianic Jew. It's semantics, but you're right."

"And Jesus died for his friends, right?"

"He died for the whole world."

"Then I can die for one friend."

"Thank God you don't have to."

"Yeah. Thank God."

"Hey, fellas." The taxi driver's voice was gruff, restless. "Ya' gonna have a lovefest back there, or do ya' wanna go somewheres?"

Mosey told him his address. Turning to Peter, he said, "I really do have a plane to catch. Mary's packing up the last of our stuff right now."

Peter sat back. "Mind if I help you to the airport? I could carry some of your luggage. Besides, I want to talk to you about this Christian stuff, ya' know?"

Mosey smiled. "Sure." Then, frowning as a question came to mind, he asked, "Hey, why'd Russell let you go, anyhow? He had the firepower to stop both of us if he wanted."

Peter smiled. "Stephen's sweet on me."

"What? You're not—"

"No, I'm not." Peter held up a hand. "But he's sweet on me."

"Wow," Mosey said softly. He thought about the moment. A sinner's sin saved a righteous man from being maimed. He'd have to ponder that one for a while.

CHAPTER THIRTY

Bill Asbury parked his Ford Fusion in front of the MacMillan home and walked to the entrance. Bob Ward, who'd remotely-opened the gate, welcomed him through the door.

The two men hugged hello.

"Jake's waiting for you."

They found Jake sitting by a patio table Bible in hand.

"Reading the news of the day?" Bill called out.

"It's all coming true," Jake said and stood to shake Bill's hand. "Thanks for coming. I need your prayer, your support, your wisdom."

"Sure. What's up?" Worry lines formed on Bill's face, then he said, "A-huh, yesterday's column."

It wasn't a question.

"You knew."

"I guessed. Who's reacting. A local court or the One World Court?"

"Sardis himself."

"Sardis?" Bill was amazed. "The World Premier's suing you?"

Jake shook his head in amazement. "Wants to be the champion of the world's LGBTQs."

"Is he?" Bill asked, brows raised.

"I don't know. Don't care."

Jake motioned Bill and Bob to take seats.

"How about I get us some iced tea?" Bob said.

"Good idea. Thanks."

Bill sat down. Blowing out a deep breath, he looked at Jake. "You're serious. Sardis himself is out to get you?"

"Well, it's his law, his declaration. He must want to make an example of me to the world, and show anyone and everyone he's in control."

"Are our American courts going to hand over jurisdiction to the One World Court?"

"Apparently. No surprise, right?"

Bill shook his head. "Guess not."

"Why stand up to Sardis with honor for the justice system or for ethics or for national boundaries?" Jake was disgusted and his face was proof. "Forget our own Constitution. Ignore free speech, the right to bear arms, or even free will. Neglect following your own religious beliefs.

"This is why our federal bureaucracies have parasitically devoured the resources and liberty of the citizens to whom they're pledged to be accountable. This is why the federal courts have forsaken the law and rule illegally and unconstitutionally—by the fiat of judicial oligarchs who've been methodically eliminating all acknowledgment and memory of our Christian history and heritage."

Bill let his friend vent. He knew Jake had to get the exasperation out of his system. They couldn't pray effectively until he did. Prayer had to begin with forgiveness. Bill would help him along the way.

As Bob arrived with a large pitcher of iced tea and three tall glasses, Jake looked at Bill. "You know what the One World Government is threatening to do?

"No."

"Lock me up and shut down the newspaper and web site."

Bill was taken aback. "Can they?"

"They'd try to shut down the television station as well, but the editorial didn't appear there—only in the newspaper and on the web."

"What does your attorney say?"

"I don't know. He'll get here in an hour or so. I wanted to pray with you first."

Bob poured the drinks and Jake took a long swallow.

"You know," Jake said, "years ago before I started Truth, I heard a preacher say, 'If it's God's plan, he'll provide the resources. If it's his calling, he'll provide the power.' I stood by that statement as a word from God himself."

"Well," Bill said, "he certainly provided both the resources and the power."

"But progress has been a battle every day."

"You've got to be like Paul."

"In what way?"

"Governments. Religious leaders. Political leaders. Idol-makers. Pagans. They all ganged up on Paul at one time or another. And yet he said he ran the race to the end for the great prize awaiting him." Bill reached for Jake's Bible. "Mind?"

"Not at all."

Bill sipped his iced tea as he turned through the pages, finding the place he wanted. "Here we are, Second Corinthians chapter eleven."

He began to read: "'Three times I was shipwrecked. I spent a night and a day in the open sea. I have been constantly on the move. I have been in danger from rivers, in danger from bandits, in danger from my own countrymen, in danger from Gentiles, in danger in the city, in danger in the country, in danger at sea, and in danger from false brothers. I have labored and toiled and often gone without sleep. I have known hunger and thirst and have often gone without food.

I have been cold and naked. Besides everything else, I face daily the pressure of my concern for all the churches.'"

Bill looked up at Jake. "I can't wait to meet Paul. A man after my own heart. Never slowed down—until he was imprisoned."

"I'll accept prison," Jake said, "if only they don't shut down my newspaper."

"Whose newspaper?" Bill asked.

Jake shrugged. "You're right. God's."

"And we have to believe God will watch over the operation, protect against its enemies, continue the truth being published."

Jake nodded agreement.

"Come on, gentlemen," Bill said. "Let's pray."

The three men joined hands.

Darek and Ty packed up the pair of two-man tents from the campsite next to Abol Bridge, while Jillian and Bethany took care of all the eating utensils and doused the campfire.

They'd put into the Appalachian Trail four days before at Katahdin Iron Works at the West Branch of the Pleasant River in the middle of Maine. They'd figured on a five- or six-day hike, and they were right on the money.

"Amazing number of people out here," Darek observed.

"Good thing there aren't even more," Ty said with a chuckle. "With Jill stopping to chat with everyone who recognizes you guys and wants autographs and selfies, we'd hardly be on time."

"So, it'd be dark glasses and floppy hats for us, eh?"

Ty shrugged. "Not a bad idea. When we get back to Boston, that's your new garb—at least when the four of us go out together."

"Good, then. You can tell Jill. She's the social butterfly."

"I hadn't thought of that." Ty shoved the last edge of his tent into its satchel. "To get Jill to *not* engage people would require a lobotomy."

Darek laughed. "Okay. Let's get serious." He pointed to the bridge, which was just wide enough for one car, although no cars had driven by since they set up camp the previous evening. "The terrain from here to the base of Katahdin is flat as an airstrip."

"The girls'll be happy to hear, especially after surviving Gulf Hagas and the last couple of days," Ty said.

Giggles emanated from the women.

Darek pointed a thumb in their wives' direction. "You and I could be a thousand miles away and these two would be happy as clams. They're like sisters."

"They *are* sisters," Ty replied, "sisters in the faith. Like we're brothers. You know I trust you more than I trust my own brother, right?"

Darek looked at him curiously. "Thanks, man. I'm honored you'd say that."

Ty stuffed his fold-up tent into a polyethylene bag. "Must be difficult, not having family."

"Jill's more than enough."

"Yeah. Same with Jess and me."

"I think as long as I have Jillian, I can live in just about any circumstances."

One the words left his lips, Darek thought them through a second time. Every word was true and now, having spoken them, the thought carried more weight.

"Well," Ty eyed him, "Rabbi Moshe Chaim Luzatto says if not for pursuit of acclaim, a person could get along with the bare necessities of life."

"Right. Bare necessities," Darek repeated. "I guess that's what we have here, right?"

"And our trusty cell phones." Ty laughed, patting a pocket in his satchel on the ground.

"Yeah, I've got mine, too. I wonder if there's any service out here in the wilderness."

"I don't know. I'm not going to try. Jess would filet me with that knife she's putting away."

Darek glanced at the women. Sure enough, Bethany was storing away a fileting knife. "What a weapon! Did they think we were going to kill a bear out here or something?"

"After the way I ran away from that bear cub yesterday?"

Darek chortled, remembering Ty's track-star speed. "You know, if mamma bear had shown up, the only way to escape would have been to fly."

"Yeah. Hey, I wonder if anyone's ever tried to design a backpack fitted with a glider."

"Don't laugh. That would be a hot seller at L.L. Bean's. I can see the ad now." He waved his hand and put on his broadcaster's voice. "Here's Tyson Cole on the roof of L.L. Bean's landmark store in Freeport, Maine, preparing to demonstrate his Cole's High-Flying Backpack. An ambulance crew stands at the ready. His wife is wearing black, just in case. We're told friends and family have written eulogies."

Ty straightened his back as if taking offense. "Actually, I'd call my creation Ty's Taking-a-Powder Pack."

Darek guffawed and slapped Ty on the shoulder.

"We noticed you boys are real serious over here." Jillian's voice interrupted the moment. Darek looked up. Both the women stood, feet apart, arms crossed, serious looks on their faces. They reminded him of his high school French teacher when Darek mispronounced a word that sounded particularly suggestive.

"I can see you've been slaving away over here," Jillian said. "Our tent?"

She followed Darek's eyes as he looked to a lump on the ground. "Well, babe," he stumbled, "I-I was packing up. But T-Ty, here. He, ah, he—"

"You see, ladies," Ty cut in, "I was explaining to Darek about my Ty's Taking-a-Powder Pack—"

A screech suddenly cut through the morning air. Winging down from a high pine tree, a blue jay glided overhead with the grace of an eagle, not more than ten feet above where they stood. He cut sideways and to the right, screeched again, then landed on the branch of another tree beyond them.

No more than a second later, the bird hopped into the air and nearly sidled up next to them, taking a perch at about eye height on a pine tree a couple of feet from Jillian.

"Whoa! Darek said, stunned at the bird's audacity.

Afraid to scare away their feathered visitor, they were silent for a good fifteen seconds. Apparently, having sized them up and given them a passing grade, the blue jay hopped to the ground next to the food satchel the girls had packed up. The bird stepped to the sack and started pecking, no, twisting the knot on the cord that kept the bag closed.

"Now, I don't know about your powder pack, Ty," Bethany said in a low tone, "but *that's* unusual."

"You think he can actually open the backpack?" Jillian asked.

"Let's watch and see," Darek said.

The blue jay cocked his head, as if he understood their conversation, then returned to his task. He pecked and picked at a knot and pulled the cord back hard. The knot appeared to loosen a bit.

"Perhaps we should give him some help," Bethany ventured, her voice low.

"I think he's plenty strong," Jillian said. "Look, he's finished."

Indeed, the blue jay had untied the knot and pushed his head inside.

"What have we got that he'd like?" Ty asked.

"What wouldn't he like?" Jillian said. "We've got peanut butter, crackers, trail mix—"

"Well, let's toss him some trail mix and save him from tearing apart the rest of the stuff that's air-packed," Bethany said, moving toward the satchel.

Sensing her approach, the blue jay stepped back out of the satchel and jumped onto a tree branch a couple of feet away. Then he yipped.

"Now that's a unique voice you have there, Sam," Bethany said.

He yipped again.

"Sam," Jillian said in reflection. "He must like the name."

He yipped again.

"Are you sure this isn't an advanced robot of some kind," Darek said. He was half-serious.

Bethany held out a hand full of trail mix to the bird. He leaned in and pecked at the treat and when he did, she stroked his side. The bird didn't object. Bethany turned to Darek. "That is a real live bird. No doubt."

"Well, then, he deserves a real live name, and I think you happened upon the right one."

Waving to the bird, Ty said, "Hey, Sam. Want to follow us to Katahdin?"

From their vantage point, they could see the top of the bold end of the Appalachian Trail. The sky above was clear except for a few wispy clouds far overhead.

"We're a day's hike away," Darek said. "We'd better pack up and head out."

Bethany opened her palm and showed the others. Sam had made quick work of the trail mix.

"Maybe he comes from California," she said.

"Why's that?" Jillian asked.

"That was California trail mix."

Flutes and tambourines playing joyful Jewish music approached from behind them and Mosey tugged Mary to the side of the Jerusalem street. Around the corner came a parade of people of various nationalities, holding up banners, waving colorful banners, singing, and clapping their hands. The throng strolled along in ragged columns four and five people wide.

"That song," Mary questioned.

Mosey nodded and smiled. "About God returning His people to Israel. About us."

"Who are these people?" Mary wondered aloud.

Mosey pointed to the banners. International Christian Embassy of Jerusalem. Bridges for Peace. Christians United for Israel. Christian Friends of Israel. Abrahamic Faith. Stand for Israel. Gratefully Grafted Ministries. Intercessors for Israel. Olive Root Ministries. National Unity Coalition for Israel.

"Christian Zionists," he said.

A Jewish man, about Mosey's height, stood beside him and nudged his elbow. The man spoke in rather fluent English, his voice deep yet soft. "These people, they get more and more each year."

Mosey nodded.

"Why, you ask?"

Mosey looked at him. Was this man a professor or something? Mosey hadn't asked, but now he wondered.

"Because the Palestinian Arabs themselves have made the case for Israel even stronger to Christians by desecrating the Christian holy sites, preventing them from traveling to places like the Mount of Olives and Jericho, and destroying Christian communities throughout the Middle East. Their terror betrays their hearts." He motioned toward the parade. "And more and more, these Christians are recognizing this Arab bigotry against them as well as the right of Jews to have our own country."

Mosey nodded again.

"You ask what a native Jew thinks about this."

Mosey laughed to himself. *No, I didn't ask.* Mary leaned into him so she might hear the exchange over the sounds of music and singing. Mosey nodded again.

"I think I'm seeing a miracle. People who centuries ago hated us—annihilated us, even, in ovens; pierced us at the end of spears; turned our land into treeless ruin—here they are singing the words of our prophet Zephaniah. They're intoning Tzion's praises, calling for our people to return home, to fulfill our call from Adonai Himself. A miracle, I say."

Mosey nodded.

"You wonder what we who have lived here for decade upon decade of anxious survival, think about giving the Muslims their own country?"

No, Mosey had not been pondering this, at least not at this moment. But now he did. He nodded.

"We who truly think things through—and don't simply throw up our hands in submission—question. We inquire, Is Islam's enemy the Jew and the West so much as the modern world that has passed them by?

"Is their enemy not the humiliation resulting from fantasies, conspiracies, and hypocrisies their leaders have devised to explain multiple age-old failures? Is their enemy not their own ideals which shun democracy; owe allegiance to their patriarchy and tribes rather than a nation of their own; ignore female intellect, and allow polygamy?"

The man shrugged and added, "Is it not that they produce children once a year until their homes overflow with offspring?"

Mosey now turned to look over this fellow. An intellectual, no doubt. Gentle-looking face. Bright brown eyes. Definitely a Jewish nose. Sporting a full beard and wearing black slacks, white shirt and Israeli-blue kippah.

"Go on," Mosey urged.

"Adonai loves the Arabs even if they don't recognize him," the man said. "They're our cousins, no doubt. But they put up with corruption. They even expect fraud and exploitation. They tolerate honor killings. They cheer when airplanes fly into buildings and kill innocents. They define knowledge as mastery of the Koran." He threw up his hands. "This is all lethal. This borders on, even exemplifies, psychosis."

Mosey was breathless. He felt like he'd just been tutored. He wanted to sit down with this man, to sit at his feet. He turned to Mary to gauge her reaction. She'd listened intently while watching and returned his gaze. That is when he noticed her eyes go wide and her brow furrow.

He followed the direction of her eyes, toward the man.
He was gone.

CHAPTER THIRTY-ONE

The Four Footmen, as they now called themselves—or Four Foot-sore-men seemed more appropriate to Jillian—were closing in on Mount Katahdin. They planned to set up camp one final night before reaching its peak which would be about noon the next day.

They'd passed a few hikers walking the other direction, and a couple more had passed them by like SUVs in a NASCAR race.

As a college-age couple whizzed past them, Darek quipped, "Someday some kid will *run* the Appalachian Trail."

"I'll be happy if I just get to the end of our little trek," Bethany said. "To be truthful, Ty, I'm glad a few of these people recognize our famous friends here and want to talk politics. We get the chance to take a breather."

"I get the feeling the ones who don't want to chat are throwing verbal darts at us as soon as they pass by," Jillian said.

"Don't be concerned, babe," Darek said. "I know people generally love me or hate me. I'm glad you're in the first group. I try to have a short memory about the second bunch."

"Yeah, a short memory about that and buying a gallon of milk when I ask you," Jillian joked.

"Funny," he deadpanned. "Listen, Jess, when by the end of the day today, you can tell people you hiked part of the One Hundred-Mile Wilderness."

"Isn't that like getting just some of the winning Mega-Lotto numbers?" she replied with a smile.

"No, you don't get blisters on your feet when you buy lottery tickets," Jillian said.

As they hiked, Sam stayed close by. They joked he was their point man, scouting out the territory.

"You'd think he'd have a girlfriend somewhere," Ty said.

"Or maybe Sam is Samuella and *she* has a boyfriend," Jillian suggested.

Behind the four hikers, always keeping a good hundred yards in the distance, a man dressed in a green T-shirt and camouflage pants kept pace. His backpack was heavier than most, for one compartment contained a Tac-Op Bravo 55 sniper rifle detachable at the barrel and the butt and well disguised.

He loved the weapon. Twenty-inch barrel with accuracy guaranteed deadly to a thousand meters. The wide foreend of the McHale stock was great for supported shooting and put a lot of weight up front. The trigger was amazing—no creep, no over-travel, and a crisp two-and-a-half-pound let-off. And why didn't more rifle manufacturers use large bolt handles like these? Perfect.

Only he'd never used the Tac-Op on live targets. This would be his first time.

He peered through his binoculars. The Fields and their pals were almost at the base of the mountain now and he swore because, once the hikers started their ascent, time would have run out for him.

Katahdin was treeless, leaving him no cover. Exposed. That had happened in Arizona once. He cringed at the memory, and his hand went instinctively to the scar left by a bullet skimming his left shoulder.

No, he'd have to make his move now. Waiting another day in this godforsaken wilderness for them to emerge back at the bottom of the mountain was not in the cards. Nor in his wallet. He had another job waiting and higher paying than this one: Jake MacMillan. Ha!

And, even if he did wait, who knew if he'd get his chance? Who'd have thought so many people hiked this dumb trail, anyhow? A trail from Georgia to Maine? What moron thought that one through?

And why do all these idiot hikers want to chat with these jokers? He shook his head at the numerous times he could have finished this job—but for all these people. They'd become the bane of his existence.

Man, this woods stuff was not his idea of fun, either. A bar, a casino, a babe at his side. A smile curled his lips. A babe at his side. Yeah.

He stole into the woods and sprinted forward through the thick forest to get parallel and beyond his prey. He had to bend and twist to keep his backpack from getting hung up in the branches.

He prided himself on keeping fit, but, boy, he'd never had to wrestle with trees on the training ground. Suddenly, he caught a branch in the face.

"Ouch!" he hollered. The branch's bristles had snapped his right eye, stinging horribly. He went to one knee and cursed a streak of words red enough to curdle milk.

On the trail, Darek stopped. "Did you hear something?"

"Where?" Jillian asked.

He pointed into the woods to the right.

"I thought I heard a yell or something, too," Ty said.

Sam let out a scream.

"Sam heard it, for sure," Darek said.

They stood still and listened intently for a minute. Nothing.

Darek shrugged and continued on, while Sam flew up higher into a nearby pine tree. They were no more than fifty yards from the spot where the trail left the tree line behind and began a quick ascent toward the five thousand eight hundred-foot-high summit.

The man in camouflage rubbed his eye and swore again, but quieter this time. Tears streamed from the corner of his eye. What a time for this to happen!

He tried to focus, but could barely even open the eye. The sunlight stung too much. *Clouds, where are you?*

His right eye was his shooting eye. He was running out of time and was determined not to let these next few minutes pass without fulfilling this contract.

He stood to his feet. Stepping forward, he squinted out of his left eye, searching for a tree with a clear view to the trail. A birch tree, rare around here, stood about ten feet ahead. He rushed to the birch, shrugged his shoulder to drop his backpack and hurriedly unzipped the compartment containing the rifle. Locking the parts together, he scrambled to his feet. One branch shot off the birch horizontally about five-and-a-half feet off the ground. Perfect.

Wincing from the pain in his eye, he aimed the rifle as best he could and looked through the scope. Blurry. He rubbed away the tears with the heel of his hand. He felt like he was aiming sideward. *This had better work!*

Taking his eye away from the rifle, he tried to spot the Fields. He squeezed his eyes shut, then opened them.

There they were. But Darek Fields was walking with the other joker and Jillian was chatting with the other woman. *Stupid broads. Never stop yackin'. Yack, yack, yack.*

Back to the scope. This'll work. This'll work!

He'd take out Darek Fields first—him being the biggest pain, public enemy number one. Well, number two, after Jake MacJerkin. *Trying to blame oil spills on Arabs! It's the oil companies hauling oil around on decrepit tankers, man. Wake up, you lyin' piece of trash. I'm takin' you out later.*

He kept the scope moving to the right, trying to get his sights on Darek Fields. The other guy was obstructing his shot, though. *Wait a sec. Just a sec.*

Then his view opened. No trees. Ah! A clear shot.

Just as he prepared to squeeze the trigger, a loud shriek just above his head made him flinch and twist the rifle. He looked up. A blue jay was staring down at him, shrieking, shrieking. He cursed, pointed his rifle at the bird, and was about to pull the trigger.

"Better put that down, son."

The voice came from behind him. He turned around warily. A game warden, complete with army-green uniform and hat, Maine Inland Fisheries and Game patch on his shirt, pointed a pistol straight at his nose.

"Put the rifle on the ground," the game warden said calmly. He was a kindly looking older man, perhaps fifty years old, twenty-five, thirty years on the job.

Would he shoot me? He fingered his rifle and considered a dip-and-roll to the ground.

Dip-and-roll with one bad eye? A better time will arise, when the warden's off-guard.

He obeyed, gently placing the rifle on the ground in front of him.

"Out here to shoot birds, are you? With a rifle like that?"

He said nothing.

"I don't think so. On your knees and your hands behind your back, son."

He swore at his own stupidity. *Should have shot the old rat!* He knelt, and with resignation, put his arms behind him. A moment later, the game warden moved behind him, keeping the pistol leveled at his head, and, as quick as spit's gone in the desert, the cuffs were on. He felt a prick of pain because they were clamped on a bit too tightly. He swore yet again.

"Gonna have to clean up your mouth, son, or those cuffs can tighten up a notch or two."

Absent for a short time, Sam flitted back to the party of hikers, landing on a stunted pine tree in front of them.

"He looks like he wants to tell us a story," Darek said.

"But, hey, he's a bird," Ty said.

They'd just re-renamed themselves the Fearsome Foursome. That was, until the ladies discovered the name originated with the defensive front line of an old National Football League team. Then they rebelled.

"Let's just watch our step," Jillian warned. "I don't want us to be the Freefalling Foursome."

They all laughed, then set out again, upward toward the northern end of the Appalachian Trail.

Darek checked his watch. "Seven a.m., folks. Lunch awaits us at the top."

"Too much to hope they have a taco stand up there?" Bethany asked.

When they reached about halfway up the rock-strewn slope, a pale rainbow appeared in the sky to the east.

"That's odd," Darek observed. He scanned the sky. Crystal clear. And hot? Temperatures rose the closer they got to the top of this broad-shouldered mountain rising ascending out of the Maine woods and wrapped arms around a basin containing tiny Chimney Pond.

At 10 a.m., Ty announced the time and asked, "How about we take a break?"

"No complaints here," Darek replied.

Everyone looked for a spot of shade, finding one beside an oversized boulder to the side of the trail. They unloaded their backpacks and sat down on rocks.

"You know, in two hours, at twelve noon here, the Feast of Tabernacles will begin in Israel," Ty said.

"Okay, you've got me," Darek said with a shrug, looking for an explanation.

"It'll be seven o'clock in Israel. Sundown. The start of the holy day."

"Is there some significance?"

"Well, God commanded the Hebrews to celebrate seven feasts—always. Four in the spring and three more in the fall," Ty began. "When Jesus first came, he fulfilled the spring feasts. When he comes again, he'll fulfill the fall feasts."

"Go on," Jillian urged.

"The first spring feast is Pesach, or Passover, remembering when the Jews sacrificed lambs and put the blood on their doorposts so when the angel of death passed by, they'd be saved. Jesus came as the Passover Lamb of God, a perfect sacrifice not needing to be repeated year after year. As John 1:29 says: 'Behold, the Lamb of God who takes away the sin of the world.'

"The second feast is Unleavened Bread, and Jesus said, 'I am the living bread that came down out of heaven; if anyone eats of this bread, he shall live forever; and the bread also which I shall give for the life of the world is my flesh.'"

They were all paying close attention, nodding as Ty discoursed.

"The third feast is First Fruits. First Corinthians chapter fifteen tells us, 'But now Christ has been raised from the dead, the first fruits of those who are asleep.'

"And the fourth feast is Shavuot, or Feast of Weeks, which we know as Pentecost when Jesus sent the Holy Spirit."

"You mentioned fall feasts," Jillian said. "What about them?"

"A lot of Messianic Jews and others believe if Jesus fulfilled the spring feasts, he'll fulfill the others as well. These all come together this month—right now—Rosh Hashanah, or Feast of Trumpets, the New Year; Yom Kippur, or Day of Atonement; and Sukkot, or the Feast of Tabernacles.

"Catching away, or resurrecting his bride—that is his believers—will fulfill Trumpets. Returning to judge and cleanse the people will fulfill the Day of Atonement. And establishing his kingdom on earth will fulfill Feast of Tabernacles, which celebrates the Lord living among his people.

Darek scratched his chin and said, "So this is what again?"

"Feast of Tabernacles," Ty said. "As a matter of fact, I've been thinking about this the last couple of nights when we've been sleeping in lean-tos and tents. During the Feast of Tabernacles, Jews around the world build flimsy booths through which you can see the sky, to remind them of their closeness to God, his deliverance during the forty years in the desert, and that life is fleeting."

"I do feel closer to God out here, sleeping under the stars," Bethany said. Darek and Jillian nodded in agreement.

"Now, picture this," Ty continued, enthusiasm catching hold. "Jesus comes to Jerusalem to celebrate Feast of Tabernacles. On the seventh and last day of the feast, he witnesses the water-drawing ceremony where the priests circle the temple altar seven times, repeating 'Hoshannah,' or 'Save now.' Jesus's name means 'salvation,' and he identified himself as the source of living water when he told the Samaritan woman, 'Whoever drinks of the water that I shall give him will never thirst. But the water that I shall give him will become in him a fountain of water springing up into everlasting life.'

"And Jesus was there during the Illumination of the Temple. Now, this was amazing. I would have loved to have been alive to see this. There were four gigantic golden candlesticks in the court of the women in the Temple—"

"Of course, golden candlesticks, court of the women. Works for me," Bethany kidded.

"Me, too." Jillian laughed.

"Ladies!" Ty pushed his hands palms down in a gesture for quiet. "As I was saying, four youths of priestly descent filled these candlesticks with pure oil, and the light from them was so bright every courtyard in Jerusalem was lit up by them."

"Wows," echoed all around.

"Now picture Jesus, the young rabbi, walking in the midst of this celebration, surrounded by Levitical musicians and choir, and religious leaders dancing and singing songs of praise and burning torches. Here was Jerusalem, lit up like the sun for miles around, and the Son of God proclaimed, 'I am the light of the world. He who follows me shall not walk in the darkness, but shall have the light of life.'"

Darek stood up. "This is amazing stuff, Ty."

"Yeah." Ty nodded and went on. "He'd come to 'tabernacle'"—he finger-quoted—"among us temporarily as the Bread of Life and Light of the World. As the Lamb of God, he'd died a sinless sacrifice for all mankind and send the Ruach HaKodesh, the Holy Spirit, to us as counselor and comforter until he returns again."

"Are you saying Jesus could be coming again in just two hours?" Jillian asked.

"Maybe. Maybe not. At certain times for two thousand years, people have thought his coming would be this year or next."

"But, at noon our time, Feast of Tabernacles begins?" Darek urged.

"Yes."

"Well, if he comes, I'm not ready," Darek said, throwing up his hands.

Ty laughed.

"No, Ty. I'm serious." Darek's voice rose, and he felt a tingle of fear.

"Probably none of us feel we're ready. But, our time could happen at any time, right? I mean, none of us knows when we might die."

"What I mean is, I have a lot of things I want to do," Darek said, showing his frustration. "I have a wife I adore and want to spend many, many years with—"

"Believe me, you'll have many, many, many years to spend with Jill."

Jillian reached out and touched Darek's hand. "Eternity, darling."

"But I want us to see the world together, sip tea in England and espresso in Italy, wine in France and—"

"Darek," Jillian cut in, "don't you think the new heaven and the earth will make this one look like a dull image of grandeur compared to the eternal?"

Darek shrugged. "I guess so."

"My bet is, yes," Ty said. "Hey, we'd better get going."

They all lifted their backpacks into place and stepped off up the trail—Darek more tentative than the others. This subject was weighing on his mind.

In the town of Millinocket, the police chief was questioning the mysterious man in the camo pants whom Warden Jeff Waring had brought in handcuffed.

Probably one of these weird militia types, out practicing "maneuvers." Small fry acting like a big fish.

He might even let the guy go free, with a warning. Save the town a few bucks on feeding him. Wasn't like the town had a whole lot of money since the paper mill closed down.

The mountaintop was in sight and the sky cloudless, but Darek's brain was foggy. *Die now? I'm not ready for that.* He couldn't wrap his mind around the idea of "going to heaven with the Lord."

"No sickness. No disease." Ty's voice interrupted his thoughts.

"What's that?" Darek asked.

"In heaven you'll have a new body, a spiritual body. We all will—we who believe. Our friends and family who've gone on before us—they'll be there, those who believe. I know you've got a great life, Darek. But heaven. Heaven!" Ty was elated by the thought of the next life, and Darek started to catch the feeling.

"No achy knee after a game of tennis," he said.

"No slice in your golf game," Ty added.

"No bad-hair days," Jillian said.

"And fingernail polish never wears off," Bethany offered. They all laughed.

"Well, I don't know about any of that," Ty replied. "But being in the presence of God will be glorious. And *Whenever* that happens, I'm ready." He looked at Bethany, who was two steps behind him. "If I go first, Beth, I'll be there waiting for you."

"Vice versa, hon."

"But I don't want to go before I play Pebble Beach," Darek said.

Ty shook his head. "There's no helping this guy."

CHAPTER THIRTY-TWO

The red telephone rang on Jake's desk, startling him out of his reflections and back to the present. He looked out the window and the monster wave still hovered, like a hungry monster ready to devour a banquet. He picked up the phone and checked the monitor.

"Darek!"

"Jake."

"Where are you?"

"Top of Mount Katahdin. You won't believe—"

"Oh, yes, I will."

"Two earthquakes just ripped right by the mountain and," Darek swallowed, "half of Maine disappeared right before our eyes!"

"Half of Maine!" Jake found himself yelling into the phone in response to Darek, who also was yelling. The reception was awful, static crackling in the audio and a fuzzy picture in the video.

"Take us live and we'll give a report," Darek said.

"Can't right now. I've sent everyone to the basement to avoid the tidal wave. I'm alone in my office."

Suddenly, Darek's image disappeared from the monitor.

In Jake's office, Jake was gone. In the basement, only two people—a cameraman and an advertising sales lady—remained, staring dumbfounded at one another.

In the elder Krekos' home in Jerusalem, where Mosey and Mary were visiting for the lighting of a menorah for Feast of Tabernacles, they were hunkered down when a mammoth earthquake struck. Instantly, the four all vanished. The match Sarah Kreko had used to light the candles was still warm to the touch, if anyone had been there to touch it.

In the huge hall where International Christian Embassy Jerusalem's Feast of Tabernacles celebration was about to take place, most of the thousands had disappeared. A couple of dozen people remained scattered about the auditorium, aghast. Some slunk to chairs, others to their knees as the ceiling began to rain down upon them.

At the Temple Mount in the Old City, the Dome of the Rock and Al Aqsa Mosque shook ferociously, then crumbled in a pile to the ground, burying everyone beneath. Beside them, the Third Temple under construction stood tall, unshaken.

The cell phone through which Peter Whitetree had been speaking with a CNN reporter, had fallen to the ground, Peter gone. Disappeared.

In the private conference room of the Supreme Court's chief justice, where the nine justices were discussing the president's request that cases involving war crimes go straight to the World Court, three of the justices had disappeared—one of them in mid-sentence. The others sat speechless, staring at one another.

In the White House, the president and defense secretary sat, taking a call from the head of the president's disaster team, trying to get a handle on the magnitude of the massive earthquakes that had carved California and the far northeastern states into the oceans. Out the office window, the sun had turned black like sackcloth.

Similar scenes unfolded around the world, where earthquakes that topped out at the maximum 10.0 had cracked, crushed, and collapsed entire cities.

Premier Sardis stood on the roof above his office in Brussels and held a briefcase stuffed with his most important papers in a vise grip. The roof shook uncontrollably, and the pilot of his helicopter was having a difficult time landing to pick him up.

Shielding his face from the helicopter's blade-wash, Sardis noticed the rising full moon had turned blood-red, like a crimson blanket had been tossed over the orb. And he swore he saw several stars in the sky fall to earth.

EPILOGUE

Eighteen hours later, broadcasting from an undisclosed place—probably in Europe—World Premier Clifford Sardis, with His Excellence, Church Universal General Secretary Howard Alphonse Bliss at his side, calmly salved the fright of the earth's population.

Every television and radio station still able to broadcast was tuned to the two men.

"A great and wonderful thing has happened," the Premier exulted, "and yet we know many people the world over are scared, anxious—even panicking. We want to calm you, to quiet your spirits."

"Yes," His Excellence Bliss said, "our Creator, in a marvelous display of his power, has removed the one element on this earth preventing us from accomplishing universal unity. Many Christians and Jews are no longer on this earth. God's purpose was to remove them—to vanquish them into utter darkness, along with their fundamentalist, unforgiving, mean-spirited, tunnel-visioned, rigid theology.

"Gone is their hatred for everyone who does not agree with them. Gone is their venom, spewed out toward other, peaceful religions—and religious leaders, I may add."

"We are here to tell you," Sardis cut in, "His Excellence Mr. Bliss and I, your World Premier, are joined together and will stand with each and every one of you, as we face a brilliant, promising future. A great new world awaits us."

Bliss, suddenly looking melancholy, said, "We know many have lost loved ones. We lament their passing with you, and can only ask you to turn your eyes toward the bright and glorious days ahead. Your loved ones were blinded to the truth, led astray by deceivers. They impeded the Church Universal and the One World Government from making this earth the place we all desire."

"Yes, there've been famines and plagues," said Sardis. "Yes, there's been terrorism, both by men and wild beasts. There've been locusts and oil spills. All these things have come to pass because evil has been trying to prevent us from delivering fairness and love to the world."

"And now," Bliss added, "great earthquakes have shaken the foundations of the earth. But we're here, standing side by side with each other—and with you—to bid goodbye to those taken from our midst and to tell any remaining opponents and oppressors, 'You will lose.'"

A few minutes later, the two men emerged from the studio into a very dark daytime in Rome. A slip of paper fluttered down from above, illuminated by a light from inside the building, and Bliss noticed. He grabbed and held up the paper to examine.

"What's that?" Sardis asked.

"From the Bible, the book of Revelation," Bliss said. One line had been highlighted in yellow, from chapter six verse seventeen. Bliss read,

> For the great day of his wrath is come; and who shall be able to stand?

—THE END—

ABOUT THE AUTHOR

MARK ALAN LESLIE

The winner of six national magazine writing awards, Mark Alan Leslie has written eleven books, including three historical novels, four modern-day mystery/thrillers, two golf books, a devotional and a Christian self-help book. His career as a newspaper and magazine editor and writer spanned thirty years before he began writing books full-time.

While AFA Journal called Mark "a seasoned wordsmith whose contemporary novels are in the class with John Grisham," Midwest Book Review cited his "genuine flair for compelling, entertaining, and deftly crafted storytelling."

OTHER BOOKS BY MARK ALAN LESLIE

<u>Chasing the Music</u>

<u>The Three Sixes</u>

<u>Operation Jeremiah's Jar</u>

The Crossing

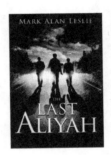

The Last Aliyah